Maker of Moonlight
THE REMIX

SUBIRA MILES

Hun Bun Luv
Publishing

HUN BUN LUV

CHAPTER ONE

Regina

My grandmother taught me never to call someone a liar or a fool, but sitting in that run-down room with my parents and their legal teams, I knew that my father had to be one of the two. He was either lying to get a reaction from me or a certified fool. There was no other way around it.

I examined the stone faces crowded around the barely-standing brown wooden table. Neither my mother nor her #156 mink lash extensions batted a beat at my father's words. Her always-fresh silk-wrapped hair didn't cascade over her shoulders with an angry neck snap in my father's direction either. No, my mother and her lips, covered in the Cherry Berry Brown Signature lipstick named in her honor, sat quietly watching the destruction of life as I knew it.

"You're not going to say anything, Cherry? You're going to let him do this to me?" I kept the pleading out of my voice and in my eyes. Strong women don't beg, but the need to plead tempted me. My dad's decisions were concrete and took several tools and a street team to break apart. My mom was always a part of my crew and had extra tools that moved my father more easily than I could. Cherry Strong would do anything for her only daughter, including but not limited to fighting her husband, Reginald Strong.

"Mom-me," I drew out the word, letting my shoulders and face droop with so much sadness that I knew victory would soon be mine. I had called Cherlissia Jameese Anderson Strong by the name Cherry since I was ten. It was what everyone called my mother because she had always hated her name. She had shed most of her country upbringing easily, but breaking away from her name took longer. Named after her Aunt Cheryl and her father, James, she didn't want to officially leave it behind completely. Cherry was her compromise. It was also the name that she had requested I call her when I was nearly the same height as her. She was 27 then, and the women around her age in my father's social circles were new to motherhood.

Saying Mommy out loud transformed our connection. It usually spurred her to crank out a solution to whatever was happening between me and my father, me and my teachers, me and the board of directors, or me and anyone in the world who made her daughter unhappy. The name mommy was my bat signal, my 911 emergency call for help, and she hadn't answered. Instead, she turned her barely creased eyes away from me and leaned over to her lawyer. Blocking her face with her hand, she whispered something to the stout woman dressed in a black blazer from two seasons ago.

"Regina," the lawyer started. The frown on my face stopped her words, and she tried to appeal again. "Miss. Strong," she corrected after clearing her throat. "All requests for changes to this agreement must be made in writing and submitted to the current owner and executive officer of Strong Enterprises, Reginald Strong. Mrs. Strong is here in the capacity of a shareholder and board member."

They were serious. Both of them. My mother, my father, and their lawyers were not playing some sadistic joke on me, but expecting me to fulfill the contract. The contract that I wished would melt through the wobbly wooden table and burst into flames.

"It's been too long, Genie." The words stumbled out in a tired drawl that my father usually reserved for close family members. He was always proper in mixed company, and he always used the best English language when in the office. His words had always been clear, crisp, and confident. *Strongs don't stutter, and Strongs don't mutter;* he would remind me in the privacy of our estate. *Your words are important. Make sure that they are heard. Make sure that you are heard.*

"Why now? Why like this?" Neither of them made any sense. I was living in a plot of a bad soap opera, and my real parents had been replaced by their evil twins that no one knew about. Their twin replicas were trying to ruin me.

"You've had your time away to help charities." Replica Reginald spoke. His words had returned to their normal astute tone.

"I am a full-time social worker with pay," I reminded him. "That's not charity, Daddy. That's real work."

"I am aware of your employment status. I am also aware of the cost of your condo and your constant remodels, your car, spa visits, and your clothing budget. Care to know why I have such in-depth knowledge of your spending habits? Of your repetitive *personal* line items?"

He had a point. The money that he provided heavily subsidized my lifestyle. I generally used my paycheck from the county on the blowout textured hair bundles that I had refreshed every other week.

"If you would like to continue reaping the benefits of the Strong name, you must use those high-priced heels that this company pays for to step up and contribute to our success. It's time to come back to lead, Regina. It's time for some hard work, and these are the terms."

My eyes darted between my mother, father, and the hideous contract. Cherry tried to hold my gaze but moved her face toward the window. Reginald Strong was unwavering.

I lifted an eyebrow in the direction of my lawyer, Micah Easton, a business attorney I used to date. I nearly lost a knee trying to keep up with his fitness obsession and love of hiking trails. All that running and sweating in nature kept my leave-out in constant need of attention. And what I wasn't going to do was live with raggedy edges. He was a fantastic attorney, though.

"My client and I will review these terms and reach out to you." Micah's platinum Rolex shifted on his wrist as he closed and zipped his leather portfolio. He was careful to avoid disturbing anything that may have been mutating on the neglected wood.

All of us looked out of place in the dusty dance hall and bar. My grandma Della, Cherry's mama, would have said that we looked *slicker than oil on a rainy day*. The defunct Shake Club had seen better days. It had been over a decade since I had even thought about the place and at least half of a century since it had been in its prime.

"Do you know why we're here? Do you know why we're in this place?" Accusation twisted through his words with an intensity that had been absent in the earlier part of the meeting. The conversation had been a matter of fact up to that point, but emotion had burrowed its way into my father's voice and eyes. It wasn't business. He had included lawyers and contracts to give me that perception, but this was personal.

"Dad." I tried to interject, but he couldn't have wanted an answer because he didn't take a breath to listen before he was hurling the question at me again.

"Do you even remember what this place means?" His fist against the table disturbed the dust layers and sent particles floating through the air.

I wanted to ignore his rude ass and end the inquisition, but the fact that he didn't think I would care enough to know the significance of where we met struck me in the chest. He had taught me the story. He had given life to what happened between the four wood-paneled walls with his words. He had given me their history, our history, and I never forgot.

The Trinity River was foul. It had always been. It smelled like someone had cooked chitlins in it, eaten them, and pushed them back out into the same water. Even as a little girl, when my father drove us out to the nothingness that lay between the shabby shack and the water, then led me by the hand over the uneven wooden steps, I knew something was disturbed about the place.

"Who would live out here?" I asked every single time we visited because it looked so run down and smelled so awful. Those were two things that I never associated with my father. He was always fresh, with something shiny dangling from him.

"It's not a house." My father would answer. *"This was a business. This is a legacy."*

Silence ticked between us as I let the long-ago memory of better times slip away into the bitter one before me.

"Well," he bit out the word through a tensed jaw.

"She doesn't know, honey," My mommy had peeked out from behind the imposter woman and was running her slender fingers over my father's clenching hand.

I knew the story like I knew my name and theirs. What I didn't know was why it mattered. I didn't know what the story of how our company started had to do with the contract.

"The carpenter Obidiah Jackson moved from Mississippi to Texas after hearing about a group of former slaves creating a town of their own," I started and watched my dad's jaw relax. "My middle name, Jenae, comes from your great-grandmother, Big Jen. She married Obidiah and started a kitchen and club for colored people in this very room, while Obie built up shacks and bought the land where he could."

His eyes softened, and his shoulders fell into their normal resting place. He didn't say anything; he just looked at my face with the same compassion that I saw when he would wake me up for school in the morning or when I won another pageant.

"Why wouldn't I remember that? How could I forget our history?"

His head shook back and forth slowly as though he had no control of the emotion that spurred it to move, and I saw the age in his drooping eyelids. The graying hairs at his temple seemed to have spread and become more prominent.

"If you remembered, Genie, then we wouldn't be here. You would care. You would do what I asked without all of this?" He stood with the agility of a man half his age, the metal chair scraping across the floor as he moved. "Fulfill the contract or watch our history die."

Confusion and uncertainty walked out of the dilapidated building with me that day. I felt just as crunchy about the situation as the sandy gravel sounded under the weight of my new shoes. My father had requested I return to the company in a leadership position. Return on his terms. *Terms.* The word didn't fully capture the gravity of what my father was demanding. Most parents pestered their children about settling down through subtle jabs, innuendo, and endless questioning. Waiting wasn't Reginald Strong's style. Resting the outcome of a problem that affected him both personally and financially on a whimsy feeling was not his mode of operation. Whatever was imperative was handled by him without room to wonder about the results. Reginald Strong did not lose, and that meant I would have to find someone to marry before my thirtieth birthday, or he would do it for me.

CHAPTER TWO

Regina

Between life in private school among the rich and ruthless and my experiences being a businessman's daughter, I had built plenty of emotional walls. I kept most people at a distance. But for the second time in my thirty years of life, I had a best friend. I loved the sweet, thoughtful Nailah, who accepted my friendship without judgment and grudgingly tried new things with me. The pregnant Nailah, the one that sat on the other side of my dressing room door in the viewing area of the bridal boutique with a pantry of food hidden in her purse, that Nailah chomped on my nerves.

It had never been easy for me to pay attention when people were speaking. Not that I wasn't interested, but my mind wondered when not in use. Most of the time, the words scrolled through in pictures. At any given time, one of those pictures could remind me of a song, and that song would remind me of a movie, and suddenly, I'd missed three minutes of a conversation. Trying to pay attention to someone who insisted on eating all of the time caused my brain to roll its eyes and move on to a different topic real quick. Between Nailah's garbled snack-filled words and smacking, my mind had gone on several journeys, giving up on trying to both hear and follow her.

"Regina!" She hollered. The sound was so clear that I saw the scowl on her newly rounded face through the door between us.

"You know I didn't hear you." Slipping the strap of another bridesmaid's dress across my shoulder, I shouted from inside the dressing room. I instantly cringed at the volume of my voice, hearing my mother's gasp in my head. *'This is not a barnyard. Use your indoor voice, dear'.*

"The groomsmen are crashing our meal today," Nailah called out, probably for the second time, but it was the first time that I had heard.

I froze, my thumb hooked under the wide strap of the silk material as pictures of the groomsmen I had met before shuffled through my mind like profiles on a Black Men With Beards Instagram page.

"Damn," I muttered as one face stood out in particular.

"What did you say?" Nailah was smacking again.

"Nothing." Even though I knew that it was something, she hadn't even said his name, and I was already preparing my body for the response his presence would bring.

I had a crush. There was no denying it. I had a full, *draw-our-names-in-hearts, smile-at-the-thought-of-you* crush.

"Are all of the groomsmen joining us?" Checking my profile one last time, I wanted to be cute just in case he walked up when I stepped out. My friend was notorious for last-minute change-ups.

"All of them." Nailah's voice was muffled again, sounding full. "Trystan, Tyson, Chad, Cairo, and Terrence." She ticked off the names that were now a familiar part of her vocabulary.

I had met most of Nailah's soon-to-be family at least once, but the thought of seeing Terrence again evoked a giddiness that I hadn't felt since I was fresh out of college, tripped over the suave Luther Boyle and fell into a puddle of hot burning feelings that scalded me for life.

I stepped out of the dressing room and faced my friend.

Sitting on a plush sofa sneaking bites of a Twinkie, Nailah looked the picture of carefree, a stark difference from her vibe just a few months ago.

"Ooh, pretty," She garbled, the words sounding just as smushed as the cake in her mouth.

"Why?" I placed a hand on my hip but then turned toward a tri-fold mirror to hide the anxiousness in my eyes.

The first time that I saw the imposingly tall Terrence, dressed in all black, with small neat locks swinging across his broad shoulders, my core started thumping with the energy of that pink bunny with a drum. He was quiet, with a cool reserve about him that beckoned me to learn more. I wanted to watch his mysterious eyes and feel the carvings of his built physique. He had a body that a superhero would envy. The defined lines of his pectoral muscles, shoulders, and forearms creased through his fitted cotton t-shirt as though they might tear through at any minute. Then, layered beneath those mounds of muscle was the most important quality of all, his heart. For most of my exes, that part was not included in the purchase of a relationship. Terrence cared for and about my friend when she was facing some of the toughest times in her life. A man who was that fine and kind was both rare and valuable, and I specialized in works of value.

"You always look good in fitted dresses," Nailah answered between bites this time.

"She meant, why are the men coming through when this was supposed to be a girls' day." Jubilee stepped out of the stall next to me in an identically colored dress. "We've all been so busy lately, this was supposed to be for us."

For the first time in my life, I had a crew. I had inherited them with Nailah, but it felt amazing in the same *'grab some sneakers to fight, bring a box of chocolate to console, or pop a bottle of champagne to celebrate'* way that I imagined it would as a kid.

I had met Nailah's five-foot-eleven-inch sister after a family catastrophe, and we had become fast friends. She was the creative kind, bold with a splash of sassy that wasn't too much. Plus, she was from the country, a small town, and when she was comfortable, she let it loose. I also loved that Jubilee looked amazing every time we crossed paths but never acted the part. I watched her season of the competition that launched her career as a top model, and I still catch an episode or two of the docuseries about her life.

"They're joining us here at the boutique to get measured for their tuxes. Everyone will partner up, and I thought it would be an easy time to meet, " Nailah smiled as she took a bite of her cream-filled cake.

Jubilee seemed to like that answer as much as I did, judging by the frown on her face, but she deflected it by turning to me and complimenting the dress I had chosen.

"That dress is everything on you." She stepped back, placed a hand on her hip, and reviewed my form before returning her gaze to her own. Twisting in the mirror next to me, she added, "Miss Independent over there, won't let me use any of my fashion contacts for this. I wish I could find something that wasn't so matronly." Her frown returned as she tugged on the thick lace and jeweled bodice of the long hoop skirt dress she had put on.

"I agree." Mali, a friend, and the groom's cousin, joined us in the center of the private room to voice her concern. "It's a good thing that we're wearing different styles in the same color. I'm not finding anything cute in my size either."

Both ladies were thick with shapely bodies that called for a double-digit size in clothing. Although they looked amazing in their everyday clothing, finding dresses in this specialty shop had been a struggle.

"I'll speak with the stylist. She said something earlier about ordering dresses in a larger size and using the smaller size in-store to try on." Nailah stated but left her hand in her bag this time instead of stuffing her face. "Jubi, you and Mali can have Regina try on a few dresses for you, and if you like them, I'll have them sent to the store for you to try on next time."

"Next time." Mali's neck reared back. "We gotta do this again?"

"If you don't find something today, we'll have to come back. Plus, we can't sit here all day, we have reservations with the guys." She reminded everyone.

Mali, Tyriq's tiny but mighty cousin, threw her hands into the air. "Here we go with them again. Can I just get one day?" The question trailed off as Mali marched off into the dressing room to take off her dress.

"For real. I did not get dressed to see men today," Jubilee added as she twirled in the thick garment that brushed over her toes. "I wore pants with an elastic waistband."

"It's not that big of a deal. Those boys aren't anything special. They'll be family soon anyway."

"Your family." Jubilee pointed out. "Your family by marriage at that. Therefore, they are men. Fine-ass men. I don't do relaxed style in front of fine-ass men. I still don't understand how you function around them?" Jubilee's voice floated up and down with her movements as she swished from side to side trying to find a good angle. She was a mountain of curves so tight that they should have come with a warning sign. Her lengthy arms, toned legs, and narrow torso were a stark contrast to her rounded chest and rap video-ready ass.

"Really?" Nailah pinged her head between Jubilee and me with disbelief ringing through the word.

"Yes," We answered at the same time.

"I'm glad somebody understands." Jubilee high-fived me as she shook the shoulder-length natural curls that had been straightened. Her long brown locks flowed over the full puffed cap sleeves of the dress. No matter how she turned. The dress was still ugly.

Nailah threw a hand across the air, dismissing the statement, and gave an unenthusiastic "That's so dirty. Terrence is like the big brother I never had. Chad could easily be an annoying baby brother. Tyson is so damn smooth, he doesn't even seem real to me, and Cairo is so quiet and cool that I barely notice when he is around. It's effortless."

Spending time with the Lewis brothers was as tempting as walking into a bakery daily while on a sugar restriction. Tyriq was cute but had been taken with Nailah from the beginning. Since I met him through her, I never let my mind escape into how good he would taste, but Terrence... That one, I wanted to know how the brooding big brother felt against my lips. His allure may have had something to do with the string of corporate-type straight-laced men I had rolled through. Most of them had accomplished great things, but they were missing something. Some were too sour, others too sweet. A few were too doughy, soft, and mushy for no reason, while a few were hardened and stale. Meeting Terrence that day left me wanting to examine his flavor profile and figure out every ingredient that made him so irresistibly tempting. I was ready to roll myself out beneath him after our quick conversation.

"Well, call me a pig and roll me in the slop 'cause honey, I'd get dirty with any of 'em." Jubilee twanged and mimicked riding a horse.

"Ok. Speak that truth." I snapped my fingers in agreeance.

Although Jubilee was a plus-sized model that had walked runaways in Paris, Dubai, London, and New York, she was still a country girl at heart and buckets of fun.

"Stop that." Mali padded her bare feet across the plush carpet and booty-bumped Jubilee. "Friends and family freaking don't mix. It gets too messy."

"I agree." Nailah piped in as she pushed her bag to the sofa, stood, and walked over to link arms with Jubilee and me. "You ladies are important to my life. We're friends, and I don't want that to change." She looked both of us in the eyes. "Let's not ever let any man, especially the men in my new family, come between us."

Jubilee playfully poked out her bottom lip but gave a serious answer. "You don't have to worry, Nailah. They're cute-looking, but I'm too busy to get close to anyone right now." Nailah smiled.

"Thank you," Mali added as she linked her arms with Jubilee.

"And my love life is already complicated as hell. No- thank you for more issues." I added, looping my arm through Mali's available arm to complete our friendship circle.

We were three very different women, but we all cared for Nailah, and that eventually led to us caring for one another. I could call Mali for counseling, decorating tips, or art insight. I reached out to Jubilee for the latest inside information on designers and fashion. They were the friends that I couldn't find at the private schools and Ivy League dorms.

They were the connection to the real world beyond the life of the rich and famous, where I never felt that I truly belonged.

"These hormones got me going soft, but you ladies mean everything to me," Nailah sniffled. "Each one of you contributed to the strength I needed to make it to the aisle and through the beginning of this pregnancy." Her arms loosened from the lock position to begin a weepy group hug. "Thank you, ladies, for being my friends. Great ones."

A wave of sniffles and 'thank you's set off across our tight hug circle as each of us inwardly reflected on why being friends was both beneficial and necessary.

"Hell yea, let me get in on that," A male voice cut through the bubble of love we had created.

Mali was the first to break free, swiping at her eyes and fussing like an experienced mother.

"Chad!! Shoo." Mali pushed at one of the men that I had promised not to entangle myself with.

"At least let me watch." Chad pleaded as she pushed him out of the area.

I leaned over to Jubilee to whisper, "Are they related to all the fine men in the world.?"

"I think so." Jubilee shook her head, but her eyes stayed on the forbidden intruder. "Mali would torture me if I even thought about a night with Chad."

I nodded my head and chuckled at the thought of how fierce Mali could be about her family.

"But," Jubilee added with a smirk. "There are some things that I can do to him without thinking."

"And this is why I love you," I giggled.

I wished that I had the opportunity to fantasize, but I had a contract to consider. There were so many complications that came with a relationship. I was in no position to even let my eyes stray toward the shadow of any man. Even though it was unnervingly obvious I would never escape what had historically been crippling for me: confident men with muscular bodies, a 'fuck the world' attitude, and 'I run shit' swag.

Chapter Three

Terrence

Before that moment, I couldn't remember ever stumbling into something great. Money didn't fall from trees, and winning lottery tickets didn't blow across my path, but when my feet hit the plush carpet of the women's showroom in the boutique, I could have been walking on streets of gold to the sounds of trumpets. I felt like the luckiest mammal on the planet when her wide brown eyes gazed up at me and her glossed lips mouthed the words, "Help me take this off."

I wasn't sure that I had heard the words. I thought that my mind had made them up somehow or had possibly pulled them up from my fantasies. Regina was perfect. Her eyes were slight at the edges with round expressive centers and the color of a rich whisky. Her nose was slim along the bridge but widened and curved enough at the end to represent the culture. Full heart lips and high cheekbones completed the face that I couldn't erase from my dreams. Her body should have been the prototype for lingerie models across the globe. She was thin, but heavy in all the right spots.

"Terrence, right?" She questioned as soon as I was near enough to wonder why the room was empty.

I nodded, of course. Even if I had been Trystan or Tyriq, at that moment I was going to be Terrence. I was going to be whoever she needed me to be. Her full taut breasts were pushed up high in the purple form-fitting dress as she turned her back to face me.

"You want me to help you out of the dress? The dress that you have on now?" My voice cracked a bit as I verified that I was indeed being given a magic bean of hope that I could touch her.

The smooth skin of her exposed neck creased as she turned her face toward me and lifted her eyes to examine mine.

"That's what I said." Her eyebrows furrowed as if determining if I were competent enough for the job. I guess she found what she was looking for as she started an explanation. "Mali went chasing after your cousin Chad. Nailah snuck off with Tyriq, and I have no idea where the other ladies went."

The dress itself wasn't extraordinary, but it had several hooks with lace tied up like a shoelace over them. For extra confusion, there was also a zipper in the mix that could be accessed from the side and was hidden in a fold of the material.

"How'd you get into this?" I carefully pulled at the ribbon sitting in the nook leading into her beautiful backside. I wanted to palm it, but under different circumstances, so I took my time and leaned on the fact that I would get to see the bare skin of her back.

"Jubilee picked out this dress. She said it was high fashion."

"Someone was high when they made this," I remarked under my breath.

She chuckled with a light breathy air that made me want to record the sound and press play again and again. It was unique, like the woman herself. I liked the way her shoulders shook slightly and her back curved forward a bit almost like a dance. I liked how the laugh was easy. She didn't have to think about happiness, conjure it up with focused effort, it just happened for her at any given moment.

"You're right. It has too much going on." She shifted a bit causing my hand to press into her skin. "I'm the only one of the group small enough to fit in this original."

She shifted her hip up to give me easier access to the side zipper and the inconspicuous hook above. I imagined her throwing it back in a different way, knowing that my musings would remain just that. Regina wasn't rude or snooty but without her saying a word, I could tell that she was classy. She was too sophisticated to give me a second glance.

"Jubilee wanted to see this dress on a body since they didn't have it in her size, so I tried it." Regina continued without acknowledging the slight tremble in my hand when I first took the tiny bra-like hook between my fingers. "I let them clip, zip, and tie me into this contraption. Then when I went back into the dressing room to grab my heels, the heifers disappeared." She took a glance at the two exits, possibly looking for her friends to return. No one showed. It was her and I with a single slender piece of cloth and a few inches between us.

I could smell something like mango and bananas from her hair and although it took me back to freshly opened boxes of fruity cereal in my childhood, it made grown man feelings heat up.

"This is a beautiful dress." It complimented her tapered waist and shapely hips giving her the perfect silhouette. "If she doesn't like it, you should think about wearing it."

"You think so?" There was a note of teasing in her tone. "Even if I have to track you down to get out of it at the end of the night?"

"All done." I touted instead of answering the question. I couldn't answer it truthfully, she was a part of the wedding party and Nailah's friend. Anything happening in the night with her would be a brewing pot of trouble in the morning.

"Thank you." She turned and took a step back to catch my eyes holding my attention with the sparkle in hers.

A silence fell between us, but it wasn't uncomfortable, just a moment to mutually examine the other person in the room. Regina was a lot to take in at once. Beyond the hair and makeup, there was the tenderness in her cheeky smirk that was endearing, almost hypnotizing, and possibly a problem for my desire.

"Hi," I extended my hand to her. "I'm Terrence, the best man."

I felt the air hit my teeth when my face lifted into a wide grin. I was giving 'the first time I touched a girl' energy without even trying, but she was that damn fine, and I was that damn eager for her to like me.

Her hand fell into the chasm of mine as we shook.

"I just let you feel me up, we're friends now," She reminded me with a simple chuckle while her hand both quickened my heartbeat and relaxed me to the point that I forgot why I shouldn't take her home with me. "And you know that we've met before today."

"I remember. You're more than memorable Regina."

The stars in her eyes winked at me and I wanted to do it again, say something that made her look at me like ice cream.

"Our meeting was brief," I continued. "As a gentleman, it's only right that I properly introduce myself."

She threw a hand across the air dismissing the notion as she tiptoed her way into the dressing room holding up the open dress. "No need for that. I know about you, Terrence Lewis."

"All good things I hope." I probably should have walked away, but I wanted to know what she had been told. What had she heard? Did she already know about my business? Was she being nice because of that? I didn't want that to be the case. I wanted her to like me, just Terrence.

The swoosh of fabric hitting the floor caught my attention.

"Nailah told me how villainous you are," She explained in a louder voice than normal so that I could hear over the door. "You know, how you stole her car, fixed everything that was wrong with it for free, and forced her to watch endless hours of her favorite basketball commentary while she was sick. You know, all of your evil deeds."

"Damn," I felt my face tighten into a frown. "All that she would tell me about you is that you're a social worker."

"That's all she told you?" Regina questioned. She hadn't opened the door then. She hadn't taken the breath from my lungs with her dope-ass body and grin while she spoke. Once she stepped through, I was over.

Regina pranced out of the dressing room on her toes and right over to me with shoes in hand. She was wearing a jogging suit that made my mouth go dry. It wasn't the ordinary tracksuit that my Nana used to wear to walk the mall. The pants were fitted at the waist and scrunched at the ankle in the same way, but the material was silk-like, and the top was missing the bottom half. It stopped above her navel and was zipped low exposing a cleavage that I could lose all of my senses exploring.

I cleared my throat as she placed a hand on my shoulder to balance herself while she slid her feet into heeled sandals. "That's it. That's all she told me about you. "

Licking my lips, I tried to keep my eyes away from her. It felt like she had gotten more beautiful.

"Nailah said that you own a garage and towing service." Her eyebrow lifted at the same time as her body and I missed the extra peek that it had allowed. With both of her shoes on, she no longer needed to hold onto me and I also missed the touch.

"That's true." I nodded.

Chapter Four

Regina

We were a good-looking group: the four Lewis brothers, Mali and her two fine-ass brothers, Nailah with Jubilee, and me. I was used to being the left-out person, the girl that never belonged to one group completely. My father was richer than most parents of my prep school classmates and for that reason it made them view me differently. Chauffeured to school by a driver, there were no awkward parent drop-offs and kisses by the door. My father arrived at school football games in a helicopter. My mom had a full film crew at every school performance. Then there were the people that tried to use me for status. I was different. It never helped that I was one of the few chocolate chips in the pack of milk-white students on campus either. While there were many multi-racial children of athletes, I was one of the few with deep chocolate skin and kinky hair that I had to straighten or get weaved. Not the same. My cousins on my mother's side all thought that I was some kind of princess from the movies, and the cousins on my father's side were old enough to be my parents. Outcast. I didn't fit in. No one was like me anywhere that I went. Somehow I felt a part of the Lewis family. I felt comfortable, like a real member of the group, and I was proud to walk next to them.

"Are you good?" Jubilee asked as we entered.

"Always." I smiled. While that wasn't the complete truth, it was true at that moment. I was alright. As weird as it was, I had already claimed them as my people. I felt good among them.

I wasn't sure if it was the fact that we looked like money or that all the men surrounding us were the walking example of 'if powerful and fine had a baby'. Either way, the hostess was too excited to say hello to our group and seat us in the private room at the two expansive tables pushed together.

Most of the men filed into chairs on the left side of the table, and I found a chair on the right side with the rest of the ladies. By coincidence or with purpose I sat at the end of the table farthest from the couple of honor but right across from Terrence.

He licked his lips as he pulled the menu apart and I noticed his thick finger push across the page as he reviewed the options. The throbbing vein there in the back of his hand made my thoughts jump to the possibility of other veiny places.

"Stop that," Jubilee whispered with a jab of her elbow into my side.

"Ow." I flinched, before whispering back. "What was that for?"

Without ever turning her head she slid her narrowed eyes over to Terrence and then back to me. "No. Off-limits"

Before we could carry our conversation further, Tyriq and his over-loud "Listen up friends and family" broke through the warning Jubilee was communicating.

We all turned our attention toward the front of the table.

"Thank you all for agreeing to participate in our wedding." Tyriq glanced at Nailah with pride sparkling in his eyes. He was finally getting her scary ass down the aisle.

Members of the wedding party responded with various words of encouragement and gestures before Tyriq continued.

"Nailah and I have decided that we will not get married 8 months from now."

Our collective gasps could have sucked all of the air from the room.

"Are you breaking up already?" One of the brothers asked. "I thought she would at least make it to the church."

Jubilee and I caught eyes before I whispered, "Did you know about this?"

She shook her head just as Nailah continued.

"I'm not running." She stomped a foot to emphasize before giving Chad and Trystan a pointed look. "And I know some of you have bets on when I'll call it off." Waving a hand in the air to punctuate her words she continued, "Don't expect any money. This wedding is happening."

"Double or nothing on the wedding day?" Chad lifted an eyebrow as he looked around the table for anyone willing to take his bet until his eyes fell on Tyriq, whose eyes tightened over his low growl. "My bad, bro."

I could see Tyriq's leg move and Chad wince so I assumed Tyriq had kicked him under the table before saying, "Nailah will be my wife. No questions or bets against it. If I have to marry her during a car chase on speakerphone, Nailah will be Mrs. Lewis and soon."

"That's right, honey." Nailah cooed and kissed Tyriq's cheek before continuing. "The where and how we get married have become less important to me than when. I want our baby to come into this world with married parents."

Nailah took a deep breath, placing her hands at the growing round of her belly as Tyriq rubbed at her back.

"Y'all know this isn't easy for me." Her eyes rolled toward the ceiling as water welled at her lower lids. "I didn't come from this." She sniffed while waving a hand in front of her as she glanced at the table members. "I didn't come from comfort, from support, from people who wanted me." She blinked down a tear while touching her belly again. "This baby is already so loved, so wanted, so cared for by everyone in this room that I don't want to wait. My baby will be the first to break generational curses of struggle and instability. I want to bring this child into the world with married parents. Instead of getting married after delivery, we need to do this before. We need to get married sooner."

More than a few tears tacked over Nailah's cheeks as she looked up to roll them back. "If trauma can be passed through generations, then so can healing. I want to heal. Toxicity won't be a family trait that runs through my family anymore. That behavior runs out with this one. We're starting anew with our union."

Everyone in the small private room had felt her sentiments, her passion for creating a life better than her own for the child she was carrying.

Tyriq pulled her into his chest and nestled his face in the crown of her head. We all needed the moment to reflect on things that we needed to change about ourselves and our families for the future.

When Nailah took a seat, Tyriq took her elbow and helped her to the chair.

"If it's important to you, then it's important to me," Terrence called out from his seat. "Whatever you want to do, we're here for it."

"We got you," Mali added.

"Thank you," Nailah sniffled before grabbing Tyriq's hand and looking up at him. "Thank you too."

The look that passed between the two of them was enviable. Nailah looked so at ease next to Tyriq. It seemed that she had found the self she was searching for and was finally able to share after the discovery. Besides hanging with Nailah, there weren't many times in life where I could be me. Rich girl, Black girl, Girlfriend, Diva, or Daughter, they were all a role that I put on and shed like clothes. So many parts of who I am, but most of me I kept close. Anytime I had dared to share in the past, it was unbecoming, ghetto, too white, disrespectful, or trashy. Everyone wanted something or someone from me and that was exhausting. I would pay anything for someone that accepted all that I am in the way that Tyriq embraced Nailah.

"We're getting married in three weeks," Tyriq announced.

"Wait. What?" Mali asked as a grumble of questions erupted from the table. "What about the venue? What about the reception: caterers, DJ, photographer?"

Tyriq shook his head. "None of that matters. I'd marry Nailah in the shower."

"That bridal march would be worth attending," Chad grinned.

"Not today Chad." Mali pinched at his arm like she was someone's grandmother in church service. She turned back to Tyriq. "You know Aunt Shirley is not having a thrown-together event in front of her sorors."

"I'm not worried about my mother," Tyriq explained.

Nailah pursed her lips.

"Not much anyway." He amended. "We'll keep the big wedding planned for later in the year, but we set up a destination wedding to get this done sooner."

"Destination?" This perked my interest. "The Amalfi Coast is beautiful during this time. Dubai, Chile? Ooh, Fiji is gorgeous."

"Wait a minute, Miss National Geographic," Mali piped in. "We don't all have a full passport book."

"We've already chosen." Nailah smiled wistfully. "I've always wanted to see the biolu-minescent bay in Puerto Rico. All of you are invited to spend 7 days and 6 nights with us, paid by us, at a full-service resort where we'll tie the knot."

"What about jobs and responsibilities?" Terrence asked. "The way his eyebrows rowed together expressed that he didn't want to shirk any of his duties. His grumpy response shouldn't have caused a tingle to shoot up my middle, but it did. I knew so many people that would run off to fun at the first chance without a second glance back or thought for those left to take care of things.

"We know that everyone has some sort of business to handle." His gaze implored Terrence's understanding. "We need you there for at least 2 days, including the rehearsal and wedding."

Terrence swiped a finger across the screen of his phone as he shook his head.

"You're my best man, my best friend Terrence."

"I got you, bro." He sighed. I could tell that he was going to do it but probably didn't want to. Maybe some time away from work would do him some good.

"We hope that all of you can get the time to come." His glance hopped across the table to each of us as hope danced across her lips.

"But you're doing this with or without us," Trystan said aloud what was already understood without anyone prompting.

"Basically." Nailah winced before speaking again. "We want you to share this moment with us, but this baby born into our union is a priority for me."

"We'll still have a big wedding later with all of our family there," Tyriq added. "So think about it. Do what you can, and fly out when you can. We'll get in touch this week to confirm dates and travel plans at our expense of course. Flight and hotel stay included."

Two servers appeared then, ready to take orders for food. I was happy for a break in the speech to work on taming my rising guilt. I had a full caseload of families to serve, review, and discharge or pass over before I had to make my exit. The realization that my father was forcing me from a job that I loved into a loveless marriage weighed on my mind as I looked at the joy stamped on Nailah's face. I wasn't sure that I could attend her wedding knowing that in a few short months, I would be doing the same for polar opposite reasons.

"Excuse me." The waitress snapped. "Mam. What would you like?"

"I'll have the Black Bean Chicken bowl," I reported but turned my head quickly when I heard an echo.

Terrence and I had picked the same meal at the same time. His thick dark eyebrow lifted in my direction with an inquiry.

"Jinx." Our eyes locked on each other as we uttered the one word simultaneously.

I didn't want to grin at him because he still held a straight face, but I couldn't help it. I found myself chuckling again, comforted by the pleased look on his face.

"Great minds think alike." He winked.

I meant to say something smart and cute but only nodded because I felt like I was melting. I was a pack of crayons in the summer sun sitting there warming under his attention.

"Anything else?" The waitress snapped with irritation. Luckily, the good vibes radiating from Terrence held my politeness intact because she was one short answer away from an unfavorable situation.

"No, nothing else for me. I would like to adjust my order though. I'll have my bowl without the chicken. No meat for me."

"Gotcha." She finally smiled with interest as her gaze traveled over to Cairo sitting next to me.

As the women flitted away to flirt with men at the table, Terrence returned his attention to me. I wanted his perusal to be an invitation to cuddle up next to him, tell him my deepest sorrows, and then use his body as a key to forgetfulness. Instead, I only smirked before asking, "What's up?"

"Interesting," He commented. "A chicken bowl without chicken."

I shrugged at his common observation of my food preference, but when he asked, "How long have you gone without meat?" It took all the years of etiquette training not to respond with exactly what meat I was missing and when I would like to sample his selection.

With a quick sip of water, I washed away my improper thoughts and gave him the real answer.

"I went Vegetarian in high school to lose a few pounds and clear up some acne before a pageant."

His eyebrow lifted. "Did you win? Am I in the presence of royalty?"

I don't blush, and the deep hue of my chocolate skin would make it difficult to see, but the burn of my cheeks after his mock bow brought to mind that it might be possible for my cheeks to pink.

"Of course, I won. You're looking at the only Miss Black Dallas and Miss South Dallas winner in existence."

"What made you stick with it? It's not an easy lifestyle."

"My grandmother had a farm down in east Texas"

"You're from the country?"

"My mom's family. I'm country affiliated, you could say," I answered, thinking of the summers I spent on the farm with my grandmother, surrounded by people who both tethered me and lifted me. "When my Nana developed cancer, she switched over to a plant-based diet. We ate from her harvest, and it was the best food that I ever tasted."

"I didn't imagine you as meatless or as a farm girl."

"Well, how do you imagine me?"

CHAPTER FIVE

Terrence

I was 100% certain that on-my-face was not the answer. When Regina Strong asked: *"Well, how do you imagine me?"* my brain scrambled for a suitable answer.

I lied. I came up with some nonsense about a smart and caring nurturer who enjoyed city life. The truth is that words were stumbling out of my mouth but most of my energy was going toward muting thoughts of clamping my lips to her core and pressing it down my throat. I tried to unsee my visions of what she might look like at the height of pleasure.

"Sorry. I have to run." Regina was putting her phone away when she stepped over to our small huddle. Her usual grin was turned down into a flat line.

"Everything alright?" Nailah's face filled with concern as she wrapped her hands around Regina's slender fingers.

Regina opened her mouth to answer but then shot me a glance as she seemed to remember that I was there. Whatever she really wanted to say wouldn't be said until I was out of earshot. I didn't leave though. It would have been mannerable for me to excuse myself, but Regina intrigued me. I wanted to gather as much about her as I could directly from the source.

"Some business that I have to take care of now," Regina stressed the word business.

I wondered what the problem was. Business seemed to be a code word for something. I wondered who had enough priority in her life to pull her away from her best friend's dinner. It didn't matter that everyone had finished eating and were mulling around chatting about accommodations and timelines. It didn't matter that the actual obligatory portion of the day was done, it was that she was leaving for a reason other than the one she chose. I could tell she had wanted to stay. She was comfortable with my people. Before her phone rang, she had been laughing at something Chad said. Then she dipped away, only to return with the excuse that she needed to leave.

"Of course. Thank you for coming." Nailah nodded, her eyebrows furrowing as she leaned in to hug Regina goodbye.

"Are you sure that you're alright?" Mali asked a school counselor, and she took opportunities to check on the well-being of others.

"I'm fine," Regina answered but only lifted one side of her face. The joy that had been emanating from her all day had been diminished. That bothered me.

"Ok." Mali leaned in for a quick shoulder touch before turning to me. "See her out. It's dark outside."

"Yeah." I nodded my head toward Regina and the exit. "I got you."

We were quiet, moving through our small group with eyes trailing over our pairing. I knew the questions would come whenever I saw them again.

"Thank you for walking out here with me," Her thick lips parted as she ran her tongue across the plump pink flesh.

"No problem." Even when speaking, I still imagined slurping her from corner to corner. I wanted to draw five-point stars across her clit, and make a game of lapping up her releases. I wanted her like that, and I had wanted her in that way the first time I met her at Tyriq's house.

"So you're a real modern-day hero?" She asked when the lights blinked on her car door, and I used the handle to pull it open for her.

"I wouldn't say that." The shake of my head could have been considered bashful. That wasn't me or my mode of operation. Quiet, maybe, but never shy. Regina was a lot, though.

"Nailah seems to think that you are." She leaned against the frame of her car and moved sleek strands of hair behind her ear. "My friend needed a friend, and I'm glad you've been there."

I gave a quick nod, not wanting to dwell on any of my deeds. Whatever I did for my family, I did out of love, not out of obligation.

"Do you know what I'm talking about?" Her eyes were already narrow and slanted some more.

"You are completely unforgettable." It was her turn to be shy at my words. "But helping is no sweat. It's who I am. It's who I was raised to be."

Nailah had some difficulty, in the beginning, carrying the baby and stayed with Tyriq after a hospital visit. Regina had popped up later that day wearing a Dallas Colts Jersey dress that instantly had me wanting to taste her from ankle to esophagus. Without any flirting or coercion on her part, it took a single one-minute meeting before I was ready to swoop her up and fuck her where she stood. Regina was fine. The problematic type of fine that came with disrespectful ass men trying to shoot their shot and the possible test of manhood knowing that she could attract someone better at any given moment.

"Thanks to whoever raised you, then." Some of her shine returned with her smile. "I can't wait for new unforgettable moments on the island."

My mind whirred as she slid into the car and shut the door.

I wanted my freaky thoughts of her to roll away with her too. Historically, Regina's kind of fine also came with crazy. It seemed like God poured more 'act right' into most of the regular girls. Fine-ass women like Regina didn't put up with shit. Women who got their way all of the time unleash a next-level type of crazy when they don't get what they want. I wanted Regina, unquestionably, but I wanted my peace more. She would have me running around looking like Tyriq, doing extreme things just to keep her happy. The only woman I had worked that hard for became my wife, and I was not traveling down the road of marriage ever again. The rest of the night, I tried my damndest to focus on the fact that my brother was so in love with Nailah that he was about to marry her twice and not the excitement I felt about seeing Regina again.

Cowardice didn't live in me, and he knew that. I would beat his pretty-boy ass without a hard breath. That was a fact. He must have forgotten that I wasn't stupid. He was deflecting. I didn't have anything to say on the subject. I hadn't spoken on it much and had continued to not speak on it. My cousin Chad is like a mosquito sometimes, and I often wanted to swat his annoying ass, but there were so many other ways to use my energy. He shoved his phone in my face the minute we pulled into the driveway. Then he tried to pull me into a verbal tug of war by asking twenty questions, but he couldn't make me stray from the important topic at hand.

"You want to drag me across the city to man up about my shit," Chad announced with a puffy chest. "But you can't even look at a news clip about yours."

"Apples and pears, man. It's not the same," I reminded him. "V isn't here anymore. I don't have any more ties to the past. You have a walking, breathing reminder out there."

"It's oranges. The comparison is between apples and oranges." He shook his head. "The Jacobs and the church are working with lawmakers to get healthcare laws changed and talking to community organizations about ways to support families who don't have enough money for medication. Why aren't you out there?"

He kept trying to swing judgment back in my direction.

Sitting in the car, staring at the front door of a small brick home, Chad had the decision to make. He couldn't be the mosquito. He had to be a man. I had done everything that I needed for my former wife. It also didn't help that her parents made it a point to exclude me from most things.

"Why are we still sitting in the car, dude?" I countered. " You pulled out your phone to show me that news clip as soon as I put the car in park because you're stalling. The situation at minute 17 is going to be the same situation at minute 32. This isn't going away. You may as well begin a new minute with a plan."

His eyes trailed up to the sky before his head turned, and I could tell that he was saying something to himself. Everything wasn't meant to be said aloud. I got that, but I also knew that we had to make a move.

"Chad." I needed him to remember that I was still there, that we still had a mission. "All the fruit and all the minutes not gonna change the fact that I don't know what the fuck I'm doing." He punched at the dashboard. "She won't call me Daddy." The anger billowed out of him as his head dropped. "I'm just Chaddy to her. The dude that she sees on the weekend."

There were times when I understood him. There were things that I didn't want to face. There were things that I didn't want to change, but they had. I wanted to give the little boy in him a pep talk and pointers about manhood. He didn't have a father worth mentioning, and that affected the trajectory of his life tremendously. Fortunately, my pop was around and stepped in to help where he could. It wouldn't replace the absence of his birth father, but it helped.

"Open the door." I let my words hold some of the compassion that I felt for his situation but didn't leave room for other options.

He shook his head.

"I don't know if I can go in there- if I can do this- if she'll like me." Chad's eyes lingered on the battered white door as he spoke. "I don't know if I'm ready for this."

"The paternity test said that you're ready. That test said that you're that little girl's father, so you're going to open that door and be that."

Even though he opened the door and stood, he was hesitant, so I took the next steps first. Chad had always been playful, the prankster of our bunch, and if anyone would get along with a child, it would be him. I wasn't sure what he was worried about. The small girl named Tia had been to a few family game nights. Tia's grandmother had recently been granted custody of the child. With Tia's mother in rehab for an undefined time, and the grandmother, who had taken in the hazel-eyed four-year-old, suffering a heart attack after being diagnosed with MS, it was Chad's turn to be responsible.

"Your daughter has a mother in rehab, a grandmother who can barely feed herself, and you. That's it." I reminded my cousin, who had finally shut the car door but hadn't taken another step. "If you don't step up and step in, what's next for your daughter?"

"Her great-aunt is helping out; at least she knows her," He pleaded, but it wasn't my approval he needed or my future that would be changed.

"Do you hear yourself?" I wanted to shake some sense into him. "What can a 72-year-old woman do with an elderly person in diapers and a kid that just got out of them?"

"I hate being forced into shit," he wiped a hand over his face.

I couldn't decide if the pout on his face was more comical or tragic.

"That's irrelevant. Your daughter asked for all of this?" He wasn't getting it. He was focused on himself, thinking about his needs and not that of his child. I felt like Chad got stuck somewhere in his teens and his body aged, but his maturity level stayed the same.

"You're right." He rubbed a hand over his face and exhaled tornado-like winds.

"Let's do this before somebody calls the police on us." I clapped a hand on his shoulder and pushed him forward. "This is a family thing. Quit acting like your momma and Mali aren't about to be at your house every day, loving little Tia to pieces."

He smiled at that, and I did too.

"True." He looked at his watch. "Patricia Ann Summers will not let her grandbaby be messed up, even by me."

Chad cleared his throat and knocked on the door.

A frail woman with a crinkled smile stepped back for us to enter and closed the door as quickly as her body would allow.

"I was watching y'all through the window." Her eyes roved over Chad with the sweet concern that only an experienced mother could show. A cautious hope stilled in her stare as she spoke. "I had to come and see about my sister and her only child. I got them squared away, but this baby gives me a run for my money every day."

Tia then appeared with a large backpack hanging from her small shoulders. Her eyes almost hung as low as the loose straps of the bag, and it tore at me to see the sadness in her. She was losing people that she loved, that she cared for, and that cared about her. She was losing her world, and I understood the feeling of loss.

"I try to be good." She whispered. Taking tiny quiet steps over to us, she added, "I can be good."

"Hey," I kneeled to clasp her tiny hands between mine. "Your grandma told us how great you are. That's why we want to get to know you better."

The instant stream of tears that poured from her face was a clear indication that my pep talk hadn't worked, but they had spurred Chad out of his comatose state, and he picked Tia up to press her close.

"I want to cry too." He admitted as he pulled the bag off and handed it to me so that he could pat her back. "I really don't know what to do, Tia, but I'm your dad, and I love you already."

That stopped the blubbering, and I watched her small arms wrap around his neck as she sniffled.

"We're going to do this together. You're coming home with me, and I'm not going to leave you," Chad explained to his daughter. Maybe it was the sureness in his voice or the way that he held her, but it seemed to make her feel better.

The weird part was that I didn't feel any better. I wasn't going home to anyone but Sandy, the aging dog that I had gotten for Valerie years ago.

I hadn't felt like I was missing out on anything before and considered myself decent with kids, but there was something instinctually significant about a father's hug that could change the world, and I had witnessed it.

Tia held onto Chad like he was her saving grace. He tried to place her in the car but her grip on his back made her yo-yo back against his chest.

"Alright," he chuckled. "I guess we'll do all of this together."

I watched as he lowered himself into my backseat with Tia's limbs still attached.

"I won't let you go, Tia," he soothed as I started the car and pulled out of the driveway.

When we arrived at his home, little Tia was asleep, and whatever fear Chad had earlier was replaced by an urgency to make his daughter feel safe.

CHAPTER SIX

Regina

Micah folded his napkin once and then twice before laying it across his lap. He straightened the personal utensils in a foldable monogrammed case that he brought with him to restaurants.

I had rushed away from Nailah's big announcement to meet with him for what he said was an important update about my impending marriage.

"There's no way out of this," Micah stated plainly.

I barely paid attention to his words as my mind shuffled through how many utensil cases Micah had and if all of them had his name on them. I hadn't seen him with the same case twice that I could remember. I wondered if he had a different set for each restaurant. I wondered if he threw each set away when he was done. That would be wasteful, I concluded right as Micah knocked on the table with his knuckles.

"Earth to Regina." His clipped tone caught my attention. "Did you hear me?"

Sipping from a glass of water, I took my time to answer his rushed request.

"I heard you, but I don't like what I heard," I answered.

"You signed the document. You have to get married." Micah reiterated. "The document has gone before the board, and they agree with your parents. No loopholes"

When I originally agreed to get married, I thought that it would be simple. With all of my contacts, friends, and exes, a husband seemed like a simple task, but none of them felt right. There was not one man in the entire reach of my knowledge that I wanted to marry, and he wanted to marry me back. Not one.

Sighing, I leaned back into the chair and let my head fall against the cloth-covered panel.

"This is only a minor setback, Regina," Micah stated confidently, his chin rising with confidence. "We can make the best of this."

I straightened to look at him and the word 'we' hanging between us. He wasn't the one getting married. My face turned up without my permission, and I was one *'What you talkin' 'bout, Willis'* statement from being a character from an 80's sitcom.

"And how can *'we'* make this better if the contract is steel?" I questioned.

"By doing what was asked of you," Micah answered while straightening his watch and cufflinks. "By doing what you agreed to do."

I narrowed my eyes. Judging from his answer, he had to have been drinking something other than water.

"Don't you think I would have if I could have?" I huffed.

The waitress stepped over to our table with a smile then and halted our conversation.

"Are you ready to order, or do you need a few minutes?" She beamed a smile as her head swiveled to me and then to Micah.

Micah's swift lift of the menu and half-smirk determined that the sweet young lady wouldn't be smiling long. "I have a few questions," he stated.

"Oh. Alright," she leaned forward to view the words on the menu as Micah pointed to a description.

I took in another deep breath, already knowing where this situation was headed.

"Is the vinaigrette for this salad made in-house, or is it bottled?"

"Fresh, sir," the waitress emphasized with a nod. "It's made every morning from our own original recipe."

She lifted up to end their shared view of the menu because she must have thought that she had satisfied his questions. She didn't know that it was only the beginning.

"Good. Good," he repeated before tapping the page. "What vegan cheese options do you have? Is the honey local? Are the pecans organic?"

The young woman blinked a few times before stuttering, "We do have plant-based cheese. The honey is local, and I am not sure about the pecans. "

Micah nodded. "Can the dish be made gluten-free?"

"I'm not sure," she hesitated.

"Then who would be sure about the food on the menu that you serve daily?" He questioned with an unnecessary edge.

"Let me ask the chef," She blurted, and then she basically zoomed away from our table and through the double doors in the back.

I'd never had an issue with being intentional about food choices, but his haughty assault on staff with difficult questions never ceased to annoy me.

Micah could probably read the displeasure on my face because he lifted his shoulders in innocence and asked, "What?".

His ability to look clueless as to why I was exasperated was a talent.

"Why did you choose to eat here without checking the menu first?"

He countered my gaze. He was still handsome, and when we were dating, that look would work some kind of magic on my mind and cause me to forget whatever irritation I was feeling.

"The wait staff should know what's in the food that they serve." He added when he noticed that I hadn't relented.

"Don't be him today, please."

"Who?" he frowned.

"That persnickety ass, who won't be satisfied until you've demeaned the entire staff or proven your superior understanding of food quality."

"Persnickty ass, you say?" He gave a mirthless chuckle. "One would never guess that you have a Yale MBA with the way that you speak sometimes. If you're not quoting the down-home colloquialisms of your grandmother, then you're speaking like those people that you quit a six-figure position to help." He put air quotes around the word help as though, it wasn't exactly what I did daily.

"That's what we're doing today?" I scooted my chair in closer. "Should I remind you of how we were banned from two restaurants for your treatment of the staff? Should we revisit your cousin's engagement party when three guys had to restrain his best man after you called him a primitive life form for eating Hot Cheetos?"

Micah had his opinions and would battle his stance to the end if allowed the opportunity. It was part of the reason that he was such a sought-after lawyer, but the main reason why we couldn't be together. He knew how to go for the jugular. Our relationship status didn't affect the way he argued.

"Or should we review the last time that you were supposed to walk down the aisle and what happened to your bank account?" Micah countered with a kill shot that shut my mouth and eyes at the same time. As my lawyer, he was the only one with the intricate details of what happened with Luther.

"Well, this has been fun," I mumbled while throwing the napkin down on the table. I had no reason to go back and forth with him. "You should have used that energy to do what I asked of you."

"Regina," his voice lifted with him as we both stood. "I didn't mean to say that. Please don't leave like this. Listen, I know how amazing you are and I hate to see you limit yourself."

I had my bag over my shoulder then and I refused to look at him.

"Regina," He pleaded. "You successfully led the repurpose of land for two of the biggest shopping malls in northeastern Texas, organized new business partners, brought in residential developers, connected the smaller companies to other opportunities. You are a star in this industry that could only shine brighter if you took your place in the sky." He pushed all of the words together quickly enough to keep me from leaving. "I hate to see you waste all of that talent. I want to see you shine at your brightest."

I lowered myself into the chair and placed my bag on the chair to the side. Micah sat as well.

"Thank you for staying." He placed a hand over mine. "I apologize for taking it too far."

The waitress came back then with answers to all of Micha's questions, and we ordered without an issue.

"Let's hear this plan." I sighed as soon as we were alone.

"You get married, but not for real." He looked proud of himself, while I waited for him to tell me something I hadn't already thought of.

"Alright." I nodded. "Are you saying that I can do a civil ceremony or something? I can have a play wedding maybe?"

He shook his head. "No, it has to be legal, but," he lifted a finger as his voice and eyes brightened, "you don't have to be in love. You just need a partner."

"For ten years though," I reminded him. "I have to stay married to this person for the next decade to remain the head of the company. That's a long time to play at partnership."

"Would we really have to play at it, Regina?" He asked.

Micah was everything that a woman could want. He had a nice athletic body, a great job, intelligence, solid support system, is wealthy, and is sometimes thoughtful. There was so much about him that I liked in general. It was the small granular things that built into the whole of him that grated on my nerves. He was often uptight, consistently boastful, and regularly judgemental. That didn't work for me. My someone would need patience.

As much as Micah annoyed me, I know that I irritated him too. We could hardly make it through it a meal together without frustration.

I wanted to feel something when I looked at him. I wanted to ignore that everything about him was perfect like he expected me to be. I wanted someone who liked me for the person that I was at that moment.

"Tell me about the other options." I purposefully left his 'we' statement where it was.

"Are you sure?" He asked taking my hand into his.

Nothing. I felt nothing.

I gave him a half-smile and nodded.

He removed his hand from mine, opened his attache, straightened his collar, and cleared his throat.

"As of the latest ruling, you have exactly three weeks left on the extension to find your husband before your father takes over."

I shook my head.

"Knowing him, he's literally got men filling out applications as we speak, I bet." I was being sarcastic, but I wouldn't put it past my father.

"He's definitely talking to some candidates," Micah nodded. "He didn't reach out to me personally, but a friend of mine was offered a business opportunity with him out of the blue."

I exhaled before adding, "And Reginald Strong doesn't throw out opportunities for fun."

As I focused solely on work and closing up cases, the time flew by. Three weeks later, I was in the car with my mother headed to the airport. I had planned to have a peaceful ride to the airport for Nailah's wedding. I planned to pop in my earbuds while I slouched in the back seat of a town car and forgot the worries associated with my dwindling days at Social Services. Chill. That's it, that's all I wanted. What I got was the complete opposite. Upon finding out that I was heading to Puerto Rico on the same day that she was heading to the Dominican Republic for her annual nip and tuck procedure, she requested we share a ride since we were both flying domestically.

"I see that you're making a habit of dressing like a hippie lounge singer." Cherry swiped a piece of hair from my face and pressed it into place, her jeweled bracelet catching the light of the sun to shine directly into my eye. "Would it have hurt to put on a pantsuit?"

I had worn a cotton maxi dress with a light blue jean jacket, chrome-colored flats, and my favorite bangles.

"Why?" I asked, already exasperated after only five minutes in the car. "I'm getting on a plane to sit for hours with people that I don't even know."

"Exactly. You never know who you might run into" Folding her eyebrows and wrinkling her nose, she placed a hand on the collar of my jacket to smooth it flat. "Which is all the more reason to stay dressed to impress."

"I wish you and daddy would stop pressing me," I grunted, slightly nudging her hand away. "Your pressure is one reason that I left the company to start with."

My mother didn't flinch at my words. In fact, she barely acknowledged them as she casually threw back the cliche that they should have been tattooed on my hand instead of repeated so often.

"Strong pressure turns coal into diamonds, and strong diamonds never break." She narrowed her gaze near my cheek. "Are you using the cleanser and toner from Lancome? Your pores are waving at me, dear."

"Can we skip the part where you criticize all of my life decisions and jump straight to why you lied to me?" I was tired of being dissected and discussed by her and my father every time we were together. Cherry had been obsessed with making me a darling debutante and my father with making me a cunning CEO. Their criticism, even though it came from love, was overwhelming, to say the least.

I had listened to them and followed most of their rules as though they had been carved into stone tablets pulled from a burning bush. Then I learned the truth. And once the truth was made clear, I didn't let them cloud the vision I had for my life again until the contract. Until my father put my free will at odds with our family legacy, I lived my life the way that I wanted to.

"Why didn't you tell me the truth?" I repeated the question since she had chosen not to hear it the first time.

"The truth about what, dear?" She answered with perfect elocution and poise. Even while sitting, my mother stood tall. Her back was straight, and her neck lifted; she looked like she was preparing for tea with the queen.

"That the company has been losing money, and that dad's investment strategies haven't been as sound as they once were."

That caused a flicker of something. It made her shoulders droop a bit and her chin fell a smidgen. Not enough for anyone else to notice, but I had spent my entire life under Cherry's tutelage. I knew her.

"We wanted to tell you, Genie," Cherry said softly, almost sounding sincere. She turned her head toward the window slightly as her mind seemed to drift off in the same direction as her gaze.

She was hiding something. She wore the same look that I saw when she was tired of talking to people at a fundraiser but still wanted to appear compassionate. As the wife of a man in the business, she had perfected the art of concealing her true feelings.

"Cut the bull shit, Cherry," I snipped.

The way her neck snapped in my direction had to set a new record for the quickest head turn by a non-possessed woman in history.

"Don't get uncouth now." Country girl Cherlissia poked out from behind the elite Cherry socialite mask. That was exactly what I wanted from her, for her to drop the facade and talk to me.

"You and dad wanted me to come back to the company by any means necessary. Returning to a flourishing company that would practically run itself was supposed to be the icing on your little cake of a contract." I reminded her.

"Nobody is trying to swindle you, chile." She tightened her shoulders and raised a finger to stab the air between us. "You need to let go of this mission work to save the children and step into your birth rite. Damn right, we put a contract on your stubborn behind. It was the only way to move you. It was the only way to save this company before it crashed and burned."

I didn't understand why it would burn. What was the problem?

She took a deep breath as she pressed a flat hand down the front of her shirt and held it to her stomach. That was a lot of emotion for her in one sitting. I watched as she seemed to swallow her irritation and sit back into the grand madame that she had become accustomed to playing.

"Mommy," I placed my hand over hers and searched the browns of her eyes. "I'm going to help. I'm going to do this for the Strong tradition and because I appreciate everything that you and Dad have done for me."

The last time that I stepped into the role prepared by my parents, I made so many mistakes. I had lost myself in the company. I had lost myself in Luther. This time it would be different. This time I wouldn't be blinded by a need to please or by love.

"We all have a role to play in maintaining the success of a legacy," My mother agreed.

I nodded. It was time for me to fully embrace my role, my insecurities included. This would be about cementing a future using the path that had been carved out for me by

Obidiah, the thinker; Big Jen, the entrepreneur; Dunbar, the educator; Josiah and Rema, the developers; and my father Reginald, who was the culmination of their wildest dreams. I would get married and run the company because they had run the race before me, and my father was now passing the baton.

"I'm glad to hear that you and that pesky lawyer will stop fighting what is inevitable," she sighed before dawning a grin. "Your father is excited about the selection process. When you get back from your little trip, we'll get it all taken care of."

She spoke about my pending marriage and CEO status as if it were an appointment at the salon, and the process didn't include the merging of two lives.

I nodded as she continued.

"He's been working diligently to find someone that can not only handle business but take care of your heart too." My mom smiled, and it was genuine. Marriage would make her happy, but it made me wonder where my happiness fit in the situation.

"I don't understand why I have to get married. I can run the company on my own."

"People like you and me were not created to walk this earth alone." Her voice was earnest, but her words still hit my chest. She didn't have faith in my ability and the words she added only compounded the hurt. "That job is tough and this world is even tougher. It could tear you down in a second."

"Then why drag someone else into the endless hours, the never-ending issue with personnel and purchases, and the non-stop grind of always trying to make a profit." I countered.

"If he's the right one, you will not have to drag him anywhere, my love." Her eyes softened on my face as a wistful smile winked across her lips. "He will be a confidant when you feel like no one of this world will understand you. He will be sturdy when you are weak, and level-headed when you are in disarray." She placed a hand on my shoulder as she explained more. "You can drive this company Genie, but I don't want this company to drive you away from what matters most."

"Like what?" I hunched my shoulders trying to stay in the realm of respect but still express my misunderstanding. "What matters to you and the 'Reginald Strong' other than the company?"

I was quite pleased with my tone and the way I got those words out without cursing until I saw her chest sink some.

"Genie, you matter more than anything. I love this company, I love your father, but you, above everything else, are my baby." Her words were gentle as she placed hands across her stomach and heart simultaneously.

Her words of affection landed on me and hit deep in the pit of my soul. I wanted to hug her, but she had stiffened again before I could even shift in the seat. She was speaking about the company again before I could even lift my arm.

"This company was developed through partnerships and that shouldn't change. It is built up through family. That's how I met Reginald. Our fathers brought us together and we fell in love," Cherry stated. "Obidiah and Big Jen- David and Hannah- Dunbar and Mary- Your dad's parents, Josiah and Rema. They worked together. They built together."

"I know the history." I reminded her.

"Did you plan to ignore that history or only plan to disrespect it? If you value the sacrifices made for you then act like it. Why complain?"

"The expectations of being the daughter of Reginald Strong were high: *Don't leave home without your hair combed*, *Situps now or saddles later*, and your favorite question *People see the package before the product, what does your wrapping say about you?*. I could call out at least one hundred Strong sayings. You and dad were so intense about the way I was perceived, my grades, and being in the community to the point that there was no space to breathe. I didn't enjoy it, I just did it to make you happy."

"And you believe that was wrong?" She rolled her neck back.

"That's not what I said, Cherry." I pressed the space between my eyes.

"Let me tell you about something wrong." She continued as though I had said nothing. "My father worked sixteen-hour days and could barely read the paper that he signed to apply. My mom filled out the application for every job he applied for. When they took money out of his check for 'supplies' and other fees, they would point to his employee handbook and say 'didn't you read it?' when he questioned them. He's why I worked hard in school, valued my education, and was able to help your father. He is why I pushed you to do well in school."

The passion of her words kept my complaints swimming in my brain. I didn't want to interrupt, even if I had a differing opinion. It was rare that she opened up to me. We talked all of the time, but not about the past, not about her childhood before money.

"My mother couldn't fix hair to save her soul or mine." Cherry gave a bitter chuckle. "She tried, but I looked like something was nested in my head or some cartoon character that had been frightened."

And in no way was that an exaggeration. I had seen the scarce photos of my mother as a child that she kept sealed in a book that was locked in a box and hidden in her closet.

Cherry slid a finger through her silky straight mane as she recalled more from her youth. "She gave me a relaxer at home once after we went swimming and my hair fell out in patches. Then when I started doing my hair, I packed it down with products and pulled it into ponytails so tight that it broke off. Guess who noticed? Guess who was teased about always looking a mess?" Her eyebrows shot higher with each question.

"But your dad won the lottery." I reminded her. "Any of those haters that had something to say back then had to close their mouth when he moved your whole family to Dallas."

"I was sixteen by then." A rye laugh laced her words. "We had been poor longer than we had been rich, and when he moved us to the good neighborhood, and the good school, I wasn't good enough. My accent, my slang, it was always something. There was always a reason that I didn't belong." She took a deep breath. "I never wanted to give people a reason to say that my daughter wasn't pretty enough or smart enough or dressed well enough."

I nodded before attempting to get my point across again.

"The people don't live in our house. People don't run our lives." I was trying to keep my emotions in check, but my frustration slipped out through a crack in my voice.

"I taught you what I knew, Genie." She placed a hand near mine as though she wanted to hold it, but had decided against it. "I taught you what I felt."

"From pain though." My voice raised to the level that warranted a lifted eyebrow from my mother.

I took a deep breath and brought it down a level.

"You taught me from a place of pain and hurt, not love."

Her chest caved as if I had physically hit her, and something like tears collected at the bottom of her eyes. "You don't think that I love you?"

"Cherry." I grabbed the hand still at her side and held it in mine. "Mommy. I know you love me, but I want you to teach me from your joy too."

She still didn't look relieved but had at least let her other hand fall on top of mine.

"That's precisely why I want you to be a part of the company again, get married, and start a family." Her grip tightened as she used her eyes to plead with me. "Moments working through crises with your father, taking trips to close deals, and absolutely everything having to do with being your mother has filled my life with joy."

I wanted to give my mother more than a faint grin. She sounded hopeful. I wanted to feel that way too, but the thought of giving up the job I loved and entering a union with someone I didn't even know, made the future seem grim.

Two hours later, I was placing my bag in the overhead compartment of the plane. If I had to fly commercial, I preferred the pods and individual space of first-class but there was limited seating. For Nailah, I sacrificed. I wasn't sure which day I would be able to get away from my office. I worked my ass off to close out my cases and say goodbye to children I had been supporting for years. The consequence of that was I had three nights to spend with my friend for her wedding and I would have to share my space with a stranger to get there.

Earbuds. Check.

Playlist downloaded. Check.

Trashy books in the tote. Check.

Neck pillow and blanket. Ready.

The only thing missing was the passenger assigned to sit next to me. When I bought my ticket, I noticed that it was a full flight, and the aisle seat had already been taken.

I pulled out a bottle of water and a pack of chocolate mints to ease into the journey ahead and hoped my prayers for a decent plane partner weren't ignored.

He shouldn't have been a surprise. We were traveling to the same destination. We were traveling to witness the same two people promise forever to each other. I should have known to prepare my heart and lady parts for the sound and smell of him. I needed to buy stock in whatever cologne he was wearing because it could be used as a tool to increase libido in women.

"Regina," My name floated from him melodically as he folded himself into the seat next to me. "It's good to see you."

My words were stuck somewhere between my rising chest and suddenly dry mouth. I would have questioned my consciousness if it weren't for the warming I suddenly felt in my belly.

I flailed an awkward wave hello with a grin that might have gotten me a quick admission to residential treatment, but it was out of my control. I couldn't put a cap on any of the awkwardness that I usually stored away.

He slid back into the leather chair with ease, as though we were in each other's company regularly. The way that Terrence moved didn't require that he say much. His presence garnered respect without a single utterance. Even in a black t-shirt and black cargo pants he wore confidence as clear as the honey of his eyes and that amped me up.

"You're a Junior Mint fan too?" He asked, nodding his head forward and eyeing the box in my lap.

"Original and true. These are my favorite candies." I lifted the box toward him. "Want some."

I probably misread the mischievous glint in his eyes as they traced a path from the box of candy to my mouth.

"I'm good." The words rumbled from his lips and fell somewhere between my thighs.

Good, he was. And I wanted to feel all of that goodness pressed up against me. I wasn't sure why the urge to indulge in him kept jumping up to pinch me in the nipples, but I wanted him to fill me up.

"But," He reached a long arm down to one of the many pockets on the cargo pants he wore and slipped his thick hand in to pull out his own Junior Mints. "Great minds think alike."

He nodded his head as he opened the box. "I think this is the second time that our minds have been great together."

Even if I had a response that didn't reveal the giddiness flipping through my insides, the flight attendant calling everyone's attention to the screens in the front of the plane for emergency directions cut our conversation short.

I was nervous about sitting next to a stranger, but being so close to Terrence and not being able to act on my attraction was overwhelming. No matter what I tried to listen to, read, or view, I kept traveling back to him. So I closed the magazine full of blurry words that I hadn't read and turned to the reason for my lack of focus.

"I thought that you would've left earlier in the week," I threw out the words without thinking. It wasn't a question, and I wasn't sure how he would take my observation. I hoped that it didn't sound judgy.

His eyes were kind when he looked up from his phone.

"I don't like to leave my shop." His words shot out as an absolute until he added and then amended. "Especially if one of my brothers isn't there to step in." Irritation stamped across his face as he spoke. "They were only getting one day out of me. I was only going to the ceremony. My mom and aunt had other ideas. 3 days out was our compromise." He shrugged. "I don't understand why they need a whole week for what takes two minutes?"

His brows furrowed with a clear annoyance for the drawn-out celebration.

It was sweet that he valued his mother and aunt so much that he agreed to participate. I wished that the only thing that I had to do for my parents was to attend a wedding.

"I feel like Tyriq wants to make the moment last for Nailah. Making new memories together. Hopefully, it will shade over some of the sadder ones from her past. The girl deserves some happiness. Why not start with the wedding." I didn't have to think about the grin that happened after. It was natural, being near him made me smiley.

"Is that how you'd want to get married?" Kindness and genuine interest radiated from his eyes as he waited for an answer.

His question hit closer to home than he knew, and I had to seriously pause to consider how I would want to get married.

"I hadn't thought about it," I replied truthfully.

"Why not? You can't tell me that some man isn't blowing up your phone or dropping mad dollars trying to impress you and claim you for himself."

"Actually no, not right now. It hasn't been this way often or long, but I am completely single."

"You? Single?" Even with hiked eyebrows, he was cute. "You must mean the single where you have men taking you out every night, but no one that you make a promise to."

"No." I chuckled. "I've been that type of single before. Had a few male associates. Hell, that's how I spent most of last year, but the contacts have been cleared." I swiped my hands across the air to emphasize my meaning. "I am single-single, as in no one in my space or that I have to answer."

"I hear that." His mouth flattened as he nodded his head. "I haven't done the relationship thing in a few years."

I almost choked on my mint.

"Wait, did you say years?" My eyes pushed forward with surprise. I didn't think he would have a harem of women, but at least one somebody he got with. "You've been single, for years? As in plural, more than one year?"

"I didn't commit to anyone, and time is life. I won't waste mine or anyone else's," He lifted his shoulder up and down. "Being in a relationship was too damn draining. I had to be something more than myself or someone different entirely. While I'm on this earth I choose to live the life that I feel the best waking up to everyday, no compromise on that."

I nodded as I reflected on the relationships that had sustained and drained me over the years.

"Relationships usually bring plenty of opportunities to compromise your thoughts and feelings for someone else's benefit." To spare the relationship with my parents, I would be giving up my life as a social worker, my passion project.

He nodded and popped a few chocolate mints into his mouth, "For a while, I didn't want to be obligated to anyone or anything but my business. I had friends but nothing serious."

"A while, huh? Have your thoughts changed? You thinking about settling down now?" I was confident in asking, but when my eyes fell against his intense gaze, something stirred in my chest, and I had to divert my sight.

Terrence didn't seem to notice my switch and he stumbled through an answer. "Yes. Maybe. A little. I don't know, I'm getting up there in age."

That got my attention, and I gave his body and then his face a quick perusal. "Up in age? You can't be more than 35?"

"34 to be exact."

"See. Young. You have a whole life ahead of you. The thirties are like the teenage years of adulthood."

"What?" His eyebrows scrunched together as he stopped chewing on the candy.

"See, in your twenties, you're a baby to being an adult. It's new, and you're getting your legs under you and establishing yourself. That takes a few years. In your thirties, though, you know the game a little better. Do you remember being 17?"

"Oh, yeah. Junior and Senior year of high school. I thought I was invincible."

"That's the 30's. You're established, you have a little money, you know what you're doing, and now you can enjoy some of the benefits of grinding in your 20's."

"I gotcha." he nodded. "Still, there's this little nagging voice that keeps reminding me that I need to build my business and a family, or else what is it all for?"

"I don't have an answer for that one, but-" I pointed a finger in the air as the idea hit me. "I do know where I want to get married."

"Alright. Share. Where?"

"My grandmother's farm."

"You, Ms. Designer Everything, want to get married on a farm?" I was almost offended by the disbelief etched on his face.

"Aht- Aht," I waggled my finger before clarifying. "Not just any farm, my grandmother's farm. There's a difference." I interjected.

"It's difficult to imagine you power stepping down the aisle with pigs and chickens running loose."

I shifted my body slightly to face him since I needed him to fully grasp what I was about to say. The small inhale of his cologne almost made me forget my words, but I dodged total mind loss and explained.

"My grandfather won something like a lottery when my mom was a teenager."

I was waiting for him to question how much or if there was a shift in the way that he looked at me, but his eyes remained neutral.

"I've never known anyone who won a lottery," he stated with nothing extra on it.

"Well, he did. It was new back then, but he took that money and sought out," I paused for a quick second, deciding to omit that the person who helped my grandfather was Jeremiah Strong, my dad's father. That's how Cherry's family was introduced to the Strongs. Terrence only knew what I had told him so far. I liked that he didn't know that my father was arena owner Reginald Strong. "My grandfather got some investment help and bought some real estate."

"Sounds smart." His words were neutral, lacking the awe that came when people realized who my father was, and I liked that. I liked that he was gathering information. I liked that I was just Regina.

"Would you expect my ancestors to be anything less than fabulous?" I chuckled, only slightly teasing.

"Nah. Not really." He gave his cheek a lazy lift, but the way his eyes scanned me and his voice dropped an octave made me want to scoot in closer and find out what sounds he made after a good kiss.

I shook off the feeling and decided that sharing more of the farm's importance was the best option.

"He moved the whole family into a fancy north Dallas suburb and put his girls in the best schools."

"So far so good," he nodded.

"My grandmother never fit in with the 'city folk'. Once their kids graduated from high school, he bought her a few acres of land in East Texas, and they built a farm on it."

I could still smell the banana bread she would make for me and hear the spinning of the warped fan that she refused to throw away. I missed her.

"When I was there, I could run barefoot anywhere. We created crafts and made messes. We had honey buns and ginger ale on the porch in shorts, and we watched the world move fast while we drank slowly. It was where I could be me, where I felt unconditionally loved. If I was starting a new love, that's where I would want it to begin."

"I like that," he nodded. "A place where love begins." He gave me a full, genuine smile with a peek of teeth showing and the kidlike, *'I got my first three-carat diamond'* joy filled me too.

CHAPTER SEVEN

Jerrence

S he was trouble. The kind worth getting into, though. I still didn't consider myself a man that luck liked, and when the turbulence started, and the plane shook with all of its might, I hoped that Regina being next to me was the beginning of a change in that luck.

"On no," Regina gripped the sides of the seat so tightly that her knuckles were turning white.

The plane did a quick shimmy as the captain's voice came over the loudspeaker to explain that everyone should buckle as the flight would be choppy for a bit.

"This can't be the end," Regina chanted to herself over and over as she buckled her seat belt.

Earlier in life, I had come to an understanding with death that when it was my time to go, he would give me some warning. I didn't have that gut feeling about myself, and I wouldn't let another person that I cared about pass away on my watch. Regina would be safe with me because I would protect her with my life. I hadn't known her that long, but the shiver that ran up my spine as the realization circled my mind reinforced it as truth.

"Hey," I placed a hand over hers as I noticed that she had returned to clawing the seat.

"This is the worst part of flying," She blurted between harsh breaths.

"It is," I replied. "Listen to my voice."

I moved closer to her, placing my mouth near the base of her ear. I needed her to hear me.

"Let's be somewhere else," I suggested. "Imagine us pulling up to your grandmother's farm."

She nodded too frantically to be calm.

"Can you see the porch? As you open the door, can you smell the grass, feel the wind?"

"Yes," She exhaled. "She's handing me her signature ginger pop."

Her breathing slowed some.

"Good."

"And she has a fresh 7Up bundt cake." Regina smiled generously before opening her eyes.

"You alright?" I asked while matching the grin that she wore.

Her shoulders lowered, and her hand relaxed under my hand.

"Better now," She nodded.

The plane shook again, and she squeezed her eyes tight.

"Look at me, Regina."

She flipped open her eyes.

"I promise that I won't let anything happen to you." I leaned over to take her other hand in mine as well.

She didn't close her eyes when the plane jumped again.

"Do you trust me?"

Her eyes traveled to where our hands were joined and then back to mine.

Her earnest "Yes." went straight to my heart.

***

"Yo'! They got some big booty hoes out here, and they run deep." Chad's voice dropped into a semi-whisper as he explained. "They're in the street, the hotel, on the beach, those cheeks moving like *womp, womp, womp*." He dropped one cupped hand and then the other in succession at the same rhythm he described how the women moved.

That's where he lost me. We were chilling in the luxurious resort bar a few hours after my plane touched down, and I wasn't interested. Most of the family had been on the island for three nights already, and Chad was giving me the play-by-play of his adventures. I wasn't paying much attention. First, if I wasn't about to get it, then I didn't want to hear it. Second, and more importantly, I was thinking about Regina. Maybe I should have expected her to be on the late plane with me. Her job as a social worker wasn't as flexible.

Still, her soft brown eyes gazing up at me beneath coal-black lashes came as a complete surprise. I had prepared myself for a mind-numbing ride that I would have to fight off memories and press down anxiety. I didn't want to go to the wedding. First, it would include interacting with people that I didn't know or come in contact with regularly. I hated small talk. There were only so many words to say about the weather. Second, no matter how elated I was that my brother had found someone to care for that would care for him back, the ache for that same opportunity had started to crack through the shell of my heart. The wedding would only make that feeling grow.

When I walked onto the plane I saw her fidgeting in her seat, then digging in her bag, only to begin tussling with a box of candy, the crack in the shell inched further. She was everything but still, and completely amazing to watch. Twice the universe had provided unintended opportunities to be close to the woman that had snagged my attention each time we were in the same space. That rarely happened. It was even rarer for my mind to float into thoughts about someone once we parted, but she intrigued me. Her friendship and fierce protectiveness of Nailah was a springboard into a pool of questions about how and why the two became close.

"Are you even listening, bro?" He slapped the table and a goofy grin rode across his mouth. Excitement crisscrossed his face as he bounced on the stool next to mine. "You gotta see the inventory out there. Dudes come talking tall tales about the Dominican Republic, but Puerto Rico? Puerto Rico bro?" He nodded his head up and down. "They got some '*mami*'s that I'm trying to make a mommy, you feel me? You gotta come with me tomorrow before tonight's outing."

That was the part that caught my attention.

"Outing? The hell is that?" I agreed to come to the unnecessary ass ceremony but to find out that we had a field trip too was overkill.

"Boat tonight, cigars with the guys, the burlesque show, and random other shit that they came up with." He ticked the instances off on his fingers. "Didn't you read the itinerary?"

"Itinerary?" I shook my head quickly to assure I was in the right reality. I hadn't seen an itinerary. "And you did?"

Was Chad smart? Yes. Did he follow a schedule or directions? No.

"Nah." He blew out a deep breath. "You know Mali shared a whole damn calendar with my ass, got alarms going off on my phone for reminders in 30-minute intervals for fittings, decorations, and activities and shit." The scrunch in his eyebrows expressed his annoyance. "Man, be glad you got here late."

I picked up the fresh two fingers of brown liquor that the bartender placed in front of me.

"I know better. Aunt Pat would have me tying ribbons, stuffing bags, and standing on ladders. I know she was directing y'all asses like a choir. Tyriq is her baby, even though Shirley gave birth to him."

Catching a later flight was better than I knew. I missed out on the bulk of the nonsense and got to ride with Regina.

I have known women like Regina all of my life. Sophisticated women that didn't befriend the friendless, un-rich kind. They ran in elite, alpha chick covens that fed off the insecurities of the meek and geeks. It made them bigger when others were smaller and gigantic when others shrunk themselves without a word or glance. Regina looked the part and spoke the same sounds, but I could tell that Nailah genuinely trusted her. That was amazing in itself. I didn't know much about Regina, only the tidbits that my soon-to-be sister-in-law shared in conversation. I wanted to know more, like how she drove the most loaded and unique Mercedes E Class sedan that I'd ever seen. She had driven up to Tyriq's home in a Maserati that wasn't even available for the general market. All of that was on a social worker's salary. She was different, and our conversation in the confines of the crowded plane only magnified how unordinary she was.

Chad was still speaking; something about a slick pimp and whores checking in and staying in the hotel. The drink was doing its job and kept the thoughts about soaring through the sky with the fly woman consistently floating through my mind.

Feeling a soft small hand against my shoulder, I couldn't help but hope that it was her. The tingle of breath at the corner of my ear made it difficult to register the caress traveling down my thigh longer than necessary. The whispered words: "I heard you were the best man" snapped my mind to attention. It wasn't the sultry sweet voice that I longed to hear. It wasn't Regina, the woman I had been trying not to want.

"Whoa there," I put an end to her feel-up real quick, my elbow effectively acting as a protractor to create a wider radius of space. "Private territory. I don't even know your name sweetie."

"Raven." Chad's Cheshire grin and devilish nod told me that he knew her before I could even ask. "You found us. You're right this is my cousin Terrence, the one I was telling you about."

He had walked over to her, hand on her shoulder introducing her like she was a college buddy or something. I did not do hookups. I wondered what he had told her about me that had her eyes skirting my body and her thinking that she could walk up on me and grab?

She nodded. "You were right. It won't be a problem at all."

"What won't be a problem?" I looked down at the cup. It was empty, but had there been something in it? I felt like I had missed something.

Before I could answer, the woman, who wasn't bad looking but very forward, was trying to climb my leg.

"No. Wait. Put your leg down." I was flustered, confused, and possibly tipsy but the woman was relentless. She was still lifting and pushing forward even as I held my arms out.

"I'm already paid for." she exhaled as she pushed against me.

"Step back," I said with a little more force. "Think of it as a come up then and go away."

"Your loss." She rolled her eyes before she sauntered away.

The keywords 'paid for' cartwheeled through my mind. I looked at Chad who was doubled over laughing, when his eyes met mine he took off in a sprint that left a 'Looney Tune' type cloud of dust in his trail.

I jumped up from the stool ready to chase and pumble the cousin that worked my nerves more than anyone. I didn't make it. Once I heard her voice, I knew that I would be sitting right back down at a table.

"Terrence," She called out looking over the rim of her oval shades. "I've been looking for you," the rhythm in her voice stopped me in my tracks.

"Hi mom," I turned to face my vacation-ready mother. She had on a water-blue linen pant-suit with a matching straw hat and bag, leather sandals, and shades that pressed against her full cheeks.

"Your fingers broke?" Her eyes narrowed as she stepped in so close to me that I could smell the White Diamonds cologne that she never left the home without spraying. "Your throat alright?" She questioned as she snapped her arms up toward my face.

"Mama." I tried to swivel away from the press of her hand, but she was quicker and stronger than she looked. "I'm fine."

"Can't be." Her hat shifted as she shook her head with conviction. "Any child that broke through my body would take two seconds and two fingers to type two words and put my aging heart at rest." She moved her hands away from me to grip her chest as though she were going to meet her ancestors that very moment.

"I'm good, mom." I started to explain, but she was already charging toward a booth in the restaurant that I was attempting to leave with the energy of a high-school athlete.

Pinching the bridge of my nose, I followed behind her.

"Buy me dinner." She huffed as she tugged her bag higher on her shoulder as we reached the table. "And any flight you find yourself on, domestic or cross the world, you better let me know your feet were put on top of the ground and not under it in a body bag."

The waiter hadn't asked for our drink order before my mom was starting in on my life.

"I love you Trunk, but I worry about you."

I groaned at the use of my former nickname. I have always been a solid guy, even as a kid, so they called me Trunk because I was wide as a tree trunk.

"I know you don't like that name, but you're my first baby. My helper and I can't help but worry about you."

"I'm good, Ma."

"Are you really? I know this has to be hard for you. Tyriq is closest to you and now he's getting a wife and child. He hasn't been around as much. I remember the sadness you had after Valerie- I don't ever want to see that again."

"Are you trying to make me sad?" I frowned. "I have a life that doesn't center around you guys. Tyriq being happy doesn't make me sad."

"I want to make sure you are aware of what you're feeling and could feel. You scared us, scared me, all of those years ago after Valerie."

My family had been worried ten years ago. I had given them a reason to be back then. I looked as confident as possible when I told my mother that I was fine because I was. I wasn't a fan of being extra like Tyriq, so I couldn't be ecstatic about the events, but I wasn't sad.

It had only been a couple of hours on the island with my family and I knew that I had arrived too soon.

Chapter Eight

Regina

I thought she was my friend. Friends don't put your life in jeopardy for a wilderness expedition. But Nailah wasn't thinking about me or my wardrobe. Nope, it was all about her seeing some glowing water.

"For real Nailah? This is what you want to do with your life?" My stiletto pumps sank deeper into the sand as I clung to the life vest with folded arms and questioned where the misunderstanding occurred. I remembered Nailah telling me that we would go out on the water to see the lights. I should have asked more questions.

Illuminated by the dimming sun and light from the nearby tour shop, I watched the other wedding party members row circles through the water in yellow kayaks. All of the boats were two-seaters. Everyone was doubled up, and I didn't have a partner.

"Come on Regina," Nailah's face drooped with the same sadness in her words. "It'll be worth it to see the water glow."

"I don't have on the right outfit for this kind of experience," I waved a hand down my torso and legs to highlight that I was dressed in a silk shirt, ankle pants, and heels. "

"You can still go. At least you have on pants," Nailah wined. "Taking risks is a part of life. If you win, you will be happy. If you lose, you will be wise."

I glossed over Nailah's quote and didn't answer the question right off because Terrence had walked by. He didn't wear a strong cologne, and I could tell that he bathed with a pine-scented soap. That part was very distinct. Whatever mixed with that fresh clean smell of him, undeniably made me pause to pay attention to him. He had dressed in black again. I was beginning to believe that he didn't own any other colors.

He lowered himself onto one of the contraptions. The tattoos on his lower arms were visible and flexing in the waning light as he held onto the dock for leverage.

"Nailah." I turned to face my friend and placed a hand on her shoulder. "I love you like a sister, but when I agreed to this, I thought we were getting on a party boat." I threw a hand up into the blank air. "Where's the yacht? A cruiser? Something bigger than a pool float?"

Jubilee and Mali were already in the water practicing moving their paddles in sync while giggling and spinning circles.

"Come on in Regina," Mali called out. "It's not as hard as it looks."

She was further away, so I yelled to her from the gut. "You two have fun without me!"

"Don't be like that," Jubilee yelled back and splashed water in my direction.

I recoiled from the water as though it would burn me at first touch. "Not today Satan." I shielded my leave-out with a hand. "This is a new install."

"Regina," Nailah tried one last time. "It's more intimate this way. It's closer to nature. This is the reason I wanted my wedding here, to see the bioluminescence."

She almost had me. I stepped closer to examine the 'boat' as she quoted 'take every chance to drop every fear". I felt compelled. I didn't want it to be said that I chickened out on an experience with my newfound posse. Nailah had tried sushi with me, but kayaking through the water in the dark was not the boating I imagined when Nailah told me about the outing.

"So I have to move the boat with that paddle?" I looked again. I didn't understand how I was supposed to enjoy the ride and workout too. "If you didn't know, I believe that most fun things don't include manual labor."

I know the tour guide was tired of me and Tyriq rested his head in his palm. I wasn't sure why Nailah wanted me to get in the water so badly, or why she wanted to squat her pregnant ass in one of those things, but I didn't. I didn't want to mess up my clothes. I didn't want to ride alone. I also didn't want to be the holdup or the problem. The rest of the wedding party was already in the water and rowing off while the groom sat waiting on his bride to get me, her friend, in on the experience.

"Regina." I looked to my left and there he was. "You can ride with me."

Between my shoes in the sand and my wobbly knees, I could have tipped right over then and there.

There were so many valid reasons to go with it, to go with him, but I hesitated.

"I can?"

He laughed. The sound rolled out from him and seemed both out of place and natural.

"'How did we get here?' The lift of his cheek and shake of his head clued me to his sarcasm.

I automatically thought of a Debra Cox song my nanny used to play. That made me smile.

"I was wondering the same thing," I responded.

"I didn't want to do group activities," he added, "but we can suffer through this together."

My father always hated when I was indecisive and my mother when I tucked my lip under my teeth. I was doing both. Although the tour company appeared mostly reputable, we hadn't discussed the weight capacities of each device, emergency plans in case of malfunction, or what to do if we drifted off from the pack. There were several unknowns. I did not like the unknown. I needed it planned out and mapped. They hadn't even given us a map. I didn't know where I was.

"I got you here safely right? On the plane, on the shuttle over?" Terrence's voice interrupted the spin of questions. "Nothing happened. I'm steady, Regina. I'm the most predictable person you will ever meet. I got this." He was reaching for my hand by then. "I got you. Trust me."

I nodded my head because I did trust him. Then I looked down at my yacht outfit.

"I don't have the right clothes." I looked back at Nailah. I couldn't kayak in heels.

The tour guide piped in quickly. "We sell swim shoes, I will get you a pair for free."

I had on pants, but I also couldn't row in the bustier and silk shirt I was wearing.

"Do you have any T-Shirts?" I called after the retreating tour guide.

"No, just water shoes." He said without stopping.

With no warning to my sanity, Terrence lifted the shirt from his body and held it out to me.

"Here," I sort of heard Terrence say. I felt like the sight of him took away my hearing.

"Thank you," I whispered as I tried not to drool over him in the sleeveless muscle shirt.

I felt it in the core of me that looking at him made things better. I slid out of my silk shirt to expose the corset underneath, folded it, and placed it in my bag. Leaving the short bra-like tank on, I pulled Terrence's shirt over it and let it drape down to my thighs.

"Looks good on you," he winked at me as he plucked at the huge shirt.

"Thank you," I grinned back at him and leaned against his arm to pull off my heels.

Terrence steadied more than my body with an arm around my side as I pulled on the water shoes. He had a soothing effect. My mind didn't race with questions. Instinctively, I felt at peace.

The guide and Terrence helped me get settled in the canoe and I was ready to go.

"Yay! Thank you, brother." Nailah blew Terrence a kiss as she did something that resembled a skip over to her husband to hug him.

"Where is my thank you?" I was appalled and I let her know. "I'm over here risking nappy roots and a wet bottom."

Nailah chuckled but was already stepping onto her canoe with Tyriq.

"You won't get wet, you won't fall, and that beautiful hair of yours will stay just how you have it. I got you. We got this." Terrence assured.

I didn't confirm with words but I honestly felt like my heart telepathically agreed with him that we were now indeed a team.

CHAPTER NINE

Terrence

My brother's smile could have powered electricity for the whole resort. Tyriq was ecstatic. The man hadn't stopped randomly rapping his happy feelings and two-stepping since he'd been on the island.

"It's for life. Got me a wife. Nailah's my girl, about to make her my world," he did a Motown era glide across the wood planks of the cabana, shrugged his shoulders, and spun around in a circle. "My world, my world."

We were gathered there for the rehearsal, but the way my brother was acting, I wasn't sure that he wouldn't burst from excitement before the actual wedding day.

The two of them had agreed to have the ceremony at dusk. They wanted to marry right as the harsh heat of the sun descended and brought a burst of color into the coolness of the night. Symbolic? Maybe. Nailah had dreamt of sunset and became frantic that it meant death or that something bad was going to happen. Aunt Pat assured her with talks of the old passing away to become new. She interpreted that the dream could represent the pain of her past setting as she transitioned into the dawn of a new joy. She capped it off with some words about a new day beginning at Midnight before the actual dawn of day. So the two decided that they were letting the sunset on singledom and preparing for the dawn of a new life filled with love and positivity. Sappy? Yes. But that was the shit my brother was on lately. Light and love.

I looked over at the grinning man and shook my head. "I don't even know who you are right now, brother."

Tyriq laughed. "I can't help it," He shrugged. " I feel-" Tyriq paused, his face falling into one of contemplation for precisely three seconds before he rotated his arms like a locomotive and slid his feet back in Micheal Jackson's Moonwalk style. "I feel light, everything's right about to marry my girl tomorrow night."

"Who wound this dude up again?" Tyson asked making his way under the pavilion. "Twinkle foot over here has been dancing for days. Your shoes got to be pissed at you right now, bruh."

"Terrence gloomy ass over here hating and shit." Chad hollered as he punched me playfully in the arm.

"Let Tyriq be happy," Trystan added. He was holding his son TJ's hand as he stepped in. "Nailah almost left him for good but then finally decided to marry him. He's got a reason to dance."

"He better hope her ass don't run away before she walks down the aisle," Chad chuckled.

I wiped a palm across my forehead already warm and wondering if we would make it through the actual ceremony.

"Stop all that cursing," Aunt Pat yelled as she walked out of the building. She moved up the path that led to the pavilion, the same path that Nailah would walk to Tyriq. "This isn't the house of the Lord, but we will not be out here showing our hind parts to these folks. Act like you have some home training."

No one on the beach behind us had paid any attention to our banter. No one had really turned their heads twice at our gathering group until Aunt Pat blasted the command for us to keep it classy.

The minister, my mother, and the rest of the men in the wedding party gathered around Aunt Pat as she plopped her fists to her hips.

"I went in there and talked to the girl." My aunt pointed her gaze at each of us in a warning. "She's going to come out of the side door today and not take the bridal march path. She's nervous, and if any one of you even looks like you're about to say or do something to send her running, you don't want to know what I've got planned for you."

Her eyes narrowed at us, and I wished that I had a fast-forward button. I loved all of my people, but I wanted to be somewhere else. Anywhere else.

Then she walked into the room. Regina. Like Prince, Jordan, Brandy, or Kobe, only one name was needed to inspire. I knew that Regina looked good on her worst day and shined brighter than new chrome on her best one. It only took a one-second glance at her bouncing onto the wooden platform and I was mesmerized.

"And you guys better show her a good time tonight at the show." Aunt Pat finished.

The mention of the required gathering broke the trance and caught my attention.

I turned to Chad and didn't have to ask the question before he mouthed, "I'll tell you later."

I let my chin sink to my chest. I almost regretted arriving nights before the event, but then Regina's forearm grazed against the skin of my hand as she popped up and down on her toes, and I thought about smiling. She was just as distracted as I was.

Regina smiled up at me. She was standing near enough that I could pull her against me and finally address the thoughts I'd been having about her. She toiled up a feeling of caution and comfort in me and I was pressed to figure out why.

The rest of the ladies, including Nailah, stepped in then as my mom and the minister took over the rehearsal. There was no time to think of anything but how I was supposed to stand next to Regina during the entire ceremony and not have impure thoughts.

After the rehearsal, the ladies went running up numbers in the spa getting all of the services. I couldn't imagine how much Tyriq was spending, but I knew how hard he worked over the years to build. I knew how hard he had worked to help me build.

Later, I met the guys at a cigar lounge on the property. All the men, including pops, gathered in a private room with large leather chairs, dark decor, and an oversized humidor full of pop's selected rolled tobacco choices.

"You didn't tell me that your wedding would be a damn part-time job," I grumbled before taking a puff of the fresh Don Collins cigar I held. "Feel like I need to submit a timesheet and shit."

Trystan's loose cackle announced that the liquor and tobacco were doing their job.

"Hell yeah," his relaxed voice floated into the air with the ring of smoke that he blew. "I'm about to hit his whipped ass for lost wages and billable hours."

"Fuck all y'all clocking-in-ass haters," Tyriq laughed as he shot us the middle finger. "My girl wanted a week-long wedding, and that's what she got. She wanted family here, and that's what she got." He stomped his foot to emphasize. "Nailah's my wife, about to make her happy for life."

"Oh, hell. Don't get this man singing again," Chad threw back a shot, grimaced and called over one of our room attendants. "I need more liquor for this. Bring out a round for the crew."

"Haters. All haters." Tyriq blustered with a laugh. "Shit, I funded all these businesses you trying to get back to."

"Real talk," Trystan lifted his glass. "The money you made hustling those players and gangsters who needed medical help, put us all on. Thank you brother. You've never been selfish with anything, and I'm glad that you found someone that is all about you. I'm glad to see you happy."

I smiled at the near ancient memory of Tyriq calling us to our parents garage one night years ago. He opened the top of mom's forgotten vertical piano and started pulling stacks of money from the top. We were all amazed when he explained that he was doing medical work for cash paying people who didn't want a paper trail. He needed something to do with the money. I had already started my downtown location, and was in the process of flipping my first shop, when we sat down to talk through making my dream a family thing. Tyson picked the locations, Trystan oversaw the contracts, I got the shops up and running, and Tyriq put a portion of the money he earned from his extra activities through them.

It didn't take long for my brother to make major money from all of the shady shit happening that no one wanted to report, but it also didn't take long for the shops to blow up. I became a master at taking sub-par shops and turning them into stunning Four Brothers locations. When we added the drive through car washes to the mix, Tyriq's under-the-table money wasn't even a discussion in expansion.

"For real." I lifted my glass. "To Tyriq. Thank you for not giving up on yourself after that injury. Thank you for believing in you, because your determination made us all better. I appreciate you. I'm happy that you're happy, you deserve this and more. Salute."

The other men in the room chanted words of agreement, lifted their glasses and threw back a shot.

He nodded his head around the room to brothers, cousins, and friends as he received the well wishes.

"Each and every one of you has helped me in some way. I wouldn't be here, ready to accept the love of my life without each of you and I want this kind of love for all of you."

Looking at the smile on my brother's face, I knew that there was no amount of piano money that could buy what he was feeling. I wasn't sure if it was the wedding event, meeting Regina, the new partnership with Strong, or a combination of it all that had me leaning into thoughts of a different future, but I felt ready for a change.

CHAPTER TEN

Jerrence

I was officially a ball of confusion. I didn't want to go at all, but I also wanted to see Regina again and made the compromise to be the last one there. Thoughts of sitting near her won over the actuality of sitting in my room. I threw on my black cargo pants, slid on a black undershirt, and a black V Neck T-Shirt before slipping into my black Nike slides.

A knock sounded at the door as I clasped my chain and I mustered up all the energy that I could for this event.

"I said that I would be there." I barked figuring that it was a family member being nosey.

Swinging open the door, I expected to see one of my cousins or brothers there to escort me. The parents were not attending the show since it was a bachelor/bachelorette party of sorts, but I knew for sure they would send reinforcements.

Regina looked up, a small smile dancing at the corners of her mouth. My face decided to mimic hers and it felt like my cheeks were attempting to stretch to my forehead.

"Hey," I found myself breathing like a runner after a race. She really took my breath away.

"Hi," she spoke back before a cloud of black fabric appeared before her and blocked my view.

"Thank you," I said, lifting the shirt from her fingers in a way that allowed me to touch her hand. We were still in the doorway, so I tossed the shirt backward into the room and onto the bed. "You could've kept it. I've got plenty."

I didn't wear my black shirts more than a few times, and bought inexpensive ones for that reason. Once they got even the slightest hint of fading, I donated them.

Regina didn't move, just stood there looking over my shoulder into the room and then back to me.

"I see." The way her eyes roved over my body, I knew that something dirty was playing in her mind. The same thing that was playing in my mind.

"You want to come?" The question was out before I could determine if it was a good idea. "In. I meant, would you like to come in my room."

The seconds ticked as her eyes darted between the space behind me in my room and my face in consideration. I wanted to flip her fine ass over my shoulder and carry her to the bed but then what? I didn't have a plan for the aftermath.

"We should get to the show," her words said that we were leaving but the hand that she placed on my chest said that she wanted to walk me through the door and explore.

"Cool." I looked down at her hand. "If that's what you want."

She cleared her throat before nodding, "It is. We should go."

We walked as a pair, which had become the norm since the plane ride. She wasn't my woman, but I stared down any soul brave enough to look at her twice while I was at her side. They didn't know us. They didn't know her and wouldn't as long as I was around.

The dine-in theater was onsite at the resort, and Regina chatted about a big surprise that she had for Nailah who was a huge fan of art and burlesque. I wasn't sure what that had to do with Regina, but I liked the melodic sound of her voice so I listened.

The rest of the crew was already seated at a long table set at the perfect distance from the stage. Orders had been sent in ahead of time with ticket purchases. All we had to do was take a seat.

"Hey, y'all," Nailah smiled.

I pulled out a chair for Regina and then took a seat next to her before Trystan made the moment awkward.

"Oh, I see you brother," Trystan's grin was mischievous. He and Crystal were across the table from me.

"What do you see?" Mali popped on a quick frown as she pried into the conversation.

"Nothing," I shot a glare at Trystan even though I was answering Mali.

Crystal rubbed her husband's arm while whispering something in his ear. He nodded at her words. His smile told me that he wouldn't bother me for a while.

When Crystal winked my way, I gave her a mini bow as I mouthed the words, "Thanks sis". She had a way of helping him identify when he had said too much that didn't piss him off.

Nailah clinked a fork against her glass to gather everyone's attention.

"I appreciate everyone making this week memorable," Nailah crooned from the head of the table next to Tyriq. "We're excited to combine our bachelor and bachelorette parties and spend more time with everyone. Thank you all for being here."

Music filled the room as a thin vanilla hostess in a sparkly dress took the stage in a flourish.

Nailah squealed. "I'm so excited!"

"What is this show about?" I asked.

"Oh, it's great! I've been here all week and seen it three times." Jubilee bounced in her chair. "I can't believe that Regina is going to participate."

"Participate?" I leaned over to Regina and whispered in her ear, "How do you participate in a show you've never seen before?"

She scooted in closer to me. I could smell the mango in her hair, and I fought the sensation to pull her soft-looking earlobe between my lips.

"Guess you'll have to wait and find out." She gave me a smile that made me reconsider taking her to my room.

The hostess introduced the first act.

"This is one of my favorite parts," Jubilee called out as a lady unfolded from the ceiling using curtains of silk. She expanded and contracted her body in the air, graceful movements helping her change positions with the beat of a slow love song.

"Nailah picked this song," Mali clasped her hands together.

Nailah nodded. "They let me pick all of the music for tonight."

It was a beautiful song about finding the girl of your dreams and taking time to enjoy the sight and experience of her, and I was feeling it.

"What is it?" I hadn't heard the song before.

"Girl of My Dreams by Chris Brown," Tyriq said as his eyes trailed over Nailah's blushing face. I didn't want to know the origin of the song's importance to them.

I didn't hear most of the song's ending because Regina had become enthralled with the act and was rolling her body to the beat of the song and making me wish I could be the seat.

The hostess returned to the stage once the song was completed with a refreshed energy in her voice and a skip in her step.

"We have plenty more in store, but do we have anyone in the audience who wants to be a part of the show?" She covered her brows with her hand and squinted as she searched through the few raised hands.

"Don't be shy. We're going to teach you a few things to share with the rest of the audience."

Regina's hand was in the air and her chair scooting across the floor before I could even process what was happening.

"Ahhh, there," The hostess acknowledged as she pointed at Regina. "You are gorgeous by the way. I think the audience would get a kick out of what we can show you." The hostess shimmied. "Are you ready?"

Regina nodded and was whisked away by an assistant.

"While we get our volunteer set up, you get to enjoy more of our great show."

The audience applauded and I was left bereft and confused.

"Everybody always loves the volunteer lap dance, and I know Regina is going to kill it."

"The what?" I nearly spit out my drink.

"The lap dance." She repeated louder as though it was just the music blocking my understanding. "At the other shows, a lady volunteer learned a spicy little dance combo in the back while the other acts were on, came out, and performed it with a guy volunteer. I know Regina is going to set some poor man's heart on fire, she has years of dance training."

"Hell yeah," Chad commented, rubbing his hands together. "this just got good."

My cup hit the table with a thud and I looked at the people who I once considered sane.

"You're letting your friend go on stage and do a freaky dance with a complete stranger that no one knows?"

Mali shrugged. "What are you so tight about? It's just a few body rolls and hip dips, nothing more than she would do at a club."

"Except for the break-away costume, it's PG-13," Jubilee added.

"She's stripping?" I knew that my face was doing something cartoonish and I didn't care. I could feel the air all the way around my eyeballs as I shook my head. "Nope. These random-ass perverts are not about to feel her up and get off on my watch."

I was two seconds from storming the stage when Mali clenched my arm.

"Chill. She'll be fine," Concern crowded her eyes as she looked at me. "You are such a big brother all of the time. You don't have to take care of everyone all of the time."

What I felt for Regina was anything but platonic or brotherly.

"Regina was on the dance team in high school and college," Nailah added. "She's always telling me about it. I can't believe that I finally get to see her dance."

I didn't say anything else to the people surrounding me because I felt like they had brought their bodies but left their minds on the plane. Either elated or nonchalant, I was the only one at the table that seemed to believe it wasn't a good idea.

There was no way that anyone was getting near her. Having her dance for me in front of my family was not my idea of fun, but I damn sure wasn't watching another man get the experience of a lifetime.

I anticipated the ending of each act, sharpening my focus to be ready for the volunteer request. My chair was turned toward the stage. I moved away from the table. My family, food, and friends were forgotten. I leaned forward on my toes ready to jump as soon as the call went out.

"You about to do the 100 meters or what?" Chad cackled.

I wanted to flip him the middle finger, but I didn't. I could not take my concentration away from that stage. Of course, the hostess was taking her sweet time walking to the center.

"She'll be fine." Nailah reminded me.

I wasn't hearing that shit. I wasn't hearing anything that any of them had to say.

The hostess did a little twirl in the center of the stage. Nobody cared about her dress change, I wanted her to hurry up and ask for a volunteer.

"You all remember that special treat that I promised earlier? Well, she's ready, and we need a male volunteer. Who would like to join us?"

I was damn near on the stage before she finished the question.

"I'm your volunteer," I interrupted from below.

She squinted, assessed my face, and smiled to the crowd. "We're going to go with the intense man rushing the stage." Her voice was chipper despite the words.

Security escorted me onto the stage.

"Take a seat," The hostess pointed to a plush velvet chair in the middle of the stage that looked like it came from the dining room of a palace.

I did as told.

Away from the microphone the peppy lady dropped her face toward mine and wasn't as nice. "This is a clean show," her words were both soft and stern. "Keep your composure." She shot a glare at my lap before catching my eyes again. "If you don't, you get to dance with Carmine the Cutter. Understood."

"Understood." I agreed because I wanted her out of my face. The bulky guy off stage didn't scare me. He just looked big. I would fuck him up with two hits before he even found something to cut with. I wanted Regina, and I would do anything to keep her safe in the process, even from me. I would control myself, not because those people frightened me, but because I wasn't sure if I could reel myself back in if I let loose.

The hostess disappeared after that. The room blacked with a loud pop of disappearing lights, and a spotlight was suddenly on my face.

I looked to the left. No Regina. The right. No Regina.

The beginning chords of Every Kind of Way by H.E.R filled the room, and I still didn't see her. My heart thumped in my chest as other parts throbbed to be near her.

I knew that I was in trouble when the crowd rolled into a series of yells and whistles. I hadn't laid an eye on a single body part but I knew she looked good.

The heel was first, a tall pointy thing that could have taken off my jaw. Regina was behind me, but her thick supple leg was over my shoulder and across my chest.

Her hands rounded my shoulders and smoothed down the front of me before I could finish registering the igniting touch of her leg.

My eyelids flew back far enough to touch my forehead when Regina jerked my head backward into her breast.

The crowd chuckled, but I felt like I had found a new home.

I could see her then. I could look into those beautiful browns that had me acting entirely out of character.

"Get him, girl," Someone from the audience yelled, thoroughly enjoying my demise.

Her hand pressed down the front of my chest again, giving my face the gracious opportunity to be buried between her mounds. Snuggling my nose near the left one, deciding that it was slightly fuller, I discovered the cocoa scent of her skin as she swiftly pulled her entire body over mine before flipping into a split on the ground in front of me.

It was over. Not the dance. Not her, but me. I was over. Done.

The way she had me feeling in public with my clothes on was too much to keep my eyes open. So I shut them, squeezed them closed as if my life depended on it, because any more of her might kill me.

A loud, "Gawd damn," from the audience had me looking to see what had happened that quickly.

Decked in an oversized white dress shirt, thigh high stockings with garters, I got a peek of the red tube top and short bottoms that she wore as she pulsed her body against the stage.

Her cheeks jiggled up and circled down to the ground as she brought her fist and body to the floor with the drumbeat of the song.

I bit the shit out of my lip as she crawled forward toward the crowd and then rolled back into a crouched position.

I blinked and she had walked back toward me.

"Take this off," She whispered in reference to a loose dress tie around her neck.

I did as told.

Regina took the silk material and slid it across me as she returned to her spot behind me.

"Damn," I wanted to mutter but said loud enough for the audience to laugh at.

She was making a show of binding my wrists as I prayed for any reason to have this woman stranded in my room tonight.

Regina was around the chair then slow rolling for the audience and I instinctively jerked at the wrist wrap. She had done an excellent job with the slippery fabric.

As she stalked toward me, I nodded. I wasn't scared. I concluded then that Regina would feel me.

"You shouldn't be up here," she whispered before a swift drop to the ground with her knees so far apart that they looked like wings. At that point I wanted her to flap across me like she was flying south for the winter. My face could definitely be her equator.

"You shouldn't be either," I reminded her in a husky drawl. She was winding upward with such skill that I think the air could have hit a climax. Then she was facing the crowd, dancing for them, and I was pleased. I received the back view as she teased the shirt off her body.

"Untie me," I wasn't sure where the growled command came from, but Regina would have gotten fucked on the stage if I figured out how to get out of the knotted silk cuffs around my wrists.

"Don't do it," She chuckled as she turned back to me. "I got you later." She whispered in my ear as she straddled my lap and bent backward so that one of her palms touched the ground. She threw the other hand into the air as she wound her body up and down to mimic riding me. In reality, her core was far enough away that I couldn't get any relief, but I was sure it looked less than innocent to the audience.

With a rhythm change, she was up again and moving across the stage. She danced more and just when I was on the verge of 'hulking out' from lust and frustration, she was behind me with a request.

"I'm about to free you," She whispered. "I'll dance around you for a little bit, then grab me by the waist, pick me up, and carry me off stage."

I nodded my head once. The mission was understood.

She performed more for the crowd, dipping, twirling, and shaking every moveable piece of her body. Then she came back to me. She came back for me.

The exact moment that my hands were free, I swooped her into my arm, using my forearm to secure her soft curves against me.

"Terrence," She squealed, probably surprised by the way I choked her waist. She thought it was a game, but what I felt was real, raw and urgent.

She wrapped her legs around me as I moved us off of the stage. The song played out as Kathy scrambled back to the spotlight.

I pressed Regina into the wall as our eyes locked, and I knew without a doubt that her show had more to do with me than the crowd.

" I still had 30 seconds left," she said softly.

" Nah. That time was up. You did enough for them."

She nodded her head as though it were underwater. It felt like we were both there, lost in each other and wading through heavy feelings to figure out what to do next.

"Is there something that I can do for you?" she asked, but her mouth was so close to mine that when I tried to lick my lip it brushed against hers as well.

"Oh my gosh!" the screech broke through our moment and reminded me of our location and the situation with my family.

"That was so amazing!" another voice howled. It was Mali.

Regina detangled her legs and slid down the front of me. I lifted an arm so that she could giggle over the performance with her friends.

In a few seconds, the group of blockers were dragging her toward the dressing room.

Regina turned back to catch my gaze and I swore she mouthed the words "To be continued".

CHAPTER ELEVEN

Regina

Nailah should have been an advertisement for the love that my parents were trying to sell. I would have bought it, and spent everything I could access to feel as content and hopeful as she did. She was beautiful, of course: hair, face, and nails done, her skin glowing, but it was the smile for me. It was the joy that radiated somewhere within her and spilled onto the rest of the crew. I wanted that kind of love: unmanufactured, unforced, unconditional. A love that made you feel good even when you weren't thinking about it.

Despite the growing belly, her chiffon and lace dress fit her perfectly. The princess-style V-neck dipped comfortably into the wide jeweled band of the empire waist over a flowy A-Line bottom. Her makeup was stunning, not too heavy, but natural and sophisticated. It fit her. I was proud of her, where she had come from, and the future that she was building for herself and her child. I wondered what my future would look like, what dress I would wear, and the mystery man I would marry.

"It's almost showtime," I remarked and placed the diamond drop earrings I had gifted her into each ear.

She exhaled a smile as her hand drifted over her belly. "It is."

"Nervous?" I would have been scurrying around the room trying to make everything perfect, but Nailah was the picture of poise.

"Not even a little bit." She shook her head as her eyes shifted up to me. "Ring or no ring, I know that Tyriq has my back… I have no doubts that whatever the future holds, he'll do everything in his power to make sure that we're good."

"Finally," Jubilee stepped over to straighten the train of the dress. "I'm so glad that you understand now."

Nailah truly did look at peace and I wondered if it was because she would now have a husband or because of the actual man who would be her husband. My parents wanted that same peace for me, and honestly, I was starting to want it more myself. Not to fulfill the contract that I signed, but to find that sureness that I wouldn't have to walk the path of life alone.

"Alright ladies, let's do this." Mali smiled. "It's time."

One by one we stepped into the hallway ready to lead our girl to wedded bliss.

"Wait. Y'all stop." Nailah whisper-yelled.

My stomach fell at the distress scrunched across Nailah's face. She was just so sure, and although I was optimistic about her marrying Tyriq, I had devised a quick exit plan for if she decided to run.

"You can do this." Mali started with an inspirational speech before she even turned around. "Don't run."

As Jubilee, Mali, Crystal, and I surrounded her, Nailah explained, "I'm not running. I just thought of something."

"What is it? Did you leave something? Do you need a relaxing pill or a shot of tequila? I got a flask in my garter. I promised Tyriq I would get you down that aisle."

"Chill, I'm getting married. No worries there. Once I walk down this aisle I probably won't be able to chat with you again before the reception." She took a deep breath and exhaled before stating. "You know Curtis is here on the premises."

I wasn't sure what spirit of giving prompted Nailah to invite him to her wedding, but she had. Curtis Green was Nailah's absentee father who resurfaced. He wasn't walking her down the aisle but he was there, along with his actual whores and some cousins. He had decided to use his daughter's invitation to build a relationship as a chance to make money off tourists and rich wedding guests. Trifling.

"Yea. I saw him and all his hoes last night." Jubilee rolled her eyes.

"Mali, I know you'll keep Cairo and Chad together. Regina, keep an eye on Terrence and Tyson. I'd be devastated if any of my dad's guests tried to take advantage of them."

"You don't have to worry about those grown men," I placed a hand at her shoulder, "but if it makes you feel better, I got you, girl."

Nailah exhaled the worry from her face, as she gave some clarity to her concerns. "I know they can handle themselves, but they're my family now and it would be too embarrassing if any of Tyriq's brothers came up with a disease, paternity suit, or a police report number for stolen items. I wouldn't put anything past my dad and those ladies he brought."

I still didn't get the big deal, but I assured her anyway in a mock British accent, "I will guard Sir Terrence and Tyson with my life in your honor, my queen." I gave a small curtsy too.

In return, I got a stuttered eye roll as she smiled. "You are so silly sometimes, but thank you."

"Alright, let's do this so I can collect my money from Chad when you make it through the whole ceremony," Mali added as she pointed a thumb toward the door.

They were expecting Nailah to have an adverse reaction to walking down the path to the altar, but it was me. I almost lost my ability to stand and see straight when I saw them. Standing at the front of the large cabana were supposed to be the men that I went boating with, but in their place were six ebony gods. They all looked like a night of delight, but he stood out. He had my full attention from the moment my eyes could drink him. I didn't hear the music anymore, I just moved. Let my body lead me to him because it knew where I longed to go.

I couldn't stop staring. I didn't know what magic potions they drank for breakfast, but all of them looked bolder, stronger somehow. Everyone was edged and trimmed, facial hair gleaming, skin moisturized, and broad bodies popping through their fitted suits. I wanted to take a seat in the audience and stare, just bask in the view. I wanted to take a few moments to memorize him standing there waiting with golden eyes and a small lift to his lips. Terrence was fwine' in regular clothes, but breathtaking in a suit with the glow of the sun at his back. Instead of stopping, I took steps and focused on the satin floor runner ahead of me. I had successfully made it to the end of the aisle when I felt the warmth of his presence.

I had never been giddy over a man, but when he slipped his arm through mine and pulled me closer to him, desire sizzled through me.

"You look beautiful," He whispered against the crease of my earlobe as he guided me to our spot.

Thank you would have been the best response, but I was too busy smiling to use my lips to form words. Once we were lined up like a choir to the left of the couple, the music switched and Nailah entered.

I had already seen her. We had been together all day getting ready, but I hadn't seen Tyriq see her, and that almost took me out. The way his face lit up, his cheeks eclipsing his eyes, nearly made me swoon. He loved her. I loved that he loved her, and witnessing it made the want for someone to love me like that grow.

"That's my girl," Tyriq said as he took Nailah's hand and licked his lips. "You're looking, good mama."

I tried to pay attention to the ceremony, but Terrence was angled right next to me and anytime one of us moved, my side boob or thigh would brush against his solidness and send a rocket of sensation through me. I swayed a little, so to steady me, Terrence placed a hand at the side of my hip. I felt his gaze on me, and I made the mistake of looking up into his eyes. I could have fallen into the deep caramel pools.

"You alright?" His words were more mouthed than loud, but he made my knee wobble a little, so he kept his hand there even though I nodded that I was fine.

The way his breathy, "I gotcha" made me shiver should have been a sign that I was in deeper trouble than I knew.

I was a horrible homegirl. Just awful. With concern beaming from her brown eyes, Nailah had specifically asked me to keep him out of danger. But there I was, at the reception, not even a whole hour later, with my panties ablaze, trying to figure out the best way for him to hose me down. That was the exact opposite of what she'd asked, but I couldn't help it. Since I saw his face on the plane, I had been trying to stop adding to the list of nasty things I could do to him. I was already on number 162 on my mental freak list when Terrence opened his jacket and unbuttoned the top button of his shirt and I thought of ten more things. I had to turn my head.

"Hey girl," Mali popped up then. Her face quickly twisted from congenial into confusion. "What caught your attention? I've never seen you sit this still." She tilted her head to the side " Come to think of it. You love to dance. Why aren't you dancing?"

I felt caught. Like I needed to pack up my dirty mind, hide it and repent. I had been stuck in the twilight zone fantasizing about her cousin for an unspecified amount of time. So long that I hadn't even moved to dance or eat or check on my friend. Horrible. The worst part was that Mali had said over and over again how difficult it was to keep female friends because of her cousins and brothers. Then there I was trying to calculate the length of Terrence's hypotenuse and how many angles we could create.

"No. I'm just taking in the scenery. The decorator did a beautiful job," I tried to cover.

"Nailah didn't even have to worry," Mali explained. "My mother was already on it. Those hoes were not getting anywhere near Patricia Ann Summers' sons or nephews tonight. She did get the Curtis crew on target with Tyriq's doctor friends though."

"That's good." I tried to smile through my conviction. I owed her that much.

"Enjoy yourself." She patted my shoulder. "Good friend duty is over."

My gut twisted again because I was breaking all kinds of girlfriend codes in my brain.

Chapter Twelve

Terrence

S itting next to Regina at the host table, I realized two things: My attraction to her was stronger than I thought, and it wasn't going away. She was stunning in her dress and the thought of her being out of it became more intriguing. I couldn't pin down a time that comfortable and relaxed happened for me right off. She had a spirited personality, smiled quickly, laughed easily, and spoke her mind. All of which appealed to me on repeat every time she batted her lashes my way.

"What about her," Regina whispered in my direction. Her smooth voice reminded me of cool jazz, a saxophone, or a flute.

My eyes followed the nod of her head toward the corner of the room where Curtis was seated. We had been playing this game for the last ten minutes: family or freak. It wasn't the most politically correct game, but as soon as Nailah's father, Curtis, who was rumored to be a former pimp, entered the room flanked on all sides by women, Regina and I locked eyes. I swear she could read my mind. There was one other man and several other women trailed behind

Curtis and the crew took up two tables in the lavish dining room by themselves. He was supposed to be bringing his family. The family related to Nailah, but it looked more like ladies that he managed.

Most of the women, including Raven, had found themselves dispersed throughout the room and chatting with the few friends of Tyriq that made the trip.

"Cousin," I guessed after looking at the conversation between the two. "A cousin."

"Nope," Regina shook her head. "She's a get-money girl."

"Why would you say that?" I tried to give most of the women the benefit of the doubt. Since I was talking to a woman, and not my cousin Chad, I kept it positive. I honestly didn't care, either way, it was another way to spend time with Regina.

"She's too close to him, look at how she's touching his arm. The way she widened her eyes and is giving him a slow blink with the lashes. That's way more than friendly. And the smile. That smile is all about sex."

"Word?" I glanced her way then, taking the opportunity to look at her mouth. "A woman's smile can say all of that?"

"Yep," she grinned at me.

"What does your smile say then?"

She fluttered her long lashes similar to the way that she had pointed out earlier before asking, "What do you think?"

"I've never been good at reading women." That was true. I had been with one woman most of my life, and when that didn't work out, I hadn't tried again.

"It's not about reading," she answered, twiddling with the strap of the dress she had chosen. "It's about feeling and much simpler than you think."

"See, right now, I would think that you wanted something." I moved in a little closer to her. "But I'm tripping, right?"

"Come on out here and wobble with me," Aunt Pat interrupted just as I was getting somewhere with Regina, even if I wasn't sure where that somewhere was.

I looked up at my Aunt who I thought would be laughing, but noticed that she was serious. She wanted me to get out on the dance floor. I never danced.

"Not this time. I'm good on that, aunty." I put up my hand giving her the stop signal. That was a full stop. It wasn't happening.

Her eyes narrowed as she folded her arms. No one said no to my aunt. I didn't say no to my aunt. Ever. Usually, she asked me to run errands and help her around the house. Dancing was different.

"Say what now?" She hit a shoulder lean that was all attitude and probably would have scared me as a kid. "Boy, if you don't pick yourself up and get out here on this dance floor and Wobble with me. Come on, it's already starting."

I noticed all of the people lining up and moving from side to side and felt my face folding in on itself.

"I don't even know what this Wobble is. I don't dance."

"Don't dance?" She repeated with a kiss of her teeth as though I had offended her intelligence. "The way you used to scuff up my floor trying to moonwalk and tap dancing in your little church shoes, you can't tell me that you don't dance. Boy, we couldn't keep your little feet out of the Soul Train line."

"That was decades ago, and you're missing more of the song standing here convincing me to join."

"I ain't worried about that song. I'm trying to figure out when you stopped dancing." She had both hands on her hips now and her feet were planted for a good long conversation. "You remember cousin Toots' wedding? You were the main one on the dance floor."

"I was seven."

"But you were good."

"Excuse me, Ms. Pat." Regina cut in.

"You're excused." Aunt Pat shot her a look that would cause armies to retreat.

"I apologize for interrupting, but Nailah and Tyriq needed us to wrap up some of the hotel payments." She explained standing up and taking my hand in a way that warmed me. "We need to catch the manager before he leaves for the night."

I stood up, grateful for the rescue, and let my aunt know that I'd catch up with her later.

"You owe me a dance nephew," she hollered at my back because I was already following Regina out of the ballroom.

Walking behind her in the curve-hugging dress took up most of my concentration, but a small piece of my mind wondered what it was we were supposed to handle for my brother. He hadn't said anything to me about meeting with a manager.

When we reached the lobby area of the hotel, she stopped and turned toward me with a cute ass grin that made me want to lick her lips and pinch her cheeks.

"So what's up," I asked, suddenly feeling the absence of her hand in mine. I looked between our hands, wanting to reach out again as I asked, "Who are we meeting and why?"

"Now, don't get angry," she prefaced what she had to say and placed her flat palms on my chest.

I placed my hands on top of hers because I liked the way that they felt there and I wanted them to stay longer.

She took a deep breath before speaking.

"I made it up." She hurried the words on an exhale. "I was trying to save you from the wobble and I lied. You looked like you were in distress."

Taking her wrists in my hand, I moved closer. Close enough that the fabric of her dress folded against my leg. "You lied to my dearest and only aunt?"

"I only did it to help. I promise." She responded in a breathless whisper. We were close. Closer than we had ever been and now we were completely away from anyone that we knew.

"Hmm. What should I feel about that?" As we searched each other's eyes, I knew that I was the reason the rise and fall of her chest had sped up and her bottom lip was tucked beneath the top one. The urge to kiss her mouth overwhelmed me, but with the way that I wanted her, starting something like that in the middle of a hotel lobby would be indecent.

I lifted each of her palms to my mouth and pressed my lips to the center. "Thank you," I said and placed each delicate hand back in its starting position on my chest.

We stood there for what seemed like enough time to float off into outer space and return, but in reality, had only been a few seconds.

"I should go," Regina said the words but her feet didn't move.

I took the opportunity to slide my hands down the smooth skin of her arms, over her shoulders, and down to circle her waist. We were in public. We were in the center of a hotel with hundreds of tourists. Absolutely no one mattered but her at that moment. There were only the two of us as I held her in place.

"Where?" I countered, wondering why she wanted to leave me. I didn't want to be anywhere she wasn't. " If you go back without me, my Aunt will be suspicious. She'll ask you questions about the business her very special nephew, Tyriq, entrusted you with and not her and why you disappeared with me." I lifted an eyebrow.

"Let's walk that way then," Regina answered quickly, hopping out of my arms as if we were teens about to get caught in the basement. "We can walk by the water and um, you know, cool off."

I chuckled to myself as she moved around the hotel confused. She walked in a zig-zag fanning herself as though she were trying to escape a maze.

" It's a little warm here. Right? Where is the door?" She asked.

She was flustered and it was cute. I liked that I made her feel something because she made me feel everything.

"Take this hall and it will lead us to the private beach." I directed her shoulders toward the glowing orange exit sign at the end of the hall.

She nodded and was walking before I could even finish the sentence.

I could've been the lead actor of a medical drug commercial for bone health or cholesterol. The ones that have nothing to do with the medicine but show happy people on beaches, in parks, and on vacation. I was smiling that hard and feeling that free. It could have all been captured on camera in slow motion with sepia filters and packaged as the definition of *Black-Boy-Joy*. The moon was out, but traces of last light still flickered in the sky as the magnetic pull of Regina had me hooked. She was still in her dress. I was still in my suit, but it didn't matter. All that mattered was reaching her. Touching her again had become a goal. I'm not sure how I ended up holding my shoes in my hand and running through the sand with the boundless energy of a toddler on Pixie Sticks, but I was. One minute, we were strolling like normal people listening to the water and watching the sky, and the next we were racing down the coast laughing like kids.

"I won," Regina shouted ending her run at a set of wooden stairs to do a victory circle.

I reached the small deck that served as a booth for beach rentals during business hours. Leaning against the stair rail, I hid my breathless pants behind a chuckle and a few words. "You cheated. You didn't say go until you had already taken off."

"Aww." She gave a mock pout as she walked over to cup my face in her hands. "Is someone a sore loser?"

I poked my tongue out and playfully licked the side of her hand. Something about being with her brought out that side of me. The less responsible, less grown-up part of me that I rarely nourished.

"Ewww." She gasped and pulled her hands into her chest. "Why did you do that?" The giggle of her question let me know that she wasn't bothered at all and was playing.

"I can't lick you?" I questioned quietly and watched Regina go from swaying in the sand to stone still.

She blinked a few times before she wagged a finger in my direction as if I were a naughty child. "We should walk some more."

I shook my head and took a seat on the upper step of the deck. "Let's chill for a minute, let me catch my breath."

Her neck reared back.

"You gotta build up that stamina, big man. That was light work. A little run." She smiled as she jogged in place.

"I have a few ways to show you this stamina. No jogging involved." I winked.

Regina's knees went from nearly bouncing waist level to stock still before she spoke, "See that's why we need to walk our hot asses around this cool water."

"You can come and sit a minute." I threw my hands up in surrender. "I promise we can stay cool, and I'll keep my hands to myself."

"Your mouth too?" She asked with narrowed eyes while taking narrow steps toward me.

"I promise to keep all of myself to myself if you come to sit down and chill for a minute."

She stopped the small two-step walk that reminded me of playing the game "Mother -May- I" and as gracefully as one could while barefoot in a bridesmaid dress, sat on the step in front of me, between my legs.

We didn't say anything for a while, only listened to the waves and enjoyed the presence of each other. I enjoyed being near her, even when we were still. As the oldest, I had grown up a little faster, worked a little harder to help my parents, and was a good example for my siblings. Hanging out with Regina, helped me realize how foreign laughing had become and how strange smiling felt.

"Who was your celebrity crush when you were a teenager?" Regina asked. The flat line of her mouth indicated that she was serious. She wanted an answer to that question.

"You do realize that I'm a man, right?" Looking at the long column of her neck as she grazed a hand along the side wouldn't let me forget that I was a man. I noticed at least three places where my lips would fit perfectly.

"I see all of your manliness." The way she turned to peruse the space where my man-defining part sat made me wonder if she was trying to test it or taste it. How willing I was to let her do either startled me.

"You had to have seen yourself with someone, right?" She lifted a shoulder up and down. "You couldn't tell me that Omarion from the boy band B2K wasn't going to roll up to my school and fall in love with me from the auditorium stage."

My face scrunched on its own and I didn't even bother to answer.

"You liked those corny dudes?"

"Oh, corny they were not." She rolled her neck.

I didn't bother to refute.

"Who's the first celebrity that you wanted to get with?" she rephrased.

"Better question. I have an answer for that. Stacey Dash." I replied before giving some context to my answer. "I'm talking about Stacey Dash circa the '90s and the movie Clueless era, not the new millennium Stacey."

Regina, placed a hand on my knee, lifted her chin to look into my eyes, and hiked an eyebrow before asking, "You've seen Clueless?"

"That's all you heard, huh?" I sucked my teeth before shaking my head, almost feeling embarrassed. "Mali made me watch that dumb shit and the TV Series too."

"That's your answer?" She twisted her lips up in disbelief.

"That's the truth. Mali always got her way."

She laughed like I was exaggerating, but I was serious and that seemed to make her laugh more.

"Mali was tough on you boys, huh?" She choked out through her chuckles.

"Was? Let her tell you, she's the boss now." I corrected her. "If Mali didn't get her way, she would go tell my mom or aunt that we were being mean to her, and we'd have to do what she wanted anyway." Mali had all of the adults wrapped around her pinky. "If I told them that she hit me, that was even worse. They would still force us to do what Mali wanted. We learned to cut out the parents and just do what Mali asked the first time."

"She worked that only girl title real good, huh?"

Looking down into Regina's eyes, I shook my head as I answered, "You don't even know the half."

Noticing the chill that slid through with the wind and Regina rubbing goosebumps on her arms, I took my suit jacket and draped it over her shoulders before continuing.

"I was glad when this little girl moved into the apartment complex down the street from us and started riding her bike in the area."

"Mali left you guys alone after that?" Regina scooted further in allowing her head to reach my chest.

"Nope, but at least when French Fry came around, Aunt Pat and my parents would send her off to find her friend if she got too bossy."

She nodded scooting in closer for warmth. Now that the sun had completely disappeared and we were still, the temp had cooled.

"Whatever happened to you and the basketball player Jermain Timmons?" I asked. The question seemed to originate from nowhere, but I had wondered about that for a while. He was a popular player and asshole who had a hand in hurting Nailah. I probably shouldn't have brought it up, but the first night that I saw Regina she was at an awards event with him.

"We're going there?" Her voice hiked a bit when she asked. "I see how you play. I gave you a sweet little question and you came back with a gut punch."

"Never that." I smoothed a hand up and down her shoulder. "Honestly, I remember seeing you hugged up with him at the Gala that night. You and he looked pretty tight."

"I can't stand his conniving ass." She shot out the words machine-gun style as if they would reach him. "He's just the standard liar and user like all the rest of them."

"All the rest?" I questioned.

"All of them." She confirmed. "I have masterfully chosen every idiot, liar, asshole, and misogynist in the metroplex. Also, a few that were so strange, I don't have a category for them."

"Nah. Not you. You seem like the type to run background and credit checks before the first phone conversation."

She shook her head. "I know how to vibe with a person too and not do any of that."

"Tell me your worst date story and I'll tell you mine." I request.

"Alright, here's one for you.

CHAPTER THIRTEEN

Regina

I was wrong. I knew it when I couldn't stop staring at his thick arms with winding veins under the smooth skin. I knew it when I felt his chest. Sitting between his legs in the dark of night rehashing bad date stories, I could feel it. I had never been one to half-ass anything in my life. In the tradition of myself, I decided then that I was going all in. If I was going to be wrong and piss somebody off for something, I was about to make it a good something to be mad about.

"There was this one guy that I couldn't categorize." I had taken off the strappy heels to let my toes squish into the sand as I recalled one of the strangest dates I ever had.

"Why not." His voice had smoothed its way up my neck to tingle in my ear. I couldn't figure out why he was so intoxicating, but I was tired of fighting it. Some things couldn't be explained.

"Short version," I explained squiggling my toes deeper into the sand. "He takes me to a book shop and I'm impressed because maybe, just maybe, he's not an idiot. He buys me the best damn cappuccino ever created and we have a good conversation about the impact of Alex Haley's Roots over some freshly baked cinnamon rolls. He pays for the treat, pulls out my chair. He's polite and listens when I speak."

"So he's not an idiot or asshole," Terrence concluded.

I had been feeling floaty since I lowered my body to the step between his trunk-sized thighs and became enveloped by the smell and warmth of him. I was cocooned by his massive body, and I'd be damned if I didn't feel like I was transforming into a being with the ability to fly. It also could have been the champagne I had a few hours earlier that night. My arm fell over the top of his hardened quadriceps allowing my back to press further against his front. It was easy like we had known each other for years.

"I was getting excited about the guy," My eyes floated over to his hand stroking my shoulder as I spoke and I momentarily forgot what I was explaining. "And um- We um- We talked about our families. He said that he admired his mother's work ethic and that his father shouldered much of the caregiving. He liked how his parents were partners."

"Not a misogynist," Terrence added with a snap of his fingers that took his touch away from me. "That's it. Why didn't you marry him?"

"If I had married that strange ass guy, then I would have never gotten the Terrence experience. That would have been tragic," I chuckled.

"Extremely tragic for me," he agreed. "I should be thanking the guy, but I want to know what happened."

"We get to my house and he asks to step in for the restroom." I continued turning my lip up at the memory. "On the way out he asks me to do him a favor."

"What? Did he want you to touch his pet snake?" The rumble of Terrence's chuckle spread across his chest to my ear. At some point, my head had landed there, in the cove between his arms and shadowed by his brawny chin.

"That would have put him in the idiot or asshole category." I cringed as I recalled the events that happened after. " His requests were benign at first. He told me that he had arthritis and that even though he popped his knuckles a lot he still needed a little extra help."

I couldn't see his frown, but I could feel the movement of his neck. I had gotten extremely comfortable, nestled there in his arms like we had been lovers over several lifetimes.

"The man squatted down, placed his hands on my floor, and said 'step on them'. I was completely confused. I've had men get on their knees before, but it was never for that reason. I gave him the benefit of the doubt."

Terrence's deep groan grumbled against my neck and the vibration moved across my body to a place not covered by underwear. "You didn't?"

"I thought that maybe it could have been that. It wasn't. I stepped on his hand and he told me to rock back and forth. Thinking nothing of it, I do. He moaned and I took it as a sign that it worked. He stood up and before I could say goodbye, he asked for one more thing."

Terrence moved his arms from their protective spot on his knees to my shoulders kneading down and pressing up in the muscles that I didn't even realize they needed the magic of his touch. "I'm glad you're here to tell this story, champ. That dude could have made you into a hat."

I popped his hand and I got a three-roll chuckle in response.

"Don't talk about me and make me feel this wonderful at the same time. Let me at least finish my story." I half crooned, half spoke, because he was amazing at massages.

"Does it end with you kicking his ass?"

"No. He asked me to spit in his eye and poke him with a fingernail file."

"What?" He stopped rubbing my shoulders. I hadn't meant for that to happen.

"Yes, he was some sort of masochist or something. He didn't like pleasure, it was all about pain and humiliation for him. Me stepping on his hand was like the equivalent of a good night kiss. Had I been paying attention when he stood up after I stepped on his finger, I would have known that he had cum all over himself."

"I've officially heard it all."

I nodded. I knew why I was single. No one understood how difficult it was for me to find a good man that was also wealthy except for those closest to me. People like Nailah, and once upon a time, Kinnesha from college, who had finally resurfaced. My circle of girlfriends had been growing and I was proud of that, but I needed a husband because of my parents. That thought hadn't escaped me and I'm sure it was written all over my face.

"What's wrong?" He asked, with the ability to read my mood already. We had known each other for a few hours of a few days, but he had assessed the change in my countenance.

"It feels like my love life is dead." I scraped my teeth over my bottom lip trying to hold in the cry threatening to come out. It was difficult to say, and even more difficult to know. I had dated so much, but nothing had come of it. My time to find a partner had been up. "It's been difficult finding and keeping a worthwhile partner."

"What do you want?"

Terrence threw the question out there as if it were simple, as if I could wish it and a man would appear. Feeling his body move forward, I wished that I could take back the entire conversation so that we could sit there together longer.

I stretched up slowly, not wanting to, but knowing that the night had to come to an end at some point anyway.

He stood behind me, an arm sliding around my waist with such a natural expectancy that I didn't question it or bother to ask what prompted him to do so. He moved us forward toward the water. I didn't question that decision either, and even though I was out front, he was leading. I was totally at ease with his direction. All I had to do was take steps.

When he stopped moving, the tidewater could reach my ankles. I leaned on him and relished being in his arms. When I returned home, there would be meetings and stress and a blitz to the altar. I sank into the peace that Terrence offered. It was limited.

"There's a full moon." I hadn't noticed until he touched my chin to lift my gaze.

Terrence looked up into the sky as well. I wondered what he was thinking then and often. He seemed to be in deep thought most of the time.

"My grandmother, may she rest in peace, believed that the full moon was a time to set intentions for the future." His eyes swung down to meet mine and questioned silently if I was open to listening. I assume he read the right answer because he continued. "It's the peak time for clarity, and the time when whatever you speak and believe has the most power."

He removed his body from mine. At first, I watched as he stepped further into the water, but then I felt an internal push to follow him. I did.

I watched, a few steps away, as he descended to his haunches. The tide waded forward and receded across his shins. I wanted to reach for a camera. I wanted to capture and take the moment with me forever. Terrence was my every fantasy in human form and I had to wonder if I had dreamed him into existence. His white dress shirt was untucked and billowed around his tight body in the breeze. Collar askew, natural light from the moon played on his golden skin. His dress pants were rolled at the ankles leaving the smooth skin exposed there. His slacks were fitted enough to display the defined muscles of his thighs and calves, but loose enough that he looked comfortable. He looked perfect.

An ache to be near him pulled me closer.

"You're not about to ask me to step on your finger are you?" I needed to add levity to the moment, to escape the deep desire that I wanted him to take his spoon and stir in me.

I was blessed with a three-roll chuckle again.

"Nah. Pretty girl." He looked up and over to drop a half-grin on my already frying brain. "Come down here with me, I want to try something."

"Now the last guy that said that-" I teased while still squatting down into the sand with him.

"Regina, do you trust me?" The honey hue of his eyes had taken on an orangish glow in the moonlight as if lit with hope.

I nodded, nearly hypnotized as he fell forward to his knees.

I pushed onto mine, the malleable sand sinking slightly to adjust to my weight.

"What do you want in a man?" he asked.

Several questions came to mind about the situation, but that wasn't at the top of my list. I wasn't sure if I was supposed to answer that.

"Are you serious right now?"

The water danced at our knees as we studied each other in the elements. Terrence was serious.

"I'm out here away from my family, on my knees in some water, messing up a good suit, to make a point. You tell me if I'm serious."

"Well if you put it that way," I responded with a sigh. I was tired and horny and overwhelmed. I didn't have time for riddles or sexy men who I wanted to sleep with but couldn't because I wanted to be a good friend and I was about to get married to a stranger.

"Regina," His palm was at my cheek lifting my head and I hadn't even realized it had fallen. "What I'm saying is, if you set the expectation for good, the good will come to you."

The slight touch of his finger against the side of my neck made parts of me quiver that should have been still.

"You are a gorgeous woman, but I'm not out here on anything foul or shady."

He didn't have to ask the question again, I had an answer. It was him. I wanted him. Right there in the dirt, I was willing to figure out how to get sand out of my hair and ass crack later. He was worth the irritation.

"What do you want in the man that you plan to spend forever with?" He was so sincere.

I focused my thought about what I knew and what I needed.

The sky didn't have the answers, but I couldn't look at him, not with tears deciding to push at the back of my eyes.

My breath was shaky. True, I had been looking for a partner for a long time. True. None of them had remotely worked out. I didn't expect the exasperation of it all to be so overwhelming.

"I need someone with the ability to forgive." I started with the hardest. "Someone with foresight. Compassion. Empathy. Passion. We have to have a friendship. Intelligence is a must. Wealth is a necessity. A legacy is what I am trying to continue building."

He nodded and smirked. "That's a tough-ass list."

I turned my face away from him, rolling my eyes as a few of the tears dropped and I sniffed. "You're making fun of me."

"Never that." Terrence used his most gentle voice but I still couldn't look at him. My tears were private. They were tears of failure. I had given my all to so many men only to get nothing but heartache in return. I was tired. I kept that to myself. I was strong, a Strong, weakness not accepted.

"You deserve all that you called out and more," his stated in a voice as soothing as the waves. "Hey, look at me."

I lifted my eyes to the stillness of his, and drew in a deep breath when he rested a hand on my thigh and another on my shoulder.

"Say it." He didn't move as the waves of water splashed over the formal wear we were ruining. "Words have power. Even more power tonight."

He bent forward to whisper at the cusp of my ear. The vibrations of his deep baritone skittering across my skin were making it more difficult to concentrate. "And if you believe and I believe, that's two of us in agreement. It has to come true. It has to work for you."

Squeezing my eyes shut, I leaned into him, letting my head fall into the base of where his neck and shoulder met. I couldn't see the moon but felt moonlight on us as I breathed in a mixture of the salty air and him.

"Me not admitting that I'm not perfect is my biggest imperfection. My someone will need to forgive me regularly. I need a leader with foresight. He'll need compassion and empathy for people, my family, and of course me. He has to be my homie for real. My someone should be smart and successful and ready to build for our future."

I swallowed the hard truth that even if I found my someone, I would be marrying someone else.

I looked at Terrence. Our knees pressed in the sand, chests pressed together, and faces nearly touching, I knew how I wanted the night to end no matter the consequences.

"And what about you?" I didn't care about the list anymore or any future man, just the man who made me feel like frosting; sweet, whipped, creamy, ready to be spread and licked.

"Honestly?" The word was gruff from his thick parted lips.

"I already told you I don't like liars, idiots, or assholes, so yes, tell me the truth. Be honest with me."

I watched his Adam's-Apple bob up and down as he swallowed.

Pure passion fueled the way that he took me into his arms and pressed his lips into mine. His tongue danced with mine as though they had a lifetime together, but I knew the reason they hadn't. I knew why our lips had been strangers. If I had tasted him before that moment, there was no way that I would have ever let him up for air.

I took the opportunity to acquaint myself with the bulky planks of his chest hiding beneath the dress shirt. When one of his hands moved up from my waist to cup my breast, I felt wetter than the water where we waded.

"I want you," he answered. "Just for tonight. Nothing more. I want to fuck you until we both can't breathe."

I felt like I couldn't breathe already, because I had been wishing for the same thing.

CHAPTER FOURTEEN

Regina

I couldn't drop my clothes in the bag fast enough. When my weak ass knees almost had me tripping down the aisle to him, I should have known that it was past the time for me to go home. Terrence was too much, a formidable opponent to my resolve that I would stay away from men that I couldn't have a future with.

Hefting the large suitcase, I threw it across the bed and dumped everything within my reach inside. Mumbling words that I forgot another person could hear, I scurried across the room gathering everything in sight.

"Oh, he spooked the hell out of you." Her chuckle should have offended me, but it was true. That was the exact reason that I had called Kinnesha, my homegirl from college. She was always blunt with me. She always told me the truth.

"Aren't you and the bridesmaids supposed to have brunch in the morning?" Kinnesha asked. Her face and voice were both coming through my phone on the bed.

"I can't suck on her cousin at night and then sip on mimosas with her in the morning, Kinny. That's just rude."

Kinnesha barely acknowledged my words, but I did catch the tail end of an eye roll when I picked up the phone.

"And skipping out altogether is better?" Her pecan brown face had twisted into a frown and reminded me so much of Nailah. "I want to see this man. Text me a pic. I know you have one."

She was right. I did snag a picture of Terrence that Nailah posted on social media of him sitting at a beachside table.

I was way in over my head.

"Regina, are you sure that you sent the right picture?"

"Of course," I looked back at the text thread to be positive. "That's Terrence."

"No that's Trunk." She replied.

I couldn't have Terrence, but the way Kinnesha was familiar with him struck a nervous chord in me.

"Trunk?" I questioned. "You never told me about no damn Trunk."

Her laugh only served to annoy me further.

"It's not like that," Kinnesha said through a chuckle. "I grew up with them. Terrence looked out for me when people would make fun of me. He was big shit on the block and no one messed with him."

"Oh," I replied, evening my reaction a little. Terrence was still a protector, it only made sense for him to be that way as a kid too. "Of all the people in the world for me to find."

"I haven't talked to Mali in years. She was my closest friend before you, and Tyson was my everything."

Things started clicking then.

"Tyson is T-Low? He's the high school sweetheart. The one you devastated by breaking up with him before move-in day?"

I met Kinnesha during my freshman year of college. My first year away from the notoriety and nosiness of my parents. Kinny was a good person and a great friend. She only stayed in school for one year, but we've remained in touch throughout the years. One of the reasons I gravitated to Nailah so easily is that she reminded me of Kinny.

"I wouldn't say that I devastated him, so much as I released him to fulfill his potential."

It was my turn to laugh.

"With all the calling and flower-sending he was doing, devastation is the only thing to call it."

"I had some tough decisions to make for me and Tanesha." She retorted.

"I know," was my reply. I did know that she made the decision that she believed was necessary back then. I let the conversation sit there because I didn't want to say anything negative about Tanesha, her fraternal twin, whom I never liked and who never liked me.

Kinnesha had left school, after everyone, including teachers, deans, coaches, and I begged her to stay.

"Terrence is a good guy, Regina. I don't see the problem with a night between consenting adults."

"The problem is that I know what I want to do. It's probably not what I should do." I let my head fall back for my eyes to find the ceiling.

I dropped the pair of furry slides that Nailah had gifted me into the case. I would have never chosen them on my own, and they were not Cherry-approved, but it was the first time since Kinny that I had gotten to wear matching outfits with friends.

"If it is truly a one-time deal, I say go for it." Her voice soothed. "I know how much you're sacrificing to go back to the company. You should take the night to enjoy yourself."

"But I can't lie to Mali." I fell back onto the plush comforter. "You know how I am with new people."

"I do, but you can tell her the truth if she asks." Kinny shrugged. "It's none of her business. Let her know that it won't affect your friendship, then move on."

"You're right." My sigh was heavy with the weight of figuring out my next decision. "Running never changed anything."

"Go unleash some tension," she coaxed. "You'll see him a handful of times after this probably."

His family got together regularly. Tyriq and Nailah would have another wedding, but I didn't go with Nailah to their functions unless specifically invited. I could handle two more planned meetings and a possible.

"You're right." I nodded more to myself than my friend. "I think I got this."

I couldn't figure out a way to get over him without letting him go through me. At least, I should experience how long he could breathe while between my thighs.

We had mutually agreed to meet in his room after having time to freshen up and prepare.

The flat line of his lips when he answered the door didn't deter me one bit. That seemed to be the position his face felt most confident in: a mix between *what-the-hell* and *get-the-hell-back*. It was somewhat endearing once it was understood that Terrence Lewis was kind.

His eyes told it all and instead of the bright light of hope that shone earlier, they burned over my face and body with a greedy passion that drew me nearer.

"Hello," his hoarse one-word answer made me look him up and down twice.

He connected his hand to my waist and pulled me into the room. He didn't have a shirt on, only a loose-fitting pair of grey joggers that clearly defined for me why so many found themselves fascinated with the particular article of clothing. The cotton material sat over his straight hips and dipped in front of his taught flat abs. The center though. That part bubbled thick along his thigh, building my anticipation for a reveal.

"You sure about this?" He asked.

"Positive." I nodded.

Our noses touched first. Then his minty breath warmed my lips before his tongue invaded my mouth. I took it, sucking and tugging at it like it just might get away.

"Alright," He nodded his head answering a question that only he was privy to. "We're about to have some fun."

He slapped me on the ass and pressed his solid hardness against my belly and I nearly wilted.

Terrence was the kind of sexy that picked at sanity, siphoned bank accounts, and slowly injured the core of a soul. I needed to keep all that was left of me intact, after him. During him too.

"Just tonight," I warned. "Nothing else. Nothing more."

His head nodded up and down but his eyes stayed right there on my mouth. "We have a little over two hours of playtime if you want to stay in the day," he half mumbled because the tips of his fingers had found their way to my nipples.

"Two hours. That's it." I confirmed. "We do this right, then we won't need a minute past midnight."

I had agreed. No other words were needed. The hungry mouth dance began again, but this time we stripped ourselves and each other between tongue play. I wasn't sure what I was doing, or how I knew when it was time to meet his mouth again. It just happened simultaneously. With each piece of clothing that moved away from our bodies, our lips came together for more.

The stark brush of air that crossed my face when he pulled away startled me. I had gotten accustomed to the feeling of him that quickly.

"I want to look at you." he took my hand in his as he drew back. "If this is only tonight, I want to make sure that I remember it for a lifetime."

I couldn't detect any lies by looking at him. He seemed to genuinely mean it. That unlocked a unnatural combination of comfort, need, and desire in my chest.

If he hadn't pointed to the inviting sheets and ordered 'On the bed', I would have leapfrogged to his neck and cemented my thighs to his face right then. Contrary to my normal 'take-charge' style, I listened. I let him tell me what to do. Curiosity led my cat right to him for the taking.

Terrence leaned his toned body forward as he pressed one knee at a time into the center of each thigh to widen my space for him.

The mounting inches of his manhood stood long and high waving proudly. I fought the urge to raise a hand in salute as it stood at attention, but that didn't stop the superhero theme song from playing in my mind.

"I like the way you open up for me." The low growl to his baritone sent tremors through me as his hand drifted over my skin.

I flexed, put my kegel exercises to use, and made my core wink at him. That was it. The moment that turned enjoyable reality into a blur of intoxicating passion.

Terrence knew his way around a clit. He didn't attack it, but damn sure made it be known that it was taken. Held hostage by his warm mouth, the way he sucked on me, made me question exactly what it was other men had done to me in the past. It wasn't the same or equal to Terrence's kiss. The way he took his whole mouth and paid homage to my girl as a whole and then individual sections with both puckers and tongue action had my neck curled backward off the bed before I even registered that he had moved. I pushed my seat further into his face because I needed the friction that his goatee created. And once the realization settled that he licked faster and applied more pressure when I pressed into him, I couldn't stop.

"Terrence." His name escaped in a tremulous moan as I grabbed onto his locks.

"MmHmm" He hummed slurping so loudly that I released more.

There was no way that I could be closer, but I damn sure tried, bucking my body against him without any inhibition or shame.

I wanted to warn him before I came all over his face. I felt it building, rising as he licked vigorously. It was ready to bubble over. I grunted, moaned, and thrashed until he clamped my waist to suction me thoroughly. Pleasure swamped my mind.

There was no air, room, hotel, or island, I was rocketed into a stratosphere of celestial bliss. I'm not sure if there was a translation for the shouted words that sliced through my throat. Tingles coursed over my entirety. Terrence deserved a knighthood, a medal of freedom for the way he led my lost super orgasm to the light. She had been locked away in a max security dungeon without windows never to be seen again. He had used his special ops to free the feeling that I thought was lost to me and I was grateful for his service to my body.

The way he guzzled down every drop had me mute and wiggling across the bed in electrified shock. With only the prelude, the introduction to his intimacy, Terrence made me mindless.

I parted my eyes slightly. I could see him, standing there rolling down a condom. I found the outline of his body in the sliver of light that broke through the curtains, interrupting the darkness of the room. He was a masterpiece, and artistically hung well. I considered if I had enough space to accommodate him.

"I've wanted this since the first day that we met." He whispered into my neck once he was back to me.

His fingers went first. I was giddy about finally having him. I half moaned and half giggled. I felt the excitement, let it take over for once. I didn't fight back, try to play sexy or unimpressed. I was genuinely impressed. I was ready for him to join our bodies.

"Terrence, are you in there?" The question came after a startling knock at the door.

He stopped mid-caress, removing his touch from my center.

I wasn't sure if the person knocking had picked up a battering ram and bull horn on the way, but it sounded as though the door would come down at any minute.

Terrence kissed my neck and I groaned. His lips were an amazing enough reason to change my life. He nibbled up to my ear and whispered "I have to get that" before another thump sounded from the door.

"But," I whimpered before grazing my hand up the length of him. "What about us?"

He groaned out a curse word just as I heard the unmistakable click of the door unlocking.

Terrence slid into his pajama pants and kicked the remaining clothing under the blanket that was mysteriously tossed on the floor.

I jumped up with lightning speed, sliding into the bathroom just in time to quietly shut the door and crouch in the corner of the tub behind a shower curtain.

"What the hell?" Terrence's voice boomed. "How did you even get a key to my room?"

"My bad bro," The intruding male voice chimed in. "Nobody knew what happened to you. We couldn't find you at the reception, didn't see you in the hotel anywhere, no answer on your cell, no answer when I knocked, so we were worried. Since you took all of this pills that one time-"

I could hear a mixture of emotions in his voice when he cut in to ask, "What do you want?"

"Chad's in jail." The very informative man explained. "He beat some dude up in the lobby after he got upset because Chad picked up his girl and did a few squats with her."

"What?" Terrence sounded just as confused as I felt.

"Apparently, Aunt Pat sent him looking for you, but he ended up talking to some girl in the lobby. When he took his shot, she challenged that he couldn't handle a thick woman like her."

"Oh no," Terrence groaned. "Tell me he didn't."

"He did. Chad picked her up. According to Tyson, who was on his way to the restroom, he rolled her over his shoulder and got through about 6 squats before her boyfriend popped up and went ballistic. You know your cousin doesn't mince words. "

"I know," Terrence's voice was gruff. "I'm fine, tell your mom and aunt not to worry. As the lawyer, Trystan, I figure you can handle Chad. Catch me up tomorrow."

It sounded as though Trystan tried to protest and that Terrence was pushing him out.

Sitting there trying unsuccessfully to keep my bottom from getting wet for non-pleasurable reasons, I realized that I should have never knocked on his door. I was getting married. I had promised my best friend that I would leave her family alone. Terrence and I couldn't make it to the finish line because I wouldn't ever want to give him up. Just a taste had me plotting ways to dip out on my dad and my duty to our family company.

When Terrence opened the door, I stood, smiled, and with as much dignity as I could muster with my bra on inside out and underwear tangled in the place I wish he could play, I told him good night.

CHAPTER FIFTEEN

Regina

I smoothed a hand over the silky pearl-colored material of the strapless top and then down to the beaded and jeweled bodice. I liked the way that it clung to the curves of my body before spilling into a pool of lace at my feet.

It was the dress. My wedding dress. It was really going to happen.

I took one more glance around the dressing room of the boutique and then at the mirror.

"Get your eyes ready for beauty because I'm coming out!" I used my best barnyard holler.

Giggles erupted from the other side of the dressing room door. While I had been binding and stuffing myself into every dress combination with a mermaid flare and a sweetheart neckline known to man, my friends were enjoying themselves.

Nodding to myself, I shuffled a few steps out of the dressing area to the private viewing room. The four women who had become like sisters to me sat singing nineties R&B songs into bottles of champagne. They, not so smoothly, switched from Beyonce's 'Dangerously in Love' to the bridal chorus.

"Here comes the bride." They sang-yelled off-key with their version of rhythm and a side-to-side sway.

"Remix!" Mali shouted before cupping her hands over her mouth to make a sloppy noise that included more spit than beat.

"Sober up lushes and look at how beautiful I am. Mali, you are not a human beatbox machine." I clap in the direction of the women in an attempt to get their full attention. "Bottles down. Eyes up. This is my moment."

"Whicky-Whup," Jubilee acted out scratching a record like a DJ and I just shook my head.

We had been there for a while. All-day was more accurate. I had been through what felt like a thousand dresses and Mali, Jubilee, and Kinnesha had been through what looked like a thousand bottles of champagne. Nailah's *'end of the road'* pregnant ass hadn't drunk but indulged in the treats she pulled from the bottomless purse she toted everywhere. She was asleep, sprawled out across the love seat, empty chip bags, snack wrappers, and candy paper acting as a blanket.

"What do you think?" I asked stepping onto the pedestal in front of a tri-fold mirror.

Kinnesha struggled to hold her head straight as an over-wide smile spread under her slow blinking eyes. From the wobbly nod she gave, I knew that the expensive bridal shop we had taken over for the day hadn't skimped on the top-of-the-line champagne. I had known Kinny the longest. The short brown-skinned woman with waist-length braids and shoulder long earrings always held her liquor and never her tongue.

"That's it, girl. That's the one," Kinny nodded, approvingly. I had missed her. Although we hadn't truly lost contact with each other after school, she had only recently moved back to the area.

I turned to face Jubilee, who let loose a giggle so loud I questioned the alcohol percentage of what the staff served, but I valued her opinion.

"Oooh, pretty." Jubilee sang. "Whoever you marry is gonna be happy when he sees you in that dress."

Glancing back over my shoulder I took another look at myself in the multiple full-length mirrors.

Fine ass bride? Check.

Veil? Check.

Dress? Check.

Groom? To Be Determined.

I was getting married, but I wasn't sure to whom. An idea wiggled in the back of my brain. There was one man that made me feel like no other. He made my body ache for his touch. If only he felt like I felt.

The crinkle of wrappers and a yawn startled me from my reverie.

"When's dinner?" Nailah stretched awake and rubbed her rounded belly.

"Hello. Don't you see all of this radiance?" I lifted my arms with a flourish and twirled in a circle. "What do you think of the dress?"

Nailah nodded. "Cute. The lace reminds me of icing. The buttercream kind. Oooh. Can we get a cake on the way to the restaurant?"

Two hours later, after feeding Nailah, the ladies and I had found our way to my favorite spa. The exclusive establishment provided a beautiful private room with a waterfall fountain, six leather massage pedicure chairs, and two manicure stations. It was the only way that I ever got my nails done. A private room or I hired a team to come directly to my home. I was a little spoiled, but money was made to spend, right?

"What the hell else do you have in that purse?" I questioned Nailah as she pulled out yet another snack pack of powdered donuts. She had opted only to get a pedicure so that her hands would be free to graze through her snacks.

Nailah had rifled open the package and stuffed a mini cake donut in her mouth before I could even finish my sentence.

"If you stay ready, then you don't have to get ready," she managed to speak.

"Nailah, I can't do you and these quotes."

She made another donut disappear before speaking again.

"Whether you think you can or you can't, you're right."

"Ugh. Swallow first, Nai," I groaned.

"Sorry. This baby makes me so hungry." Her huge engagement ring and wedding band twinkled in the light.

"Leave her alone," Mali piped in. "Let her have those snacks or the world will suffer for it."

I shook my head.

"I am so ready for you to have this baby." It was true. It was also very selfish of me, but I wanted my friend back.

When she joined the Department of Child Protective Services, I was assigned to help her navigate the new role. Somehow, Nailah became the little sister I never knew I wanted. I hadn't longed for siblings, I was fine soaking up all of my family's love and money by my lonesome. I didn't realize how much I missed having a best friend until Nailah came around. She and Kinnesha were a lot alike. Before the baby and marriage, Nai and I hung out all of the time. Usually on her sofa or mine, because the girl was a hermit before me. Still, popcorn and chocolate on the couch tasted better with a best friend.

"Really? *You're* ready for me to have this baby?" She scrunched her face as she chewed. "At least your womb hasn't been taken hostage and made into a jungle gym."

Mali, who was Nailah's cousin by marriage, leaned over to speak into Nailah's stomach.

"I just can't wait to see her my God Daughter's face," she cooed, her long Senegalese twists dangling over Nailah's belly.

"Correction." I snapped. " You mean my God Daughter. She's already your cousin Mali. You can't have all the titles."

"How's the search coming?" Kinny abruptly changed the subject.

I knew that she was trying to keep the peace, she was a classic avoider, but the topic was still touchy. I was doing all of the right things to prepare for my new role as wife and CEO, except having a successful relationship.

"It's all in Reginald's hands." I took a deep breath in and exhaled harshly trying to breathe away the anxiety of letting my father loose in the world to choose a man for me.

"You're not even trying anymore?"

"You were there Nailah for the crazy, I'll date anybody, just give me somebody with a body and money that landed me crawling behind Jermaine Timmons."

An unmelodic chorus of groans sounded through the room.

"Right. And at the end of the day, I need someone that I can tolerate." Even as I said the words they tasted funny, and felt weird, but my choices were limited. "The kind of love that my mom and dad have, like Nailah and Tyriq found, it doesn't exist for me. I want some pretty babies and someone to help me run the company. Fuck love. I'm looking for the right partner to help me build."

"I thought that you didn't care that much about the business?" Jubilee frowned even though she was quickly building an empire of her own. She still actively worked the runway as a model, had a reality television show, brand sponsors, and a possible movie deal.

"I didn't back when I felt like he was invincible, you know? I felt like I could do my thing in the world because he would be there to keep the earth spinning forever."

I didn't like to talk about my family and our wealth. I had sworn the ladies to secrecy. If anyone did an internet search, they wouldn't find many if any connections to my father. And even though I shared the same name as a prominent businessman no one ever put the two together. I trusted the women in the room.

"My father made some bad investments, and the company took a big loss last year. Strong Acquisitions and Realty has been bleeding money since then and he reached out to me. He wants me to do this for him, for his legacy, for our family, and I couldn't refuse."

"You are so choosy. It's hard to believe that you're letting your dad sift through business partners until he finds one for you to marry." Jubilee winced as skepticism clouded her face.

I understood why she wouldn't want her father to choose her husband. Curtis Greene was a womanizer who didn't take care of his responsibilities. My father had given me everything that I had ever asked for and more. He was the kind of man that I looked for.

"Real recognizes real, and my daddy is a real one, so I trust him." Mostly.

"Do these men know that they're competing to be your husband?" Nailah, who had finished her snack, asked. She was on her open-and-honest journey.

"Not at all. They're building a business relationship and those not chosen will never know that there was an option."

Nailah lifted an eyebrow. "Do you get any votes in picking the winner?"

"I do. My dad has narrowed it down to five men. He won't give me any information about them yet, but once he whittles the list down to three, I decide from there."

"You don't have to do this, Regina. Love is the essence of life," Nailah added. "Aren't you worried about living life in a loveless marriage?"

I didn't answer. Speaking my fear out loud wasn't easy. I wasn't supposed to be scared.

"Why are you doing this?" Mali asked.

"I guess-" I looked away from my friends and focused on the small ticking hand of the clock on the wall. "Part of me believes that maybe my father will find someone good for me. I sure as hell hadn't been able to." I look for comfort in their gazes again. "There's a tiny piece of hope in the corner of my spirit that wants this to work, that hopes whoever my dad chooses will eventually love me and I will love him too after some time. I hope that this option works for real love."

I hate the sympathetic look in their eyes.

"And if it doesn't?" Nailah asks.

I didn't have an answer to that question either. I had the dress, the venue, the date, but I didn't know what I would do if it didn't work. I would never leave my father hanging, but at what cost?

Chapter Sixteen

Terrence

Shutting the hood of the car, I stood up to my full height. I wiped my hands on the towel tucked into my waist, and looked around my shop. Years ago, we had expanded from two to six car bays; each lift had a car, and more cars parked outside. Then we expanded shops throughout the states of Texas and Oklahoma. It took time and hard work, but I had accomplished what I had set out to do. I had made the money that I felt destined to make, but something was missing; there was an ache that I couldn't work away.

Circled the car with me were eight inexperienced teens whom I mentored. I had started the group two years ago in an attempt to mend a part of the hole in my heart. I would never have kids of my own, so I thought I could help the ones that were already there. They were working on a rust bucket I found for them to overhaul for practice. The kids came by after school to assist my employees in the supply shop, car bays, or car wash, and I paid them a little above minimum wage to be apprentices; as long as they stayed out of trouble on their high school campus, and stayed for skill training once a week after hours.

We started Brothers T Auto Care Group together. Family had molded me into the man that I was. I realized that many boys in the neighborhood that I grew up in, and where my car shops serviced, didn't have that luxury. If nothing else, I wanted to give them a skill that would help them build a better future, and a hobby besides sports that kept them out of trouble. It also helped me feel useful, so it was a win-win.

"Mr. T., you got a shop over on the west side? Over there off of Hampton?" Daquan, of my YAM's, or Young Aspiring Mechanics, asked that Friday night.

The boys thought it was hilarious to call me Mr. T., after the character on the A-Team television series. Other than my muscular build, I looked nothing like the character. First off, I wore my hair in locks and the television character was near bald. I let it slide because I knew it was a sign of respect.

"I own a shop over there." Stuffing my hands in my pockets, I wondered what the kid was getting at.

Skills training was over and most of the teens had straggled home already. My brother Tyson and two of the YAM's were in the shop's lobby. We were all waiting. . Daquan was waiting for a ride, Trevion was waiting for the bus, and I was waiting for a customer. I promised to give a late vehicle pickup. Tyson was stuck waiting to close out the day's transactions.

"I've seen that shop. I ride past it sometimes on the bus." Trevion added. He caught the bus home but never seemed like he wanted to leave. He was always the first to arrive at the shop after school without fail every day, and the last to leave every night. If I had the shop open, he was there.

"My homie was wondering if you do this at all your shops," Daquan asked squaring his shoulders and standing with more confidence than his years should allow. "You know, hire kid labor?"

"It's not kid labor." I corrected him. "And make sure you don't call it that in front of anyone else. You'll have the feds running through here checking ID and paperwork. It's a paid internship, and this is the only location. Having teenagers near all of this equipment is a liability, and I don't trust anyone else to oversee it."

Tyson cleared his throat.

"Well, I don't trust anyone who stays in the city longer than three days a week to run the program." The amendment to my words didn't straighten the look on Tyson's face.

"Better," Tyson grunted as he continued pushing buttons on the computer register.

"That's messed up, Mr. T., I know you're making that bread with cheddar stacked on top," He reviewed my attire. "Even though you don't dress like it, I know you got bread. You could hire a special teacher just for your shops. You could build a training shop just for kids like me to come to after school and work."

"Don't count my pockets." I looked over at the small kid with big ideas. " I do alright for myself, but the liability cost for a shop full of teenagers?"

"Yea. I mean, it's not unheard of. Some high schools have it as a class, but I don't have space to fit it in my schedule because I'm taking advanced courses."

"It sounds good youngin', but that's a lot of money you're talking about. For every five kids, we would need at least one instructor." Tyson piped in.

"We got all that we can handle right here."

Daquan shook his head. "This is a great program Mr. T., and I have been in a lot of them. My momma puts me in everything. You should do this all over the city."

"This is my favorite place." Trevion layered on with an enthusiastic nod.

"I know some kids that would work hard for an opportunity like this. And then-" The sound of the city bus turning the corner interrupted Daquan's words.

"That's my ride. See you tomorrow Mr. T., I'm out," Trevion nodded his head up in my direction before bounding through the door to the bus stop in front of the shop.

"You could make an actual difference with this," Daquan wasn't letting up. "Like with Trevion. His mom just got out of that drug rehab place-" He snapped his fingers a few times before finally throwing out the name. "Grace Lake, that's it. She's been there at least twice this year, and it never sticks. Why do you think he's always up here? And Do' Boy, he got a baby on the way. He uses the money he makes here to give to his girl."

I knew about Dorian, AKA Do' Boy, getting his girlfriend pregnant. I had talked him into finishing his last year of high school, allowed him to come in regular hours on the weekend to work tire rotations and oil changes, and gave him a slight bump in pay. Trevion's situation was news to me. He rarely had much to say.

"Even if you don't do the training center, think about adding another group. It's not a lot of options out there and-" Daquan stopped speaking. The abrupt silence was startling because the boy talked non-stop even when he had nothing to say. I noticed him blinking a few times.

Looking over at him, I noticed the beginning of tears welled at the bottom of his eyes. I let him have a moment.

I placed a hand on his shoulder. As tough as the young men in my shop acted, they were still little boys. Because of their bravado, society sometimes forgot. I couldn't.

Daquan blinked again and cleared his throat before beginning. "They got my cousin."

He paused and looked around the room. I could tell that the incident was fresh and he was still struggling with it. In the last two years, I hadn't lost any students, but some of them had lost family members and friends.

"He won't have any more chances." Daquan continued. "What if he had come to something like this with me? Maybe he'd still be alive."

Light from two cars pulling into the lot shined through the storefront windows.

"That's me." Daquan pointed his thumb toward the door.

"I'll look into expanding," I call out to the very persuasive young man.

"That's what's up." He nodded.

"And if you ever need to talk-" The rest of my words trailed off as Daquan nodded.

"I know Mr. T. You're the real deal."

He was out of the door then, and the woman coming to pick up her car after hours slid right in.

Rachel was a newer customer. Most of the clientele at this location had been with me since I opened, but I still offered her the OGC, original garage crew, perks. She was a single mother and had an odd work schedule, so I stayed later to accommodate her. It's not like I had someone to go home to.

"Thank you so much." Rachel gushed while sliding a hand down my shoulder and my entire arm. "I don't know what I would have done without my car tomorrow. I already had to bum a ride today."

"It was no problem." I pat her resting hand, remove it from my wrist, and then move behind the counter.

"You have a nice shop." She said leaning forward, her low-cut blouse putting her breasts on display.

I could tell what she was doing, but it did nothing for me. Not that she was bad-looking. There had been only one woman on my mind for the last few weeks.

"I appreciate you." She drew out the words punctuating them with a syrupy smile.

"And I value you as a customer," I gave a slight smile before handing her the keys.

She lingered a little longer before the quiet awkwardness of the moment pushed her through the door.

"Youngin' had a point," Tyson interrupted the quiet. "I'll research the financials on our end, but you should look into a sponsor or partner to help you expand."

I wait for the rest, for him to dive into his normal spiel about my life.

"That's it?" I lift an eyebrow.

"If you're waiting on me to talk shit about letting that 'hot and ready' walk through that door, you can stop. I got nothing to say about you wasting away as a monk. You don't wanna wild out with women- shit, or even one woman- that's on you."

"You have nothing to say about that, huh?"

"Well, since you asked-" Tyson stepped around the counter. "When are you going to move on? There's got to be a woman that wants your 'standard black shirt and cargo pants' wearing ass. If I hadn't seen you in a suit myself, I wouldn't think that you owned anything else."

My brother didn't know that one woman had wanted me recently and that I had wanted her back. I couldn't stop wanting her. She made me smile. I never wanted to have enough feeling inside to smile again.

"I get mine and don't have to do none of that prissy shit you do." I reminded him.

Of my three brothers, Tyson was the smoothest. He dressed like he was about to audition for the role as an English Duke. Picky as hell, the only time he wasn't walking around looking like the prom king was when I made him put in time at the shop.

"Check back with me when you own more than two suits." My brother retorted as he started turning off the lights.

I flipped Tyson the middle finger before replying.

"I have work to do. This shop doesn't run itself." I had an office. I didn't have to take his shit out in the lobby.

"Correction." Tyson issued the words to my back. "This shop doesn't run itself, but it could. The other locations do well with a management team and my supervision."

That caught my attention and I swung around to face his smug ass grin. He and my family had been on my case for the last year about leaving the shop, my shop in the hands of another manager. What would I do every day if I wasn't in the shop?

"There you go again."

"You don't have to be here. We're not small-time anymore." He reminded me. "We have regional managers now. Your nails could be as clean as mine and your clothes could be close if you step out of the pit and into life again. I promise it's not as scary as it looks."

Starting my own business had been a rocky risk that I had to work hard to smooth out and expand. I was proud of what I had accomplished despite the naysayers, but even I hadn't dreamed that I would be riding through a course with one of the top real estate and business developers in the state. After meeting with my brothers and me, he asked about my golf skills, and he had been a mentor since. It was encouraging that he saw something extraordinary in me and had become somewhat of a mentor over the last few weeks.

"Come now." Reginald Strong stopped the cart on a green mound near the club doors. Sitting in an arrow straight position with a gleam in his eye, he turned to look at me.

"I would like to think that we've built a rapport with one another at this point. We've been golfing for a while now." Mr. Strong encouraged.

I didn't feel comfortable telling him about my nightlife, but I wanted to keep the business opportunities open. Besides operating a tow service, we signed a deal to add a Brother's T Spotless Car Wash on the arena property as well. Valet patrons would be able to have their car washed and detailed during any event.

"You have to have a woman somewhere." he prodded.

I let the lift of my cheek break through the silence. My face could only respond in one way when I thought about her, a smile.

"That's what I thought." He chuckled as he reared back and bounced his head in a nod.

"It's not like that." I waved my hands in protest. "It's nothing serious, nothing exclusive at all. So far, it was only one night. But it was a helluva night."

Mr. Strong pulled the cart forward to park in the shade of a tree.

"Having a good *woman of the night* is an important part of life. It's even an important key to marriage," he explained, his face tight and serious.

I had never claimed to be as smart as my brother Tyriq or as great with putting puzzles together as Tyson, but Reginald Strong's words made me check around the course for hidden cameras. I couldn't have heard him correctly. I read somewhere that he married his wife nearly 35 years ago.

"Let me explain." Settling against the smooth leather seat, Mr. Strong folded his fingers together before continuing. "A marriage can be like running a business. The wife is a trusted manager and has many important roles and functions. But your manager is going to need an assistant. Just like you don't want to overwork your employees, you don't want to *overwork* or burn out your wife."

I scratched my ear before taking a few moments to review the words in my head. *What did I hear?*

"By *work,* you mean..." I tumbled my hands in circles around each other. "You mean sex?"

He gave a hearty chuckle. "I think you've got it there now. The right *worker* can be very useful to a man. But you got to find the right one. This new generation of night ladies," he shook his head. "You all call them side pieces or side chicks, I think. They don't know how to stop talking. Back in my day, you could have two or three different families and no one would know until the funeral."

He gave a slight laugh, but I cleared my throat. I was surprised. He never gave the impression that he cheated on his wife before. His words didn't match what I had observed about him.

"No disrespect sir, but if I ever marry, there will only be one." I hid my apprehension behind the lift of my eyebrows. "Once I say 'I do'... I won't be with anyone else."

Tense seconds of stark quiet ticked by and frayed at my nerves as he inspected me with narrow eyes. *Had I offended him? Would my offense affect our partnership?*

A smirk lifted at the corner of his face.

"I understand," He grinned as he clapped a firm hand against my shoulder. "I like your integrity. Stick to what you believe, son." He nodded his head toward me before returning his hand to the wheel. "I wanted to see where your head was. If a man will lie to the woman he lays next to every night for his own needs, it makes me question how that man does business with someone he sees occasionally. It seems like you have a pretty good one on your shoulders. I like that."

The tension in my shoulders loosened as I relaxed at the thought that he was possibly testing my character.

"Speaking of integrity-" I began, figuring that it was as good a time as any to discuss my plans. "I am expanding my mentoring group, and I wanted to know if you would be interested in partnering with me or making a donation?"

"I'll have my new Chief Operating Officer contact you about the project." He answered as he pushed the gas and moved the cart forward.

It almost felt like a brush-off. I dealt directly with him on every project. Why would he suddenly pawn me off on a random understudy?

"Don't worry. I have funded many mentorship groups in the past. I am working on a pseudo-mentoring project myself."

I felt like there was something the old man wasn't telling me, but I let the feeling pass and listened as he continued.

"I'm working closely with my new COO who will eventually step into my role."
****

"Found you!" TJ shouted as he bounded through the sliding porch door, his tiny limbs working overtime to catch up to his energy.

I had taken a seat. There was no way that I could match his energy. I had learned that the best children's games let them do most of the work. Little Trystan was roaming around my mother's house looking for me while I chilled out back sipping.

"You sure did." I played along. Hiding on the back porch was the most inconspicuous and comfortable place that I could sit and think without TJ finding me quickly.

"Tickle, tickle." My nephew twisted his tiny hands in circles against my stomach.

"You have to laugh, Uncle T-Rex." His two front teeth were quickly covered by his falling smile as he folded his arms and huffed.

"I don't laugh little man," I pat his shoulder.

"Not even for tickles?" His eyebrow lifted as though he couldn't believe that such a thing happened.

"Nope, not even for tickles."

"Why are you sad?" Those tiny fingers spread across my knee and his observant eyes surveyed me. "If you take a nap, you can feel better."

I let the corner of my mouth crinkle at that.

"Go find your mom and get ready for dinner," Trystan told his son as he stepped through the door and took a seat. "Grandie has a special treat for you."

"Yay!" Trystan Jr scurried through the door with a grin pressing against his chubby cheeks wide enough to hide his eyes.

I swiped my finger across the phone screen and thought about calling her. Regina. What was supposed to be a passing infatuation that buried itself below my consciousness, turned out to be an experience that I hadn't been able to forget.

"You losing the shops?" Trystan had been talking, but I was lost in my thoughts.

"What? Losing the shops?" I questioned. "Why would I lose the shops? They're better than ever right now."

"I've only seen you this confused twice in life." He lifted his hand to count the instances on his fingers. "The first time was when you saw Jenny Thomas walking down the street with Chad while wearing your letterman jacket. The second time was when you first opened the shop and had that tax problem so you thought that the IRS was going to take your business."

I shook my head.

"Why would you even go there?"

Trystan knew how to bring up random facts from the past that no one else wanted to remember.

"Those are the only two things that make you look that way, women or money. I would ask if it was a woman, but everyone knows that you haven't been with anyone since Valerie died."

"Go away," I murmured. I never understood how he could be so smart yet so simple when it came to practical conversation.

"It's about a woman?" His voice leaped as high as he did from the chair. "You got a girl?"

"Not exactly." I considered the word to use about the vivacious woman that had been on my mind. "I might ask her out. I was thinking about dating."

"Holy shit! You're turning in your monk card?"

"Chill, man. You can't say a word, especially not to mom."

He slid two pinched fingers across his mouth and pretended to lock his lips.

"Your secret is safe with me." He answered.

Trystan was a ticking time bomb when it came to secrets ready to explode words at any second.

"Where's the party?" My brother Tyriq asked as he stepped through the door.

"Not out here," Trystan answered. "Terrence is out here trying to fight back the love he has for his new woman."

I shouldn't have been shocked that it took Trystan less than a minute to flip his lips, but I was.

"That was a record," I mumbled.

"What?" He hunched his shoulders. "I didn't tell mom."

I walked away.

In the living room, Tyson sat starch straight in his plaid suit shuffling a deck of cards like a Las Vegas dealer.

"You out here throwing cards for fun?" There was no one at the table with my brother

"The champ is here," Chad announced as he slid in from the kitchen, pulled out the chair I had reached for, and sat down.

I elbowed my cousin in the shoulder as I made my way around the table to another chair.

"We're about to play Tonk, you in?" Tyson called out as the cards folded between each other.

"I'm in," Tyriq called from behind me. "Anything other than sitting alone with Trystan. That fool just asked me if I was going to Briana's wedding."

Only Trystan would ask a man about attending an ex's wedding. That woman had made Tyriq's life hell and almost cost him Nailah.

"How did he get Crystal to marry him?" I questioned.

"I've been wondering that since he brought her home." Tyson agreed as he dealt the cards.

Family game night had been happening for as long as Valerie had been gone. My mom, Shirley, and her sister, Patricia set up the tradition. Aunt Pat had three children: Mali, Chad, and Cairo. Even though they were my cousins, we grew up more like siblings.

I could always tell the exact moment that Nailah entered a room. My back was toward the door, but the look in my brother's eyes changed. It was beautiful and devastating the way that Tyriq loved Nailah. No matter what was happening, he always made sure that she was good first, that anything she needed was taken care of. I had loved Valerie, she was the only woman I had ever loved, but it wasn't all-consuming like it seemed to be between my brother and his new bride.

I was right. Tyriq's smile was due to Nailah entering the room, but she wasn't alone.

My brother stood to greet his wife.

I didn't have to turn around to fully comprehend who had accompanied her. The sweet-smelling mix of vanilla, mango, and jasmine caught my attention the second she was near.

"Hey, family." Nailah greeted cheerily. "Sorry, I'm late. Mr. Lewis here refused to let me shop by myself, and anytime Regina and I get together the stores stock up and celebrate. Y'all remember Regina, right?"

While Tyson and Chad turned to glance at the woman behind me, I knew to keep my eyes forward.

"Who wouldn't remember Regina?" Chad's eyes roamed in her direction too long.

"Hey." Her melodic tone reminded me of her moans.

Regina didn't step into my line of vision, just orbited somewhere in my midst and that bothered me. I felt pulled to her.

I dropped a card on the table, bringing everyone's attention back to the game.

"Are we playing or what? If we don't hurry up, those two will sneak off somewhere. "

Tyriq chuckled as he reclaimed his seat and Nailah wiped lip gloss from his cheek with her thumb. Her swollen belly bumped against his arm slightly and he turned to rub the spot where they had made contact.

"Nobody's leaving the game," Tyriq said as he picked up his cards.

My brother had left the game as soon as he met Nailah. When she whispered something in his ear and he smiled, I knew that cards would be over soon.

She waddled back the same way that she had waddled in, but the way Tyriq watched her, I figured that we wouldn't even make it through the first round.

"Fine ass women do travel in a pack. What's up with Nailah's friend? Regina can jump on it anytime." Chad inquired.

It took all my restraint not to snatch his lips off.

"How's Tia?" I bite out the words. Talking about his daughter was the only way to get Chad's attention when he got stuck on a woman.

"We're figuring it out," He smiled. "I already have her room decked out in her favorite color, peach."

I never thought that my kid-like cousin would get to a point of excitement about having his four-year-old daughter live with him and tackling single fatherhood.

"Is her mother getting better?" The woman had dropped off their daughter at Tyriq's clinic some time ago. Tia's mother was in a rehabilitation facility. Luckily Nailah, a social worker then, was able to connect the young girl with her grandmother, and after a DNA test, Chad.

"Tyson helped me get Misti checked into a better center. The one she had been in before, Grace Lake, was terrible. I want her to get better for Tia's sake."

"That's very mature of you."

"Food's ready!" My mother called and all the cards hit the table simultaneously, the game was quickly abandoned.

She had been in my dreams, on my mind, and then she was walking around my mother's home. She looked better than the food. My appetite craved her and sitting around pretending like I didn't know her body inside and out was driving me crazy.

"You alright?" My mother asked. "You're usually on your second plate by now."

"True." My cousin Mali, the only girl in our group, pointed a fork in my direction. "You're usually quiet, but tonight you're quiet-quiet."

"The shop has been busy."

"But you like it when the shop is busy." Mali narrowed her eyes. "The only time I see you smile is when the shop is crazy busy."

Everyone in the room seemed to agree, most nodding their heads or murmuring over their food.

"He only looks like that when-" Trystan began but was interrupted.

"The baby just kicked!" Nailah exclaimed.

Just like that, the family had forgotten that I was even in the room, and I took that moment to slip away.

Me: Meet me in the restroom.

Regina: What will you do when I get there?

Me: I just want to talk to you.

Regina: We can talk at the table.

Me: In private. Please.

Five of the longest minutes on earth passed before a slight knock on the door announced her presence.

I yanked the door open and shut it with the same motion. I could only give her a few seconds, allow her space for a span of breaths just to take her because I wanted to be in her.

"What's so important that I had to make up a silly excuse to -"

She didn't finish the words. I probably should have let her, but I kissed her. She kissed me back. Regina parted her lips and slipped her tongue into my mouth and kissed me back. She had missed me too. I hadn't imagined the night we shared or the emotions that came after.

We were tangled together in an instant. My hands cupped and massaged her lush curves. Her fingers fondled across the planks of my back and then my waistband.

"Regina." I pressed her name into her tongue before pulling it into my mouth.

Her hand slid over my member reminding me of why I couldn't get enough of her.

"I thought you said one night," she asked between pants, the mounds of her cleavage rising and falling rapidly beneath the top of the low-cut dress.

She agreed to one night. I thought it would be one and done. It had been in the past.

"We didn't get our one night. What do you want right now?"

It took self-control to keep my hand at her side, planted at her waist while I waited for a reply.

"We made the rule, so we can break it." Her eyes darted back and forth across mine as if reading my reaction.

"Damn right." I agreed and the kissing resumed. Our tongues found each other for a sensuous reunion and danced to the melody of our want.

I hadn't known how much I had missed her body.

Regina had her legs around me in seconds and I walked her over to the counter so that I could free my hands to explore.

Clothing was moved, my belt unbuckled, and her skin uncovered.

Regina exhaled a moan that instantly steeled me.

I felt like I didn't have enough hands and fingers to touch her everywhere that I needed to. Massaging her breast, gripping her ass, and pushing between her thighs had me ready to escape somewhere with her and never look back.

Our mouths crashed together, noses smashing, lips popping as we found our rhythm and the best way to taste each other.

She squirmed in response to me finding the button to her heated center, but we didn't drop our kiss. We pushed together more, tongues turning, bodies bucking, restraint breaking. Feeling the petal-soft insides of her walls as she soaked my hand enlarged the ache to bury myself in her. I wanted to get lost in the sensations her body elicited.

"Oooohhh" she gripped my arm as her body tightened around my fingers. I could tell that she was close. The scrunch of her eyes, grit in her teeth, and quickened breath made me increase the pace. I wanted her to get there. I wanted to see the look of bliss explode across her face.

Regina pressed against me and she panted out, "So. Good. Oh so good."

Her soft moans made me want to poke my chest out like I won a medal.

A loud knock at the door had Regina jerking her head up and interrupted the most exhilarating moment I'd had since Puerto Rico.

"Terrence you in this bathroom?" Aunt Pat banged on the door again.

I loved my aunt, but at that moment, if Regina hadn't scooted forward and opened her legs wider to get my attention, I probably would have cursed her out.

"Yeah," I answered Aunt Pat as Regina circled the hardened nub of her clit in my view.

"I'm trying to find that vegetable girl that didn't want none of my pork chops." Aunt Pat called out through the door.

Regina licked her lips as she rolled her hips against her hand. "I'll eat your meat though" She whispered.

"You say something?" My aunt asked.

"Just me aunty," I grunted.

There was a pause, and I groaned again.

"Work that one out baby. You need some of my special chocolate?" She was referring to the laxative she often carried in her purse.

"I just need a few more minutes." I pleaded in a fake guttural tone.

"You didn't have any of Crystal's deviled eggs tonight, did you? Her recipe will have you going and stopped up all at the same time." She questioned. "I'll be back to check on ya."

"I got it, Aunt Pat."

Regina burst into a fit of laughter and I even added a chuckle.

"You're a mess."

I was a little sad when she stood up from the counter and fixed her dress and underwear. I didn't want to miss the chance to be with her again.

"I did that for you. Aunt Pat would have thrown Holy Water and anointed your head with oil while burning sage if she had caught us in here together."

"Let's finish this somewhere else then?" She suggested fixing her appearance in the mirror. "I can sneak out of here and leave Nailah with Tyriq."

I liked the idea. I wanted to be with her and touch her, but I also needed her to know that this wasn't a forever situation.

"Regina," I slid my arms around her, locking that lush body in place. I needed her close to me as I explained my thoughts. "I like you, and I want to continue to have a sexual relationship with you."

"But nothing else." She finished for me. " I agree. I like you too. I like your body even more. You can be my midnight man."

I nodded, liking the sound of that.

"Since we're giving out nicknames." I thought for a few seconds before nodding my head. "Bloom. You can be my Bloom."

Her eyebrows were knotted. "Where did that come from?"

After pulling the base of her earlobe between my lips, I explained. " I liked the way you always open up to me."

She leaned into my ear. "Alright. You're in."

I took four steps back and rubbed my hands together. I had plans for her.

"Two hours. I'll text you the location and leave a key at the front desk."

Her hip pushed back like she had something to say about it, but I left before she could rebut. Regina knew what it was.

CHAPTER SEVENTEEN

Regina

I don't rush for anyone. I don't move faster than I want to for anything. Mastery is a process, and I am well worth the wait. However, the matter with Terrence required a different sense of urgency and time management altogether. After the family dinner, I went home to get my body all the way together so that Terrence could completely ravage it apart.

He didn't know what he started. Terrence wasn't ready for the events that I had planned for that bed. On my way to him, a group of grannies nearly got the business because they blocked the elevator call button. As they completed a headcount and randomly yelled through the lobby for a woman named Claudia, I thought that I was going to blow a gasket. By grace, they caught the hint after only one neck roll and over loud *"Excuse me"*. Once in the elevator, I jabbed at the buttons. I felt like I could have jogged up the stairs quicker than the machine was pulling me up. I moved down the hall with precision. I bet the entire floor could hear the intensity with which my heels hit the carpeted hall. Our room was at the end, off to itself. A utility closet and a brick wall enclosed it. The perfect location to cancel out the screams of passion itching at my throat to be free.

He was a release from all the tension in my life. He was a release from the day-to-day sadness that I carried from being a social worker. He was the ultimate release into a world of satisfaction.

My heart rate increased with each step. He had already been down this hall. I could smell his cologne. He was in that room and he was waiting for me. My cookie twitched at the thought.

I readied my room key; there was no time for fumbling for it at the door.

When the lock light on the door flashed green, I felt like I had just opened a bank vault. Money had never made me feel as good as Terrence, so in a way, he was more valuable. I nearly leaped through the door as I opened it, but his presence stopped me in my tracks.

Terrence was standing near the window looking like his carved body had just descended from the sky. Thin, grey cotton pajama pants hung low around his waist. Beams of light highlighted the tattoos on his biceps and the smooth line of his jaw. Hands behind his back, his face held determined eyes and kiss-ready lips.

"Take off your clothes," he demanded. The rumble of his voice vibrated over my skin and I nearly melted.

The door closed behind me with the same thud as my heartbeat.

Terrence didn't move. I didn't either.

Did he get finer? Was that even possible?

I saw the lift of his eyebrow in the moonlight. He was not a man to say things twice, so I did as he asked. Whether he took the lead, or I did, the outcome would be the same. Pleasure.

I stepped out of my heels first.

His eyes traipsed over me as I slid down the zipper of my dress.

"Can you help me?" I whispered at his hungry gaze.

He swiped his tongue across his bottom lip before tucking that lip under his teeth. He slid one hand into the other in front of him and drew my attention to his center. I remember how rough his fingers felt but how gentle they touched.

"You got it." The words are quick, low, and heated and the middle of me pulsed at the thought of having him.

My dress formed a circle over my toes as it pooled around my ankles.

I moved toward him. Anxious want spiraled through me.

"Nah." He placed a hand up to stop me. He pointed to the thin scraps of lace still covering me. "That too."

I unhooked my bra, shimmied out of it, and threw it at him. Panties too.

He caught them both.

He tucked my panties into the pocket of his pajama pants. He dropped my bra to the floor.

I advanced toward him again.

He lifted his head in the direction of the large plush-looking mattress and head-board. "On the bed."

"You coming with me?" I asked.

I didn't have to, because he finally moved his body near mine. He was finally in my orbit, finally near my pull, and I couldn't wait to get him in my atmosphere.

He obviously couldn't wait either, because he stepped behind me so quickly that I thought he had teleported. It was like magic. It was as if he had wiggled his dick to instantly reappear behind me without his feet ever leaving the floor.

I slid my back against his front, my head falling back against his chest without my permission as he kissed my neck. He stretched his hand across the skin of my stomach and down to my middle. His fingers tripped around my newly trimmed landing strip as I anticipated him pulling into my terminal. When his finger landed between my folds, I jumped at the jolt of pleasure. It hadn't changed. The last time wasn't a dream. He still made me feel like a fiend.

Wrapping an arm around my breast he guided both of our bodies to the bed. It's a damn shame, but I almost melted from the warmth of being tucked beneath him.

Nearly engulfed by his large frame, there was no place that I would have rather been. Pressed between the soft bed and his rigid body, I knew then that it wouldn't be the last time.

His hand was still between my thighs, touching me and I pushed against it. I already heard the sloshy sound his fingers caused as he played with me.

Slithering his hand up and across my belly, I felt the wet effects of his touch, and disappointment floated over me. I knew what that hand was capable of doing.

He flipped my body over so that I could see the want in his serious mahogany eyes. I missed his fingers between me. I wanted him to touch me again. I would have agreed to anything to get that feeling again.

"Whoever we are outside of this room doesn't matter," he reminded me. "You're Bloom and I'm Midnight. Regina and Terrence would never do this.

"I got it." I understood that he wanted to keep some distance between us and make the visit less personal, but it was too late for me. No matter what I called him, he was a need for me. "As long as you agree to keep doing this." I placed two fingers where I wished he were and gave him a visual.

"I'll call you King Anaconda, the damn Prince of Pleasure; just keep making me feel..." I took a moment to moan. Even my fingers felt magical when he was in the room. "Like. This."

His eyes raked over my body and I knew that I had his attention.

He parted my lips with his mouth, nestled the length of himself right against the seam of me, and then I could finally breathe a sigh of relief.

Midnight may have been in control but I closed my eyes to explore his mouth and tangled with his tongue as if I would never be able to kiss him again.

A condom appeared and my fingers automatically floated into the air to roll it over him. I didn't have any power over that anymore. That piece of him exposed my lack of restraint. When I wanted something, I got it, and in that manner, he was no different. However, the hunger that gripped everything in my gut and below when I was near him was distinct.

Pushing the latex over his girth, I listened to his slight intake of breath. He was feeling it too. It wasn't one-sided.

Midnight was not a vocal lover. He didn't say a lot, but the way he touched me explained his feelings thoroughly.

He moved a hand over mine to push it away and finished the task. I was too transfixed to sheath him quickly.

"Lay back."

He was ready and so was I.

Resting my back against the soft comforter, I spread my legs for him without question. One knee at a time he fell on the bed and pushed each thigh further back.

Some girls liked a long man, and Midnight had a length on him, but what kept my toes curled and my mind in a fog was how thick his length felt when he moved inside of me.

With one hand holding onto my waist, he inched into me at a blissfully tortuous pace. I gasped when he found his way in, but too quickly he pulled himself out again.

"Oh, you're playing games tonight huh?" I questioned.

Lunging back inside of me was his reply. When he swooped down to simultaneously take my breast into his mouth, I shuddered.

Fuck it, he can play. I'll be his slide, swing set, merry-go-round, and the whole damn playground. That was what I was waiting for.

I clamped my legs around him to hold on. From the intensity of his thrust, he had some things that he needed to work through. At the rate that he was going, he might have worked through me, like just pushed through my entire body.

"Damn 'Night. You miss me or what?" I huffed out.

A double-pump into me was his answer and I shut the hell up because the world was folding in on me. Another one of those would end me, and I didn't want to let him go. I didn't want it to be over. But it was coming, I was coming.

The juicy catch and release that our bodies played, kept the pleasure mounting and my back arching. My head and neck lifted and fell back all on their own. My toes were crinkled and my eyeballs rolled toward my brain, but I wanted more.

I bounced with him, rode on him like our parting would cause the world to end.

"Let it go," he demanded before switching the tempo on my sprung ass.

He went from a pump to a roll that made time and location a blur.

"Damn. Shit. Ok." I wanted to look down between us to see if it was real, but I couldn't control my eyes. Was he real? Caught between this world and the white light of joy, I shook my head like a lunatic.

"No," I whined, not wanting to fall so soon. My body betrayed me.

"Shit," I stuttered out the word as my body tingled, shredded apart into a million pieces, and then brought itself back together again.

He let go then too. His bullish grunt grew into a roar as he broke into me so fiercely that I exploded around him for a second time.

CHAPTER EIGHTEEN

Regina

After waving back to the security guards watching me for reasons other than my safety, I waltzed through the halls of the high rise building. I rode the private elevator to the executive suites. The atmosphere of Strong Tower was starkly different from the hallways of the Child Protective Services building. Filtered humidified air, sunlight, and smiling faces were the standards.

On the top floor, heads popped out of offices and over cubicle walls as I swished through in my brand-new heels as though I were leading a dance number in a musical. Everyone greeted me with waves and warm smiles, and I was pleased with the decision to return.

I settled into the plush office chair that once belonged to my mother. Once she decided to stay home and participate in board duties only, her office became mine. It was in the same place that I had left it, right next to my father's. At my request, it had been remodeled, but it still felt like home. As much as I wanted to hate it, to not want it, being back at the family company was more gratifying than I imagined it to be. I loved my work with families and the children I helped, but I felt the adrenaline pushing its way through my bloodstream. The business was in my blood.

"Regina." My father entered my newly painted and furnished office with a smile. "It looks like you're settling in. How does it feel to be back in the professional world?"

I never imagined working for my father again, but turning down his offer was not an option.

"The coffee is better," I smirked, but I honestly missed my tiny office at the county and the lukewarm iced coffee that Nailah would bring for me.

"It'll take some time to get adjusted. We'll ease into community projects before stepping into some major realty ventures."

"You think I can't handle the specs for the cricket stadium?" I made sure to keep my voice even and drop the secret knowledge. I wanted him to sit with the fact that I knew and he hadn't told me. He and my mother had been holding on to so many secrets in the name of what was best for me, and it was tiresome.

My father lifted an eyebrow before rowing them together.

I returned his eyebrow hike to explain without words that '*Yea, I knew about that*'

"I know that you can manage whatever comes at you, but the last time that-" My father took a deep breath as if the pain that caused me to leave the company also affected him greatly.

"I won't leave again, Dad. I understand things better." I pushed out a smile as I spoke. "Sacrifices have to be made sometimes for the betterment of the community and family."

Parroting his words usually made him smile, and he didn't disappoint me.

"Good." he nodded, the slight sadness from earlier erased from his face. "Community projects are scheduled today. Our ten o'clock would like to do some work with the elderly and he's the first candidate."

I blinked as uneasiness settled in the pit of my belly. It was time to meet the marriage prospects.

"You've narrowed it down to three?" The hitch in my voice gave away the slight nervousness that I felt. I wanted to be stone about it, and not concentrate on the sentimentality of the partnership I was working toward, but my anxiousness curled in my chest, taking up most of the space I had reserved for bravery.

"You'll meet two of them today." Excitement shot across his face as he nodded. I hadn't seen that kind of joy since the basketball arena was built. "These are some stellar candidates."

"So, it's time to send out a save-the-date?" I inhaled and exhaled the words quickly. My father's gleaming approval as he looked over me squashed out some of my nervous energy. The self-reminder of how much my parents had sacrificed for me, and how I had left them to pursue my dreams for some time brought in a brigade of confidence that the process would indeed turn out alright.

"Six months from now, you should be walking down the aisle." My father's gleeful clap came as a shock. He had always been so serious at work, so stern. it was good to see him lighten up. His chipper mood and words lifted my spirits too. "I can't wait to stand with my baby girl and watch her take her rightful place."

My father continued to gush about the three men he had selected as we moved into the conference room, but my mind ran through thoughts of Terrence and our time together. He was supposed to be a fling. I couldn't care for someone while waiting to marry someone else.

"Your 10 AM group is here." Charla, my father's assistant, chirped when I picked up the phone in the far-right corner of the room.

"Please lead them in."

I took a steady breath to bolt down the last of my jumpy nerves. One of the people that walked through the door could be my husband. Even if there was little or no love involved, he could be my life partner.

I closed my eyes and readied myself.

"Ready?" His comforting hand on my shoulder made me feel taller, stronger, and more sure than I was. Reginald Strong had that effect on people. He could make others feel like dignitaries without diminishing his presence.

"As I'll ever be." I exhaled and opened my eyes.

My father stepped forward first to shake hands with one woman, an older grey-haired man, and then finally, a tall, slender man in a tailored suit.

Oddly, the man's skin reminded me of peach pits. He was brown with round reddish cheeks that I figured women probably loved to pinch when he was a boy. He was cute, a cherub charm surrounding his smile, but he walked as if he were wiping mud from his feet and his knees were stuck. *Ugh.*

"Clayton," My father greeted the long man with a grin and a pat on his back. "I want you to meet my Chief Operations Officer and daughter, Regina Strong. She's heading our community outreach and is your point person for the project going forward."

"I'm Clayton Stewart," he extended both hands to capture mine in a warm wrap. "It's nice to finally meet you, Regina. Your father speaks highly of you."

"Nice to meet you as well. Let's get started." I nod toward the table.

The first time that I met Terrence, all of me knew that I needed to continue knowing him. His composed demeanor had eclipsed the room. There was never a question of Midnight as a leader.

Clayton smiled a lot. He had great ambitions, but the power didn't exude from him like Terrence. He was giving *'can I sell you some insurance'* energy versus the *'here are the terms of the deal'* power that I wanted.

I reminded myself that I didn't want to be overly emotional about the marriage anyway. It would be a partnership.

Clayton Stewart was unremarkable. I could easily keep my brain from falling apart and the nickel between my knees. During our conversation about expanding services for the elderly, he seemed old himself. He was sitting in front of me in the fit body of a thirty-four-year-old man but with the speech pattern of a man nearing a century of life. At least, that's how I felt. His pace was so slow as he spoke that I had forgotten what we were discussing twice. When the old- young man ambled out of our conference room, I had to shut the door.

"Really, daddy? You thought 'Can't *Move* Clayton' was a match for me?"

"He may not move at your speed, but sometimes slower is better."

I didn't expect his face to be serious. That sloth of a man had to have been a practical joke.

"When have I ever done anything slow?" I questioned as we stepped through the conference room door.

"Exactly," My father threw his hands in the air. "Your fire leads you to make rash decisions. That can be detrimental to business."

He still had some issues about me leaving the company years ago, but my departure wasn't a spur-of-the-moment decision.

"With someone steady and patient at the helm, it could balance you and the company." He added.

I lifted an eyebrow at my father's unbreaking gaze. He was serious.

"Anyway," I chose not to belabor the subject. The first candidate was a 'no'. "I've met the tortoise. If candidate number two comes jumping through the door like a bunny, I'll have you committed."

"We're meeting the next young man at a restaurant. He's a little unconventional, but I like that about him."

"He can't be worse than *'I've fallen, and I can't get up,* Clayton'." I mused.

He was absolutely worse than Can't Move Clayton. He wasn't supposed to be a husband's place filler. It took me seconds to spot him. His freshly retwisted locs were pulled back at his neck, and his fire-gold eyes blazed even brighter.

I felt it when he found me. It made me breathe differently. I both wondered and knew why he was sitting in that chair at my father's favorite table.

From the look on his face, he had no clue why I was walking next to Reginald Strong but stood to greet us as I stepped closer to the table.

"Play nice, Regina." My father whispered as we walked. "He's not your normal type, but-"

My father was clueless too. He wouldn't have known that my friend Nailah had married this man's brother. He wouldn't know that this man made me feel impossible things and had buried himself in me repeatedly.

"I understand." But I didn't. How could my father want me to marry him? Why did my father believe the same thing that a tiny corner of my heart was beginning to feel: this man was meant for me?

"Terrence Lewis, this is my daughter and new COO, Regina Strong. Regina, Terrence is one-fourth of the multimillion Four Brothers Investment Group. He and his family own and operate a string of automotive care facilities."

Sliding his scarred hand across the smooth trimmed hair on his chin, Terrence examined me for seconds that felt like an eternity.

All the moisture from my mouth magically appeared in my hands. I smiled weakly as I slid one sweaty palm against the other. I needed to touch him. We wore too much clothing to be in the same room, but he looked better than good. He was dressed in a tailored suit and a slight scowl.

"Hello, Ms. Strong. It's a pleasure to meet you." His deep voice rumbled itself to the space between my thighs and I bit my lip in an attempt not to moan.

He was going to act like he didn't know me.

"Hello, Mr. Lewis." I smiled.

Concentration became a foreign concept as Terrence spoke passionately about his current program for kids and his plans to expand it. He was one of the sexiest men I knew, had a brilliant mind, and had an open heart for humanity. The lethal combination had me sipping water every three seconds to keep myself cool and my hands from reaching under the table to touch him.

I did everything but drool as he completed his signature slow beard rub. He did that when he watched me undress. He did that when I smiled at him. It was like he was contemplating something devious, and that simple gesture turned me on.

"What do you think, Regina?" I heard a far-off voice resembling my father's ask.

My brain had been somewhere lost in the memory of what it felt like to be in Terrence's mouth, drank in, and guzzled between his lips. Terrence rendered me speechless during the daytime and the night.

"Um. Well." Most of my food was still on the plate where most of the words from the pitch had fallen. I had heard enough to know that Terrence Lewis wasn't just some slouchy sex machine with no ambition. He had goals, he had dreams, and he had success on his own. I was wrong about him. He wouldn't need me for his survival. I wouldn't be his sugar mama. I wouldn't have to stand guard over my credit cards and watch my bank account or the business for fraudulent activity with him. It wouldn't be like before.

I took another hurried sip of my water.

"Thirsty there aren't you?" He observed.

I shot him a sharp-eyed glare. It was meant to be a scowl. It was meant to ward off any other sarcastic ass comments, but the commanding look in his eyes reminded me of how direct he was when he took control of my body. Then the suit and the cologne all seemed to swell into an overwhelming symphony of feeling.

"Excuse me." I blurted and shot my horny ass away from the table.

When I safely locked myself away in the private restroom, I took a deep breath.

I had to end the lunch and end the crazy notion that Terrence was my husband. I had chosen Terrence. I enjoyed Mr. Terrence 'Midnight' Lewis, which meant he had to be all wrong. I had chosen wrong so many times, that I knew with all of my heart that I would choose wrong again. My father thought Terrence could be the right one for me.

I don't know how long I stood there staring from the marble counter to the mirror trying to figure out where I missed exactly who Midnight was. He didn't dress like a millionaire. A multi-millionaire. We had never been on a date; I had just assumed. I had never been to his shop, never asked anyone questions, or searched his name on the internet. I thought I knew what I needed to know about him.

The knock startled me from the whirlwind of thoughts spiraling through my mind.

"Occupied."

"Regina." His call filtered through the barrier and slightly into my soul.

I looked toward the door as though the lock would twist on its own.

"Open up." He requested and I had no option but to oblige.

"Did you know?" He entered the restroom like it was his home, shutting and locking the door behind him.

He always looked intense, but the stern look that tightened his face was one I wasn't familiar with.

"I didn't know that my father was working with you." The words rushed out quickly. "I didn't know who you were."

"Is that why you didn't tell me who you were?" His voice rolled around the small room like thunder, low and dangerous. He was angry, or hurt at least. "Did you think that I was going to come after your money? You'd let me do all those things to you, or better yet, do all those things to me, but not mention that you are the daughter of one of the most successful businessmen in the state? "

He hit a nerve. Sure, I had not been truthful, but I am more than my father's daughter. We had agreed on a casual thing.

"That's how you wanted it too," I reminded him. "We kept it light on purpose, remember? And it's not like we had a lot of conversation between humping and grinding."

His gaze trekked over my face before he broke the silence with, "That's all you have to say?"

"What else do you want me to say?" I nearly yelled because I was confused and didn't understand why he seemed so bothered by me keeping my life private.

He didn't blink and the absence of his words gave me time to see the disappointment in his eyes. "On the island, that was a fling. That was a one-and-done." The consternation in his voice reached me before his tight large body made its way to hover over me. "I thought what we did last time was the beginning of a friendship."

"A friendship or a fuck-ship, because I distinctly remember us declaring that we wanted to make time for screwing each other only."

Lacing the fingers of one hand through mine, he drew my body against his with the other. Being pressed against his familiar warmth started to liquefy me and fire up my desire to stay that close to him.

"For either one, honesty was required." He explained.

I barely caught his use of the past tense before I met his lips for the sensual kiss that made me feel light every time.

When he pulled away, turned, and moved for the door, dismissing me like I didn't matter, like he was done, something snapped.

"Wait." The panicked yelp was all that I could get out as the fear of not knowing him intimately anymore gripped me with an intensity that shouldn't have made sense in the short time that we had known each other. I didn't have the right to want his perfect body, kind spirit, chill attitude, and obvious business success to remain a part of my life, but I selfishly wanted everything about him to be mine. At least the time I had before I became a wife.

He didn't wait and I couldn't let him leave.

With one leap, I hooked an arm over his shoulder and was on his back, those years of dance classes finally becoming useful in my adult life. I wrapped myself around his wide back like I was supposed to be attached.

"Listen." I held tight and spoke into his ear.

"Regina." It didn't sound right. That wasn't my name from him. That wasn't what he was supposed to call me.

"I'm your Bloom," I reminded him. "Don't do this. I didn't mean it. I didn't tell anyone."

His shoulders moved downward, relaxing, so I continued.

"It felt good that you liked me," I couldn't pinpoint why my head resting on his neck felt like comfort or why gripping the expanse of his broad chest made me feel that I could keep him. "I liked that you liked me just because I was me."

He didn't throw me off or move to leave, so I held on. I didn't know what spell he had put on me, but I couldn't let it go. I couldn't let his stability go. Everything in my life was changing. With a new job and a possible new life as a wife, I needed to hold onto something for myself, so I held onto him.

"Regina, get down." He rubbed a hand across my arm.

There was hope. I didn't hear the same anger as before.

"Nope. Not until you promise not to walk away. You have to promise that we can at least talk about this."

His harsh exhale made me look toward the ceiling, thankful that he was relenting. I didn't have to hope for much because I had almost everything, but there wasn't another Terrence laying around.

"If we're going to continue this, you have to be honest."

Feeling like I had him in my grasp, I slid down so that my feet were touching the ground.

I considered telling him all of what was happening, telling him that my father thought that he was a good catch for me to marry, but I knew that wouldn't go over well with him. If I told him that I was looking for a husband, even if I already knew that he wasn't the one, he would split in seconds. I couldn't gamble with losing his night skills, not when I was possibly about to enter into a loveless marriage.

He faced me; his eyes were softer then.

"You want this?" His hand moved between us. "You want to keep our sessions going?"

"You want to lie and say that you don't?" I smirked.

He looked me over, sliding a hand over my hip and up to my waist.

"I'm not ready to give you up yet." He said with those lips that had kissed me everywhere.

"What are we gonna do about that then?" I asked and then watched the mouth that had made my body feel heavenly as it pushed in for a kiss.

CHAPTER NINETEEN

Terrence

I had done dirty things to his daughter, and for a quick second, I had a difficult time looking him in the eye. Fortunately, when Regina left the table, Reginald received a phone call. Thirty seconds into the call, he left to handle the situation. Relieving was an understatement. I had barely heard him above my simmering rage. I felt like she had played me, that she lied to me because I wasn't good enough. It shouldn't have mattered, but it did. It shouldn't have stung, but it did. As soon as he was up from the table, I was at the restroom door where Bloom had runoff.

We ended up at the same hotel in the same room that we had been in before. The feeling of pushing into her amazed me. I wanted to believe it was because of the few women I'd been with since Valerie. I wanted to believe that the joyful pleasure invading me was a fluke that would fade, but I knew better.

It was not supposed to be like that. She was not supposed to be a weakness, someone that I thought about beyond the night. I should have left when the moon was out. Daylight had broken through the sky, but I couldn't tear myself away from her. I had time to slip away before she woke, but the magnetizing pull of her body held me there.

I had never known a woman to talk so much, that even sleep couldn't keep her from running her mouth. She swished her lips in a circle and mumbled more incoherent words. She was cute even then. A good portion of her makeup had rubbed off when I had her face planted in the sheets, but she was still amazingly beautiful.

I leaned back against the pillow. We had done everything early. My wife Valerie passed away nearly ten years ago when I was twenty-four. I had been with a few women since then, but no relationships, nothing consistent. Whenever I was with anyone, it felt wrong the next morning. Always. The next day regret would dig in as if I had cheated. That was with other women. With Regina, there was no remorse. The emptiness was missing. I didn't know how to feel about that.

She scrunched her face and then pursed her lips.

I didn't know how to feel about her or if I even wanted to.

I took a few minutes to freshen up and decided to slide on some boxers and slip back under the covers with her. Maybe we could try daylight. Maybe we could talk.

Her eyelids stuttered apart and then widened with horror when she recognized me.

"You're here," she shrieked while scrambling from the bed.

She grabbed her bag from the door area and zoomed into the bathroom.

"Good morning to you, too," I spoke at the slamming door.

"No!" She yelled from inside the restroom. "I reject your good morning!"

I heard the water running from the faucet and the rustle of cans and bottles being shifted from one surface to another.

"You didn't see me." She hollered through the door. "Erase the image from your mind."

"What? Why?" I yelled back. Regina was gorgeous, and I liked the innocence of her face without makeup.

It sounded like she was brushing her teeth, when she gurgled out, "No one sees me without my makeup."

When she emerged nearly fifteen minutes later, dressed in a silk nightgown with her hair and make-up refreshed, I inwardly smiled. She looked like she was about to walk the runway in a lingerie showcase.

I wasn't sure what to think when she slid back into the bed as a different version of the soft unmade beauty, she had been only a few minutes ago.

"Good morning." She finally replied and leaned her body closer to mine.

At that moment, the world was in her eyes and the key to happiness was on her lips. Something about her drew me in, and the more that I tried to identify it, wrestle that unnamable pull, it slipped away from me.

"You're still here." She smiled.

Instead of answering, I traced a thumb under her cheek. Surprisingly, it was where I wanted to be.

"Is that a grin for me?" I asked.

The light caught the Whiskey brown of her eyes as her smile widened.

"Maybe."

I lifted an eyebrow.

She chuckled while pushing the tips of her pointed nails against my chest.

"You know what it is." Her grin turned naughty as she traveled her hand over the panels of my stomach and then below.

She traced a soft jagged path across my hardening member, and I groaned. This is where we landed every time.

"What makes you smile?" She asked before taking my bottom lip into hers for a gentle pull.

"Definitely that," I remarked when I had my lip back.

"Good answer. Now tell me, what makes you smile?" Her nipples spoke to me at the same time and I skipped the tip of my finger around her breast.

"My family sometimes." I shrugged.

"Do you ever laugh? You always seem so serious."

"Life is serious." I didn't think much about my answer until she removed her luscious skin from my reach.

She shook her head no and sat up in the bed to grab a pillow.

I gave her a sideways glance when she began pressing the pillow inward like an accordion.

"What are you doing?"

She wrinkled her nose as she squashed the pillow together from both ends this time and gave a small grunt.

"You'll see." She said and then pulled a small feather from the pillowcase. "No one should ever go through life as seriously as you do."

I liked her idea more when she straddled me and then pressed her breasts against my chest.

Placing a hand against her thigh, I leaned my head back as she kissed my chin and then my neck.

Then- *What the hell?*

I felt a feather brushing against my side and I wrinkled my eyebrow.

"Are you trying to tickle me?"

She sat up with a pout and folded her arms over her chest.

"It doesn't work if you expect it."

"It won't work because I'm not ticklish."

I clasped my hands at her waist to hold her steady as I pushed against her core. She was playing, but I had other games in mind.

"Nope." Regina rolled off me.

She climbed out of the bed moving her plush ass out of reach. "Your serious self is about to laugh or something. Get up."

I watched the energetic woman bounce over to her bag in the bathroom and return with a phone.

"Come dance with me."

I swung my feet to the floor but waited to see what she had in mind.

The song *I Like Your Smile* by *Shanice* played from her phone and she reached out to me with her free hand.

Her upturned hand was as enticing as any other part of her. Touching her anywhere had started to become a need.

"Dance with me." She requested before she shook her shoulders while doing a two-step.

"I think I'll watch."

I do give a half-grin when she rolled and winded her body up and down to the beat.

The woman was finer than frog hair.

"You're not human if you can listen to this song and keep a sour face." She moved closer to me and pulled at my arms.

Relenting, I stood. She was right. Her excitement was contagious and the movement of her hips hypnotizing enough to make any man do whatever she asked.

I allowed Bloom to tug my arms around her waist to rock with the sway of her hips.

Looking into her eyes caused something to stir in my chest. *Was this the living that Tyson was talking about?* Maybe I could do this with her, just Bloom. She made me forget. She made me feel.

"I'm gonna get you singing and dancing and smiling before you know it," she challenged.

"Those are some big goals."

"You're a big man." She pressed her body into mine and whispered up into my ear. "I go big or not at all."

I wasn't sure if I was rocking on rhythm, but we were moving together. We found our own pace together.

"You always have on this chain." Regina flipped her pointed nails under and over the gold necklace as we continued to sway.

"Jealous?" I joked.

"Kind of," she laughed. "I bet this necklace has seen some things and could tell some stories."

"Not really. I have a couple."

"A couple you say?" She said, reaching up to unhook the chain. "Let me hold this one then."

Gently, I removed it from her hand and asked, "You want to wear my chain?"

I felt like I was asking more when she lifted her shoulders in a shrug, tucked her head, and answered the floor rather than looking at me. She was cute when she was bashful.

"Yes, I do," She said looking up at me finally. "If you want me to."

"Yes, I do," I answered without thought, and felt like more. "I want you to wear it."

I placed the jewelry against the flat surface of her chest and fastened it.

"Thank you," Regina slid her hand back and forth across the gold as she beamed down at it.

I was proud of her, of us, and suddenly our secret didn't seem like it should be that anymore. Instead of addressing that notion, I took her back to bed.

Still fumbling to catch her breath, Regina rolled into the crook of my arm and pressed the back of her body against the front of me. She fit perfectly, and I pulled her closer as emotion pulled at my thoughts. *What was she doing once we left our space? Who would she see? Was I the only man that got to hold her body so close? What if I wasn't? What if I was?*

**

My dog, Ginger, nudged her head against my fingers and then positioned herself underneath my hand. The dog wanted my attention, but sitting in the den of my home staring at what used to be my favorite game, I could think of nothing but Regina.

Ginger, an aging Golden Retriever Labrador mix, shook her head against my palm.

"Not right now, girl," I muttered, looking down at the unfinished Scrabble game.

Valerie and I had a habit of taking pictures of our games. I had taken a picture of our last game together, too. The one we never finished. I took out the board and replayed it sometimes over the years.

I had played the last word during that game. It was her turn that night, but we stopped playing once she got sick. The game, just like the two of us, had never ended properly. Sometimes, I felt like I hadn't started again, like I stopped playing the game of life once she lost hers.

Everything in the room was the same, like a shrine. Valerie and I had spent the better part of many nights plopped on opposite sides of the sofa reading, at the table playing Scrabble, or simply chatting among mugs of coffee and cocoa. She had been in all of my honors classes in High School. We were two of the few black students that took advanced classes, and we stuck together. We understood each other.

Getting married after high school, despite our parent's warnings, seemed natural and right. The pregnancy that followed two years later, right before my twentieth birthday, brought us even closer.

I did rub Ginger's head as the memory of why I purchased the cute little puppy returned.

Valerie hadn't been able to carry our baby to term, and although our daughter never made it into this world alive, Ginger had been a small comfort after some time passed.

I inhaled the smell of the books still crowding the shelves. They still held a little bit of her.

I scrolled over the letters splayed on the game board. A word on the board made me do a double-take to review the letters again. I blinked, examined the letters closely, and quickly looked around the room.

Scrabble with Valerie had been epic. Games could last for days. We had even bought more letter tiles to add to the bag. I wondered if the word had always been there.

I pulled the letter tiles from the last holder that Valerie had ever used. I would have sworn that there were no other words to be made, but Valerie had 3 tiles left- E, L, and V. I had memorized the letters on the board and the ones that were left to play.

Cautiously I looked over the word 'SLIP' on the board and added the L above the I and the V and E below it. It spelled LIVE.

I had to get out of the room. The word had jumped out at me. Over the last ten years, I hadn't noticed it, but it was so apparent now.

My feelings were as jumbled up and scrambled as the letters had been in the bag. Every day without her, I had been grabbing blindly at pieces and playing whatever shook out. Everything except business had been unclear. I wasn't sure if I could jump back into the ambiguous again.

Tyriq lived in one of the most expensive neighborhoods in the city. I pulled up to the unnecessary gate that my brother refused to let anyone have the code to, pressed the call button, and waited. Although my brothers and I were nearly stair-stepped in age, Tyriq was the closest to me in temperament. We had always been close, even with his new marriage and baby on the way, we still made it a point to kick it whenever time permitted. His home was the perfect escape. Plus, I had a few questions for Nailah about her friend Regina.

"Hello," I yell at the box. "Open the gate, bro."

The gate opened a tiny bit and then closed before opening back up and then closing again. Honking the horn, I jabbed the call button. I thought inheriting a child would mature him some, but no.

"Say the magic word," my cousin Chad's voice sparked through the box.

"Now. Stupid ass," I barked.

I heard his annoying laugh before the gate opened fully and I drove through.

When I walked into the media room, I learned the reason for Chad's presence.

His daughter, Tia, sat in a small plastic chair between Nailah's legs getting her hair braided.

I waved at the small girl with big round eyes, earbuds in her ears, and a tablet in her lap. She smiled politely and let her attention fall back to the video.

She still didn't know us because of the situation between Chad and her mother, but I could tell that she was warming up to the family more. It would take time.

"What's happening, big cuz?"

I ignored Chad's greeting and the mischievous cackle and opted not to curse him out. He was always playing.

"Where's Tyriq?" I plopped down next to the extremely pregnant Nailah.

She gave me a grimaced grin.

"I needed some Neapolitan Ice-cream and Blackberry pie so he ran out to find it," Nailah explained without blinking. She was serious.

"What?" I started to question her food choices but shook my head. "Whatever makes you happy."

"It's crazy, I had never even had a blackberry before I was pregnant." She pulled a finished off a braid with beads and then picked up a comb to part another section.

"Can I ask you something?"

"Shoot." I looked over at little Tia who was lost in the images on the screen, her earbuds secure. "Why didn't you tell me that Reginald Strong was Regina's father?"

She shrugged as though the fact didn't alter my entire newfound sex life, as though the information didn't obliterate my world.

"It's not my story to tell, plus - why would it matter to you? Better yet, why do you know? Her father is extremely private about his wife and daughter."

Her eyes narrowed as she appraised me, and my brain scrambled to come up with a plausible answer.

"Well, you know. When we were golfing. He had said." I stuttered. It had been a long while since I was under investigation by a woman with a cause. It had been a long while since I had something to hide.

"Mr. Strong doesn't even keep a picture of his daughter and wife in the office." She added. "Regina said he's always had this irrational fear that she would be kidnapped for ransom because she's his only child."

"Well, uh." I couldn't think of anything else to explain it. I needed to talk to my brother. I should have started with him. Nailah was a cool person, but she was like the other women in my family: part detective and full-time investigator.

My ringing cell phone saved me from Nailah's eyes. A picture of the Night-Blooming Jasmine flower appeared. No name, but I knew who it was.

"I have to take this." I was off the couch and into the hallway before I finished the words.

"I bet you do," Nailah called out over Chad's hyena-like chuckle.

"I need your help." Panic strained her hurried words.

What she told me made my heart drop.

CHAPTER TWENTY

Regina

I looked over at my mother like she had stepped off a spaceship from another universe. The woman in front of me was not the same woman who warned me that my tongue would grow bumps for every lie I told and subsequently fall off. She couldn't be the same woman who made me walk back into a grocery store with a purse that I had slid over my shoulder without paying for it. She couldn't be the same woman who lived by the creed 'I'm rich Why lie?'. That same woman looked at me in the face and told me that everything was fine when I called her earlier that day, but there had been something wrong then.

"The police." I insisted. "We need to call the police right now."

My mother, who had paced a hole in the floor, was on the way to rubbing all the skin off her hands and was gnawing a hole in her lip, looked tired. In the history of her story, she had never looked tired. Standing there in workout clothes instead of her Neiman Marcus special, a ponytail instead of a fresh-pressed mane flowing across her shoulders, she looked like she was getting ready to teach a Zumba class. When I walked through the door, her appearance immediately worried me. My mother wore silk to sleep and stilettos to the kitchen. She set my icon status in motion. I was the true example of 'she get it from her mama'. Cherry Strong was always put together. When she told me that my father had gone missing, I nearly had a panic attack.

"He hasn't been gone for more than 48 hours. There's no evidence of harm from someone else. There's no evidence that he harmed himself." She ticked off each statement on her fingers as though she had heard them a few times already.

"Let's track his phone," I suggested while pulling out my cell.

"Can't." Still pacing, she lifted a small black cell phone from her pocket. "He left it."

"I'll be right back," I sighed and hurried toward the ringing doorbell.

I didn't have time to notice how fine he looked when he stepped through the threshold, his gold chain swinging against his chest, locks swishing over his shoulders, or the mind-numbing scent of his cologne wafting directly into my brain. I didn't have time to pause and stare, but I did for a second. Only for the first second, because in the next, I was wrapped in his arms being buried in a hug that I didn't know I needed.

"Terrence," I exhaled into his chest. "Thank you."

Taking a few steps back, his eyes washed over me. "Are you good?"

I shook my head, and those warm lips pressed against my cheek in a fashion so normal, that it felt expected.

"I don't know. More numb right now- Nervous." I explained while enjoying the fact that his hands cupped my shoulders.

He kissed my cheek as if it were normal, as though scout missions for my father and tender kisses happened every day.

"No worries. I got you." He assured.

I nodded because I knew what he said was true. Whether or not we found my father, I instinctively knew that he would have my back. I had seen him with his family. He took care of things.

My mother barely noticed when Terrence and I entered the kitchen. She barely paid attention when I introduced the tall, unwed man next to me as a friend. This is how I knew that shit was serious. My mother was not matchmaking.

"How long has he been gone?" Terrence asked.

"At least twelve hours. He doesn't have his phone, and he took his 74' Corvette that doesn't have any type of tracking system." I recited the facts that I had learned recently from my mother.

"Does he do this often?"

"Not at all." I crossed my hands through the air as I shook my head. "He's in bed every night before 9. This is the first time that I-"

"It's happened more than once." My mother cut in; her voice so weak that I hardly heard her.

"What did you say?"

My mother looked as small as her words had been, but that didn't matter to me. The words '*Not the first time*' were taking time to register.

"It's happened a couple of times, more often now." Her hands twisted into one another even though her words were bolder.

"Really? No one thought to tell me about this?"

She looked up at me, her eyes brimmed with tears, and my heart hurt. She was in pain. She was wearing her angst, and that was what we didn't do. The phrase *Never look like what you've been through,* was invented for her.

"Be honest. What's going on?" I always felt like my parents and I had a decent relationship. We talked about most things, and I was never scared to tell them what I was thinking. I respected them, and I thought the feeling was mutual.

"I'm losing him." Tears slipped from her eyes then, and she didn't reach to stop them. Not even a pat or tap of her fingers. She just let them fall from her face like people weren't standing there. "He has early-onset dementia, and the symptoms have been- It's more noticeable lately."

"What!?" Good thing Midnight had been near. If not, the floor would have seen where my weave started and where my real hair stopped. His warm presence kept me steady and upright but didn't change the growing pain in my head.

"Yes. We found out some time before we decided to present the contract to you." She swiped at the tears finally as she moved toward me. "They think it may be the Lewy body version that comedian Robin Williams had."

It all made sense, then. The schedule mistakes, weird changes in his character, not remembering where he kept things for years, and-

"The marriage," I said more to myself than anyone else.

My mother confirmed my spoken thoughts with a nod.

"He wants to be there when you walk down the aisle." She worried her hands as her eyes buried into mine. "He wants to be present. He wants to teach you all he can while he can."

"So, you both lied?" My brain couldn't let those thoughts enter to compute. The words stood right outside of understanding, taunting me. It was too much to process at one time. Thoughts and feelings clashed and careened through my mind, warring for clarity.

"After the way that you left the company and stayed single since the end of your engagement to Luther, we knew that it would take an act of God to bring you back and down the aisle in time. We were desperate."

She reached for my hands, but I pulled back closer to Terrence.

"I don't even know who you are right now." I couldn't wrap my mind around it. "How could you keep this from me?"

I noticed her head fall first, the bounce of her hair as her chin hit her chest. Then it was the slump of her shoulders and the deep cave of her chest. I had to register it piece by piece and take in the evidence in sections because as a whole, it was not the norm. It was unusual and I wasn't sure what to make of it. My mother was wilting, not just crying. She was melting right in front of me like a cartoon character.

Confusion about the scene, empathy for the woman in front of me, sadness for the leader I loved, indignation at their lies, and rejection at not being included in their trust circle. Emotion after emotion stormed through me. I didn't know which one to feel first or if I had a right to feel any of them. My father, as I knew him had an expiration date. *Who would I lean on? Who was I in a world that his name created for me but without him?*

The sobs broke my thoughts. *Who was sobbing?*

Shaking out of the shock that stilled me, I moved closer to my mother, who had fallen into a bar chair with her face buried in her hands. My mother, who loved her beauty more than anything, had covered her face. I wanted to cover her, and make her feel better, but I wasn't sure if I could.

"You've been at this by yourself for a while now." I finally said to her. Cherry had taught me to fake it until I made it, so I put on my boss voice and took charge. "I'm here. Terrence is here to help me. You should rest a bit and let us take this on."

When she lifted, I held in my gasp. Her tear-soaked face tore at me. No one would have ever used the word distraught to describe my mother before then.

"Alright." Wrapping her arms around my neck, she stood and whispered, "I'm sorry, Gene-Pie. I didn't mean to hurt you. I just-"

Her tears fell on my shoulder before I heard her sniffle again as she let more of her weight rest on me. I hugged my mother close. Imperfect for the first time in my memory, but she was mine.

"It's ok. We got it from here."

I walked my mother to her room. Terrence moved in tow behind us like a safety net because either one of us could completely fall apart at any minute.   Once my mother settled in bed, we left to search for my father.

In the car, Terrence and I didn't say much to each other. I had an internal dialogue going on that felt deeper than the seafloor. As he drove through the city, I pointed out all of the hangouts that were prominent in my father's routine, past and present.

"You're getting married?" His eyes roamed the road as the dotted lines passed us by. Terrence kept his same cool.

We had just turned away from what used to be the Shake Club, the dilapidated place where I was first made to sign the contract. I had hoped that we could have found him there. I was reaching and thinking of everything, any spot that I could.

"Yes." I sighed. I hadn't wanted to tell him because I knew that it would be the end of us. However, after learning how much my parents had been keeping from me. Honesty was better.

He responded with a nod and another question, "You left your father's company?"

"That was years ago." Angst twisted in my gut and crawled up my throat. I stopped the words, just like I stopped working for my father. "I had-"

I took a deep breath before starting again. Even though my emotions were flooded by memories and overwhelmed by the present, he deserved the truth.

"Turn here," I instructed.

Terrence pulled the truck into a deserted gravel parking lot and silenced the engine.

"Tell me." His words were an invitation to let him in.

"My father knew that I wouldn't come back to the company or consider marriage unless there was an incentive. Things were bad. I lost my relationship and left my position in the same year. I ran away from everything corporate or relationship-like for a long time. That's why I used my undergrad degree to get hired as a social worker. It felt like the opposite of what I was doing. Last year my father came up with this ultimatum: Come back to run the company with a husband, or he would cut me out of everything, the inheritance, the company, everything."

"That's cold."

"It's not as cold as it sounds." I found solace in the brightness of the stars. I finally understood that my father meant well. " I don't even care about the money that much. I have trust funds from both of my grandfathers, and my mother would never let her only child be without. "

"Then what is it?" His fingers grazed the side of my shoulder as if they needed to be there. My eyes latched on his because I knew they needed to be there.

"My father is a proud man. His family helped build this community. Black-owned grocery stores, banks, and properties lined the area and were prosperous. The Strong family owned a few of them. He's carried that legacy into the empire he has now, but he's getting older. He needs some help. He needs me. He would never say the words out loud, but that company is his other child, a part of his blood as much as I am."

The kindness in his eyes comforted me, so I continued. "You do anything for family. I would do anything for him. There's never been a time in my life that he hasn't been there for me, and I don't want to ever disappoint him."

"You could never be a disappointment."

I had been worse than a disappointment before. I had been taken advantage of, but Terrence didn't know.

"He used to take me to this specialty donut shop sometimes. They make pretty donuts that they put in a gold-colored box and wrap with ribbons. As we ate, he would tell me, *'Each day is a gift. Take time to untie the ribbons'*. I was always moving so fast, and when I got overwhelmed, that's how he calmed me. That's how he centered me. When the world was too much, he gave me a new focus, a reason to smile."

It dawned like morning in my mind.

"I know where he is."

It pierced my heart that he stared right through me. His eyes were open, but his mind looked like it had closed up shop. Terrence helped me get my father, who came along with ease, into the extended cab of the large truck. He knew who I was but acted as though he had just been sitting there waiting for me to come and pick him up. We rode home in silence.

My mother's hug seemed to wake him up. He smiled at her tears, wiping them away with his thumb.

"You were always so emotional." He said in the voice that I knew. "Let me take you to bed, dear. I hate to see you cry."

"You can't wander off like that, Reggie. You scared me." My mother reprimanded him.

"Don't worry yourself about that. Genie's back now. She's going to take care of things."

"I know. Go ahead to bed, Reg. Let me say good night to my baby and her friend." My mother kissed my father's face before turning to Terrence and me.

"Thank you." She patted Terrence's shoulder. "I'm so glad she had you to call."

"Any time. I'm here to help if either one of you needs me."

That won him a smile from both ladies in the room.

I wasn't sure that my mother was feeling slightly better until she bent forward to hug me and whispered, "He's really cute, and your father likes him."

After my parents left their room, I walked Terrence out to his truck.

"I appreciate your help. I'm going to stay here with them tonight."

"Makes sense," he nodded.

"I feel like I owe you the entire truth."

"About-"

"All of this." I whirled my hand in the air.

"That would be nice."

"My father developed partnerships with different young businessmen around the country in hopes of finding someone for me to marry."

His eyebrows tented as he choked out the word, "What?"

"He narrowed the search down to three men for me to choose from, two of which he's already introduced to me."

There was a pause before he slowly pointed to himself and spoke, "You and your father met with me."

I nodded. "I'm supposed to pursue one of the three for marriage."

"So, me- he wants you and me-" he moved his pointer finger in his direction and then mine, and stopped the motion right above my heart. The little organ beat big beats and felt like it would jump into his hand any minute.

"Yes," I cleared my throat. "I am supposed to choose one of the three men my father introduced me to as a husband."

It felt good to get the words out, but my hands twisted around each other as I waited for his response. I wanted to continue being with him. I wanted to be in his presence, at least until I had to make a decision.

"You want to marry me?" He asked.

I had to remind myself to breathe because both the air and my tongue felt thicker. I wondered what the words would sound like coming from him with a different tone. The weight of the fact that no one would ever say those words to me in love hit my stomach first and then caused the rapid patter of my heart to slow and feel like it was sinking.

"I didn't know my father had included you in his top three list until he introduced us." I kept it flat and business-like because that is what it was.

"Top three? Like Star Search or the Bachelor?" he shook his head. "What do you want from me?"

I placed my hand on top of his, willing the words to walk across our bridged bodies from my mind because I couldn't say them.

"I don't share," he moved my hand away. "And I don't want to get married again. *Ever.*"

"But, what if- We can-" I was about to beg. Regina Jenae Strong was about to beg again. But I had to boss up real quick, ignore the pricks of hurt stinging my chest.

Cruelly, he kissed the words from my lips. Instead of just feeling good, it felt like goodbye.

"We already knew what this was," he stepped back and rubbed a hand over his beard as his eyes perused my body for what was possibly the last time. "I'll see you around."

CHAPTER TWENTY-ONE

Regina

I should have known when we boarded the charted plane to Houston. I should have known when he mentioned 'stadium' to the driver, but the magnanimity of where we were going didn't hit me until we were parked in front of the mammoth coliseum. If I had not been sure that something was wrong with my father's brain before, I was certain of it at that moment.

"Hell no," I didn't make it a habit to curse at my dad, but at that moment, he needed to understand that we were beyond a 'hard pass' situation.

The flat line of his lips and steel-straight eyes expressed how much my words didn't phase him one bit.

"Give it a try. Meet with him and his grandfather once, and if he doesn't impress you, then we'll let it go."

I looked toward the mega stadium and then back to my father.

"Are you sure that you're feeling alright?" My dad had returned to work and his mission. I didn't want to question his sanity, but I was confused.

"I made this decision with a clear mind." His words are stern and sound like the father that I have always known, not the one I rescued from the donut shop a week ago. "His family owns a sports team. We own an arena. They are good people."

"His family is great. Hendrix is not."

My father looked away from me, his gaze straying toward the window.

"I'm scared." His words were so soft that I almost didn't hear them. I wasn't sure he had said them. "I'm scared to leave this earth without seeing you stable and my legacy in good hands."

"He's horrible," I whined.

"But loyal," he replied. "He helps run a large business. He understands how to handle the pressure of great family history. He understands the responsibility of being a black man with power in this state."

"But will he understand me?" I questioned. "I can do this for responsibility. I can do this for your legacy, but I want to find a friend in the man I marry. I need that for me."

"One hour, Genie. Give him an hour to impress you. If he doesn't, we'll move on to the runner-up."

I would have rather eaten a vat of slimy worms or licked OxBalls. Put me up against the worst of anything before putting me in a room with him. Hendrix was a damn terrorist. He tortured me as a child, annoyed me as an adolescent, and completely decimated my prom.

Walking through the familiar halls of the stadium brought back memories. As a kid, I often traveled with my father. Back then, I was his buddy. Wherever he went, I did too. It was like being with a superstar. People made way for him, and greeted him with smiles, hugs, and kind words. He made decisions on car rides and deals in the sky while flying between major cities. We had been to arenas and stadiums across the world. I had learned from the best, and I would give my father nothing less. Even with the knowledge of how his mind was changing, I would do whatever it took to protect him. We were partners in this. So, I replayed every sacrifice he had ever made for me on loop as motivation to keep sane and smile at Hendrix.

When the point-toe of my stilettos found their way in front of Hendrix for the first time in years, I forced a grin. The men stood when we entered and the light handshake that Hendrix provided was not inspiring. He was still nice-looking. Fresh cut, popping waves, and a slick suit but the heart wasn't there. The sparks didn't come, and my gut kept still. But that was a good thing. I wouldn't fall in love with Hendrix.

I took my seat, and the men followed in succession.

Leonard Wilson was not the spry angry man that I remembered. His scowl had fallen flat. His rounded face was milder, with sleepy eyes and a soft demeanor.

Hendrix was still fine, but I didn't trust him. This was the same person who came to a family dinner with a saltshaker that was full of sugar to hand me just so he could laugh when I covered my food with it. When our families went on a vacation together one year, he snuck into my hotel room while I was napping and snapped a picture of me waking up to the sound of an air horn. Then when the awkward part of puberty had finished for both of us and we reconnected at a fundraiser, he asked me to attend his senior prom with him. I found out when the girl that his parents forbade him to bring as a date showed up and threw a cup of tea on my dress. He used me as a front to meet another girl at the prom. He had been the instigator, but I got in trouble for molly whopping that girl's ass across the dance floor. I had attended the best schools and taken etiquette lessons from pageant trainers, but I knew how to fight too.

"You're looking healthy, Regina. I'm glad to see that the personal trainer and those braces paid off."

That's how he started the conversation. That was Hendrix 101. Even though his height had changed slightly, not much else had. I always hated his backhanded compliments and wanted to backhand the smug grin off his face. For the sake of my father, I only took a breath.

"I still have my trainer's number if you're looking to get in shape."

"Hendrix, why don't you tell us a little bit about this new project?" My father piped in.

Hendrix leaned forward, rubbing his hands together, as he told us about a string of sober living homes and rehab facilities he was expanding.

"The need is great, and insurance companies and the government are paying top dollar for long-term beds," Hendrix explained. "I've already been approved to house people who are on a deferred adjudication plan and have to prove their sobriety or face jail time. I have partnerships and people lined up, but not enough facilities."

"Where does a relationship with Strong come in?" I asked, trying to ignore the way his eyes brightened at misery.

"Mr. Strong, you are the king of real estate," Hendrix continued to talk to my father as if I hadn't asked the question. "As you can imagine, some neighborhoods are not excited about the idea of a rehabilitation facility near their homes. With your zoning and licensing connections, we could take over the state. We could become the Wal-Mart of treatment centers."

I had to blink a few times to make sure that I was in the right place. We were supposed to be looking into philanthropic proposals. Everything that Hendrix had to say was about the money that he wanted to make from people's pain.

"Your venture sounds like it has more to do with lining your pockets than community outreach. We are currently working on expanding our community partnerships that don't exploit the same people that we want to help." I said, rather than, '*No dumbass, we're not about to pimp poor people to get money from the government.*'

"Mr. Strong, I assure you-" He addressed my father again.

"Let me stop you right there." My father's stern gaze was unwavering. "You've made your appeal to me, but this smart young woman sitting next to me will soon be the head of the company. She's being gracious enough to humor an old man with a few last days and an opportunity to show her the ropes. You want your project financed," he lifted an eyebrow, "it's not my ass that you need to kiss."

My father was not apologetic once we were in the car, he seemed satisfied with the way that meeting went.

"How can you possibly be smiling right now? Hendrix is a pompous prick whose only objective in this world is to be rich and famous. He has no heart."

"But you do," my father added. "You don't need a *yes-man*. You need someone who is not afraid to make a deal, not afraid to take a chance, and who can balance out your kindness with some sensibility and bottom-line thinking. You have the stubbornness of your mother. You need someone to stand next to and not on top of."

"Daddy, Hendrix is-"

My father waved a dismissive hand in the air.

"Genie, if you don't like him, then you don't like him, but time is running out."

I didn't want to take his call, but I did. I sure as hell didn't want to meet for drinks in the hotel restaurant, but I agreed. I was looking for a partner to help me run the business, not someone to fall in love with. Keeping my objective clear, I dressed like I was going on a real date, and plastered on a smile.

I was early on purpose. The waiter, Rod, and I had gotten well acquainted with each other in the nearly empty establishment as I ordered drinks and appetizers. I had to get my mind together. There were some things that I needed to find out about Hendrix that words couldn't tell me. How a man entered a room gave a lot of information about him, and I made sure to be at the perfect angle to scope out Hendrix's stroll. I liked a sure man, the kind that walked straight but took his time. Not anxious about how his greatness would be perceived and is cool with any situation that may pop off. I was attracted to confidence, which kept a kindle of spark between Hendrix and me but made me burn for Terrence.

Was I going to give him up? He had made it clear that we were through, but I couldn't think of an ending for something that was never supposed to begin in the first place.

Midnight had a *'cross me if you dare to'* kind of walk. His face was stuck on *'I wish a fool would'* mode, but there was a softer side.

I wasn't far into my drink when the waiter who had become a pseudo-friend during my time at the table rounded the corner leading a dip-strutting Hendrix to my table. He moved like a reject from the movie Hollywood Shuffle or like he was impersonating George Jefferson. *Had he always walked that? Eww.*

"A scotch neat," Hendrix lowered himself to the seat ordered.

"I'll have another Merlot and some more water as well."

"Sure thing." Rod smiled. "I'll give you two some time to look over the menu and be right back with your drinks."

Hendrix nodded in Rod's direction before picking up his menu.

"You're still a drinker, I see. Still throwing back with the boys."

I counted to three in my mind to push back any attitude.

"I have a glass of wine here and there," I answered. "I noticed that you ordered a scotch."

He looked up from his menu.

"But I'm a man."

"I'm a woman," I responded. "Glad we got that cleared up."

He gave a slight frown before placing the menu on the table and changing the subject.

"Your father tells me that you volunteer as a social worker."

I don't bother to hide rolling my eyes.

"I've maintained a career as a social worker for five years," I explained. "Well, I had, anyway. As you know, I'm returning to the company as an executive."

He chuckled softly.

"Back in the big leagues." He stated. "Not an easy place to play."

"I played there as a child. I learned how to braid hair and underwrite a loan at the same time. Hell, I made my first million-dollar transaction before I had a car."

"Good for you," he gave a slight shrug as he picked up the menu to peruse it again.

The stiff silence dissipated with the waiter's return. We took our drinks. Hendrix lifted his glass for a toast.

I lifted my glass as well.

"To new partnerships and the prosperity-"

My cell phone chimed interrupting his words and I lowered my glass down to attend to it.

"Sorry about that. I meant to put it on vibrate."

"Is there something else more important than I am right now?"

Really?

"It was a silly media notification. This one was about Naeem Matthews."

He nodded before sipping his drink.

"The basketball player, right? That's been big news lately. It's a shame what they did to him."

I stopped my drink in midair. *Had I heard him correctly?*

"What did they do to him?" I had to blink my eyes a few times. "Naeem beat his wife for years."

"They persecuted him in the public eye for something he did in private," Hendrix explained with a flourish of his hands. "He was given a twelve-month sentence for one assault because of other abuse allegations that he was never prosecuted for. The system beat this man down over some stuff that people knew about for years and didn't care one way or the other until it proved to serve their interest."

I frowned, and Hendrix must have taken that for confusion. I understood. I didn't agree. He went on to explain anyway.

"In short," Hendrix faced his palms inward and closed together to demonstrate a small distance. "He was the Colts' golden boy until they couldn't get the money they wanted for him in a trade. Suddenly, his past and present aren't in line with the team's beliefs. They found a new way to get out of the contract."

I gulped down some more of the drink. Liquor was required to listen and even speak to him.

"That's not what happened at all. I was there," Was all that I could manage to say. It was easier than trying to explain that not only had I dated Naeem's friend, my father owned the arena, and my best friend was also involved with him.

"Answer this." He tapped at the table, his eyebrows dipping right when his finger did. "What would you do if you saw a man kicking the tires on his car?"

I took a deep breath before answering. "Nothing."

"Right, because he bought it. That man is going to take care of that car. He pays for it, buys the gas, and the car is his to do with as he pleases. Agree or disagree?"

"Agree."

"If a man wants to destroy his property, who are we to say that he cannot?"

I looked around the room to see if anyone else heard his words because my mind had to be playing tricks on me. *Was he comparing a woman to a car?*

"Cars don't have babies or feelings-" I began before the jackass interrupted.

"They don't have mouths either." He added before moving his hands together in a praying motion as if he needed supernatural power to try and explain a concept to me. "But they still serve a purpose and have to be guided and driven just like women."

I took a beat to re-run the boldness of his words through my mind before responding.

"You'd be guided and driven directly to an ass-whooping if you try that shit with me." I leaned in close and looked him in the center of his eyes. "Also, please note that I kick back muthafucka."

He met my eyes with an intensity of his own before grinning. "You always were feisty. I used to enjoy that about you."

"Enjoy this then." I stood pushing the chair back and moved around the table. I had moved far enough for him to get a good view of my ass when I heard the words that stopped both my steps and tracks.

I was seething, but when I turned toward Hendrix he was leaning back coolly in his chair.

A sneaky grin slipped over his face as he sipped at his water.

"You're going to have to watch that dirty mouth of yours if we're going to marry."

That was the needle that scratched the record of anger spinning in my brain. No one was supposed to know about the marriage prospect of my father's plan.

"Who says I would marry you?" I asked still standing a short distance away.

"Take a seat."

When I didn't move he sighed and reverted to his normal routine.

"I won't tell you anything unless you have a seat. If you want to know who the leaky faucet is in your camp, you'll have to enjoy some more time with me."

I wasn't convinced but was also interested in how he knew what was happening.

He lifted both his hands in surrender.

"I promise to play nice." He attempted an innocent look but it came off mare as constipated.

I took a seat anyway.

"When Reginald mentioned you stepping up to lead the company, I did some fact-checking," Hendrix took on a business tone as he spoke. "A reliable source relayed that Papa Strong is indeed looking to leave the reigns to his daughter but only if she has a husband and is married within the year."

I wouldn't let his words affect me. My family had been intertwined with him for years. We had mutual acquaintances, friends, and staff. I wouldn't question where his knowledge leaked from, I would just plug up the whole.

"Again, who says I would marry you?"

"I'm here, aren't I?" He countered.

When I didn't respond, he continued. If he wasn't partially correct, I would have walked away, but I sat and listened.

"I'm laying my cards on the table here." He leaned forward. "My grandfather favors my cousin to run the company. He thinks that he's more stable."

I scoffed. Jared was stable and more. He was completely the better man and happened to already be married to his long-time girlfriend.

"A marriage between you and I would provide access to the real estate connections and image boost I need while securing control of your father's company for you."

"But we would have to be together." I couldn't have scrunched my face together any tighter if I was stuck on an elevator with a pack of unwashed teens carrying buckets of raw fish they caught while they baked in the Texas heat all day.

"In name only. I know how to play the game Genie." My family nickname eased off his lips as though he had a right to use it. Maybe he thought it would endear me to him or remind me of the bonds that our families already shared, but it only spurred a dull ache in my right temple.

"I'm under no illusion that there would ever be true love between us." His shoulders lifted in the manner of a stereotypical mobster saying '*capisce*' as if his suggestions were (a) my best option and (b) my only option. " This is a partnership agreement."

Considering Terrence would entertain the thought of marriage and Clayton was an odd duck who moved like molasses out of the water, I thought it best to keep Hendrix in my top pocket until I had a move. If nothing else, he knew how to play a game and give the world a show.

"You've given me a lot to think about. I'll be in touch concerning my decision." I finally acknowledged.

"Make sure it's soon. The Jacobs' Anniversary Party would be a great place to introduce the world to us as a couple."

CHAPTER TWENTY-TWO

Regina

When the ladies arrived with bottles of liquor, I knew that my impromptu get-together was about to become a sleepover. Drunk was an inescapable destination, but first: advice.

"I swear you change furniture like you change clothes," Mali commented as she, Nailah, Jubilee, Kinnesha, and I settled onto my overstuffed living room sectionals.

"Change is inevitable and all that, but I don't think I've seen your apartment the same for more than a couple of months. The last time we were here everything was white and I was afraid to sit down or touch the sofa," Nailah commented.

It was true. I got bored with things quickly, clothes, cars, furniture, and men. Well, most men.

"I am living in Rose Gold and Misty Rose until the day I say I do. Got the wardrobe lined up and two new bags. I switched it up for the wedding."

"Is that why we're here?" Kinnesha picked up a bottle of champagne and a bottle of Vodka. "Are we celebrating a groom announcement?" She lifted the bottle of champagne and then switched to lifting the bottle of Vodka, "or gearing up to kick ass?"

"Either way, we got your back," Jubilee, who wore a silky one-piece jumper with strappy heels, added.

"You gonna fight in that?"

"Tennis and jeans are in the bag." Jubilee patted her designer backpack. "Stun gun and zip ties too if the situation gets a little rowdy."

"Slow down Charlie's Angel, no covert missions today. I'm having trouble with my dad's picks, that's all."

Kinnesha lifted the Vodka. "Gotcha."

Nailah pulled a stack of shot glasses from her purse and lined them up on my living room table.

"Why do you have shot glasses in your purse, Nai? You shouldn't even be drinking." I questioned.

"Gotta stay ready."

"Never mind that. What's wrong?" Mali's school counselor's background showed up in her voice. "When you told us about your dad's diagnosis, I was a little worried about his choosing skills."

"Dear old dad was lucid throughout this picking process and is very clear in his reasons. Two of them are horrible romantic matches for me but balance my business sense and there's one that I feel like I could fall in love with."

"Wait." Kinnesha stopped pouring the Vodka. "Do I need to get the champagne? Shouldn't you be happy about possibly loving someone? As lonely as I am, I'd be two-stepping into his arms."

It felt like someone had sucked all of the air out of the room. Kinnesha looked like she wanted to take the last part of her statement back, and the eyes of my old friend fell on my new friend's cousin.

"You had options, Kinny." Mali reminded everyone. When Kinnesha returned and I first reintroduced her to Mali, there were a few tense moments around how Kinny disappeared on them and left a mess of Tyson. Mali was protective of her family, of all the guys. She and Kinny got along, but she never let an opportunity pass to slip a reminder about how hurt Tyson had been.

"We're here about Regina." Kinnesha only let a small bit of sadness seep onto her face before she returned to pouring. In college, I remember her dreaming about her hometown love. Leaving him was hard for her, and I knew that she had some regrets. "Still, possible love is a good thing, right?"

"You don't understand." I closed my eyes and took a deep breath. "Midnight is one of my father's picks, the one that gives me 'curly head chubby cheek' baby visions. The one that I have powerful chemistry with. The problem is that Midnight is Terrence."

I could hear the clock tick on the wall.

"What?" Mali choked out. "Terrence, Terrence? As in my cousin, Terrence Lewis?"

I felt a little shameful, a tiny bit.

Mali's face went through several stages of confusion.

"Oh, that's- Ewww."

"That's it. Pour me a shot," Nailah requested.

"You can't drink while pregnant!"

"I can't think about you with my brother-in-love sober either. I have to erase all the nasty shit you ever told me somehow."

"You better not mess up my god baby. Grape Juice only Nai." I warned, even though I knew that she was playing.

She rolled her eyes and frowned as she pulled a bottle of juice from her purse.

"Let me get this straight," Mali's voice rose at the same pace as her body from the couch. "This whole damn time, you just been smiling in my face and fucking my cousin?"

I considered her a friend, and although I didn't lie, I didn't tell the whole truth either.

"You know that Terrence is a very private -"

Her neck roll was already in progress before she spoke. "What you won't ever have to do is explain my cousin to me. You are new to this."

Deep breathing was becoming my new norm and I used the exercise to center myself enough to let Mali finish. She was upset. I hadn't given her the truth about my relationship with Terrence. I knew she wouldn't have liked it.

"I know who he is," her finger jabbed the air as her neck bounced back and forth. "But if you were bold enough to tell his bedroom business, you should've been bold enough to let me know that you went behind my back to sleep with him after I specifically asked you not to."

I nodded because that was true even though I didn't fully agree. We were full-grown adults that didn't need permission, but I also understood that she asked me to consider her feelings about a situation and I didn't.

"I could have handled it differently." I reached for her hands, but Mali kept them planted at her hips. " I didn't want it to cause a problem between us. Terrence and I had agreed to a fling and since there wasn't a future, I thought it-"

"And now you see a future with him?" Confusion replaced the anger on her face, and her eyes blinked rapidly enough for me to understand that her brain was computing something. "You think that he'd want a future with you?"

I would have rather seen her angry than the look of pity that dawned in her eyes when I admitted my hopes to her. It was a *'bless your heart'* moment without the words. She didn't believe I had a chance with Terrence.

Mali sighed before finding her seat on the sofa again. "Tell me about your other options."

"Yeah." Kinny added, "Let's see the lineup."

"My dad gave me three options. Number 1: Clayton."

I cast pictures from my phone to the television and showed the ladies the first man my father introduced to me as a prospect.

"OK." Jubilee weighed her head from side to side. "Not bad. He's cute. A clean-cut, babyface is not what I pictured you with, but-"

"He's old," I exclaimed. "He walks like a scarecrow and speaks at the pace of dripping molasses. He looks young, but everything about him is reminiscent of the senior-ist of senior citizens. Y'all know I'm about the *snap-to-it*."

"Maybe he could slow you down."

"Or maybe I would lose all my money buying him energy drinks. Who knows?"

I swipe to the next picture.

"This is candidate number 2: Hendrix."

"Alright now. Yaaas. He's fine." A chorus of positivity escaped amid a flurry of snaps.

"Hendrix is cute, but we have history," I explained. "We grew up together, his family is part owner of a football team, and he runs a couple of different businesses on his own."

"That's a good thing, right? He already knows your family and what the company is about. He has a history in business and sports."

"But he also cuts me off, speaks over me, and acts as though men are superior to women."

The ladies sigh.

"Well shit, more Vodka anyone?" Kinnesha asked.

"Then there is Terrence." I'm the only one to swoon when I put his picture on the screen. He was family to the ladies. "He's a multimillionaire businessman, which my friends conveniently neglected to tell me. He's caring, fine as hell, and smart."

"There you go. Pick Terrence." Kinnesha picked up the champagne. "Let's celebrate. To Regina and Terrence!"

"It's not that simple Kinny." I could feel Mali's hand on my shoulder as she explained. I didn't look at her, but I knew that the pity look was back. "You know that Terrence was married once before. His wife died during the time we'd lost contact. He promised that he would never get married again."

"Well, shit, we're going to need another bottle of vodka for this."

"Do you know why he doesn't want to try marriage again?" Nailah asked Mali. "He's such a great guy. Grounded, giving, and intelligent."

"Losing Valerie changed him." Mali's voice was quiet and infused with sincerity. I could see her mind drift back over the changes in her cousin comparing the versions. I wish I had known the other him too. I enjoyed the updated, albeit bugged, version that I met at Tyriq's house.

"Is that why he never really smiles?" Nailah rubbed her belly as she spoke. "He's always been nice to me, even when others weren't. Whenever he did turn up the corners of his mouth, it seemed like it was extremely hard to do."

"He was always serious," Kinny answered. "Even as a kid, he would make us line up in the kitchen single file for dinner and orchestrated chores when Shirley was working odd hours."

"Kinny's little homeless ass was always at Aunt Shirley's house," Mali commented.

"So were you. Now what?"

Mali sipped a little more from the shot glass as she rolled her eyes. "Terrence is the oldest of the brothers and cousins so he got stuck babysitting all of us. A lot. He had to be responsible while all the adults were doing what they had to. Valerie was kind of his escape from home life and a friend at school. He was the only one that got into the fancy math academy up there with all those rich kids."

"He went to Valley Vista Prep?" I was shocked. "They were our rivals in the private school division every year."

"Full scholarship. He got noticed because he won the gold medal in the state Math Olympics. His public school beat Valley Vista two years in a row before they reached out to Aunt Shirley to have him take their entrance exam."

"And they accepted him?" I was in awe. Terrence was a mechanic millionaire who had a prep school education. I never would have guessed.

"Accepted is a strong word. He went to the school, but there were a handful of black kids and only two others there on scholarship. Valerie wasn't a scholarship student, but they hit it off and stuck together."

I had gone to expensive private prep schools, so I understood what it was like to feel different among your peers. My dad was in a tax bracket that not many people of any race ever reached, so our circle was small.

"Everyone was surprised when he brought Valerie around his junior year of high school." Mali continued. "He didn't have a lot of girlfriends. He wasn't like Tyriq and Chad who dated two or three rotations of girls at a time in high school. They had an A-Team and a B-Team. Chad even had a C roster. It was sad."

"Oh really?" Nailah piped in. "I need to ask my husband about these teams."

Mali smiled. "Girl please, Tyriq found you and hasn't looked back."

"Nailah already got a man, back to Terrence."

"Everyone tried to talk them out of getting married young. Valerie's parents tried. They didn't like Terrence because our family didn't have any status socially or financially." Mali shook her head before continuing. "I won't lie and say that they didn't have their good times, but Valerie started to resent Terrence a little. Once they got married, her friends were living the fun twenty-something life taking trips, clubbing, and hanging out while she was *stuck* with my serious cousin who was trying to save money. Terrence was working super hard to buy their house. Anyway, being poor and boring bothered her, and it bothered him that he couldn't make her happy. Then she died, and I think he blamed himself. Her parents blamed him."

"Wow." I had to take a shot after that. I should have had a novel of words to say to that. He had never told me that about his wife's passing. He had never given me the details of his feelings. I never pried or tried to get him to explain either, figuring it was too deep to discuss for our shallow relationship. While I had assumed we were in kiddie pool territory, Mali's explanation of Terrence's past let me know that our relationship barely splashed in the puddle level.

"He's a big ol' teddy bear with a big heart behind his growl," Mali explained with a hint of compassion. "Valerie broke him in a way that I don't know will ever be repaired. You need to cross Terrence off your little game list."

"It's like that?" I was astonished. I was asking for her help, not her judgment. "Do you think I would hurt Terrence?"

"Hell yeah." her voice rose. "All of this is for show. You can't even commit to a damn sofa. What makes you think you can commit to marriage? Your shallow, *spin the wheel and pick a partner* game was funny until it included my family."

"You think I'm not good enough for him?"

Silence saturated the room as Mali met my unwavering glare with one of her own.

"I think he's not over Valerie. I think that you are everything that he could fall for but never recover from." Mali's steel words and sharp eyes sliced at my heart. "If you aren't looking to love him for the rest of your life, don't drag him into this mess."

We sat there for stretched seconds without saying a word before I finally spoke.

"I'm not-I do- because Terrence is-" The right words caught in my throat, and I sputtered out something else in resignation. "I care about Terrence, and I care about your friendship Mali."

Deflated, I slumped back into the sofa. I felt like I had finally found my tribe, and I didn't want to lose them already. I wouldn't lose friends over a man that I couldn't have. Even though Terrence had already removed himself from my list, I still held out some hope that I could change his mind. I had changed it once before.

Terrence had lost a wife once. Our marriage would be in name only, even though I liked him a lot. I didn't want to hurt him. I didn't want to marry him only to leave him.

Tough decisions had to be made. I had a company to save, a father to monitor, and a life that didn't allow time for the exploration of emotions. I needed someone who could walk into a position with little help and support the day-to-day operations of the company. I needed someone who would look good on paper and my arm but leave my heart alone. I needed someone that I couldn't damage.

CHAPTER TWENTY-THREE

Jerrence

I had never been anyone's father. All the words that sped through my mind were either inadequate or would probably come off as rude. And I wanted to help. I wanted to correct the situation, but I wasn't sure where to begin. I couldn't get past the resounding *'What the fuck?'* of the whole scenario. I didn't wake up that morning with a child.

His shoulders dropped in the chair across from my desk, his eyes falling on anything but my face.

When I got the call that my son was in trouble and I needed to pick him up, I had to look at the phone twice and double-check who they were looking for. When the woman on the line said my name again and checked if I was the father of Trevion Cane, I agreed and went to pick him up. We rode to the downtown shop in silence and sitting in my office, I needed answers from the young man from the group of boys that I mentored.

"What made you call me?" I settled on that question before blurting out, "Better yet, why did you tell them that I was your dad?"

His round cheeks drooped with remorse as he faced me for a quick second.

"I'm sorry about that Mr. T, I didn't know what else to say." He looked out of the window. The bourbon colored centers of his thin slanted eyes landed on everything but my face "I always have to do the school information updates. Every year I have to leave the part about who my father is blank." He shrugged. "This year, I don't know. I was like, it would be cool if -"

He didn't finish the sentence. I could tell that he was battling with something inside as he blinked a few times and swallowed hard.

I didn't press him, just let him sit with those emotions. Children were not meant to be adults and he had obviously handled many adult responsibilities in his time.

He sniffled before continuing. "I didn't think they were gonna call you. I don't ever get in trouble."

The flash of hurt and desperation that cracked through his voice reminded me of how fragile even some of my toughest mentees could be.

I thought he might cry if I pushed or demanded complete answers, so I softened my tone when asking about why I was the one that the school reached out to.

"Why didn't they call your mom?"

I watched his gaze float upward as he picked at the edges of his nails.

"My mom- she has some troubles sometimes and she can't be around." His eyes drifted between his hands and my face. "Her friend let us stay with her, but she said she doesn't want her name and number on anything. She has a one-bedroom with three kids and it's against the rules to have more people in there. My mom is already tripping again, and I don't want to get kicked out."

I understood.

"They have to talk to an adult. I didn't have no one else." He finally admitted.

His eyes widened. They were red from the strain of holding back tears. I moved to sit next to the young man who was battling so much.

"Don't kick me out of the group Mr. T., please," A few thug tears had escaped from his eyes. "I know you said we had to keep our grades up and not be in trouble to stay in, and I lied to them about being your son, but I don't- I don't have anyone else. I don't."

I gave Trevion's shoulders a quick squeeze, before letting my shoulders relax.

"You call me whenever, for whatever you need," I assured him. "I'm gonna always have your back, group or not."

"But I can stay in the group?"

"Yeah. You're one of the best engine techs. We can't win the competition without our engine guy."

I didn't have to work on cars, but it helped soothe me, so I took Trevion to the garage and talked to him like my father talked to me. Working on cars with my dad taught me patience. It taught me commitment and how to see something through to the end. That's what I would do for those boys. I would see this program through. I would help Trevion, Daquan, and Do Boy, but there were others out there like them.

"Thank you, Mr. T," Trevion said a few hours later as we closed up the shop.

Playing golf with Mr. Strong had become a weekly thing. Since the night that he had wandered off, we had become closer. He told me stories about his life that I related to lessons about business and manhood. He shared interesting tidbits about money management and making connections with people. He had become a mentor. As much knowledge that I gave to the young men that I worked with, spending time with Mr. Strong taught me that there was still so much to learn. I noticed that he forgot some things and said the wrong words sometimes, but he was himself. I would help him where I could.

"Where are we on the funding for the young mechanic's program?" I asked. "It's been on my mind lately and I was thinking about expanding the program into a small center for young men who have some difficulties."

Mr. Strong lifted an eyebrow, a sign that he may have been interested, so I continued.

"The center would have free and low-cost trade education but be taught by men who look like the youth they serve. People who can mentor the boys into men. I was also thinking that the center could double as a low-cost rental space for minority-led businesses. Those entrepreneurs would contribute hours as mentors and provide training opportunities as a part of their low-cost rent agreement."

"Hmmm." He pressed down the grey hairs filling his mustache with his fingers. "And what would this center be named?"

"I'm not sure, but the Reginald M. Strong Empowerment Center has a nice ring to it. People donate to foundations and colleges all the time to have their names on the building. You could help people for decades by influencing them through positive programs."

"Regina has already chosen her project for this year." He scratched his chin.

It was over. Regina and I had been playing a game for a while, and someone else had won. That stung. She had chosen her husband, and even though I couldn't marry her, an ache bloomed in my chest. I missed her.

"No disrespect, but you're still the boss. She can have her project, and you can have yours."

"You're right, I'm still running the show." He nodded his head as if reassuring himself. "I like the impact that this project can make, and I want to partner with you to get it done. That means securing the land for the center because we're building state-of-the-art from the ground up, with no half-stepping. I'm talking permits, blueprints, guiding a team for construction, all of it."

"I've gone through the process of expanding our auto parts chain. When we built the Brother's T custom shops, I worked the process from a dream in my mind to products on the shelves."

"Good. Good." Reginald nodded. "I'm hiring you as a consultant, for now. We'll figure out your title in the company later. There's a conference room near me that I'll have turned into your office within the week."

"Right." I nodded slowly. I hadn't thought about that. I wouldn't go to the shop every day. I wouldn't tow cars or work the register, or do inventory. It's not like I didn't have people in place to take care of that stuff. Tyson made the rounds to the shops and met with managers and supervisors often. Something about the change nagged at my gut. The shop had been my entire life for years now.

"As long as I can still have my time to work with my group, you've got a deal." I finally agreed.

Things were changing quickly. I wasn't with her. As quickly as it had started, it was over. But she had happened. We had happened. I missed her. In a short time, I had gotten used to her. I had never meant to get that close to her.

In the middle of my Regina thoughts, my brother called me. Tyriq was about to be a father for the first time. Nailah was in labor. While Trystan already had two kids, the void stung stronger now that the brother closest to me was building his family and stacking up titles that might only be a dream for me. Husband. Father.

Once at the hospital, I gladly sat in the waiting room to direct family and friends who came to visit. Mostly the waiting room mimicked my life, people stopped through, but no one stayed long. It was just me staring through a window into the night, my thoughts lost in the space beyond the glass. When she entered, I saw her reflection. It bothered me that an image of her was the best that I could hope for. She was gone too, but still in front of me. That ache tugged at my chest when I walked over, and she greeted me like we were ex-co-workers who never ate lunch together. I missed her. She had chosen her husband, and I couldn't have her anymore. I couldn't marry her. I wouldn't be pushed to do something so long term so quickly. I didn't want to share her. Apart was the only option left. Life without her was the only choice that I had. Knowing and unknowing Regina had added another rung to the depth of my loneliness.

"Where's everyone?" she asked before I could let go of a word.

Her effect on me hadn't changed. Her angled face and curvy body hadn't stopped making me feel light just because I couldn't see her naked anymore. Regina still made me want to grab her by the waist and anchor inside her for a day or five.

"My mom and Aunt Pat are in the delivery room with Tyriq and Nailah."

If I could have looked at anything other than her, I would have. My eyes were stuck there, gliding up and down her athletic tights, T-shirt, and trainers. We were alone together, and talking was something that we didn't do. Her eyes called to me and the only reason I let my gaze tear away from the hypnotizing brown pools of seduction was to watch the sharpening buds of her nipples through her T-shirt.

"You can't look at me like that," was what she said, but I felt the heat of her stare on my lips.

"Like what?"

"Like you'll gobble me up in three bites."

She shifted her weight to one leg as she plopped a hand on her hip. That movement only served to spark memories of her skin and the way it felt pressed against mine.

My laugh was unintended.

"That's funny to you." Her pouty lips were both entertaining and enchanting.

"It's funny because it's not true." Closing some of the space between us, I moved a hand to trace the line of her arm. I felt that was innocent enough. "You know for a fact that I savor everything I put in my mouth."

She moved nearer like I had a string pulling her in, but it was the opposite. She was a lifeline, a tether to a happy place that I couldn't unbind even though I had tried.

"You joking today?" She gave me a laugh, but it was a tension breaker. She slid around me out of my reach to play with the vending machine.

"Straight facts. You're a delicacy, Bloom."

That caught her attention.

"Regina," she corrected quietly.

Her whisper made my body harden.

"I'm Regina and you're Terrence. There are no more twilight meetings in hotel rooms. No more Bloom."

I was glad to have her near again. I kept my hands to myself even though they were itching to feel every piece of her.

"Can you sit with me? Is that an option for us *Regina*?"

I took a seat in one of the wide wood-based, blue canvas chairs. She was still standing in the same spot but watching the chair as though it would swallow her whole if she sat in it.

"You're the one who said that we couldn't be together if I was getting married." She finally stated. Her feet stayed planted in the same spot that they were when I first asked her to join me.

"Are you still getting married?" It wasn't a question that I wanted to ask, because I already knew the answer. I already knew that she was going to follow through with whatever it was that she had set out to do. Regina didn't back down from anything, except me it seemed. She had backed away from me and that hurt.

"Yes." She said the word plainly, not the menacing response that it was. That yes was an act of treason in my book. She made me like her, want her, and crave her, knowing that she wouldn't be available.

"I don't share." I reminded her. "Almost flunked out of kindergarten because of it."

She laughed. "You are hilarious and no one knows it." That unfroze her somehow and she found her way into the very chair that I had asked her to take earlier. She found her way closer to me. That endearing smile and her nearness felt right, felt comfortable, felt like it would be mine again.

"Just you, Bloom," I remarked.

"I am not your Bloom anymore." The smirk playing at her lips convinced me that although we were on pause right now, I would get my chance to play again.

"We'll see."

While I was honest about not sharing Regina with anyone. I also knew that whatever lame-ass dude she got to agree to her crazy marriage scheme wouldn't last long. She didn't half-do anything. Her body always told me the truth and I knew that it would be caressed by me again. I didn't mind waiting.

She moved back to the snack machine on the other side of the room.

"I can't believe they're doing this, having a baby. A whole other human that you can't send back is about to appear from her body."

"Think you'll ever have a kid?"

She shook her head and looked away.

"Not anytime soon. Taking this position is going to require dedication and time for the next few years."

"You'll be good at it."

Her eyes met mine.

"At what?"

"Both, but I was speaking about leading the company. You have a good head on your shoulders."

"Thanks."

"Your dad is going through his thing, but he wouldn't have put you in charge if he didn't believe in you. Plus, he'll still be around in some capacity for a bit. Me too, I'll be around if you need me."

The desire in her eyes brought me to my feet. Back to her.

"You know, for anything business-related," I say, but move closer to her in a non-business manner.

I slid a finger along her jawline. Her fingers grazed the back of my hand.

"You can't touch me like that and then tell me it's only business." Her lips fell against my palm and the gentle press made me want more.

My breathing grew ragged as our bodies drew against each other. It had been too long since I was inside her. I needed to feel her.

"I miss you." Words that I felt but meant to keep tumbled out before I could hold them back.

Looking up into my eyes, Regina dropped my hand and I felt the warmth of her mouth near my lips.

"Yo! Where the party at?" Chad's voice interrupted the tender moment.

Regina zoomed away from me.

"Is the baby here yet?" Mali's words trailed off when she stepped into the waiting room. Her eyes darted between Regina and me. The death glare she'd perfected over the years landed on Regina.

That was interesting because she and Mali were friends but were not looking friendly.

"I'll check the nurse's station for an update," Regina slipped out of the room and I didn't see her the rest of the night.

CHAPTER TWENTY-FOUR

Regina

There should have been a parade, in the middle of the day, in the middle of the office, complete with confetti. My college band should have been marching through the halls playing renditions of the top twenty hits like a scene from the movie Drum Line. I deserved a prize for staying upright after my father's surprise announcement. I didn't explode when my father told me the news. I was controlled as a woman who had chosen to marry a man that she didn't like and found out that her ridiculously fine but unavailable lover would be in the next office daily could be.

"I've had a few conversations with Terrence Lewis, and I like his proposal." My father started the conversation. We were in his office reviewing business plans at the table when he started speaking my nightmare into existence.

"I do too, but I've made my decision." I reminded my father. We planned to partner in whatever project my fiancé chose.

"I think you and Hendrix could be a forceful team together." He nodded matter of factly before he leaned forward and clasped his hands together. I recognized this from when I was younger and he wanted to explain things to me about life.

"I want to be transparent with you, especially since you are moving forward to handle more aspects of the business." He started.

I wasn't sure about what he wanted to tell me but it seemed so serious. It seemed important to him, way more important than the fact that I had chosen a husband, something he had been begging me to do for over a year.

"Whatever it is dad, just tell me." I sat up straighter, preparing myself to be blown back by a bomb of shocking news.

"I've hired Terrence as a consultant to create a community center in my honor. I'm having conference room three turned into his office." My dad explained. "He's moving in this week."

I had to re-listen to his words in my brain after he repeated them twice. The conference room was right between my father's office and mine. *What had changed?* He wanted me to work with Terrence and I needed to understand why. I had barely survived him at the hospital.

"By moving in, you mean he'll be here, daily, as in a part of the team here?"

My father nodded. "He'll see the project through from planning to staff."

I scrolled through the different processes in my brain and totaled up at least two years. I would have to look at Midnight, smell his hypnotizing cologne, and not touch him for two years. Part of me wanted to throw the parade that my father didn't because Terrence would still be a part of my life, even if Midnight wasn't. The other part of me wanted to fall on the floor and throw a full foot-kicking, lung-shredding tantrum.

"But why?" I managed to ask through the scurry of thoughts.

"Why not? He's refreshing and the project he's working on will-" My father shrugged. "I haven't always done the most popular thing but I've always tried to do the best thing for my family- This community center will allow some atonement for some decisions that I had to make that were less favorable."

I had been privy to many of my father's decisions and knew that some of his actions couldn't be covered by any earthly grace. This center sounded important to him, and the fact that he trusted Terrence to lead the project was thought-provoking.

"The cricket stadium will be a testament to my tenacity in business, but it won't change anything in the community that I came from. That's what I want."

"And what about me? Did you think about what I want, or how I would feel about any of this? Did you think about how Terrence working here would affect me?"

I was trying not to shout. I didn't want to yell at my father, but he was too damn unbothered. He was too sure that Terrence was supposed to be a part of our company, and that he was supposed to remain an integral part of our lives, of my life. That concerned me.

"Is there something that I should have considered? Something that I don't know about you two?"

My father had caught me. Stuck in the middle of feelings that I should have kept hidden, I could only stare at the man that knew me before I knew myself and grimace before trying to backpedal my way out of admission.

"Uh. No. He's just a friend- It's fine- It'll be fine." I stuttered through the explanation, suddenly feeling exposed.

I knew then that he knew. He had to. He wore the same expression as he did when I was six years old and I told him that I didn't know who wrote my name on my bedroom wall in my favorite color.

"Which one is it?" My father questioned. His eyebrow lifted higher with each word.

"Fine or going to be fine?"

My slow answer was louder than my actual shaky, "We're fine. It's fine."

He nodded and a look of understanding brought his hiked eyebrow down to its normal position and his mouth to a smooth slightly curved line.

I turned to leave so that I could go back to my office and panic in peace. His request caught me before I could completely exit the office.

"Go see him." The three words weren't much, but the way my father mashed them together left no room for argument. There was no room for consideration of my feelings or debate, just like when he told me I couldn't go on a trip to Barbados with my boyfriend and his inattentive parents when I was sixteen. He had given an edict that I was required to follow.

"See who?" I asked without turning back. He didn't need to see my eyes.

"I'll let Terrence know that you'll stop by his shop tonight to review the project outline."

He had picked up his phone and was heartily greeting Terrence before I could pick up my jaw and tuck away my feelings.

I had never been to Terrence's shop. For as much as I knew about his lips, tongue, and fingers, there were so many other things that I didn't know about him. I hadn't expected the body shop, auto repair, parts shop, and car wash to take up the entire damn block. I knew he had his own business, but I had imagined a small two-stall garage in a renovated gas station. What I stood in front of was an empire that rivaled national chains like Pep Boys and Auto Zone, and I was impressed. When I realized that this wasn't the only shop that he owned, I fully understood what my father knew a long time before I did. Terrence was a businessman who masqueraded as a mechanic for fun. He may have dressed like

Eazy E in black t-shirts and cargo pants, but he was more like Jay Z, a mogul. I found a parking spot near the auto repair garage where I was told I could find him.

"I'm here to meet with Terrence Lewis," I explained to the woman standing at the counter. Her nametag said Chyna and she was the basic kind of cute, music video background, community celebrity noticeable.

Terrence had never mentioned her before, but the look of desire that crossed her face when I mentioned his name, told me that she wanted to be a problem. Her over-bright makeup made a statement too, but I was working on being less judgmental.

"He's unavailable." There was a smile on her face, but I spoke Bitch thoroughly. She was blocking.

"He may be unavailable to *you*, but he's expecting me," I countered because I didn't appreciate how she was trying to play me like I wasn't important.

Her head tilted to the left and the smile was still there.

"Only employees or family are allowed beyond this point. Not even employees interrupt Terrence during group."

Really? The way she referred to him as Terrence irked me.

I lifted a pointed nail at the oblivious young woman about to tell her a few words when I heard a familiar voice.

"Regina," Tyson called as the front door jingled closed behind him.

I turned to face the suave man who in the past would have been more of my type. He was always decked out in the smoothest designer suit, decadent ties, with expensive shoes and socks. He was the clean-cut image of what a businessman was supposed to be. He was everything that used to appeal to me. The Regina from a year ago would have been all over him, brother to an ex or not. A few months with Midnight and no one else could quite measure up.

"Tyson." I extended his name and poured all the extra that I could into the simple one-arm hug that he gave. Chyna needed to know who I was.

"Glad you made it." He said. "I had to step over to the carwash and left our new front desk manager, Chyna, in charge." Tyson turned to the woman. "Chyna, this is Regina Strong of Strong Realty and Acquisitions. Friend to the family."

I placed an innocent hand over my chest and squeezed my shoulders up as I replied, "You know I love the Lewis's. We're family."

Tyson nodded as he walked behind the counter, pulled a bag from a cabinet, and placed it in front of me.

"Terrence wants you to put this on before you come back."

My nose wrinkled without asking, and I pulled the peach coverall from the sack. I wear the finest couture clothing; only pure blend fabrics have touched my skin since the beginning. I break out in hives at the sight of any mass-manufactured garment.

"Terrence found it, especially for you. He got it embroidered and everything as soon as he knew you were stopping in."

Tyson pointed to my name stitched over the right breast pocket of the one-piece cardboard-like suit. I had determined that it was a coverall. Men had asked me to wear a variety of things, but that was the first time I had ever been asked to dress up like a mechanic.

Normally, the whole outfit would have been a 'no', but to spite the basic bitch in front of me, I agreed.

"He knew exactly what color I would love and everything." I threw some extra excitement in for Chyna.

"You can step into Terrence's office to change."

Chyna's gasp was incentive enough to walk with Tyson and put on the hideous jumpsuit. I kept the *"Checkmate. Even his office is available to me"* though. #Growth.

Nothing about Terrence Lewis was what I expected. He had a sofa, a small restroom, artwork, flat-screen television, and drapes. Even though it was housed in a shop, his office was homey and pristine. Pictures of his family were everywhere. I stepped to his large desk and noticed a picture of his parents, and then one faded photograph that caught my eye.

It was a younger Terrence without the dreads, a standard tapered haircut, khakis, and a button-down shirt. He looked so, so square. Like a cookie-cutter movie version of a good guy nerd. Dressed like a neighborhood car salesman, he looked nothing like the tattooed rough and rugged soul that had whipped my pussy into submission. In the picture, he reminded me of Tyriq, wholesome, and boy-next-door-ish. The picture was folded in the frame, and I couldn't tell who Terrence's arm was around, only saw a piece of a dress and a church. I knew that church. It was the Jacobs' church.

A knock at the door startled my snooping.

"Terrence also bought some socks and tennis shoes for you," Tyson said through the door. "I'll leave them right here."

I dressed quickly and slid on the perfect-fitting socks and shoes. I placed my clothes on a hanger in the small wardrobe near the restroom. His jacket was hung there along with a pair of black cargo pants and two t-shirts. I wondered what it would be like for our different lives to intermingle.

I dismissed the notion; Hendrix was my future.

"I didn't believe my brother when he said you would show up to an auto shop in a power suit and stilettos." Tyson chuckled as he guided me down a corridor toward the garage.

"What's wrong with that?"

"Have you met Terrence?" Tyson continued finding the situation hysterical. "He's serious about this shop, and if you thought you were gonna sit clean behind a glass window to observe, you miscalculated. Even when I come to the shop, Terrence has me in coveralls running the desk, towing, and tire changing... and I'm part owner."

Thoughts of getting dirty with Terrence Lewis scrolled through my brain as we reached a solid door and I was completely unsure if I was ready for it to open.

"Here is where the dirt begins and my tour ends." Tyson smiled and pulled out a pocket watch. "I've got meetings scheduled. We're looking for a good media and public relations firm to help with branding and a few commercial ads."

"Let me know if you need some recommendations."

He nodded.

"Go get 'em." He winked.

I planned to observe, just watch what he did to keep teenagers engaged, but as soon as I stepped in, I was pulled in too.

Tools, machines, and equipment lined the walls and took up space in the simulation bay, and eight young men huddled around an Oldsmobile Cutlass with Terrence at complete attention.

He was picking up car pieces as various voices called out names to the parts.

His eyes were up and on me as soon as the door finally pushed closed. His gaze had his students turning to gawk as well.

"Welcome." He said. "This is Ms. Strong, she's-"

"This yo' lady?" One of the young men asked.

"Are you on Love and Hip Hop," another one inquired.

"I see you, Mr. T," the young man closest to him commented.

"Terrence and I are friends." I smiled.

"Ooooh, the Friendzone."

"But I got friends though. Some other people can see." Terrence shot back. "What yo' friends look like?"

"Aight, Mr. T." He nodded his head with a grin.

By the end of the class, I had successfully learned the function of an alternator and agreed to be the race team cheerleader.

"That was fun," I commented as we watched the last student, Trevion, hop on a bus. "I enjoy it."

"My father wants me to learn more about this project, get an overview."

"Is that the only reason you're here?"

It was hard to think when he was looking at me like that. Those golden honey eyes with flecks of oak and green sprinkled throughout were austere. They were hypnotizing.

"Come to dinner with me." He requested before I could answer.

"Do I get to choose the place?"

***

I automatically frowned when he pulled into the parking lot, avoiding the deepest holes and broken concrete like a pro.

"Terrence?" I looked up at the faded sign of the establishment and then down at the dilapidated display board. "They don't even have all the letters on their sign. What is UN PA CIEN?"

"The more letters missing, the better the food. No advertising just word of mouth." He said and turned off the car as though he expected me to get out. "The Kung Pao Chicken at Ming's Cuisine is superb."

He kissed his fingers like he was a chef describing the great taste of a gourmet meal.

"More jokes, I see."

"Only for you, Bloom."

"I am not-" I started to explain for the hundredth time to call me Regina, but gave up.

Back in my business suit and red bottoms, I was completely overdressed and unsure about leaving the car.

Terrence had come around to the passenger side door and opened it before I had completely made up my mind to exit.

"You trust me?"

His eyes were sincere, his hand was outstretched, and I felt like the question was about more than the restaurant.

Falling into his gaze, I pushed my hand forward into his and slid down out of the super large truck. We were close again, face to neck, and the radiating warmth from him filled me with want.

"I promise I won't let anything happen to your body." he smiled as he hovered above me. "I got some things I need to do to it in the future."

Lingering near him a little longer, I laughed. I would be eating someplace new.

"Come on." He said keeping my hand as he pulled me forward toward the door.

"You know I don't eat meat, right?" I reminded him as he opened the door to Ming's Cuisine for me.

We walked up to the cashier and he answered: "I know you're special Regina. They have this fire tofu and mushroom dish that I tried by accident. I think you'll like it."

"Tall Terrence," the small Asian woman behind the counter exclaimed as she pulled Terrence down for a hug.

I learned two things right then: one, Terrence frequented the place enough to be family, and two; the woman did not have an indoor voice.

"Finally, you bring a pretty girl to see me." She shook her small shoulders in my direction as she grinned.

I think Terrence blushed.

"This is my friend Regina," he said and it pricked at my heart. We had been more, and I wanted to be more to him than a friend.

Terrence paid for our meals and picked up our drinks. Before I could walk away, the woman behind the register grabbed my hand, pulled me close, and told me what I already knew and what continued to bother me.

"He always leaves a good tip, got big hands, and a wide smile. Tall Terrence, he's a good man," she said in a non-whisper.

I laughed at that and thought about just how good Terrence could be. I found Terrence in a booth and took a seat.

"You look scared," he commented.

"I ain't never scared." I half spoke and half sang like the rapper Bone Crusher.

"If you say so."

"For real, I went to an HBCU. I'm not as prissy as you think"

"Howard?" He guessed. "It's full of rich people, so that doesn't count."

"I am a Panther baby, Black Fox."

"Get outta here. For real?"

"For real. My father had me in private prep schools my entire life. When I graduated high school, he agreed to let me complete my undergrad at a Historically Black University if I went to an Ivy League school for my graduate degree. Best decision I ever made."

"And why is that?"

"It felt like home," I said wistfully. "I was one of the few chocolate chips on the drill team in my prep school. We wore big petticoat skirts and cowboy hats and did big kicks like the Rockettes. I had to wear the same pale nude tights and bright red lipstick as the other girls. Nothing matched my skin tone. At A&M, everything felt like it had me in mind. We wore costumes and wigs to match our routines and every week was something different. Hell, for every song we did a different stand dance during football season. We shook everything and left it all on the field during halftime. It was like living in the middle of Beyoncé's Homecoming. Best three years ever."

A server placed our meals on the table then. Terrence and I said thank you at the same time and the server retreated.

"So, you like big bands and dancing?"

"I like HBCU Bands and dance." I corrected.

We both took a few minutes of silence to ingest the great-smelling food in front of us. I hummed with each bite.

"Good huh?"

I rolled my eyes at him, refusing to give him the satisfaction of being right.

"The young men that you mentor seem nice."

"Some of them are."

"What made you start the program?"

"I always dreamed of the ideal family, wife, kids, dog, and the whole nine. That idea got shot out of the sky like hunting season. Still have the dog. Since I probably won't have kids, I thought I would help some of the ones already here. One of the kids inspired me to expand my little idea, and then when I spoke to Reginald, I thought about making it bigger: A center to cultivate leadership and small business, give advice, space, and training."

I was more than a little impressed with him.

"So how did you end up a mechanic?"

"You say that like it's a bad thing." He frowned. "I own businesses and I provide a needed service in my community at a reasonable price."

"I know, but you seem smart."

He placed his fork down.

"Smart people can't be mechanics?" He asked. "I went to college. I have a degree and I worked a corporate gig for a couple of years. The suit, tie, and briefcase too."

"Really?"

"My dad worked as an airplane mechanic and wanted better for us. College was cool. I got a good job with a good starting salary, but it was ruthless long hours away from my family and wife. I was always at work, preparing for work, or socializing for work. I made time for her where I could. We had our never-ending scrabble competition and morning coffee, but- When she died, I wanted something different, something that I enjoyed."

"That's understandable."

"My pops and I used to fix up classic cars together and that's what I enjoyed the most. Now I do something that I love every day, and help people along the way."

"Careful your heart is showing."

"Never said I was heartless, just don't want to fall in love. I have too much heart, so I gotta keep it put away."

I nodded and there was more silence as we finished our food.

"I made a decision." I blurt out dropping my fork.

"Wow. What's his name?"

"Hendrix."

"Hendrix, huh? Sounds very metro-sexual-hipster-ish."

"You sound very salty-ish right now."

"Nah. I'm not salty- You know what? Congratulations. I'm sure you and Hindenburg will do great."

CHAPTER TWENTY-FIVE

Terrence

The scenario played out in my head in a thousand different ways. When Regina said that she had chosen someone, it hurt more than knowing it. The entire ride back to the shop, my mind was consumed by what could have been. She had become a necessary liberation. I thought it would be a temporary break, and she would notice how her body longed for mine. She would come to her senses, and we would continue in our escapades.

"Is she the only one here?"

Regina's question broke through the swirl of my thoughts. I was just parking the car when she nodded toward the clear windows of the shop.

"Chyna, your manager. Is she the only one here?" She asked with folded arms and narrowed eyes.

I frowned a little because I was unsure of the notes of jealousy playing in her voice. She was getting married but had an issue with Chyna?

"She's taking over most of my duties. My first store and my last store to let go of." I looked toward the building. "So yeah, she's the first one here and the last one to leave."

"Doesn't she have a man or something to go home to?"

I shrugged before opening my door and jogging around the front of the truck to open the passenger side door for Regina. "I don't know, but she's not married."

"Of course not." She murmured as I shut the truck door.

Awkward seconds ticked by, while I waited for Regina to move toward her car. Her long lean legs looked scrumptious in her heels as she stood there in the moonlight.

"I'm gonna head in the shop for a few to close down some things and clean up the mess from my class."

"I can help." She offered.

I didn't mean to laugh in her face, it just happened. That was the most hilarious thing I had heard in a long time.

"You're going to help me clean the garage?"

"Yes. I know how to clean." she lifted her head in defiance. "I'm not just some spoiled rich girl."

I took a deep breath and wondered at fate before answering.

"Aight, Ms. Clean, you and your power suit can come with me."

Chyna was working with the screen on the cash register when we entered. The quick look of dissatisfaction that swept over her face made it clear. She had a small crush on me.

"Terrence. I'm so glad you're here. I need your help with adding the new coupon code to the system."

"Sure." I looked back at Regina. "Do you want to change in my office?" I knew that my face couldn't convey all of the confusion that I felt. I couldn't decipher if Regina was being obstinate for the sake of being stubborn or jealous that another woman was interested in me.

"I'm good right here." Her feet planted, face set in a flat line, Regina made it obvious that she would not be going anywhere. I assumed that it was due to her boss nature until she added, "A little dirt won't hurt." That's when I knew that she was jealous.

"Alright then." I walked around the counter to stand next to Chyna, making sure there was a respectable distance between us, but I could still see the screen. "You were almost there, just tap the three dots at the top and choose the add option."

Chyna shifted her weight to her right leg bringing her backside closer to me.

"This one?" She chose the right button without a problem.

I nodded, but since Chyna couldn't hear that nod, so she turned to look at me.

"Should I touch it?" she asked in a tone that could have been tempting if she weren't an employee or this had been months earlier.

"Yes. That's right."

I locked eyes with Regina when I heard the tap of a heel and the clang of metal bangles on her wrist. Her mouth was pursed into a fish face as though she were biting the inside of her cheek. I wanted to laugh at her annoyance. She was getting married, but she had an attitude about me speaking to Chyna. Hilarious.

"Yay!" Chyna squealed and turned to grip my shoulders. "Thank you, Terrence! You always know what I need."

Gently, I unclipped the unwanted grasp and patted Chyna's hand.

"Alright." I ran a finger under the collar of my T-Shirt. "Well, Regina and I'll be in the garage straightening up the mess from the group."

"I can help," Chyna offered.

Regina answered, "That's ok Tokyo, I got him taken care of. Let's get this finished Night so you can get me home."

I knew Chyna had gotten to her then. For her to call me Night in public, was a clear indication to anyone around that she knew me personally.

"Aight." I didn't question it. I wasn't into Chyna in the least bit. All of my thoughts were geared toward Regina anyway.

As soon as our feet hit the garage and she shut the door, the atmosphere changed. She turned on those heels and pushed her face up to mine.

"Your little assistant is cute."

She didn't mean cute, and we both knew it.

I hooked an arm around her waist and pulled her against me.

"Why are you playing with me, Bloom? You know I'll open you up right here."

She only blinked, and I reveled in the fact that I made her speechless.

"Why do you think I'm playing?"

I don't know who moved first, but her lips were closer to mine with each breathy word she spoke. Then I was exploring the inside of her mouth, tangling my tongue with hers. It had never been tender between us, it was a clashing of passion, extreme magnetism joining our two bodies together because natural law mandated it every time that we were near. There was no other outcome when she was next to me.

We both had points to prove. Regina was determined to show that she was someone special in my life. I needed Regina to understand that she couldn't live without me, that marrying someone else was wrong.

She moaned into my mouth, and I knew that she was loud on purpose. Chyna was still on the other side of the closed solid door. She couldn't see us, but my girl wanted to be heard, so I gave her a reason.

The lacy bikini underwear she wore came apart with two tugs once I had her situated against the car.

"Midnight." Her whimpered version of my name energized me to get her in my mouth quicker.

With the bend of her knees on my shoulders, I traced my name across the center of her with the tip of my tongue.

Between languid licks and strong sucks against the pebbled nub of her core, I reminded her of things that she was acting like she had forgotten.

"Who am I?" I asked before sipping the messy juices of her enjoyment.

"Midnight." She whined while simultaneously squeezing her thighs around my face.

"Who are you?"

"Midnight's Bloom."

That's all I needed to hear, to know, and the way that I ravaged her after the proclamation was all that she needed to remember.

Something primal charged through me when I felt her legs begin to quake and I exchanged the quick flick of my tongue for sinking strokes that dismantled her logical speech patterns.

"Oh. Good. Always. Yes." She squirmed to press harder against me. I felt her body racing to release. I let her take control of her ecstasy, let her use my face to find bliss. She didn't let herself down, pushing her pulsating pussy into my mouth like it would run away if she didn't feed it to me.

I knew the exact moment that she climaxed, felt her warm wet rush when she flooded my lips. I didn't drown though, just lapped that goodness right on up.

Adjusting myself, I gave her a few seconds to gather herself before asking, "You wanna take this to our spot? This would be a lot more fun with a bed."

She hesitated a little, twisting her skirt down and flattering her shirt.

"I shouldn't have let you do that." She was shaking her head no while speaking to me but I felt like she was scolding herself. "That was wrong."

"Wrong?" I stepped to pull her into my arms. "Bloom-"

I had never seen her look so lost. She just kept shaking her head as she pulled away from me.

"I'm still getting married. I have to."

"Why?" The demanding bass in my voice must have shocked her because she jumped before looking me in the eye. "Why do you have to get married?"

"I signed a contract with my father," her voice pleaded as her hands flopped at her sides.

Regret stamped across that pretty face of hers, and I fought the urge to kiss it away.

"If I don't get married in a few months, the board will get to choose the next leader," she explained.

Pricks of pain pranced through my chest as the realization set in. She was ending us. I had finally found someone that I felt comfortable with, who helped me feel like a person again, and she would belong to someone else.

CHAPTER TWENTY-SIX

Terrence

I turned the metal ratchet that my father had handed over even harder, tightening the bolt down further and further. The tension winding through me was just as tight and coiled. Everything that I had worked for was so close. Business expansion, community development, mentorship, and all the things I cherished. All the things that my family instilled in me as life necessities were in my grasp, were right there on the other side of a fiery woman who had scorched her way across my life.

"The car didn't do it." My father's gruff voice cut through my thoughts. We were working on his crystal blue 1972 Buick Electra 225, better known as a Deuce and a Quarter. It seemed that both my father and I were on the verge of having dreams come true. Although he had three other cars that he had rebuilt over the years in a garage out back, the Deuce and a Quarter was his crown jewel.

"I know." I huffed back.

Answering didn't keep me from twisting.

Deftly, he stopped the tool and took it from my hands.

"You tear up my car and I'ma have to tear you up." He couldn't whoop my ass, but I respected him enough to let him believe that he could.

"Let's talk about it, son."

"Talk about it?" My elbow bumped against a car part and I winced.

"Yes, that's what adults do. Talk about their thoughts. You can throw in some feelings sometimes too."

He bent at the waist to use the ratchet to tighten another piece near the motor.

"I thought the point of this," I moved my hand across the plane of the car. "That us fixing cars was to not talk about feelings. You know, let the work take your mind off the issue until it goes away?"

"Well tell that to your face," he said, pointing the tool in my direction. "It's doing some kind of droopy, pathetic thing. The last time I saw that look was when you found out cheap cologne didn't go on the places below the waist."

My brother, Trystan, had to get it from somewhere.

"It's not that." I picked up a rag and wiped at random blemishes on the car. "It's a woman."

My father, who had turned his attention back to the car, quickly popped up. "You say you got a lady?"

"She's not my lady. In the past, she was-" I paused to consider the words I would use to describe Regina to my father. "She was an option for fun, but she's a coworker now. She's boujee, bossy, and smart-mouthed-"

"The good ones usually cause a little trouble."

"Yea," I nodded. "She's also considerate, hilarious, and fun to be around. She makes me laugh."

"Then what's the problem?"

"She wants to get married, and has to do it pretty soon."

Pops only grunted.

"I don't know if I can ever get married again."

"But you considered it, and you considered it with her?"

I nodded my head to affirm. I had thought about her in that way. I could see her as my wife. I could imagine being with her day and night. She would make a hell of a partner.

My father grunted again before speaking.

"You've always been good at whatever you put your mind to." He leaned his forearms on top of the car roof. "When you left that good-paying job to open your first shop, I thought *That girl done passed away and took my son's mind with her*, but it worked. Then when you started buying up all these little shops, fixing them up, and naming them Brothers T, I was skeptical, but you made it work. In less than ten years, you created an empire. All of us are better for it."

"But what if I fail?"

He shrugged. "Haven't you failed before? What did you do then?"

I understood what my father was saying, but he didn't understand what this failure could cost.

"With the way Valerie passed," I squeezed my eyes shut. "I wouldn't want to be the cause of another heartache." Other words got stuck somewhere between my heart and lips. My sanity and heart were on the line. I struggled through regaining myself after Valerie. I wasn't sure that I could do it again.

"That wasn't your fault." My mind knew that he was telling the truth, but everywhere else was still trying to buy into the notion. "Even if it was, don't you think you've locked yourself away for long enough?"

My office at Strong was nothing like my office at the auto shop. I could fit my entire original garage in my new shiny office that even came with an en-suite restroom. I could live in the deluxe executive suite. Between the plush sofa, conference table, and a huge television screen that connected to all the brand-new devices they provided, I felt more like Tyson, my dapper brother, than myself. I felt like I had stepped back into the life that had been scratched off track, the life that I had originally worked hard to achieve.

"I never thought that I would step away from the day-to-day of Brothers T," I explained to Mr. Strong as we rode in the back of the chauffeured car. He had offered to take me to lunch to celebrate my first day. I had thought about Regina and whether she would be there. Her office wasn't far from mine, basically next door, but I hadn't seen her.

"I'm glad to have you here." Reginald's robust voice filled the car. He had been a man of power for a great portion of his life and his authoritativeness spilled into every detail of his appearance and actions.

"You're glad, even though your daughter will be hiring someone else?"

"I told her that she could make the decision. I just gave her some input." He looked out the window then. "I like the way that you handle yourself. I like that you are a hard-working family man with a genuine spirit. I still think that you could have been a good match for Regina, but since I was already pushing her to do this for selfish reasons, I wanted to provide her with some choices."

My thoughts traveled back to the beauty of Regina.

"There's a banquet coming up. There'll be a lot of important philanthropists there with big hearts and even wider wallets." Reginald turned to me. "I believe in what you're trying to do. You may not be my son-in-law, but I want you to be a part of the Strong family in some way. Come to the event and let's generate some buzz for the center."

I wanted to ask if Regina would be there. I needed to keep a level head, stay focused, and her presence usually made that difficult.

"Regina will attend. She's guiding my last business project: a new stadium." He smiled in my direction. "I'm glad that I have you two on my team. If I -"

His words trailed off and he frowned, rattled his head around, and then cocked it to one side.

"I- you and my Regina should-" He blinked but didn't finish the sentence.

He stared off into space for a bit longer than normal. He had been doing that more often now, not finishing sentences, zoning out while we were playing golf.

"My daughter is complicated." Reginald broke through the stark silence with overloud words that seemed to pick up where he left off several minutes ago. "I had to push her into finding her way."

He swung his usually bright coal eyes away from the window to land on me and nodded.

"She'll get to where she needs to be and I need you to be there when she does." The stern flat expression that cloaked his face belied the importance of his words. He was preparing her and possibly me for a change.

I grew up with men. My dad had three brothers who were several years older than him. My grandmother had explained to me in a random moment before her death that my dad was her 'change of life' child. She wasn't expecting him but was happy to love him all the same. My uncles were old school, and while they were alive and able they taught us how to be men. They taught us about manhood, brotherhood, and Lewis-hood.

I had no clue what Reginald Strong meant about Regina and her complications, but I did know that he was testing me. He was sizing me up with his stare, trying to measure if I would bend against pressure. I didn't. I wouldn't. I met the center of his pupils with my own until an understanding was formed without words that I wouldn't fold if a time came when he needed me to stand.

When we pulled up to a renovated two-story office building, I looked over to Mr. Strong.

"I thought we were going to lunch?"

"We are." He leaned forward to speak with the driver. "This isn't the bistro, why have we stopped here?"

The driver's face was full of concern as he swung his gaze back to Reginald.

"You instructed me to drive here, sir. This is your tailor. You said-"

"I know what I said," Reginald flared as he bit out the words. "I just bought a suit yesterday, why would I have you bring me here?"

The young man looked nervous at Reginald's sudden rage. It was awkward for me to see my mentor slipping out of his normal self.

"I need some new suits." I piped in. "If I'm going to attend the dinner you mentioned, I'll need some suits."

Mr. Strong pivoted his eyes toward me before allowing his head to follow. With crumpled brows, he reviewed my attire.

"Yes. You do. If you are going to work with me, you'll need to look the part." He nodded as both his shoulders and face relaxed. "Very well then, let's get you fitted."

"That's a plan."

The driver swallowed and let out a sigh.

Mr. Strong had gotten out of the car when I patted the young man's shoulder and said: "Thank you."

"No, thank you." His eyes were wide as saucers as he shook his head. "I can tell that he trusts you. Lately, he's been more- unsure about things. He gets upset about it and blames me, but I'm only doing what he tells me. It's like different people are battling to be him."

"How long has this been happening?" I inquired.

"The first time I noticed it was after my birthday, so less than a year ago." The driver shook his head. "I thought I was trippin', and then it happened a few more times. I ain't say anything because I need this job. Strong has been a good boss, and the benefits I get here keep my daughter with asthma pumps."

I nodded and patted the young man's shoulder again before giving him my business card and two hundred dollars in cash.

"Mr. Strong is a very private man, so let's keep his 'unsure' moments between us and these four doors. Contact me if anything seems out of sorts. Your job is secure; I'll make sure to speak with his daughter about the situation."

Pictures of them greeted me before I could get two feet in the door. Their haunting grins menaced me as I pushed through the front desk area of the hotel. As I made my way through the grand building, her parents' smiling faces sat on large golden easels, were plastered at eye-level around columns, and mounted perfectly flush on the ballroom doors. The broken part of me, the part that was still a work in progress, that had survived the havoc after her death, but still shook when I walked into the hotel, that part of me wanted to take off in a sprint and not look back. My steps slowed and my mind raced as I neared the ballroom. It was their anniversary party. Strong didn't mention who the party was for and for the life of me I couldn't understand why I hadn't asked. I had been so caught up in the business possibilities that I didn't even consider who the function was celebrating.

Valerie had always looked like her mother, short slender nose, striking tight eyes, and full pouty lips, but wore facial expressions like her father. I could see traces of her smile in the photo outside of the ballroom proclaiming 'Happy Anniversary Pastor and Sister Jacobs'. Before Valerie passed away, her family had made their dislike of me crystal clear. Afterward, their disdain was palpable. I hadn't taken care of their daughter. They had trusted me with her and I had failed them, just as they had predicted. The last words that Dianne Jacobs said to me as they lowered her daughter, my wife, into the ground replayed in my head. *I should have took my baby and locked her away the moment she told us about you. You weren't there when she needed you the most, and she's gone because of it.'*

I couldn't make my feet move forward into the room to face them, to face the walking memories of her. I turned to leave. My mind rotated through a list of plausible excuses for not showing up as I moved through the empty hallway. There would be no witnesses to my escape. Mr. Strong would be upset, and I would miss some partnerships, but facing Dianne Jacobs was not an option.

"Would you listen? Slow down." The words had come from a man's voice.

I hadn't taken two more steps before I heard Regina's unmistakable attitude. I turned around to see her exiting the ballroom.

"Go find you some business." Her voice was as brisk and annoyed as her steps.

"Dammit Regina, just put the jacket on." The man whisper-yelled as he rushed after her.

"I have one father." Her neck rolled back and her voice rose with frustration that the man in front of her didn't seem ready for. "Just one and he is not in this hallway."

"For the sake of me and him, cover this trampy piece of cloth up." He pushed the coal-colored hunk of material toward Regina's chest. " Put the damn jacket on."

I was content to watch the scene unfold, to let Regina argue with the guy she had chosen. That was until his hand formed a grip on her arm, tightened to the point that her skin bubbled over his bony fingers, and he yanked her to him. I didn't have a claim to Regina. We weren't in a relationship and had stopped all friendly activities, but I wouldn't stand by while he touched her like that. She was too special to be handled like that. She deserved better.

I stepped forward then, just a little closer to the two. I knew that Regina could handle herself, but something turned inside of me. Twisted.

My feet moved me nearer to the pair and my fist tightened before I could even think to do so.

"How are you, Regina?" I spoke to her but eyed the fool who had grabbed her. He needed to understand that she wasn't alone in this world. Regina wasn't some woman without her voice or a force of people behind her. If he couldn't respect her voice, then I would resort to force.

His eyes adjusted to my height and steady glare. His weak-ass knew it was a losing battle, so he made a wise decision to drop his hand.

"I'm fine, Terrence." Her voice was icy as she cut her eyes in his direction before stepping back from him and closer to me.

I cringed at the use of the name. I missed the way that she purred the word *'Night'* in my ear.

"You're Terrence Lewis." The creep stretched out the hand that he had tugged on Regina with. "You're the new consultant."

I shook his hand with an extra tight grip.

"You've done your research," I observed. I already knew who he was. Hindenburg. The lame-ass Regina had chosen to marry.

"I'm aware of all major new hires to the company," he slid his hands into his pockets and reared back. "Even temporary ones."

"What role have you been hired for?" I asked, knowing he had no official title.

Regina patted a hand against my shoulder and interrupted the space and opportunity that I was giving the idiot to speak up or step up.

"Terrence, would you be a dear and walk me back into the ballroom? I wouldn't want to embarrass anyone."

There was a slight hesitation on my part. I didn't want to enter the party. Valerie's parents were in there, but I also didn't want to wimp out and leave Regina with lame-ass.

It was the way that she slid her slim hand around the bulk of my forearm. It was the way that she pulled in close to me and the expression of need that she gave without any words. It was the rapid pace of her heartbeat and the tightness of her voice that made me agree.

"I got you." I pressed a hand against hers. "I'm always available to you."

I made sure that he could hear the words too. I needed him to understand that although she took the actual steps on her own, Regina had an army behind her. Forget thinking twice about harming her, the thought should never generate in his mind to disrespect her.

She moved first. I stayed a pace behind to sneer at the trifling jerk and remind him to check himself in the future.

"It's all good my man." He tried to add a chuckle to his words as he threw his hands up in surrender, but there was no joking about the situation.

There wasn't a need to answer him, so I focused my attention on Regina and the fact that I was about to attend an event that I hadn't thought of in over a decade.

We moved into the ballroom together, and I could feel his beady ass eyes burning holes into the back of my head.

Damn right, Regina walked away with me. I made up my mind at that moment, that no matter how my last relationship ended, I was ready to start over. I wanted to try again with Regina, even if it meant failure. Seeing her with Hendrix had triggered something. She had chosen him, but I knew she needed me by her side. The moment that she stepped away from him, the moment that she leaned into me for protection, I knew that I would never stop covering her. I knew that I would never stop caring for her. If anyone would support her in a fake marriage or any marriage, it would be me, not some sleazy dude who tried to control her wardrobe. I wasn't sure how to tell her that I changed my mind, so I walked next to her, determined to be by her side until the best time came for me to reveal that I could do it. That I would do it. I would be her husband on paper until I was a husband for real.

The room was everything that someone of status would dream of. Large chandeliers, vivid decorative centerpieces, beautiful lights, and coordinated covered chairs. There were people everywhere. The Jacobs were a big deal. I knew this when Valerie and I started dating. They reminded me of their notoriety when Valerie and I wanted to get married, with every mention of them in the paper or on the news, and each smug grin that reinforced that I had married out of my league. They were influential.

"Thank you." Regina broke through my complex thoughts with simple words.

"What happened?" We scooted through the room together with nods and smiles as she gave small cues with her body as to the direction we should travel.

Just like in the bedroom, she let me lead, but I always listened to know the next step.

"This dress." She frowned. "He didn't like my dress."

I looked her over, her noticeable curves and round breasts. Even though just a small portion of her breasts peeked out through the sweetheart neckline, the skin-tight clingy material made it impossible to miss her knockout body. *What man wouldn't like her in the form-fitting dress?* She looked damn good and thinking about what she allowed me to do to that lush body cut through my concentration like a hot knife through butter.

"To credit his consistency, he doesn't like my drinking, cursing, or my sense of humor either," Regina added before she ordered a cocktail from the bar.

"All of your finer points," I joked.

"He wanted me to wear his jacket to cover up all of this." She flared her hand across her breasts, drawing my eyes to the place where I had once spent time nestled. "Such a prude."

She received her drink, and I placed a tip in the jar before we moved back into the flow of the growing crowd.

"You chose to marry him," I countered. We needed to talk somewhere private. We needed to talk about my past and our future together out of the public eye.

For once Regina was quiet. I shouldn't have said that because I didn't give her many options in that department, but it didn't make her being with someone else any more bearable. Before I could apologize, Reginald and his wife swept in and took to our sides ushering us to the front of the room.

"So glad that you could make it Terrence," Mrs. Strong beamed. She was next to me as we found our table. "There are a few people that I want to introduce you to."

Two seconds later, I knew who those people were, and all I wanted to do was run.

Her eyes were so similar to Valerie's that I had to hold back a gasp.

Mrs. Strong opened her mouth to make the introductions, but Dianne Jacobs spoke my name first.

"Terrence?" She blinked a few times and squinted. "Oh, my word, honey look. It's Terrence."

I didn't know what to expect when we saw each other. It had been years since I handed over most of Valerie's belongings to them. I hadn't kept their daughter. I couldn't return her, so I gave them what I had left of her. What they had left.

Regina and I had hardly been in the room long, but I couldn't stay. Facing the Jacobs' was more than I bargained for.

"I left my phone in the car," I blurted out awkwardly as I made my exit. It was the best excuse that I could come up with.

I was near the front of the hotel when Regina reached me.

"We both know how to exit, huh?" She gave a weary smile. "What's going on?"

I hadn't moved fast enough, and I wouldn't have stopped for anyone else but her.

"I should have turned around when I saw their pictures."

"The Jacobs'? How do you know them?" She asked slowly as if the answer was forming in her mind as she spoke. "Valerie. The daughter that passed away, she was your wife?"

I confirmed her conclusion as Regina stepped closer to me and placed a hand on my shoulder. The worried look on her face bothered me.

"Valerie and I married young," I explained trying to find something in the lobby to look at unrelated to their event. "She left this earth while she was still young, but she was a Jacobs."

"I don't know what to say besides that I hurt for you," she said wrapping one hand around mine and placing the other on my shoulder. "Maybe you should talk to them."

"Do you know what they said about me?" I ground out the words while trying to restrain my resentment and the mounting residual anger over the situation. "They shut me out and treated me like I'd done something wrong. I did what I thought I was supposed to."

I cleared my throat hoping that she didn't catch the hitch in my voice.

Regina wrapped her arms around my waist as she looked up into my eyes. With all the gusto that she could muster she stated, "Respectfully as possible, fuck them."

There was no way that I could avoid chuckling at that.

A few church members were still entering and shot a glare in our direction at her words.

"Fuck them too." She added.

That made me laugh.

"I mean it." Regina added. "I don't care about this being a church event or him being a pastor. You're the most caring person that I know. You take care of kids that aren't even yours for free. You give from your heart. If you took care of your wife only half as well as you take care of your family then I know that whatever took her from this earth was out of your control."

I lifted my head to look toward the ceiling, feeling like Regina was a divine intervention, a sign that I needed to move past the hurt.

"If you want to walk out of this door right now and not look back, I'm with you." Regina continued. "If you want to walk back through the door to get this money for your group, and make these connections for your business, then I'm with you. I'm for you. I got your back and I'll be by your side if you need me. It's about you. Don't let them be the determining factor."

I swallowed.

Regina let go of me then, took a step back and looked me in the eye.

"Do you trust me?" Regina held out her hand, her eyes wide with expectation, as she waited for me to answer.

Looking at her hand, I thought about how I had asked her the same question before.

I didn't want to go back in there and face that rejection again, but I placed my hand in hers.

"I don't know about in there," I answered truthfully. "I trust you here."

She smiled.

"Believe that I have your back. Cherry will take the pastor's wife down if she steps out of line. Moms don't play about hers and you know that my father handpicked you to take care of his company and his daughter."

"But you didn't choose me," I reminded pulling her closer to my body.

"If you can't walk back into that room, were you and I really ever an option?" She asked while smoothing the frame of my mustache with her thumb. "If I said yes to you would you say yes to me?"

I didn't answer in words but pressed my mouth against hers. She was inviting as always and welcomed my tongue to what felt like home. The kiss was soft at first but the need to be closer to her surged through me and I pulled her into me. Her arms were around my neck and nothing else mattered.

I wanted to say yes to her, to feel invincible next to her. I wanted to fall into the only woman that saw me hurt and confused but didn't make me feel less for it. She pulled away too quickly for my liking, but I knew that wasn't the time or place to discuss us.

"Regina," I huffed. "We should talk."

"Tonight is about you and the Y.A.M.S and the company," She was stern and her eyes determined. "This, me and you, can't happen right now."

"I ain't worried about your man," I let her know. No bull shit. I didn't care who she had arrived with, I was ready for Regina.

Her eyebrow lifted as she responded, "Me neither." With grace, placed a hand on my cheek and chest as if pressing the confidence she had for me into me. "I'm worried about you. I think that you need this, you need them."

"Nah," I shook my head. "You got everything that's going to make me feel better." I tweaked at her nipple through the dress. "We are in a hotel, you know?"

When her expression didn't change, I sighed and let my head drop. That's when I noticed it, the gold chain, my gold chain.

I ran a finger across the metal. It looked sophisticated on her, elegant with her formal dress where it looked strong on me.

"You were out here rocking my chain and walking with Hindenburg," I stated because it wasn't a question. She had worn it on purpose.

She lifted the necklace and her eyes to mine at the same time.

"Don't worry about all of that," she grinned. "As I said, I got you. Also, maybe I needed a little of you with me tonight."

We went back into the ballroom, and being together made it better.

Diane and Pastor Jacobs were waiting with the Strongs. Both of them looked distressed as all eyes turned toward us.

I walked over to the group and when I smiled, she smiled and pulled me in close to her for the warmest hug I could remember. Something in my chest cracked and fell away. Wrapped tight by the smaller woman my mind strayed to find when this had ever happened before. I wrapped my arms around her too and accepted this first-in-a-lifetime greeting.

"Oh Terrence," she repeated over and over in a sing-song voice.

I wasn't going to cry in front of my new boss, so when tears pricked the back of my eyes, I blinked them back and stepped out of the embrace.

Dianne held onto my arms, examining me like a long-lost relative that showed up for Thanksgiving. When I saw traces of her tears against her cheeks, I knew that they were the result of an internal battle making their way to the surface.

"You've been on my heart." She breathed, both hands crossed at the heart as though she could show it to me. "And here you are. Look at God."

"Amen." Pastor Jacobs said stepping closer to his wife. "Dianne was just praying for you the other day."

Both of them were just as serious as they had always been but the judgment that seemed to fill their faces when I was younger had disappeared.

Mrs. Jacobs rubbed at my shoulder like she wanted to hug me again and I felt the sincerity in her solemn demeanor.

"I didn't know how to or if I should contact you. So, I prayed. We didn't do some things right when Valerie was alive and after she died either. I said some things- I needed someone, something to blame." She moved her hand and swiped at an errant tear.

Pastor Jacobs rubbed circles in the center of his wife's back as she spoke.

"That was my only baby, and I loved her-"

"We loved her with everything in us." Pastor Jacobs joined in.

"I loved her too." I insisted. They had to know that. I had spent so many years trying to prove just how much I loved Valerie to them, and I needed them to know that I meant it.

"We know." he nodded before Dianne continued.

"I was hurting and we iced you out when you needed our support more than anything," her eyes circled upward over her pooling tears before she let them fall back to my face. "I apologize for that, and I know that you did your best for our baby."

She took my hands between hers and I had to look up at the sky to keep the tears back.

"Valerie is at peace, and you should be too." Diane stated.

A piece of me was mended right there in front of half the city. I had felt so broken after her death, so useless. Opening the shops, and mentoring the young men, gave me purpose again. My family started meeting nearly every week to play games and eat food to get me out of the house. Hearing and feeling the understanding from the Jacobs was like another piece had slipped into place for a rebuild of me.

Their reassurance was something I didn't know that I needed.

CHAPTER TWENTY-SEVEN

Regina

I nearly fell on the floor when Mrs. Jacobs and Terrence hugged. My Terrence was their past son-in-law. Cherry, Daddy, and I all exchanged glances of disbelief as we watched the First Lady mess up her pristine makeup to deliver a heartfelt message. My family and I had never met Valerie. My father joined the church nine years ago as they expanded from a well-known ministry into a megachurch. He had caught wind of their super-plex ambitions, which included a stadium-sized praise facility, grade school, senior living apartments, and health care center. My father wanted to be on the ground floor and went above and beyond to befriend the pastor and his family. We had learned about their daughter's untimely passing, and although there were pictures of her, there was no mention of a husband. There were no pictures of her and Terrence anywhere.

I rubbed my hands over each other and watched as both pastor and wife hugged the man that I had grown to care about.

Somewhere along the way, my father's attendance at the church became real. It was no longer an act when he stood and lifted his hands. He walked with the pastor diligently, sought his counsel, and guided him in the business world. He became a friend and a believer. He credited Pastor Jacobs and his wife for being the real deal.

Mrs. Jacobs excused herself. "I have to assemble my glam team; I'll be back shortly."

My mother and I settled at the table as my father, Terrence, and Pastor Jacobs stood and spoke nearby.

"Fine young man." Pastor clapped Terrence's broad shoulder as he spoke to my father. "Known him since he was a pimple-faced freshman chasing after my daughter."

I cringed. I didn't want to be jealous or feel any negativity toward the deceased, but his daughter was the reason I couldn't have what I wanted. More than ever, I felt drawn to Terrence. We fit. He didn't mock the way I spoke or chastise me for my style. I could be me, free of criticism from him. Physically he was with me, he had given me every part of him, but not the most important piece. With Terrence, there was no pretending. I could fall in love with him. I knew it when he brushed my face with his fingertips in the morning, when he couldn't find the beat in a song to dance, and when he cracked lame jokes that no one understood but me. I would fall in love with him. I also knew that he wouldn't be there to catch me. I knew that he would let my heart slip and shatter.

"Thirty-five years. Amen, good people. Amen." Pastor Jacobs spoke as he loosened a button on his suit jacket and placed his hands on the podium.

Everyone in the room had taken their seats by the time Pastor Jacobs stood proudly at the front of the room on the stage and the First Lady sat next to him on a high-backed mock throne.

Like in life, I was stuck between Terrence, on my left, and Hendrix on my right. I only wanted one of them, but it seemed like this wouldn't be the end of our awkward meetings if Terrence continued to work at the company and I married Hendrix.

"It hasn't been easy, has it baby?" He looked at Mrs. Jacobs.

Although she was agreeing with how hard their relationship had been, her smile was wide like sunshine. I couldn't help but remember waking up next to Terrence and I understood her grin.

"It's been blessed though. Not free of stress but fulfilling." He tapped the podium before he glanced at his wife. "Don't she look good y'all? Stand up, Diane. Alright, hurry up and sit back down. I don't wanna give anybody any ideas. Sorry fellas, she's all mine. I'm a pastor, but I fight for mine."

"How crass," Hendrix scoffed in a low voice.

"I think it's cute. He's just joking."

The audience laughed. They were used to our pastor's humor.

"She shouldn't even be on the stage with him." Hendrix's words came out in a sneer and it made me wonder if he would want the same when we were married. I wondered if he would want me to sit in the background somewhere while he ran the show or if he thought I would be a quiet nonparticipant in my family business. That's when it hit me how much I didn't know about Hendrix. We had grown up together and I knew the basics about his history, but I couldn't explain his core beliefs or even say that I shared any of his values. I didn't know what he valued. I had chosen him based on my father's word, our past, his business knowledge, and ultimately his availability to marry. Sitting next to him at the table, I wasn't sure that even my father's declaration was enough to make me go through with the task.

"It's their wedding anniversary though, he's supposed to," I stopped talking because he completely turned his gaze away from me and shook his head mid-sentence.

He had dismissed me without a word. That was strike two.

My mother caught the murderous glare that I shot my date and gave her head a subtle shake of 'no'. My mother was not for the drama, unless it was necessary.

I gave my attention back to the pastor; Hendrix was going to make me curse him out in front of my parents and all of the church members.

"We've come here to celebrate love and commitment, how faithfulness will lead to a life of fruitfulness. I almost stopped believing. I almost stepped away from my calling. Y'all don't hear me. Some of y'all perfect saints never wanted to give up. Some of y'all never been on your knees in prayer wondering why you were chosen to carry the burdens."

He batted at the air and looked away as the crowd responded with 'Say that' and 'Preach Pastor'.

I could feel Hendrix's distaste. We may have been dressed for the red carpet, but we still had foot stomping, hand clapping, hand raising souls.

"I almost stepped right on out of the pulpit and shunned the blessing of having my wife. Some of the newer members don't know. Some of the original members may not remember, but my only child, my sweet baby girl, transitioned, got her wings, and went on to glory ten years ago."

Terrence folded his top lip over the bottom and his gaze dropped to the table. I placed a hand on his arm when the pastor continued.

"During this time of celebration and reflection, thinking about all the great years and triumphant moments, I feel a sense of sadness. Not just because my daughter is gone, but because I shunned the man that she loved. When I look at my wife, I can't imagine life without her. In my pain, I didn't see him as a young man who had lost his wife. Through my grief, I did some un-pastor like things, said some not-so-nice words, and felt some real harsh feelings for this young brother when all he did was love my daughter and follow the path before him. That realization shook me and weighed me. My son through love is here tonight."

The audience applauded as the pastor smiled in our direction.

"Terrence Lewis is here tonight and I'm so proud of the smart young businessman that he's become. I know Valerie is proud of you. I'm grateful for the healing tonight. I wish you all of the happiness and joy that you can find in all of your future endeavors."

When the pastor looked from Terrence to me and winked, I pulled my hand back to my lap. *Had he noticed something between the two of us?*

"Alright y'all, let's eat and then move our feet." Pastor and Diane walked down from the stage among claps and whistles.

"They look good standing there together." My mother smiled and scooted closer to me. We were the only two left at the table.

I shouldn't have looked. I knew Midnight's body with my eyes closed. All of it. Every inch. Standing there with a fresh lineup on his beard, his locks braided back neatly, and a tailored suit, Terrence activated more of my want for him. He was self-assured, a hand tucked into his pocket as he listened to the elder men speak. There wasn't a trace of the emotions that had played out earlier. Power encapsulated the three as others in the room began clamoring to get closer. Conversations happened near and around them, but nothing broke through the hold that Terrence took once he spoke about his passion: Helping the community.

"Why isn't he the choice again?" Cherry asked.

I turned my eyes away and played with the napkin on the table as I concocted a simple answer.

"According to his cousin, he's not over his ex," I bit at my bottom lip recalling the conversation that Mali and I had. She was resolved that Terrence was defective, unable to love again after Valerie. With a sigh, I added, "I don't want to live in her shadow."

"Understandable," my mother nodded her head as she looked over the man I wished was mine again. "But I sure would have fun trying to bring him out of the shadows and into the sunshine."

Before I could gag at my mother, Hendrix was next to me with a shawl.

"Wrap this around you and introduce me to the pastor," he insisted and I wanted to swat his mosquito-acting ass away.

I'm not even sure where he got the chiffon wrap, but I was tired of arguing with him. Between juggling the daunting tasks of pressing down my desire for Terrence, containing the rage Hendrix evoked, and ignoring the possibility that my father could not be at the next anniversary party due to his health, my emotions were burned out for the day.

The rest of the night went like that. Terrence captivated everyone he met and Hendrix tried to gain an audience while using me as his entry.

"No one wants to talk about money here Hendrix," I explained what I felt he should have already known after the fourth group of business-affiliated people dispersed with a sudden interest in drink refills. "You have to talk about our projects as though they are already funded and ready to go. Show your excitement, show how much you don't need them, and then they will reach out during business hours because they want to be a part of this wonderful new thing that you are doing."

He should know better. He had grown up around business all of his life.

"I know how business works, Regina." He nearly spat through clenched teeth. "If your little friend wasn't in here hogging up all of the investors with his golden boy routine then there wouldn't be a problem."

Terrence, although occupied with a conversation, had made a point to find me with his eyes throughout the night. Every once in a while, he would smile in my direction, making the droning voice of Hendrix bearable.

"Pay attention," Hendrix growled. "No wonder people are walking away. If you're making goo-goo eyes with that fool, they're going to wonder about him too. You chose me, so act like it."

The chuckle came out from a dark place inside of me. It wasn't my normal laugh. It sounded more like emergency glass shattering, alarm bells ringing, or crazy escaping.

Hendrix immediately took a step back.

After a night of listening to his dribble and condescending remarks, mixed with a few drinks, I had it. I was done and he was about to get what he had been poking for. Church association or not, he had tap-danced all over my last nerve and hit the red button on my wrath.

As soon I twisted my mouth and lifted a hand to put Hendrix in his place, I was being tugged away by my shoulders.

"Dance with me."

It wasn't a question, but a command. Pressed against the warmth of his hard body, I had no option but to oblige.

"He don't know me," I repeated with a twist of my neck and roll of my eyes at Hendrix's disrespect. My blood was still boiling even though I was next to the man that I wanted to be near.

"Relax, HBCU." Terrence laughed. "I do know you. I could see it in your eyes a mile away, that you were about to blow. He was about to get all of your years of hood training from college right in front of the deacon board."

We were standing near the dance floor now a safe distance from Hendrix.

"Dance with me." he requested again and I looked at him. Those honey eyes were fixed on my mouth and all the madness of the night melted away. The building frustration fell away. Terrence was the only one left as though he had always been the only one there.

"You don't dance." I reminded him, but my body moved closer. My mind was already lost on him, and everything else was following.

"You need a dance, and I owe you one." He said, sliding his hand around mine. It was warm, sending currents of need for him straight to my core.

"For what?" I whispered. I wanted to gain control of my breath again.

We were moving then, walking into the crowd in the designated dance area.

I didn't feel my feet anymore as he wrapped his bulky arms around me.

"For this. For pushing me into living again. I wouldn't have walked into this room if I hadn't seen you."

I rested my hands on his shoulders as we swayed from side to side. Terrence truly had no moves on the floor except the two-step. Even then, he seemed to be counting in his head, but that didn't matter. He was out there for me. He was on the dance floor looking foolish for me.

"You're bad at this," I mumbled into his shoulder because my face felt good there. All of me felt good with him.

"Thank you for that encouragement. I'll keep that in mind the next time I pull you away from embarrassment and possible viral rant."

I stopped talking then. The mix of his baritone, cologne, and soft music scrambled my senses and it took all of my dwindling power to remain upright with my legs closed. Terrence could get it on the dance floor, and I wouldn't have a sliver of shame.

"Bloom."

The name pushed electricity through my body as I was reminded of the origin. He liked the way that I opened for him. I liked that he was opening up to me, that he was trying new things for me. I liked that he listened to me.

"Do you want to marry Hindenburg?" He asked the question against my earlobe so close that it felt like he had jumped inside my brain. It was bad enough that I already felt like he was inching his way into my heart.

That was the only question that could have broken the moment. The question that brought reality crashing back. I was supposed to marry someone and it couldn't be the man that I wanted.

"You know me so well, what do you think?" I pushed away from Terrence because I was tired of playing that game with him. It hurt too much to be so near the man that I wanted more than anyone else to be my partner during this charade and not have him. He had been a friend, he had a head for business, he knew how to talk to the community, and he had a heart. He had made the cut with my father, but he didn't want a future with me enough to let the past go.

I made myself scarce for the rest of the night. I didn't return to Hendrix, but I couldn't be near Terrence either. There were hallways to explore, bathroom walls to be held up, and a room that could be rented for disappearing at a small fee.

CHAPTER TWENTY-EIGHT

Regina

Hendrix made the bottom of my feet itch. Just looking at him made me twist up my face like onions were being sliced over unwashed asses in a locker room after a game. I wanted to try for my father. I wanted to like him just enough to tolerate his overbearing ass. No. There was no way. Monday morning came quicker than I wanted it to and since Hendrix was already in town for the anniversary dinner, he decided to join me at the office bright and early.

"I know you were a little put off by my words the other night, but I have confidence that you can get the hang of being a respectable woman that knows how to support her man quietly."

That was how we started the morning. That was how he greeted me.

When I turned and walked away, dismissing his ignorant salutation, he followed.

"What's first on the agenda?" He questioned. "I need to speak to you and your father about the new Cricket Stadium. I know the representative is here today for a preliminary conversation."

That caught my attention. It was information that hadn't been broadcast. Select people knew about our dealing and he wasn't on the list.

"My grandfather." He answered the question before I spoke it. "As a team owner, he hears things about opportunities in other sporting areas."

"This isn't a meeting for you to crash Hendrix." I tried to explain gently even though he had not spared my feelings once.

"Your father already stated that you are taking over things and to defer to your ass for kissing as needed." He smirked because he knew that my dad was doing the hokey pokey dance out the door. His left arm and left foot were already there.

Those words should have done something other than turn my stomach. I didn't want his lips anywhere near my face, ass, or space in between.

His pleading eyes found the one last soft spot I had left concerning him and I agreed to let him tag along. After all, I needed to gauge his business acumen in a meeting anyway.

I nodded and kept walking to my father's office. A happy Hendrix was right on my heels not missing a beat.

When I entered with a guest my dad quickly hid his surprise.

"I thought that you would be attending this meeting alone, dear." He observed.

"Hendrix volunteered to sit in and provide some insight from a team owner perspective." I bluffed and shot my father the sweetest smile that I could. He would know that I was faking it, but I also needed to know if the man I could marry would at least match with me business-wise. Socially we were as incompatible as two could be, but this was for my father and our family business. If Hendrix could cut it in the boardroom, I would forgive the tension we had in every other room.

"Very well then." My father nodded.

The meeting went every way but well. Hendrix spoke over me at every turn, made subtle jabs at the visiting gentlemen's accent, and completely ignored the overview I had briefed him on before the meeting started. He made us look both dumb and arrogant, which completely pissed my father off. My father was always cognizant of the way we behaved and made sure that we spoke well and dressed nicely. We presented the best of ourselves at all times because he never wanted to add any validity to the stereotypes.

When the meeting was over, my father just stared. I thought something was wrong, that he was having an episode. As we stood in a circle near his desk and the familiar crease in his forehead appeared, I realized he was fine, just at a loss for words. The whole meeting had been equivalent to a nightmare.

"Hendrix," my father spoke slowly and pushed up his glasses. "You were a guest in my house, and as such, I expected a level of respect for myself and my daughter that was not shown here today."

"Mr. Strong, I understand-" he interrupted.

"And if you already understand, then you're not listening, you're not learning. That's the problem. I'm looking for partners. Do you know what a partnership looks like? I need people who can listen. When you talk, you're repeating what you already know. Listening wins loyalty. We need to learn more about the client and cater to their needs."

The intensity of my father's voice rose with every syllable he spoke.

"With all due respect, I am a grown man, and I-"

"Take your grown-self out of my office! Matter a fact, get out of my building, and don't step foot in my city until you learn the real got-damn meaning of respect!" My father loosened his tie and was so close to Hendrix that I thought he would hit him. "I run all of this shit boy, not you and your penny-valued brain. If you blow up this deal-"

His hands flailed as he yelled. My father rarely yelled, but then he was falling, quickly. He fell so fast that I couldn't catch him and his head hit the large oak desk. He slumped the rest of the way to the ground.

"Daddy!" I screamed. I felt it. I saw it. His eyes were closed and he wasn't moving. One second, he had been the frustrated father I remembered, and the next he was motionless on the floor.

Hendrix froze next to my shaking frame. I was screaming, crying out words that I don't remember, but I remember Hendrix standing mannequin still. I guessed that my hysteria was enough to bring Terrence running from his nearby office because I had never called for him. Terrence was just there.

I didn't know why Hendrix had stuck around because it was Terrence's voice that I heard over those screams. My screams. My sobs. It was Terrence who sat me in a corner, spoke to the paramedics as they wheeled my father away, updated the staff, and gave them options to go home with pay. It was Terrence who got in contact with my mother about my father's medical history on the paramedic's cell phone and arranged for a car to pick her up while he drove me behind the ambulance. He did all of that while I watched from another place outside of my body because my father had fallen. I couldn't deal. I had always considered myself strong, but at that moment I couldn't hold more than the tissue to my face. The man that had cherished me had fallen, and I didn't know what to do with that.

Hours had passed and no one could give me definite answers about my father. People had called my cell and even come by the hospital, but I was numb. None of them mattered. Their presence didn't change what had happened or how I felt.

"You gonna drink that coffee or just finger the cup?"

I heard him. He was sitting next to me in the waiting room because I couldn't sit in my father's hospital room. I couldn't see him like that, couldn't watch and wait as my mother did. I couldn't be still, kept reading all the numbers, touching all the cords, asking random people about anything that seemed abnormal. Apparently, people that take out the trash in the hospital wore scrubs too and had no idea about the side effects of head trauma on a patient exhibiting signs of early-onset dementia. I hadn't been sure where Terrence had disappeared to, once he got me situated earlier, but one call from my mother and he was there ushering me out of the room and to the cafeteria to get coffee.

Their version of coffee was disgraceful, but it was something to do with my hands. It was something that I could do, something that I could control. I kept spinning my finger inside the circular bottom of the cardboard container.

"That's not funny." I didn't look at him when I spoke, I just kept watching the door and waiting for something to change or someone to tell me this was just a dream.

"She speaks." He laughed. "I was beginning to miss that pretty voice of yours."

I won't lie, I did crack a smile because his compliment thawed me a little.

"There it is," he said, taking my hand in his and pressing his lips to the skin there. "I needed that smile."

As quickly as I took my eye away from the door, my mother was rushing through it.

"He's awake and asking for you," My mother was moving at a near sprint.

Leaping out of my seat, I dropped Terrence's hand and was next to my mother before she finished the words.

"Oh my God, finally."

I was already dragging my mother toward the room when she called out to the man I had left behind.

"You," she pointed to Terrence who had stayed in his seat." He asked for you specifically."

I didn't care who my father had asked for, we all went to his room.

It looked like he had aged years in the hours it had taken for him to wake up, or maybe it was the lighting and the absence of his permanent suit.

"Kiddo," my father laughed when Terrence entered the room. He was sitting up like he hadn't been laid out a few minutes ago. "Come over here so we can cut the mustard and chop about the cheese."

His words were slower, hoarse, and slightly unclear. He used words that didn't make any sense to me, but my dad seemed confident in them.

I looked at my mother, who lifted her shoulders and whispered: "He woke up like this."

"How are you feeling?" Terrence asked, stepping forward to the bed.

"Got smog on the nog'," he tapped a fist against his forehead." I need your help."

"Anything."

"There's a big, large-" he motioned his hands far apart to demonstrate. "There's a big-money thing. It's at the place with the queen because they want to play bowling with baseball when we make the field. See them and seal it."

His words didn't flow in their natural pace and his choice confused me. Terrence seemed to follow, even when my father's face turned serious.

"Take care of my flowers. If the sky opens, you standstill," He leaned back into the pillows then, as though he had reached the end of his energy, but his eyes remained open.

Something passed between the two of them that had me confused as hell and my mother dabbing at her eyes.

When my father lifted a trembling hand for Terrence to shake and then pulled him in for a tight hug, I wanted to break that shit up. Wouldn't be any passing of torches, because my daddy was coming home dammit. He was not allowed to give up.

"Come here." My father motioned to me and Terrence and then hugged us both. "Team."

After the doctor assured me that my father would be alright and able to return home 'soon', my mother suggested that I go away. She would stay at the hospital and hover, but I had to go. Even my father shooed me away with a cryptic sentence about opening doors at big buildings. Terrence translated that to mean keeping the business going.

When we arrived at my apartment building, I had Terrence drive me into the parking garage just to extend the time that I was with him. The time when I wasn't alone and had the comfort of him near. I couldn't go up. I didn't want to be by myself with my thoughts. I didn't want to figure it out alone.

"Terrence," I placed a hand on the door handle but didn't step out. The words were just as stuck as I was. My eyes fell against the lavender color of my favorite pair of Ferragamo pumps. I had the very best education that money could buy and I couldn't figure out how to express that I wanted him to stay, that I needed him to wrap those big ass trunk arms around me and hold me in place.

The sound of the truck door opening caused me to look up. He was standing there in front of me, eyes full of something that seemed like compassion and concern. He wasn't ditching me. He wasn't dumping me off and running away but standing and waiting. He was waiting for me and that filled me with both relief and wonder.

"How about I hang out with you so that we can work out a statement?" Terrence asked.

I nodded because I truly didn't want him to go. I didn't want to be without him.

CHAPTER TWENTY-NINE

Terrence

We sat on the sofa of her huge three-bedroom apartment, scribbling out a plan for taking care of her father's business schedule, a statement for the staff, and the start of a plan for the Cricket Stadium. We drank coffee and bounced ideas back and forth in a match of intellect. A few hours in, I couldn't take it anymore. I was used to her. If Regina didn't laugh at least once every thirty minutes, then there was something wrong with the world. My world was not the same without her joy.

"Did you hear about the guy whose whole left side was cut off?" I asked and shut off my laptop, moved to the corner of the couch, and motioned for her to come closer.

"What?" her face twisted in confusion, but she didn't resist coming closer. She moved her notepad to the side and slid into my arms. "You said that his left side was cut off?"

"Yea, but don't worry," I deadpanned as I brought her body against mine. "He's *all right.*"

She paused before mumbling the words out loud.

"Alright? All right." She repeated.

Finally, the burst of laughter that I had missed more than I realized punched out of her. "That is so corny." Regina howled through a cackle.

I couldn't help but join in, chuckling loud from the pit of my stomach because that's where the happiness grew from. Being with her brought me so much joy that it spilled out. It couldn't be contained.

"You know what would be great right now?" She mumbled while snuggling deeper into my hold.

"Sex?" I answered only half playing.

She tapped my thigh with her knuckles but didn't move.

"No, not that," her voice was soft and playful. "When I was a kid, my nanny-"

"You had a nanny?" I interrupted.

She frowned, and I couldn't help but place a kiss at the corner of her jawline.

"Yes, now listen." Her eyes closed as she slid a hand along the side of my leg, and she smiled. "My nanny would sneak in these hard, flat, flower-shaped shortbread cookies that had a hole in the center of it."

"A cookie with a hole in it?"

"Yes," she replied. "They made perfect rings on my fingers. Those were the best cookies I ever had in my life at the time. I used to put one on every finger and bite off the pieces."

"That doesn't sound like a classy rich girl Regina thing." I laughed. "It actually sounds a little unsanitary."

"Oh, I was all about the unsanitary back then." She sounded tired, but that didn't stop her from telling me more. "I used to ride my bike with my candy necklace and candy bracelet every chance that I got to hang out with my cousins."

"Was that often?" I asked.

"Before I hit the double digits, my parents never let me miss a summer."

"You were riding around in the summer eating candy off of your body?"

She nodded her head slowly before mumbling, "Yep."

I frowned at the thought of a pre-teen Regina eating candy that lived on her neck while she rode her bike in the Texas summer sun.

I wanted to ask more but realized by her soft breaths that she had fallen asleep in my arms.

We needed to talk about the contract and our future, but the day had been long, and I was content to end it with her.

She was my peace. Calm rolled over me, pulled me out of the rough with the tide, and left me smooth. I woke up with her in my arms, and I didn't want to start the day any other way.

"Good morning," she stretched the words with her body.

"Morning," I responded with a kiss on her forehead.

"How did I end up in bed?" Regina questioned as she wrapped her arms around my neck.

"I woke you up, and you walked."

"I have no memory of this," She snuggled in closer and pressed a kiss on the underside of my jaw. "But I am glad you made it here with me."

"Me too," I squirmed as Regina pressed pecks against the skin of my neck because it was a new tingly feeling.

Then she changed my view of life with one small action. Regina rumbled her lips against my skin.

I full on burst into loud rolls of laughter as she blew raspberry kisses across the left side of my neck.

"Regina," I huffed in between the spaces of laughter. I tried to scoot my neck away, but I couldn't escape the feeling. I couldn't escape my feelings for her. "That tickles."

The more I laughed, the more she kissed, and I thought I would never stop laughing. I felt like joy had a cut-off point, that a person was allowed a limited supply of happiness in this life before it ran out. With Regina, I felt like joy could be never-ending.

Finally, I folded her entire body in a hug and rolled over so that she would stop.

"I found your tickle spot," Regina sang, repeating the words like a nursery rhyme.

To end the screeching, I kissed her. She may have danced well, but singing was not her calling.

"You did find my only tickle spot," I acknowledged. "And, I found my heart. I found you, and I don't want anyone else to be your husband. I don't want to do another day without you."

"I don't want to be without you either," She confirmed while pulling her arms from my hold to wrap around my neck.

"Can I be your fake husband?" I asked.

Without hesitation, she chuckled out a "Yes."

"Really?" I questioned, almost expecting her to tell me no.

I didn't know if Regina felt what I felt, but I knew that everything about our relationship would be real to me.

"Yes. I can't believe you're going to do this." She beamed as she sat up in bed. Excitement radiated from her. "Wow. I think we can do this."

"We are, and we can."

"Ok. The wedding date is already set a few months away, and right before my dad's official retirement. We need to find a house. I can finally send out an announcement with a name!" As though she just remembered that I was there, she asked, "We have to be together for the next ten years."

That's when she looked unsure. That's the slight second that she looked scared.

I pulled her down to my chest because I needed her to hear my heart when I told her, "As long as you need me, you got me."

I craved Bloom, the sex goddess who took me to unvisited levels of pleasure. I admired Genie, the daughter, and her devotion to her father. I enjoyed silly Regina, the witty friend to my sister-in-law who tried to make me laugh, and I respected Ms. Strong, the fiery businesswoman who understood how to implement complex business plans with ease. In name and on paper, at least, she would be mine.

Later, I made sure that she and her mother were comfortable when visiting Reginald and then distracted her from the pain afterward.

We fell into a routine that concluded with me falling into her each night and our lips finding each other every morning. We rode to work every day, watched movies, and ate dinner together at night.

Regina had gotten the representative to consider giving Strong one more chance. He agreed to keep the already tentatively scheduled meeting in front of the England and Wales Cricket Board, but our presentation would have to be stellar. We knew of one other company, GP Holdings, that would be presenting the same week as us, and because Mr. Strong and his daughter were counting on me, I needed to make the deal.

After checking in at Strong, I left for a meeting with Tyson and Tyriq at Brothers T. There were too many variables happening at once. I was traveling out of the country for the first time. I wanted to seal a deal for my mentor, who was literally losing his mind. I also had to not mess up his business or my own.

My brother Tyriq had always been a good guy, my moral compass sometimes. My brother Tyson was all about business. If anyone had any ideas about how to win in my situation, my brothers would, or so I thought.

"Does that look like the Deep Ellum area to you?" Tyson pushed a phone with the picture of a woman standing in front of a bar closer to my face. "I think that's Main Street. What do you think?"

"I think that I want you to pay attention!" I snapped. Kinnesha Rawlings and Tyson dated all of high school, but Tyson had loved her since elementary school. She had some family issues, and not only left the state but left him too. Her possible reappearance in the area had my brother acting like a bootleg detective to find out if the possibility was true. "Besides, don't you have some connections that can look her up?"

"I'm not trying to have her investigated. How would I tell that story to our grandchildren?" He explained so matter-of-factly, that I almost questioned why I asked.

"Kinny got you bugging out here." I shook my head. "Grandkids, my dude? You haven't talked to her yet."

"She might be back in Dallas." He looked up at me for just a second. "Her profile popped up on my social media's 'people you may know' list for no reason yesterday."

Tyson slid his finger across the screen to scroll through a generic profile with a few shared articles. "The page is sort of new, but there's no location on it." He explained.

"Did you hear anything that I said? I have real feelings for Regina." I looked over to Tyriq. His focus had drifted to his phone as well. "Tyriq?"

"Huh?" Without a clue or care about what I was going through, he scooted closer. "Let me ask you this, do you think Nylani has my ears?"

He pushed his phone closer to my face as well, an enlarged picture of my newborn niece covering the screen.

"Hey! Pay attention."

Tyson finally unglued his eyes from his phone to speak.

"I got you. I'll teach the Y.A.M's this week, work out their schedule, and get them paid. I'll make sure to keep an eye on Trevion. Chyna got the shop on lock all ready for the day-to-day stuff." He ticked off the tasks like they were simple. "Go on the trip, quit being a coward, and let the girl know how you feel. Problem solved." Tyson finished the rest in nearly one breath. "Now," He pushed up his phone again, "does this look more like Love Field Airport or DFW International? I think Kinny might be a ticket agent."

I wanted to shake him but knew that he was just a guy who wanted a girl that he probably shouldn't. Since I was swimming in those same uncharted waters, I couldn't be mad at him. I was taking a step away from my brothers, my business, and my boys, all that mattered most to me so that I could help Regina. I didn't even kid myself that my idea for going to Reginald about the community center wasn't partially a way to keep tabs on Regina.

"You guys are useless. Let's get out of here so you can get back to your women."

"I was about to roll anyway. 'Lani is awake." Tyriq, who had been absolutely no help, announced as he stood.

"I'm surprised you left little Miss Nylani Monique's side for this long." I slapped hands with my brother and pulled him in for a quick clap on the back. "Fatherhood suits you, even if it has taken over your brain."

My brothers and I walked to the front of the store, each of us smiling for entirely different reasons. Our worlds were changing for the better.

Chyna's frown greeted me as soon as we made it to the front lobby. That was unusual. She made a habit of smiling at me and being extra kind.

"What's up?"

Chyna shot her eyes to the left, her arms folded across her chest.

"I tried to get him to leave," she huffed. "But here he sits."

To my credit, I didn't rush his ass and cave in his face like I wanted to. I took a few seconds to casually stroll over to Hendrix, who stood up as I approached and asked him a question.

"What do you want?"

"Your disappearance," he grinned. "But I'll settle for your resignation from Strong Realty."

"Not happening."

I moved to step around him, but he slid over to my path.

"Listen, I have an opportunity to work with GP Holdings. I can get you connected to some real money. Reginald is already on the bench, and we all know Regina doesn't stand a chance without you showing her the way. Strong is folding in on itself. Come work with me."

It boggled my brain that someone as smart as Regina thought that marrying Hendrix was a great idea. Why couldn't he see her brilliance?

"No company stands a chance with you." I countered before gears began to grind in my mind about which company he had been working for all along. "Did you purposely tank Strong's meeting with the rep?"

His eyes didn't deny it, nor did his mouth.

"Why would I do that to my future wife?" Hendrix placed a hand across his heart as though it pained him.

The word wife grated across my ears and amped up my frustration. I didn't know what kind of game he was playing, but I was about to put an end to it.

"That's not happening."

"Your resignation or my wedding?"

"Either," I answered. Regina and I hadn't announced our decision to marry yet, so no one knew, and I wanted a front row seat when he found out.

I could hear my brothers gathering closer like I couldn't take Hendrix's twerp ass on my own. He must have noticed because he hurried to his point.

"A promise is a promise, and you can quote me on that. Reginald may ice me out of his business, but Regina is still going to bring me into the family." His grin was sinister. "Step away, get ill, but if you go on this trip then things won't end well for you or her."

He nodded forward as he stepped backward toward the door.

"I don't give a shit about your threats."

"But you will." His eyebrow lifted. "Don't say that I didn't warn you."

My brothers suddenly found time to be interested in what was happening to me. We walked back to the office, and I explained again what I had already tried to get their input on for the previous hour.

Regina called me right after my brothers were all caught up.

"What are you bringing me for dinner?" She breathed into the phone.

"Hello to you too. How was your day? Mine has been taxing?" I was being sarcastic. I liked that she had called. It didn't matter that much what she said, I just enjoyed her voice.

"Terrence, I'm hungry." she exaggerated the words in a whiny voice, and I imagined her stomping her feet as she spouted.

"So, I'm your food delivery driver now?" I asked. Giving her a hard time had become my daily ritual, and acting like a brat had become hers. "What if I were going somewhere else tonight? Your dad is back home in his bed, and things are as normal as they can be. The office is running fine-"

"Please," she asked again.

Saying no to Regina was never an easy option, and I was comfortable being with her.

By the time Tyson parked at the international airport, I was ready to find Regina, sweep her into my arms in classic movie style, and bend her back with a kiss. She had left the apartment early that morning to check on things in the office and meet with her lawyer, Micah. I offered to go with her, and we travel to the airport together, partly because something about her suave attorney irritated me. There was something wrong about him, but I hadn't determined if it was jealousy or intuition that told me so. Regina knew how much of my sanity needed to stop in to visit my favorite shop before the trip. Giving up on the idea of us riding together, we went our separate ways. I saw that Chyna had everything under control, and my brother jumped at the chance to take me to the airport.

For some reason, Tyson and I had hopped out of the car with the same energy: get to the girl. When he pulled out a rolling suitcase from his trunk, I was even more confused.

"I got this," I said, placing a hand in the air to stop him. "You don't have to walk me in bro. I'm grown."

"I know." He frowned. "What do I look like walking yo' big burly ass to check-in? I'm trying to see about a friend today."

"Why do you have bags?" I pointed out.

He waved a dismissive hand in the air as he power-walked ahead of me.

"I got some things in play."

As we walked further into the terminal, I didn't ask anything else about his trip to nowhere to uncover unquestionable things because I spotted Regina. I saw her there looking good as hell. With a mass of wavy hair pulled up and wrapped into a bun at the top of her head, light makeup on a fresh face, glossy nude lips, and dressed in tights and an oversized midriff sweatshirt, I knew that I made the right decision. Standing next to her, in an airline agent uniform, was Kinnesha Rawlings.

"Is that- Does Regina know-" Tyson sputtered. He had seen his first love, and a glitch occurred in his normally smooth operating system.

"It is, and I'm not sure how they know each other," I answered as the ladies chatted comfortably with exaggerated hand motions. They were oblivious to the commotion that their very existence had caused for my brother and me.

"That's Kinnesha." For a second, I thought I saw cartoon hearts bulge from his eyes as he grinned. "She's back."

Regina must have sensed that we were looking in her direction. We were far enough away not to be noticed right off, but it only took a few seconds for both Regina and Kinnesha to swivel their heads toward us.

"Oh shit. She's looking. Laugh." He prompted me to join in his fake revelry with a tap to my shoulder.

"We are too grown for this shit," I protested through a half-smile and gave a light chuckle anyway.

Regina's eyes drew me closer and Tyson joined in step as though he were just as infatuated with Kinnesha.

"She's back, and I need a chance to get on her good side." He mumbled.

"I wondered why you're wearing so much cologne just to take me to the airport. You even got all trimmed up and baby-faced. That's cute and all, but I'm not trying to be a part of your stalker games."

"Yo, just play along. I want to see if she's still the woman I remember and if she's interested. That's it." Tyson had stopped walking to plead his case. "I figured out that she worked here from a post. I was going to casually drop in to grab a ticket with whatever airline counter she was in front of and try to get things poppin' again."

"But if she doesn't want you, then this is the end," I confirmed. I was almost worried, but I remembered how close they were and all that he was willing to sacrifice to be with her before she ghosted him.

He nodded in agreement, "But who wouldn't want me?"

I shook my head as we made it to where Kinnesha and Regina stood.

"What's up, French Fry?" I greeted.

"What's going down, Hash Brown?" Kinnesha responded just the way she did as a kid.

Kinnesha and I laughed through a hug. It was good to see her. She was always around the house as a child. Before she was Tyson's girl, she was French Fry, the skinny kid who lived in the neighborhood.

"Oh, so y'all close-close then?" Regina acknowledged before she elegantly swept Kinnesha back, leaned in for an extremely tight hug, and kissed my cheek.

"Kin-Kin was like a little sister to me growing up." I leaned down to kiss Regina's forehead.

"Kin-Kin, huh? I'm going to remember that." Regina chuckled. "Thank you for doing this. I appreciate you taking this trip with me."

"I always got you." When I whispered the words near her ear, I felt the shiver from her body where my hand rested on her back.

"Tyson, it's good to see you." Kinny proffered her hand to him for a shake. "What brings you here?"

"Terrence is heading out now, and my flight is later," he motioned to his bag. "I figured that I may as well chill at the airport. Hey, we should catch up over lunch since I'm here pretty much all day."

"That sounds good. I have an hour before I need to be at the counter. I got here early to drop off Regina."

"How do you know each other?" I asked Kinny.

"Regina and I went to college together. She was my roommate freshman year until-" her voice faded off before she stumbled over the last few words. "You know, well- We were roommates."

"Wait. This right here is crazy." Tyson crossed his hands through the air as he blinked his eyes in confusion. "Walk me through this. Regina, you met Kin in college your freshman year?"

Regina, still snuggled under my arm, nodded her head.

"Kin, is Regina the rich girl that took you to Jamaica before you, well before you left?" He clarified.

I could see the pleading in Kinnesha's eyes before she said anything to Tyson. Tenderness laced her words and added to the sound of remorse. "I didn't keep in touch with anyone, Tyson."

When both their voices muted through the long leering glance, Regina popped in to give a suggestion.

"You two should go ahead and find a good spot now before Kinnesha has to go," Regina winked as she looped one arm through mine. "I need to get this one on a plane."

I sent up a silent prayer for my brother and Kinnesha who had once been like a little sister to me. Coupled, we said our goodbyes and went our separate ways.

CHAPTER THIRTY

Regina

The scream originated in the depths of my soul and traveled out with such a resounding burst that I shocked myself. I should have known that he couldn't walk away honorably and lick his wounds. No, he had to be a terrible human. I should've never entertained the thought of working with that slimy snake of a man.

Terrence was out of the restroom in a flash, a towel half wrapped around his taut skin to catch the rivulets of water cascading across the muscles that I never forget exist.

"What's wrong?" His hands were on me, but not in the way that I had been daydreaming of only thirty minutes ago. He patted at the column of my neck as he lifted my head, then tapped my shoulders, hips, and legs as he spun me in a circle.

"Terrence," I tried to get his attention. I assumed he was searching for the wound that caused my blood-curdling yell. "I'm fine. I'm alright."

I tugged Terrence up from his bent position, where he was inspecting my legs. "Look at me."

Terrence and his towel stood, and both my eyes and libido saw him this time. I hadn't ever stopped wanting him, but with my attention needed in so many places at once, I didn't have time to notice his appeal as much.

"There's nothing wrong with me physically," I explained while working on remembering the exact reason I was not humping Terrence every opportunity that I had.

"What happened?" He asked.

There it was, the care that made him different. I would say that it glowed from him, but it seemed that I was the only one that could see it.

"This asshole just destroyed our family name and everything my father has been building," I felt like nothing would ever get right. I found a husband to keep the company but there may not be a company left. "The deal is over."

"Talk to me. What deal?" Terrence went straight to the point.

"The one we're here for." I reminded him. "The one my father-"

My ability to speak caught up to how fine he was, and became mesmerized as well. It's not like I hadn't seen his body before, but the way he glistened under the dimmed room light pushed the pause button in my brain.

"I can't focus while you're in that towel." I swirled my eyes up to the ceiling.

He dropped the towel.

"Better?"

Did he refocus my attention? Yes. Was I still a little frustrated? Of course.

"No," I whined and plopped down on the sofa as he put on some shorts, and I refocused myself. "This is so messed up,"

"Regina." His fingers traced the side of my face before he sat next to me in a pair of basketball shorts and a cotton shirt. "You haven't explained the problem, really, and honestly, no matter what the issue is, you'll be ok. This is one project."

"I know, but it may be the last one- the last project that I get to work on with-"

My father was slipping away, and this was the last deal that we would have together.

"I want to make him proud," I closed my eyes and exhaled. "It's not happening right now."

"Most things broken can be fixed, and if it can't be fixed, maybe it can be mended. And sometimes, it was broken to be replaced with something better."

The coolness of his voice and the smoothness of his hand pressing up and down my spine relaxed some of the tension.

He made sense. I let more of the frustration dissipate when he slid his arm around my waist to pull me into the familiar warmth of his chest. I had been there so many times over the last few days. He had been my comfort, my sounding board, and my motivation to keep going when I felt like I wanted to fall into the fetal position and cry.

"You can do this," He stroked his hand across my shoulder. "Your father will be proud of you no matter the outcome. He knows how much effort you put into this for him."

I nodded against him before he released me.

"Let's see what the damage is," Terrence insisted.

I picked up my discarded laptop and took a seat at a small table near the window. Terrence placed a hand on my wrist after he pulled a chair next to me.

Pushing play on the video clip sent my anxiety back into orbit. I couldn't help but think about what the information would do to the legacy of my father and the future of the company.

"The Reconstruction era in United States history was one of the most extensive periods of growth for freed persons of color." The woman in the video spoke over vintage black-and-white photos of well-dressed African Americans. "During this time, freed slaves established and maintained communities where they not only survived but thrived. What happened to those communities, and why don't we talk about them?"

"What does this have to do with your dad and the deal?" Terrence asked.

I shook my head, not wanting to answer just yet, and we continued to listen to the video. It hurt when I heard the words, but the truth of human nature could often be painful.

"One particularly booming area in North Texas was the unincorporated town of Promise, boasting two black-owned banks, four churches, a drug store, a movie theater, and a school in the early 1920s. By the time that Reginald Strong and a group of investors came along to haul the land for the arena space, only an underperforming school and less than twenty dilapidated homes remained."

I looked over at Terrence, expecting him to scoff or something, but his face remained neutral.

"This isn't that bad," he shrugged. "Your dad helped buy up land to build an arena."

The investigative news segment was close to thirty minutes long so I slid the bar underneath the video further into the segment. The blue-grey hair of an older woman filled the screen.

"They sent the only black man in the group to talk to us." Her voice was strong and sure. "He told us about all of this money and relocation expenses we would get. In the end, our land was stolen, Reginald Strong stopped taking our calls, and we were put out of our homes due to eminent domain. Mr. Strong and his fancy words were only a cover while they took what we worked hard for and demolished the first school in the entire county to ever educate black children."

I ended it there. Terrence's face had changed slightly, but he looked more concerned than horrified. It's comforting that he asks questions first and seeks to understand versus my slide into hysteria.

His fingers grazed the top of my ear as his eyes fell on me. "I feel like I'm missing pieces to this puzzle," he added softly.

I wanted to clear my consciousness of the shame, but I wasn't sure what he would think of me after. I didn't want his opinion of us to change once he knew, once he understood what my family had sacrificed for status.

"Talk to me." His request came with a warm rub of his hand against the column of my arm.

"I was just back from college when people started whispering about what really happened when the stadium was built." I took a deep breath before telling more. "He knew. My father knew what they were doing to those people. He knew that they pulled him into the project because he was black and because he had ties to the community. His great-grandparents had one of the first businesses in that area. The town was unofficially named Promise because many of the people that settled there had witnessed slavery or were born right after. They used to say that having their own area for themselves was the closest thing to the Promise Land they would get to on this side of the grave."

"I can't imagine how good that felt." Terrence said. "Ownership after witnessing another human being owned."

"Right," I added. "Obidiah and Jenny bought up any acreage that white people didn't want, especially out by the Trinity River and near cemeteries. They acquired several properties and later passed them down to his grandfather. That's where Strong Realty started, and he finished it. Part of what his family had worked to build, he helped to tear down what was left."

"Damn."

"Those people trusted him." A hitch escaped in my voice when I admitted part of the truth that hurt the most. "I trusted him."

"Is that why you left the company?"

I nod. It was one of a couple of reasons.

"I had worked with him all through high school and every summer through college. When I came home, I started full time, and he brought me in on the deal." I answered.

"You knew too?"

I shook my head.

"I didn't know back then when it happened. I thought that the residents had been given above- market value for their homes. I found out later that wasn't true. I was serving the homeless. One of the women I recognized from the community came through the line. It confused me because she should have gotten nearly half of a million dollars for her home and corner store. I asked her about her situation later. She told me that they barely got the price that she paid for the property and that she couldn't afford a home because of price increases and the loss of her business."

I felt his smooth hand rub across my shoulder.

"It didn't make the news when it happened. Once members of the original investment group started to die off or have financial troubles, more information trickled out. Enough details to spark rumors and cause questions," I explained. "It wasn't just one or two people that fell on hard times after that. More than a few people got pennies for their land. It wasn't broadcast. My father's business partners made sure of that, but people knew."

"People like Hendrix Wilson and his family."

"Right."

Terrence slid two fingers against the skin of my chin, carefully lifting my fallen head.

"The meeting is still on. We can only fix a problem that we can see. Luckily, we got a whiff of this issue before we were in front of the clients. Let them bring it up, I got your back. It'll work out how it's supposed to."

"My father took advantage of people to get ahead. He took an opportunity that damaged the lives of others for that stadium, for the money."

"It also elevated his company to another level and provided opportunities for other businessmen. It provided an opportunity for me."

That night, we reviewed our presentation and then composed answers to possible questions about the scandal. I enjoyed the back and forth in the development of ideas that we accomplished. Working with Terrence made me feel smarter. He listened to my ideas and helped me think through possible pitfalls. He didn't criticize me, although he did chuckle when I suggested a foot relief station for women at the stadium. Honestly, I wore heels everywhere, and sometimes my feet hurt. I would have loved to dip off during a game for a foot rub and then catch the ending with my guy. We fell asleep together, wrapped in covers and each other as though that was the way it was supposed to be.

The meeting started well enough. After handshakes and introductions, Terrence and I tag-teamed a walkthrough of our strategy to bring their stadium to life and then partnered with companies to sustain it. We were in a groove, harmoniously switching through slides and responding eloquently to questions. Then the real question came. The representative who had visited my father's office brought it up.

"What about the acquisition of land? We hear that Strong has some less-than-above-board dealings. We will not associate ourselves with any negative press."

"We'll see that the negative publicity is handled and assure you that the Strong Company prides itself in transparent business practices. Where this project differs from the previous endeavors is that Strong is the lead investor, where we were a minority partner before." I answered.

"Life is our greatest teacher. You get the benefit of our experiences and our determination to make this endeavor stellar." Terrence confidently jumped in. "As a partner, you would receive weekly reports and have access to personnel in handling each aspect of the cricket arena."

"We'll consider this information. Due to the recent development, we have some concerns. I'll be honest; we are considering other partnerships. We'll be in touch in the upcoming weeks."

CHAPTER THIRTY-ONE

Terrence

I had to look twice, blink three times, and touch her skin to make sure that what I saw was real. Little droplets were leaking from her face. They resembled tears, and they were odd on her cheeks. Her streaked makeup was evidence of their existence, so I had to believe that Regina was crying.

We were on the sofa again, where we had been the night before. Pulling her into my arms, I stroked her shoulder.

"I'm messing this all up for him." She sniffled. "I'm not doing this right at all. Hendrix only did this because of me. That segment would have never run if I had just played nice with him."

"You didn't do anything wrong."

I didn't know what to do with a pissed-off and crying, Regina. During the car ride back to the hotel, she cursed out Hendrix using all the words she had been storing up for the last few days during her 'no cuss' challenge. In the elevator, her face changed, softened, and then once in the room flooded. I didn't know what variation of her would emerge next, and I wanted to keep her safe. I wanted her tears dry and to soothe the doubts and fears plaguing her.

Her shoes were the first to come off, then her suit jacket, and after that, it seemed like she shed a piece of her sanity too. Rubbing her back, I finally got her less tense.

Her phone dinged and danced against the table next to us.

"Don't answer that."

She reached out to grab the device anyway. "I'll just check the messages. It could be my mom or someone calling about my dad."

She picked up the phone and rolled her eyes.

"I should have known that his sneaky tail was up to something." As she sat up, her eyebrows furrowed. "Hendrix sent me dates for two social mixers that he wants me to attend with him. He just blew up my life, but he wants me to go schmooze with him. How much sense does that make?"

Her mouth dropped when I slipped the phone out of her hands and put it on an end table near me. She needed to chill and remove herself from that energy. Hendrix wasn't important. London wasn't even that damn important. Her well-being mattered more than anything.

"I got something for Hendrix, don't worry about him." I slid the small throw blanket she had brought for the plane over her legs. "I already checked in with your mom. Your dad is fine, and I told her to call me if she couldn't get in touch with you."

"You and my mom are cool like that now?" She leaned back into my arms, but her face stayed fixed with concern.

"Just a little." My hand wore a path down the side of her slender frame, following the beat of our breaths. Her being next to me burrowed into my side, felt as natural as blinking. It occurred without thought. My feelings for her were there without any effort or awareness on my part. We happened.

The fact that I had given Cherry my number just in case Reginald had any more episodes, and she needed to get in touch with me wasn't important at that time. My priority was her well-being. "How're you feeling?"

"Like, I failed at something expected of me," she tilted her head down slightly.

"This isn't over," Lifting her chin, I gave her my biggest smile with hopes that she would smile back.

I hated that she was so down on herself. I didn't see her as a failure but as a fighter.

"Planning always makes me feel better," I wanted her to hear the hope in my voice, the longing that I had to support her. "One man, in particular, had a problem with your father's past. If we could somehow turn his opinion, then we can salvage it."

She nodded slowly, and I prayed that my hope would vine us together and lift her spirits. Then an idea sprouted. More work wouldn't be the answer. We'd been working non-stop.

"Get changed." I requested. "Fuck Hindenburg and his antics. Let's go out, enjoy the city and spend another day here. I'll have the room extended another night."

"You're right. As my friend Jubilee would say, one sad clown won't stop the rodeo." she stood up from the sofa in a power pose, the blanket I placed on her falling to the floor.

"I got you. Let's take some time to live it up in the city."

An hour later, Regina and I walked into the city looking like the American tourists we were. Regina was in tennis shoes and a T-Shirt. She had spent time trying to make me smile and I wanted to do the same. I wanted to do something nice for her but let her take the lead.

"So first, we have to get food." Her sneaker-clad feet bounced to the same beat of her words. "I found so many places within walking distance, but one spot has -"

Once Regina started, she got excited, and a flow of words replaced the tears that were there earlier. That made me smile. I didn't pay attention to much of what she said, just that she held my hand while she said it. We were together in the daylight, and it felt good. It felt right.

Regina, the GPS on her phone, and her words led me down a major street and a smaller less crowded street. The cobblestone under my feet was nothing compared to what had been in my heart.

"You're going to love this." She spoke as she stopped in front of a small restaurant. "I found it while you were changing. Look."

I stopped next to the excited woman rolling back and forth on the balls of her feet.

The restaurant seemed standard, a refurbished two-story building with an awning, patio, and small tables out front.

"What am I looking at?"

Regina popped her hands on her hip. "A neighborhood spot. You like those, right? Going to dives with good food? They have good reviews and home-like cuisine. I found this place, overlooked the five-star restaurant, and forwent the chauffeured car to walk. Aren't you proud of me? "

I chuckled at that. Regina was the gourmet and kissed her cheek.

"Very much so. Thank you."

We settled at a cozy table. I was content to listen to Regina talk out her plan of attack on the department stores, but a nagging feeling had me check my phone. I shouldn't have. My mood quickly descended. There was a text from Diane Jacobs. She had asked to keep in touch with me during their anniversary party, and I had agreed.

Diane: Today is always so difficult for me. I loved her so much. I found her wedding photo and thought that you must be hurting too. You loved her too.

Be Blessed.

I didn't respond because I didn't know the words to type. Her text reminded me of something I had been too busy living to realize I had forgotten.

Amid all that, Regina had still been speaking, but suddenly there was silence, and I noticed her watching me. I wasn't sure when she had stopped talking, but she must have missed my attention. Before she could mouth the question that her eyes were already asking, the waitress appeared.

"What a cracking couple? And you're a fit fella. The two of you together are a bit much for the common eye." The chipper waitress complimented us after taking our order. She gave me an extra wink before she slipped away.

"I thought you were trying to cheer me up. Your entire mood changed when you checked your phone." Regina observed.

"Today is the anniversary of Valerie's passing."

"I don't know what to say."

"Not much to say."

"Tell me about her. She had to be remarkable to capture your heart."

"She was a catch. Pretty, smart, funny. Being the oldest comes with a lot of responsibility. My parents depended on me to help with my siblings, but Valerie worried about me. She kept it fun even when I was thinking of the consequences. I never knew what the day would hold with her. She would wake up and want to paint or drive to L.A. I could talk to her about anything."

"I'm glad that you could experience that happiness. I've never been so lucky." She took a sip from her drink. "How- you know- how did it end?"

I gave a grim wince of a smile. Remembering Valerie was easier now. The stabs of pain that used to pair themselves with the memories were absent.

"I vowed to love her and take care of her in sickness and in health, but when she was sick-."

Regina reached across the table and caressed the top of my hand.

"She had the flu, and the medication was $100. I laugh at the price now, but when we first started, that was expensive. I went with her to that doctor's appointment. I remember the doctor explaining that it could or could not work." My eyes found the napkin holder on the table and then my fork, her spoon, and finally, her eyes. They were kind, and she was quiet. "I complained about the price, so she didn't get the medicine. She got worse but didn't go back to the doctor. That was another co-pay just for them to tell her the same thing. I should have made her go or just bought the damn medicine. Something. I disappointed everyone."

Regina took my left hand between the two of hers. "I don't think you could disappoint anyone."

A sorrowful chuckle was all that I could manage at her using the words I had once said to comfort her.

"I don't know about that," I inhaled and tried to reign in all of the emotion I had let spill. "I know what this venture means to you. Your father is sick, and you want to make him happy. If I had known those last days with Valerie were the last, I would have done all that I could to make her happy every minute."

She nodded, and I continued.

"I will do everything that I can to make sure you uphold your promise to your father."

"Even if it meant that we- "Regina started but stopped when the waitress came closer with our food.

"So lush you two are. I would chat up the both of you in the club." She chatted while she added plates to the table. "Enjoy the food. I'll be back to check on you soon."

I wondered if Regina had been thinking about what I was thinking.

"Whatever you need. I'm here to support you any way that I can," She finally said with care as she settled her hand over mine. "No matter what that looks like."

We walked through the shops, pointed out landmarks, and avoided any serious conversation for the rest of the day. I wasn't alone for the first time in a long time. I had someone who didn't mind listening to me wonder about car models out loud or said nothing at all. I could listen to her rattle on about random things, each topic adding a layer of like to the mounting pile of emotions gathering for her.

"Sea lions are severely scarier than clowns, I don't care what anyone says, but both can be found in circuses." Regina continued about the worst California vacation that she had as a child. "When that clown tried to pull me from the front row to pet that water monster, I took off. Instead of running out of the tent, I ran right into a pack of clowns. I passed out. It scarred me for life."

Without thought, the laughter rolled up and out of me as I imagined a miniature Regina scared of anything and running through a circus tent for her life.

"So it's a *no* on a visit to the Sealife Aquarium, then?"

She didn't bother to answer, just grabbed my hand and pulled me across the street as she chirped excitedly, "Look. Come on. We've got to go here."

Regina had the energy of a toddler on Mountain Dew and Skittles, and I couldn't help but to absorb some of the joy that bubbled over from her.

"Forbidden Planet?" I read the sign while keeping with Regina's brisk pace. "What are you trying to drag me into?"

"It's a game store." She answered as we entered through the large glass doors. "We should get something to play with while we're in the room. What's your favorite board game?"

It didn't take a second to answer. I already knew the best way to honor my belated wife and enjoy time with the woman I would wed.

We had barely dropped all of our bags off at the front counter of the hotel before Regina was dragging me out of the door for another expedition. In general, I wasn't a 'go-out' type, but when it came time to move around, I didn't hesitate to be by her side. There were some limitations, though.

"I'm not putting that shit on my face." I pushed Regina's outstretched hand away.

"Come on. Please." She pouted, and her lip looked like it might detach from her face.

Begrudgingly, I took the London Bridge-shaped glasses, slid them over my eyes, and then looked at her. She had been pestering me about the souvenir glasses for about 3 blocks.

Regina tried to hide a giggle, but I caught it, and I snatched the lame spectacles off. She snapped a picture or three before I could hide the hideous things in my pocket.

"Nailah and your brothers will love this." She said, tapping at her phone.

I reached for her device, but she did a quick spin and slid out of my reach. I reached again, but she twirled away with a giggle.

"Boom. Sent." She laughed louder as she skipped backward a few steps, and I had to move faster to reach her.

"See, now you have to pay," I finally scooped her against me with one arm and reached around her to take her phone with the other.

"Nope," She tried to wriggle away, but I kept her pressed against me.

"Give me my phone." Regina finally squirmed her way around to face me.

"What do I get?" I didn't intend for my voice to drop that low, or for my words to drip with lust, but I'm glad that it happened. I'm glad that her eyelids dropped and her pulse increased. When she licked her lips, I fought the urge to take her tongue.

"What do you want?"

Our faces were closer, and I didn't care about holding the phone away, just holding her. Wrapping both arms around her waist to keep her close, to keep her as near to me as possible, I answered.

"You. I want to love you. I don't want this to be about business. I want us to be for real."

Regina rubbed a hand across my chest, before looking up into my eyes. I could tell she wanted a brother too, but her stubborn ass wasn't about to say it.

While I was lost in thoughts of our future, she plucked the phone out of my hand and ran.

"Gotta be faster than that big man," she chuckled with a quick sidestep that kept her out of my reach.

It only took a second or two before I had her in my arms blowing kisses on her neck. The kind of kisses that I had come to find out also tickle her.

Everything about the day melted away: no dads, business, or idiots trying to sabotage business to worry over. Airy joy filled me with each roll of her laughter. I didn't want that to ever end.

"Let's get on the London Eye!" She pointed.

"What is that?" I wouldn't deny her but I also needed more information.

She extended her long nails into the distance, but I sure didn't know what she was talking about.

"That big ass Ferris wheel over there?"

"It's called the Millennium Wheel and you stand up instead of sitting down in buckets. It's essentially a Ferris wheel but it's also an observation deck. We can see the entire city."

"Let's go."

Miraculously we got into a capsule that had about 10 people without too long of a wait. The glass-encased pod was tall enough for me to stand up straight with room to spare and wide enough for a couple more people to enter. Even with the few people around, in my mind, it was just us.

Immediately Regina put all of her attention on the scenery staring out of the glass and not looking at me.

"It seems like the entire world is out there." She glided her head from side to side, examining the cityscape.

When I stood next to her, she made an effort not to look my way.

"I feel like it's right here."

I leaned in to kiss her neck. I missed the taste of her. She didn't seem to notice. I assumed that she was just really into the beauty of the city because she truly looked amazed.

"At this very moment life is happening," Awe floated out with her words. "Lives are ending and beginning right now. We have to live while we can. You know?" She turned to me then, her eyes glistening. I felt like she could see into my heart. "Just live."

Those words shocked everything in me, and the hairs on the back of my neck rose. Live. One word that I noticed on my Scrabble board. One of my last words with Valerie.

Our bodies found their way to each other, and I draped an arm around her.

"Let's do it." I didn't think about it, I just said it. It felt right. I had been underwater, and she was lifting me. The day had as needed as the first breath of air after drowning. "Let's do this for real."

The skies should have opened up with rays of sunshine pouring into our pod because that's how my heart felt, open and refreshed.

The day went by in a blur of laughs, food, and fun. Regina didn't comment on my request to not restrict our relationship. I wanted to let the love come, even though it felt familiar to us already. We fit in a round of Scrabble after changing into lounge clothes, playing Scrabble, and then climbing into bed.

My mind wouldn't let me rest, so I decided to lay it all out for her.

"I worked hard to fit in when I started prep school," I told Regina. I'd talk to her if she didn't talk to me. If she wouldn't agree to marry me, I'd show her why she should. "I tried to fit in with kids with more money, looked different, and lived different lives than I did."

"You mean to tell me their fathers didn't have fifteen purple Crown Royal liquor bags filled with pennies around the house, and their mother didn't put foil over all the leftovers?" She chuckled a little after detailing what she'd witnessed at my parents' home the few times she'd been over.

"Nah, those rich kids didn't know about putting grocery bags in trash cans or seven ways to make Ramen Noodles taste better." I took a deep breath. "When I married Valerie, I was still trying to fit in. I was trying to be the perfect man and husband for her. When she passed away, I wasn't finished yet. I hadn't achieved my goal, and until that point, I had never failed at anything. Everything that I put my mind to, I accomplished. I didn't get to reach my goal with her or for her. I was like a car with a good motor, but I didn't have my paint job. I needed some interior work too, but she died. She left before I reached my full potential."

I felt her head nod against my chest before she asked a question.

"If you were trying to fit in with the prep schoolers, the business world, and a church girl, how did you end up with tattoos and locks?"

I liked that she asked questions and even more that I had answers. I had thought about those things for ten years. I had no one to explain my conclusions.

"After the sadness, there was anger. I let my hair grow out and got it twisted. I got one scrabble-piece tattoo with the letter V on it in her honor, and I couldn't stop after that. Wearing black clothes every day worked out for my business and my washer. My career had been part of the problem in our relationship, and I stepped away from it to do what I enjoyed. I took the time to be me outside of the first son, big brother, and husband. I rebelled against the good clean church image I had built for her. I think they were trying to make me into her father."

"Do you think that's what I want to do, turn you into Reginald Strong?" Regina asked.

"I found Mr. Strong. I admired him before I knew you. I'm not trying to take his place, but I value his advice."

She hummed and snuggled in closer as I rambled on.

"You're like Valerie: smart, well-educated, giving, prissy as hell."

Regina swatted at my shoulder, and I pecked a light kiss on her forehead before I continued.

"I guess there's a type that I fall for and even care about. I tried to keep some barriers between us because of that. I felt something for you from the start. That laugh, your wild mouth, that sexy ass walk, how driven you are, how you care about family, all of that, all of you, woke me up out of the fog. I had been drifting through life before you."

"Can you do this? Can you love me, Midnight?"

"I think I already do."

I felt the rise and fall of her breasts against my side. She was silent, and I took that opportunity to tell her more.

"Instead of worrying about how this will end, I want to enjoy the time that we have together, what's in front of me right now."

I put myself out there. I put my entire heart on the line and Regina just stared at me.

"Say something." I prompted.

"Promise not to break me." Her soft words brushed across my soul and I instantly wanted to keep her safe forever, even from me.

"Bloom, I'll do everything in my power to make this last forever." I pushed my face down to graze my lips across her forehead. "Stay mine. Be my wife and I'll make sure that you won't regret it."

As she took a deep breath, I held mine.

"Alright. I'm in. Wherever my heart leads, I'll follow."

CHAPTER THIRTY-TWO

Regina

I wondered how many women agreed to marriage while lying in bed with a half-naked man. Terrence had me ready to give up my entire life after a few minutes tucked beneath him. Midnight had my mind doing the Cupid Shuffle and my hormones doing the Wobble, but I felt I had made the right decision. He wanted to marry me. He wanted to be with me for real. The contract didn't matter. At least, that's what I told myself.

Right before the trip to London, I met with Micah to discuss the status of my father's terms. When I sat down to order at one of his favorite and familiar restaurants, Micah was bursting with excitement. It took him less than thirty seconds to explain that the board had a change of heart after considering the negative press that could ensue if it were ever leaked that a female employee was required to marry to lead. He explained that my father relented without any rebuttals. I immediately went to see Reginald after that. I didn't understand why my parents would put me through so much only to renege on the requirement. Simply put, it was Terrence. My father felt confident in my skills and comfortable with Terrence's ability to look out for me.

I didn't have to marry anymore. Terrence didn't have to marry me, but I wasn't sure what to tell him that would make him marry me anyway. So I lay there and let him pour out his heart as I willingly gave him what he had already taken: my love.

It took ages to make it to the DFW International airport and even longer to gather all of our things to get to a familiar place. His dog Ginger would come to stay as well. I was ecstatic when he explained that she went to a daycare every day and had been through obedience training. My shoes were safe.

I unlocked the door, but he dropped our bags off in the room and sprawled across my sofa without hesitation. He was already acting as if my space was his own. The thought of us building a home together was comforting, and when he lifted his arm for me to fall onto his body, I was sure I was making the best decision.

A Friday night at home, in his arms after a long-ass plane ride, was a slice of heaven.

"I'm beat," Terrence said, "I'm not picking up Ginger until tomorrow."

"Let's not move until tomorrow, okay? I just want to stay right here."

Something about speaking my plans out loud makes the universe decide to plot against them. I shouldn't have said anything. I should have kept the words under my tongue because Terrence's phone buzzed on the table no sooner than I finished my sentence.

I looked at the phone and the name 'Moms' flashing across the screen and knew he would answer. I moved to get up, but he hooked me back close to him.

"Nah. Stay right here. This won't take long."

Securing me with one arm, he reached for his phone on the coffee table with his other. He had become an expert at that, keeping me close.

I was just getting cozy, falling off into that fanciful space of contentment, when I was jolted back into reality by his words.

"I know, Ma, but I can pick up Ginger tomorrow. That flight was long, and we're tired."

I couldn't hear his mother, but in my mind, she had to have come back real quick with a *'who the hell is we?'* response based on how he started explaining.

"I'm at Regina's. We're together. I know it's game night. Mom, we're not staying all night."

I hopped up so quickly he didn't get a chance to hypnotize me with those bright eyes and smooth words.

"No," I said as soon as he hung up the phone. "You are more than welcome to leave, but I am not facing your aunt and mom tonight."

"It's not like you haven't met them before."

"I haven't met them as your girlfriend. You just told your mom that we're sleeping together."

"What? I just said that we're together."

"You told her that you are at my house and that we are 'we' now. Believe me, she caught all of that wordplay and read between every letter."

"Bloom," He moved toward me, his pitiful rounded eyes drawing me in before his arms took me to his chest. "Come with me. I want my family to know how important you are in my life. "

He nibbled at my neck on purpose. I should have kept my eyes and ears closed. I should have said no, but his kisses told me to do otherwise. He was too sweet, and I had already asked him to do a million things for me. The fact that he no longer had to marry me sat in the back of my mind nudging me to do whatever he asked.

"I guess so." I agreed. "I need to take a shower and get myself together. I'm not carrying this airport funk over to meet your people."

"Fine, as long as we make an appearance. It's going to be great."

His excitement was contagious, and I was smiling against the anxiousness of being introduced as his girlfriend.

I showered and dressed first since it took my man less than fifteen minutes to wash, put on all his clothes, and be ready to walk out of the door. Terrence was getting dressed when I left the apartment for the parking garage. I had some bomb-ass gold bracelets that I wanted to throw on with my burgundy maxi dress and gold hoops. The last time I had worn them, I took them off in the car because they kept getting in my way of the steering wheel.

"Damnit. Where are they?" I flipped open and shut several storage areas before finding the jewelry under the seat.

I had just closed the door when the king of bitch-assness showed his ashy face.

"I told you to be back last night." His sneered words were as dark and tight as his roving eyes. Hendrix walked up to me like he was there on the night I was conceived. My father didn't even come at me like that.

"You couldn't be talking to me." I sidestepped him and moved toward Terrence's truck. I should have just waited a few minutes until I could have had an escort.

"This marriage won't work little darling, if you don't play by the rules."

I spun around and unleashed.

"I make my own damn rules. The quicker you understand that I don't need you or your approval, the better off you'll be. And let me make this clear for your simple ass: No. No to helping you, no to a business partnership, and abso-fucking-lutely no to marriage. Get your-"

Before I could go full 'Waiting to Exhale' and curse him out Angela Bassett style, he grabbed me by the arms. He did it so quickly that I missed his hands moving. They were by his side and then pressing me against the bed of the truck without warning.

"Bitch, this is not a game," He growled. "My future is riding on this partnership, and you're going to pay up one way or the other."

I didn't let his words scare me for two reasons: 1- Whatever he did to me, my father would rain down hell on him for and 2- Terrence had made it to the parking garage. Hendrix had gotten a few dirty words out of his mouth, but when Terrence yanked him up like a rag doll, Hendrix's teeth looked like they would fly out of his face.

We were on the fourth floor of the parking garage and when Hendrix found his head dangling down over the concrete barrier, I heard him call on every deity he could summon.

"First and final warning," Terrence thundered. "Don't put your thoughts, words, or hands-on my girl."

"Ok. Ok. All right." Hendrix whimpered. "I won't bother her again. Just let me up."

Terrence had always been gentle with me, but the sinister look that dawned his face was one that I never wanted to see again.

"Nah." The word was simple but held the promise of demise. "You the the type of bitch that don't listen. You the hard headed type that don't know when to shut the fuck up and sit the fuck down. You think you're hard because you got a little flash and money."

I couldn't see Hendrix's face anymore, only his body. The grip of his hands on the barrier and pointed toes pushing to find footing on the ground said he was scared.

"You ain't hard." Terrence reminded him. "That concrete, though, that shit will knock you soft. That concrete will make sure you don't put your hands on my girl again."

"I won't I promise. Regina, Genie," he cried out. "Tell him that he can trust me."

"What did I tell you about talking to her?" Terrence didn't bother to look in my direction. "You already messed up."

"I'm sorry. I didn't mean it. Ok. I'm done. I promise." He pleaded.

"Go to your car, drive away, and find a different purpose in life because this ain't it."

Hendrix's feet hit the ground, and he disappeared as quickly as he had appeared. As far as I could tell, anyway because Terrence had me scooped into his truck and was examining me within a few seconds.

The rage that danced in his eyes earlier had dissipated, and worry had replaced it.

"Did he hurt you? Are you all right? I swear I will-"

"I'm fine, Night. Let's just go to your parents."

"You sure."

"Yea. It's the least that I can do to thank you."

He kissed my cheek.

"It'll be great."

It was not great. In thirty minutes, I had effectively pissed off Aunt Pat by turning down her fried chicken and made Mrs. Shirley roll her eyes when I accepted a piece of her Pineapple Upside Down Cake, but put the pineapple to the side and only picked at the corner with a fork.

"You're going down in flames." Nailah gave a slight chuckle when she whispered the words.

Terrence was embroiled in a heated game of Spades with his brothers and I had escaped the burning disapproval of the matriarchs and slipped into the back room with the mothers and babies. Nailah was rocking baby Nylani in her arms while Crystal sat on the queen-sized bed and patted her daughter's back as she fought the sandman.

I just sat in the quiet, rocking in the extra chair next to Nailah.

"I know," I whispered back. "They loved me before."

"Because you weren't dating one of the brothers."

I shook my head.

"Don't worry," Crystal said with stealth, "they didn't like me much at first."

That shocked me. Crystal was married to Terrence's younger brother Trystan. She was pretty in a modelesque way. From her eyebrows to her cheekbones and her pointed chin, everything about her was angled and sharp but put together like a painting. As a high-powered attorney, she even had a sharp mind, but she was sweet and gave Shirley the first grandbaby. How could they have disliked her?

"Are you serious?" The words came out in normal volume and set off a round of 'Shhh' from the mothers.

"Yes," Crystal responded quietly. "I'm older than Trystan by five years and his mother questioned my motives at first. Once they saw how much I cared for him, they warmed up."

I nodded. Mali had already voiced her dissent. She didn't want me anywhere near her cousin, and I wasn't sure that I could change that.

"Let's see if we can sneak out of here," Nailah murmured, as she turned on the baby monitor.

We moved out of the room with the sleeping children and into the family room with success.

Pops had turned on some music and was pulling Mrs. Shirley off the sofa when we made it in there. I always thought that they were a cute couple. Before I could take my seat on the sofa, Terrence caught my eyes and nodded me over to the table where he and his kinfolk had switched to playing dominoes. He lifted his arm and pulled me across his lap.

"You back there practicing for our future?" It wasn't his words that caught me off guard, more the nibbles into my neck between the words.

The sound of dominos raining down against the table broke my trance.

"Yo, this can't be real." Terrence's cousin Chad shouted.

All of the chatter seeped out of the room as everyone turned to look at us. Even the music had stopped to get a better understanding.

"What? Y'all fools act as if you've never seen someone in love before?"

"No," Chad shook his head from side to side slowly. "Not you. Not like this."

My heart nearly beat out of my chest when Terrence patted my leg signaling me to stand up.

He stood then, took my hand, and led me to the middle of the room right next to his parents.

"If you don't know, this is Regina Strong. I love her. And," he stretched out the word like a drum roll before he spoke again. "We're getting married."

His mother blinked so fast and hard that she could have cooled the room with her eyelashes.

"You said what now?" She fastened a hand on her hip as she spoke.

I felt the same way as his mother, a little confused. He had just thrown the love word out there several times in sixty seconds and we hadn't discussed it once. I wasn't sure if he had mentioned it so his parents would understand why we were getting married or if he felt that way about me.

"I was hurting for a long time." Terrence started after a deep breath. "Then I was numb, I couldn't feel anything. I didn't want to feel. I was just floating. Then I met Regina."

When his eyes fell across mine, I could have melted into the floor right then. His sincerity tipped the faucet behind my eyes, and I felt the tears pooling near the base of my lids. He continued speaking and I continued trying to blink away evidence that I was human.

"I didn't know how gray my life had become until she colored it with her smile and that laugh. I couldn't imagine doing this again with anyone else. Regina Strong, I'm ready to be your husband."

The girls in the room seemed to all swoon with me. Even Ms. Shirley's face softened as she closed in on her son.

"Is this what you want?" She asked.

"Yea mom. Regina is it."

"Alright then," she nodded as she stepped away from Terrence. Without warning, I was pressed into her ample bosom and she smashed her cheek against mine. "Welcome to the family Regina, and don't worry, I'm gonna find a cake that you can't get enough of."

I wanted to tell Shirley that her best creation was standing next to me and I couldn't stop putting him in my mouth but figured that was a bit much. I said, "Thank you" instead.

"Turn the music back up." Pops smiled as he pulled his wife into him. I saw where Terrence got that.

When the intro to Shanice's 'I Love Your Smile' sprang from the stereo, both Terrence and I grinned.

"Do you ever laugh?" I asked just like the first time we heard this song together in the hotel.

"I do, now that I'm with you." He answered.

I wanted to pack his fine ass up right then and take him to my bed, but I let him wrap me in a hug so that we could sway together. It was his version of dancing, and I liked our little side-to-side two steps. I loved anything that involved me being pressed against him. I loved anything that involved him. I loved him.

CHAPTER THIRTY-THREE

Terrence

I t had been a long day of house hunting with Regina, and the term 'house' is used loosely. We were visiting single-family towns it seemed. Every estate had sprawling acreage, pools, entertainment centers, a lake, and multiple dwellings. I was impressed that the Banks family had a pool house on "The Fresh Prince of Bel-Air", but what I saw on the home excursions with Regina couldn't even compare. I had to swallow my angst about her father providing our home as a wedding present, but the sugar that eased the bitter pill was the way that Regina lit up at each location. I found solace in the fact that I would maintain the property and joined in Regina's excitement. After the fifth tour, we settled on a two-story property with a lush green landscape and fountain out front. I was excited about bringing my father out to fish in the lake and hosting a family get-together in the party room that included a full bar and disco area. We had a little less than five months until the wedding but our move-in date would be closer to thirty days. Life was coming together in ways that I had never imagined it could and I had Regina to thank for it. I wanted to take her somewhere special to celebrate.

"Are we going to help Shaggy, Scooby and the crew solve another mystery or go to a Texas chainsaw auction?" Regina asked from the passenger side of my truck.

It was seven in the evening and we had been driving to my surprise for an hour. Regina was getting impatient.

"Neither." I grinned. "But it's worth it, I promise."

"Where is civilization, Terrence? How can we have a date without a building or people or electricity?"

"We're only an hour outside of the city."

"Are you sure? There's nothing out here." She waved a hand in front of her to accentuate how desolate everything looked.

"Do you trust me?" It was a real question, and I waited for her answer.

"I do. Yes, I trust you," she huffed. "But that doesn't mean that I won't question you, or that I'll let you lead me to a well-intentioned death."

"Good enough."

When I turned into a drive-in movie complex, Regina didn't say anything but I could tell she was relieved to see the destination. When I helped her from the cab of my truck, uncovered the truck bed, and set up a futon mattress with covers and pillows, I could tell that she was pleased. When I pulled out my backpack of snacks and drinks, I finally got the smile I was waiting for.

She opened up the backpack as I climbed in next to her.

"Aww. You packed us some snacks. What is this?" She asked holding up the silver bag that looked like a kids juice pouch.

"I brought mixed drinks," I explained grabbing another packet of liquor and pointing out the liquor content.

"Terrence. Look at me, sweetie." She waited until my pupils were lined up with hers. "These are not the good mixed drinks. Nothing good can come of foil packet liquor."

"Mali swears by them."

I stole a quick kiss from her lips before falling back and summoning her against me.

"I guess I'll try something new. What else do you have in this wilderness survival pack?" She fidgeted her hand through the bag and nodded as she placed items neatly in front of us for easy selection. "I must admit, I like my movies in air-conditioned rooms, but being out here under the stars with you is kinda primal. How did we get lucky enough to have the whole screen to ourselves?"

"I know a few people." I bragged. "The owner is part of the small business coalition and he hooked us up."

"So, what are we watching?"

"We're starting with Fame -" She didn't even let him finish his sentence before she hopped in with joy

"With my play-aunty Debbie Allen? I love anything that she choreographs, directs, produces, or acts in. She's the whole reason I finally watched Grey's Anatomy. " Regina said in a breath.

"Ok. I guess I chose the right movie to start us off. It's a double feature. I know how much you love HBCU bands, so our second feature is Beyoncé's Homecoming special."

She bounced up to her knees with excitement radiating from her face.

"You're about to get a show, cause I know every step." She flipped her hand back and forth, mimicking the infamous move in the Single Ladies video. "All my single ladies."

I patted the space near me as the first movie started.

"Speaking of single ladies," I took a deep breath and reached into the pocket of my pants for the small black box. "I know why we started this journey, but the closer we get to the finish line, the more I'm convinced that I should have asked you to marry me that night on the island."

"Right after I beat you in a foot race?" she grinned.

"Right after." I chuckled. "I promise that as long as we're together I won't stop trying to make you smile as bright as you did tonight. I call you Bloom, but you helped me to bloom. Will you grow with me, Regina? Officially?"

I opened the black box and listened to her gasp.

"Terrence," there was a warning in her voice and apprehension in her voice. "This ring is huge. You didn't have to do this."

"I did it because I wanted to, not because I had to. I did it because I want to be with you." I reminded her. "I don't know everything, but I know me, and all of me wants you."

Her eyes met mine and the caution that had been swirling there before had dissipated.

"More than anything else in this world, I want to be with you too." Regina's words matched the pace of the tears streaming from her eyes.

I quickly slipped the ring on her finger before Regina bowled me over with a hug around my neck so tight that I nearly hit my head on the truck.

"Thank you," she repeated against my lips, cheek, and neck. "Nothing is better than being here with you."

Her lips tasted like the berry gloss she wore on the weekends, but the taste of her tongue kept me addicted.

"Nothing?" I questioned breaking the kiss to slide her body beneath mine. "Not even me, over you?"

"Hmm." she kissed along my wrist and forearm. "I may need to adjust my list."

My ringing phone stopped my hand just as it was reaching for her center. I had made a point to answer the rare calls I received after business hours since my mother had been in a car wreck about a year ago.

"Hold that thought." I kissed Regina's cheek before accepting the call. "Hello."

When I heard the voice on the phone and what she had to say, I instantly knew that our movie night was over.

"Let's go. I'll fill you in on the way."

The grim look stuck on Nailah's face was confirmation that shit was bad. She met us at the front of the hospital holding a paper cup of coffee in her hands and worry on her shoulders. We greeted each other with quick hugs and hellos before I asked the most important question.

"Where is he?"

"He's in there with her, but I wanted to ask."

"No, Nailah," I answered quickly. "He's not my son."

Before Nailah had married my brother, she had been a social worker. That's how she and Regina had met. Nailah still had a few friends in the Department of Children Services, one of whom had been on duty tonight and a bridesmaid at her wedding. When Trevion arrived at the hospital with his unconscious mother and told the social worker that 'Terrence Lewis' was his father, it caught her attention. The Y.A.M's had been introduced to my brother before, so when the social worker asked if Tyriq Lewis was his uncle, she reached out to Nailah.

"Do you think my mom would have let me hide a child for seventeen years?" I asked.

"Stranger things have happened." she shrugged.

"He's part of the mentoring group, and I told him that I would look out for him."

Nailah nodded. "His mother is stable but still unconscious, so you would be responsible for the two."

"Two?"

"Yes. Trevion has a little sister, Amaya, she's eight. Both of them are here. They don't know that I reached out to you. Sandy can take them to a foster home without you even seeing them, but if you decide to take them, you would be responsible for them until their mother is better. There's also the possibility that she won't get better. She could be unresponsive for days or weeks."

"Damn," was all that I could manage to say.

My eyes darted to Regina. I knew in my heart what I wanted to do, and what I wanted to say, but Regina wanted to focus on the company. We had only talked about children briefly, and she mentioned that they would not be in her near future.

"I know that he means a lot to you," Regina started as she looped an arm around mine. "We're in this together, so - yeah. Let's do it. It'll probably just be a couple of weeks. How bad could it be?"

"Are you sure? I've been staying at your apartment, and I know that you like things to stay neat and in place. Having a teenager and an eight-year-old would change the way that we function."

"Terrence, everything is changing the way that I function these days, and maybe that's a good thing. Would I volunteer for this situation? No, but I know you. I know that you take care of things for people and that if anyone can make this adjustment work, you can. I can bend a little bit for a little while. It won't be forever."

I was so proud of her.

"Thank you. You won't regret it."

"Alright then. Sandy had to run and check in on another case, but you'll just need to sign a few things and you can take off."

Nailah opened the door to the social worker's office, and before I could get out a word, there were two small arms wrapped around my waist and a face pressed against my stomach.

"Daddy!" the little girl that I assumed was Amaya shouted. She hugged me so lovingly that I was almost convinced that she was mine. She looked up at me with brown eyes and blinked. "Mama got sick, can you take us?"

"Uh, sure, but Mrs. Lewis here already knows the truth, so you don't have to act."

Nailah winked at them as she grabbed the papers from Sandy's desk and handed them to me to sign.

"Oh." Amaya let go of my legs and dropped the syrupy sweet smile. "Tre told me that I had to play pretend. I acted like I was a girl who was happy to see her daddy in a movie. Did I do good?"

"You did great." Trevion approved and his sister smiled.

"I don't want to go back to the kid farm," she added.

I handed the paperwork back.

"Kid farm?" Regina asked.

"Yeah, whenever Mama got sick, they would take Tre and me to the kid farm, where all the extra kids live."

Trevion was putting his backpack on as he said, "Thanks, Mr. T. Come on, Amaya."

I was more than a little confused when Trevion reached for the door.

"Wait a minute," I looked at Regina for confirmation and then back to Trey. "You don't have a place to go, and I'm not letting you roam the streets."

"I got it, Mr. T," He confirmed with confidence. "I needed an adult to sign us out. Mya and I know what to do. You don't have to worry about us."

Regina spoke up then.

"It's late. Come with us tonight, get a good night's sleep, and then you can come up with a plan tomorrow. There's plenty of space, and Mr. T and I were just about to grab some burgers."

"At least tonight," I added to Regina's fib because she doesn't even eat meat.

Amaya shifted her gaze from Trevion to Regina.

"Do the burgers have bacon on them?" She plopped a hand on her hip as she questioned.

"Of course, bacon is required," Regina answered with exaggerated astonishment. "I always love a good milkshake but can never finish one."

Amaya bounced on her toes as she raised her hand and wiggled her fingers. "I can finish the milkshakes."

"It would be great if you came to share with me," Regina smiled.

"We want you to stay with us." I directed the statement to Trevion.

"Can we Tre?" Amaya added. Her voice was sweet again, like when she ran to me earlier. He looked at his little sister and then back to me.

A moment ticked by before Trevion sighed.

"Mr. T, you don't have to do this."

"I know that, but come with us anyway."

He gnawed at his bottom lip, watching the hole in the top of Amaya's shoe move from side to side as we waited.

"We won't be trouble," he answered with an assurance that chipped at my heart. "We can clean anything you want, and we know how to stay quiet. You won't even know that we're there. Amaya doesn't know how hard it can get."

Water wells at the bottom of his eyes, and he quickly brushed his face against his shirt.

"I gotcha Tre," I pulled him to my side in a one-armed hug. "And you know I mean what I say."

Trevion nodded in agreement, and we left the hospital together as a unit.

CHAPTER THIRTY-FOUR

Regina

I woke up the following day to a sweet aroma. I loved when Terrence cooked in the morning. It was the closest feeling I could find to my grandmother's porch. But when I turned over to see him next to me, I instantly wondered who the hell was in my kitchen. Dinner had gone well with the kids the night before. The little one, Amaya, had a mouth on her, but she was sweet. I liked her. Trevion was quiet most of the night, but I could tell that Terrence stepped up and added a piece of his youth back.

"Good morning, Miss Regina," Amaya called out as she expertly flipped a pancake in the skillet. I wouldn't have been sure she could reach the stove without seeing it with my own eyes. Amaya looked like a miniature-grown person who was drowning in my 'display only' apron with a towel on her shoulder.

"Good morning, Amaya," I replied, stepping closer to the stove and eyeing her work. The girl was good. No mix anywhere, no dripping batter on my marble countertops, and no mushy pancakes in the stack neatly placed on a plate. I was impressed. "Where did you learn to do all of this?"

"Lindy's house. I used to make breakfast when Mama was asleep. Tre likes the frozen kind you put in the microwave, but I make my pancakes fresh."

She was indeed an eight-year-old little woman.

"Well, can I help you finish up? I'll make bacon and eggs."

She placed a hand on her side where a hip would be before she asked, "Can you cook?"

"Yes," I nodded, unsure why I wanted to answer her. Miss Lady had a way about her eight-year-old soul that surpassed her years. I didn't do a lot of cooking, but I knew the basics.

"You're so pretty, and you gotta be hella rich to live here."

Her language caught me off guard, but I wasn't her parent, so I wasn't sure what to do.

"I do well and cook enough," I responded with a lifted eyebrow.

"When I get rich and pretty like you, I'll never cook again." She flipped one pancake and poured the batter into the pan for another. "I'm going to eat at every restaurant and have a chef that cooks all of my food."

I grabbed the mushrooms from the fridge and joined the little lady near the stove.

"Sounds like I need to visit this future home of yours," I chuckled. "I know you like burgers with bacon and fresh pancakes. What else do you like?"

"I like you and Mr. T a whole bunch. Tre told me about how much Mr. T. helps him. This is the best place I ever got to stay in." She said the words nonchalantly like they wouldn't melt my heart.

"You can stay here," I offered. "I have plenty of space."

The happiness that sparked in her eyes nearly melted my heart before her expression fell back into tough-girl mode.

"Tre said we have to go today." Amaya busied herself, wiping the counters and then avoiding any eye contact.

I didn't bother trying to convince her, but I knew a conversation with Trevion was imminent.

We finished breakfast together, chatting about food, which turned into conversations about cookies that led to talks about candy and me hopping in my car with the little cutie to make a superstore run. I usually had everything delivered, but it suddenly felt like an adventure.

When Amaya and I walked into the store, I instantly felt judged. I wore clothes with foreign names. Amaya wore too-large jeans, a stained shirt, and shoes that her big toe burst through.

She didn't seem to mind. The prospect of walking down the candy aisle and picking out her snack had stars in her eyes.

"And I want the jelly beans that smell," her smile spread as quickly as her feet moved forward.

Seeing mothers with their hair and nails together while their children looked neglected crossed my mind. I reminded myself that she wasn't my child, just a visitor. Fortunately, I didn't have to figure out how to bring up clothing. I didn't want to offend her.

Right before the candy section sat a mannequin of a young girl with a sparkly outfit and headband. Amaya's eyes drifted toward the outfit and lit up.

Amaya didn't say a word, but I could tell that she was restraining herself.

"Do you like sparkles too?" I asked.

She shifted her eyes away from the mannequin.

"Only a little," she held her fingers together as she twisted. "Tre told me to be good. He said *don't look at nothing, don't touch nothing, and don't ask for nothing*, just do what Miss Regina says," she mimicked her brother in a sing-song voice that made me chuckle.

I didn't grow up that way. Whatever I wanted in reason, I got. If it wasn't reasonable, I still got it, but just on holiday. The clothes weren't expensive. I could buy the entire children's section for what I spent on a handbag.

"But did you ask for anything? I didn't hear you ask for anything. It doesn't hurt to look, right?" I lifted an eyebrow. "Let's see if they have it in your size."

"I won't ask for anything," She put a hand over her heart as if she were saying the pledge.

I was trying not to hand my entire wallet to the kid because she was so cute, so I smiled at her instead.

"I wanted to try picking out some little girl clothes anyway. I'm a godmother now, so you can help me practice now for when Nylani gets older. You would help me out."

She seemed to like that idea better. She wouldn't defy her brother, who had been doing all the parenting.

"I'm going to pick some pieces, and you tell me if you like them. For helping me out, if you like it, I'll buy it for you."

Lil' Mama knew what she liked and had no problem choosing. I bought her clothes, shoes, accessories, and candy we were dying to eat. I was used to men taking me on shopping sprees and buying me things, but it felt good to give. It was fun.

When we returned to the apartment, Terrence and Trevion watched a sports documentary on the couch.

"Did you buy the whole store?" Terrence asked when he turned his head to us, fumbling through the door with bags and boxes.

"There's more in the car. Would you and Tre grab them?" I asked.

"Tre, why don't you bring up the rest of the bags," Terrence nodded in the young man's direction. " I need to talk to Miss Regina right quick."

I didn't like the look on his face when he guided me back to the bedroom.

He took a deep breath and gave a wince of a smile before speaking.

"I know you agreed to have the kids stay with us for a little while, but it looks like it might be longer. The doctors don't think their mother will wake up anytime soon," he cleared his throat, "or at all. They are moving her to a hospice facility for end-of-life care. Tre is 17 and wants to live independently, but Amaya could be with us indefinitely."

That stunned me. As a grown woman, I fretted over losing a parent. Trevion and Amaya were much younger and had to deal with much more.

Terrence studied my face, so I kept it as neutral as possible. I enjoyed playing around with Amaya, but I wasn't sure about becoming a mother to her.

"What do you want to do?" I wondered out loud, but I had a gut feeling what his answer would be.

"I'm going to take the legal steps to keep them with me, maybe even adopt them if that's the case," he answered.

He was serious. He wanted to adopt two kids. I didn't know what to say. I hadn't signed up for motherhood.

"I don't know what to say," I stumbled over the words. "I'm rebuilding a company. This isn't the best time to start a family."

He moved his eyes toward me, sadness registering there.

"Look," Terrence took my hand, "I didn't have kids when you agreed to this, so if you want to back out, I understand."

"They've already been through so much," I insisted. " I don't know how much I'll be around to help."

"Take some time to think about it," he said and pulled me closer to kiss my forehead. "I love you and I care about them. I know what I promised you, but-"

I lifted a hand to touch his cheek. I wanted to wipe away the torture plaguing his face.

"Terrence, I understand. Give me some time to think this through, but choose them. Choose the kids."

I kissed him then and he took my cheeks into his palms to bring me closer and deepen our connection. It felt like goodbye even though we hadn't said it out loud.

There were other things to do besides think about Terrence and his kids. I still had a life, and my father was slowly losing his. For the first time, my mother reached out to me about helping her take my father to the doctor, so I responded by joining her at the appointment. My father's symptoms had accelerated, and I began to worry if he would make it the four months to my wedding.

"I've seen Luther around the doctor's office a couple of times," my mother said as we drove. She was sitting in the front seat next to me. My dad was securely safe in the backseat.

"Why is this the first time I've heard about this?" I didn't like this new secretive mother.

"I didn't want you to be upset," she answered. "He's married now. "

"He married the sauce queen?" I kept the *'Screw that dumb hoe'* I wanted to say in my brain. I can't believe she fell for the okey-doke. Luther and his grand plans.

"I didn't want to upset you," she repeated. "I know how you can get about him." My mom explained. "But you have a good man now, so poo on him."

I did have a man. It wasn't enough that Terrence came with widower baggage the size of his damn dually truck, but then he ended up with kids too.

"You're getting married soon, right Genie?" My father sounded more childlike than his usual self. That made my heart ache, but I didn't know how to answer the question. I didn't have to marry Terrence. My father had already brought him on as a leader. The company was in good standing.

Because it had been that kind of day, when my parents and I walked into the office building that housed the doctor's office, Luther and his wife were right near the front waiting for the valet.

"Regina. Is that you?" he squinted his already narrow eyes as though he could barely recognize me. The asshole had 20/20 vision the last time I checked, and I had only gotten finer over the years, so his act of confusion was annoying.

Everything about Luther was average, and I do mean everything. He wasn't too tall or too short. He wasn't fit, but not pudgy either. What caught my attention about Luther was his flash. He had the most expensive of everything. Anything pretentious and overpriced, that man would buy. He only wrote with Montblanc pens and only signed documents with his Sentryman Resin Rollerball edition that cost a whopping $500. I liked nice things, but I wasn't completely wasteful. I assumed that's why he set his sights on me, why he needed me in his life.

"Hello, Luther." I nodded in his direction. Then I noticed that his wife was pregnant. I cut my eyes toward my mother, who had neglected to tell me that the couple was expecting. "Goodbye, Luther."

I turned on my heels, gathered my parents, and walked away. We didn't get far before I heard "You'll see the bigger picture for the greater good soon."

I didn't know what that meant at the time, but I knew that I wasn't trying to run into his procreating ass again.

CHAPTER THIRTY-FIVE

Terrence

I never liked the game Limbo, the chance to win dwindled at every round. I despised losing and felt like I was on the verge of losing in two major areas of my life. I had just gotten Regina, but I could lose her by adding two kids. Amaya and Trevion had gotten comfortable at Regina's, so we stayed there instead of returning to my small two-room bungalow home. Regina and I were still working together and sleeping together, but she hadn't given me an answer about our future. Then there was the conversation that I had with Tre. I wanted to get a pulse on how he was handling his mother's prognosis. The sad part is that he wasn't fazed much. He said that he knew it would happen sooner rather than later. He was more concerned about the people left at Grace Lake.

It was time to start clearing some problems. I swiveled side to side in the massive office chair and then put in a call.

"What's on your mind brother?" Tyson greeted me when he answered my call. He sounded like he was outside somewhere.

"Where are you?"

"At the airport, I'm about to grab a ticket to Austin and hit the rounds on a couple of the shops there."

I frowned and looked at the phone. It wasn't like Tyson to hop on a plane for a city that was four hours away by car.

"You always drive to Austin." I reminded him.

"Today I'm flying. You called me, so how can I help you?"

I was about to tell his young ass a thing or two when it dawned on me why he would have been so pressed to visit the airport.

"I bet Kinnesha is selling the ticket."

"Hanging up in 5, 4, and 3-" Tyson threatened.

"Chill out, Super Fly. I told you that Trevion and his little sister are staying with me. His mother isn't doing so well and he's convinced that it was the actual rehab facility that caused her overdose. "

"Really? What makes him think that?"

"She had been arrested and sent to Grace Lake again instead of jail. The day that she overdosed, Trevion had taken his sister there to visit her. When Tre called her out for being high, she told Tre that she got more drugs in rehab than on the street. "

"That's crazy, but how can I help?"

"I know you got those investigative skills. Will you find out some info for me? Who's running the facility? Are there any rumblings of impropriety?"

"No problem. I'll hit you up when I find out something."

With one less thing on my mind, I went to Regina's office.

Her secretary was out, so I walked straight in to find her gazing into her phone.

"What you looking at?"

Startled, her eyes popped up from the screen.

"I just sent a picture of Amaya to my girls. I had her looking to fly for school this morning, somebody had to see my work."

"Is that right?" I didn't know whether to interpret her words to mean that she liked taking care of Amaya or she liked showing off.

"Yeah, this morning was a hoot. After you left at the crack of dawn to check on the shop, we had a 'get ready with me' session. I showed her the proper way to wash and moisturize her skin. We worked on the perfect pucker to get your lip gloss right and of course, I taught her some of my smell-good secrets."

"So, it went well?"

"Yep. I sent them off to school via personal driver looking and smelling like a million bucks."

"Sounds like you're enjoying being a guardian."

"Ehh," she shook her hand from side to side. "It's a'ight."

Bloom and I never really ran out of words to say, but an awkward silence spread between us as I kept myself from asking her if she was willing to take on Amaya, Tre, and me for the long term. I changed the subject.

"I have a last-ditch effort to try and save our cricket stadium. They're still taking meetings and they haven't made a final decision yet, so in the meantime-"

Regina sat forward in her chair and the floral scent of her perfume drifted near me. She licked her lips and I wanted to join her. I liked licking her.

I cleared my throat and refocused.

"We talk about looking on the bright side of things, so I bet we can put a video together about all of the people that benefited from the arena. If a video is what got us in this mess, why not flip it and use it for good."

"I'm interested."

"Not only did your father create programs for felons to re-enter the workforce, but he also has partnerships with several high schools and colleges for internships, sponsors the MLK parade, and funded a charitable organization to help those that were displaced."

"I hear what you're saying, but-"

"But what? We get some of the people that he helped to speak about the positive things, throw in some clips about his other deeds, and have some media outlets run it. We can push clips at the game and on social media. I thought we could do an owner's spotlight at halftime or something. We wouldn't even have to send the information to the panel."

Regina's face tightened as she sat back in her chair. "I don't like it. I hate it when people mess up and then try to cover it up with money."

"What's wrong with taking a difficult situation and highlighting the good that transpired because of it? A couple of things didn't go as planned, so what? Why are you trying to run away from it now?"

"This is not about us Terrence." she shot back. I didn't challenge Regina often, but she was wasting time.

"Isn't it? You want to complete your father's last project. You need a partner to lead this company. You need a husband before his mind leaves. Am I the man you want?"

Fear constricted in my chest as I considered that she could say no.

"I'm sure that I want you Terrence, but I'm still not sure about jumping into motherhood. And I was going to let the deal go because I'm not trying to do some slick shit to get them on board. The fact that you're trying to spin this has me questioning it even more. This business can change you."

"I am who I say I am. This ain't a front." I considered my clothing and adjusted my words. "Maybe the suit is, but this is me. I already have millions. Having more millions is icing but it's not the cake. You're my cake."

She plunked her hands on top of her face, expressing her frustration with a grunt. "I apologize. The whole thing just reminded me of something that my ex would do."

"I know you're not comparing me to Hindenburg." I couldn't have been any more insulted.

"Ewww. Never that," she frowned as she placed a hand on my shoulder. " You are beyond comparison. I was referring to the other reason I left the company, Luther Boyle."

There was so much that I didn't know about Regina. We had been together a short time, but my feelings for her ran deep.

"Tell me more."

She sat up in the chair folding her hands together as she settled in.

"He worked for Strong Reality in accounting during the arena purchase. I had finished school and was back full-time. After running into each other a few times, Luther asked me out. My father didn't like that we were dating."

"Which made you want to date him more," I added.

"Absolutely. After a year, we were engaged. Six months later, when I went through his phone, not only did I find out he was cheating on me but stealing money from the company as well. His entire purpose for getting close to me was to get to the money."

"Did you prosecute? He's doing time somewhere, right?"

"Nope. I never mentioned the money to my father. I replaced most of the funds from one of my trusts. I didn't want to look that naive in front of anyone. I did make Luther resign."

"Whatever happened to him?"

"I'm not sure, but I'm telling you this because you are such a genuine person. I love that about you, and I don't want you to start twisting the truth just to win."

"It's not like that. My ambition had already become a wedge between Valerie and me. I was focused on getting to the next goal, getting more money, trying to prove that I was worthy."

"Worthy to who?"

"Myself, her parents, my wealthy classmates that walked into positions because of business connections with family and friends. I hustled for everything, but when Valerie died, none of what I had could bring her back. None of what I acquired could bring back my joy."

"Keep talking all that enlightened stuff, and I will lick you right here in this office."

"Tell me again, when we get home tonight."

"We won't need any words then."

"Seriously Regina, I'll press the deal if you want, but anything that goes out to the media is factual. Having integrity and you by my side is more important to me than winning. It's your decision."

I left her office then. All of the decisions rested with Regina and I wouldn't be able to relax until our future was decided.

I did most of the heavy lifting for Trevion and Amaya. They were going to be mine anyway. I didn't want them to get too attached to Regina if she decided to leave me, leave us. They had suffered too much trauma already. Still, Regina found time to hang out with Amaya and make her feel like a princess. We did typical family stuff, like watching movies and going for ice cream. I had introduced the kids to my folks during the family game night two weeks earlier. Trevion was impressed when he found out that Chad created one of his favorite video games. Amaya loved Mali's twists, and Mali promised to take her to the shop and get her hair done too. My mother and Regina bonded over Sock-It-To-Me cake, and Aunt Pat made a Lentil soup that we all enjoyed. Everything was great, except she still hadn't given me a clear answer about our future. We were pretending again, this time to hold off the sadness of our inevitable demise.

Game night had rolled around again. The crew and I rode together in my extended cab truck and went our separate ways as soon as we hit the door. Regina was already intertwined in my existence. Two of her closest friends were my family. I wondered what it would be like for us to be apart and she is still around for me to miss.

I popped my head into the office area where Trevion had set up his game system. He and Chad were supposed to play later.

"You alright in here?"

"Great," he rushed as his concentration remained on the game.

He nodded his head up at me without removing his eyes from the screen. I chuckled at that and walked out to the patio where I found my father. He was puffing on a cigar and chatting with Chad and Tyson about the neighborhood when I walked up.

"Hey there, new father." Pops bellowed as he patted me on the back. "You need a cigar."

"I'll pass for now," I smirked and considered if I was a new father. Trevion had mostly been his own guardian, and Amaya had too. He was slowly relenting some of the responsibility, even taking a used car that I loaned him because he refused to accept it as a gift, to hang out with friends.

It was good to get outside in the breeze of the night with my family. The thought that I wouldn't be returning to an empty home, filled my chest and felt better than any artificial source would. I felt good in the world.

"When is the wedding?" Tyson inquired.

The pride and peace that had been building inside me plummeted with the thought that there may not be a wedding.

"Do we need to get a special kind of tux? Tyriq had us in those specially made ones." My father added. "Took a while for those to come back."

"Yea. I looked good in that suit and pulled a few ladies that weekend too." Chad added. "Regina got any friends?"

I wasn't thinking when I threw out "Just Jubilee and Kinnesha that I know."

"Not Kinnesha." Tyson was always smooth. His line name when pledging to a fraternity was Dapper. He was anything but cool when he responded.

"Oh, Lil' fine ass French Fry? She grew up real nice. I saw-"

"I said not Kinnesha." Tyson shot the words out tough man style. "I got that already."

Chad just chuckled at Tyson's angst, and I was thankful that the attention was off of me.

"You think you could get her back before I get to her?" Chad teased.

"Make a move and see."

Pops held up a hand, signaling us to hush. "I can still fit my tux is all I was saying. Do we need to get another one?"

He was a practical man. He and my mom were not hurting for money, but he still saved a penny where he could.

"You don't have to worry about the details yet. We still have about two months until the day. I'll fill you in when I know more."

I was hoping that the conversation would end there. Of course, it didn't.

"How did you end up with these kids anyway? Are you sure Tre ain't yours? He kinda looks like us in the nose." Chad threw in for extra annoyance.

"I'm positive that they didn't come from me."

"If they are with you, then they are with us. We'll love them the same, just like they are blood."

"Damn right." The men agreed with some version of the words.

"Thanks."

Pops took a swallow of his liquor and nodded in response.

"Speaking of the kiddies. I got some info about Grace Lake. Why don't you grab Regina and meet me in the dining room?"

I found Regina in the room where the mothers, Crystal and Nailah, had taken over. She and Mali had been in separate parts of the house the whole night. It was odd that she always gravitated to the kids but acted as if she didn't want any.

We sat at the grand twelve-person dining table that was quickly becoming too small for our growing family.

"Tell us what you got." I prompted my brother.

He had set up his laptop and adjusted a pair of frameless readers on his face. He cleared his throat.

"Grace Lake is managed by a group named GP Holdings." Tyson began.

"Wait, isn't GP Holdings one of the companies we're up against for the stadium?" Regina peered in my direction and I could read the dismay spreading across her face.

"Hendrix mentioned GP when he charged into my shop. He's working for them and tried to get me to join."

"I learned that GP is run by a former Strong employee. Do you remember Luther Boyle?"

"This can't be happening," Regina responded as she placed two fingers at her temples and began to massage. " He used to work closely with my father and me in accounting."

"He started GP or Greater Picture Holdings right after leaving Strong."

"Greater Picture? That's what he named the damn company?"

Tyson and I watched the fuming Regina jerk up from the chair and start a pace around the table.

"He used to tell me that stupid shit all of the time. I swear it's one of his favorite lines." She huffed. "According to him, I didn't get the bigger picture of why a man like him was created for the greater good."

I was thoroughly confused. "What?"

"Luther is ridiculous," she shook her head. " When I found him cheating on me with the saucy barbeque bitch, he fed me a line about how he was kingdom-building and pooling black wealth. According to his plan, he would unite the wealthiest families by getting several heiresses pregnant. These children would then go off into the world healthy, wealthy, and whole to create a new black super culture. In his version of reality, having a slew of kids by rich women was going to uplift the race. That was his greater picture."

"He's one person though," I added, still not getting how his having kids would change things.

"He thinks of it as a domino effect," Regina's nose folded down in disgust as she spoke.

"His partners may also be involved," Tyson piped in as he tapped on the keys to his keyboard. "Gerald Rogers and Princeton Lowndes are listed as investors of GP and have new kids under the age of three."

"They're probably in on it as well." Regina sounded defeated. " I remember Luther going off about the same families having all of the money and prestige. This was his way of spreading the wealth to include him and his friends, I guess."

It was messed up what the group was doing, and no one would be able to fully understand his purpose but him. I wanted to know how all of that madness tied into a rehabilitation facility.

"That answers a few questions about why you aren't together anymore, but what about Grace Lake?"

"It's a cash cow. They get millions of dollars to run facilities that they put thousands into. They use the centers to fund their escapades and as showpieces, too," Tyson answered. "Luther was going broke and partnered with Hendrix about two years ago."

"Don't they need a license to run facilities like that?" Regina stopped pacing to ask.

"In the state of Texas, as long as they claim to be a faith-based program, they only have to register with the Health and Human Services Commission, it's not as rigorous."

"That's why he was so pressed to get in good with the Jacobs', to help him legitimize his faith-based facility." Regina dropped her head. "This is too much."

"We still have an issue." I reminded. "How do we get them to shut down?"

"You can still report infractions, even without a license, the Health and Human Services Commission can still investigate a complaint."

"Tre said that the staff denied his mother and other patients food to cut costs, and didn't provide any counseling or support for rehabilitation. They were locked in their rooms and only given water. "

"Maybe Tre can make a complaint on behalf of his mother or get some of the women to tell their stories," Regina added.

"Fuck that. This sick-ass dude has hurt too many people that I care about. Who do we know that still takes pay?" I nodded toward Tyson as I stood. "I'm tired of playing."

"Birdie and his people still run for hire," Tyson responded. "I know one of his spots where his girl gets her nails done."

"What is happening here?" Regina asked, her eyes ballooned and her arms spread in the stop position like a crossing guard. "No one is hurting anyone else. No violence."

I stood as close to Regina as humanly possible once she dropped her hands to her side. Our eyes connected, and I connected our hands because I needed her to catch the full understanding of what I needed to do.

"Did Luther threaten you?"

"Well," she grimaced.

I nodded.

"Hendrix threatened me. Did he threaten you when he showed up in the parking lot unannounced?"

"Yes, but-" Regina started but I cut in.

"I'm not losing my wife." I was resolute in that. "I can't lose another wife."

"I'm not your wife," Regina shot back. "This isn't even real."

"Yet. You're not my wife, yet," I added before recognizing the look of regret in her eyes. "Or has that changed?"

"Terrence," she spoke quietly, "I need to tell you something."

I was already shaking my head before she could finish saying my name. "Don't hit me with the bull shit excuses. Are we doing this or not?"

Those foreign tears were back again present and pooling at the lids of her eyes. Each one that fell was a knife to the gut.

"I want to marry you, night." She huffed as the tears continued. "With everything in me, I want to be your wife."

I couldn't wipe away the water that tracked down her face quickly enough.

"We can do that," I assured and attempted to pull her closer. She was mine and it pained me to see her hurt.

"That night on the island, in the water," she looked up at me. "When I asked for the man that I needed, I wished for you. I prayed for you."

Her words eased out some of the anxiousness crowding my chest and churning my gut. Her angst concerned me.

"Then tell me what's wrong, so that I can fix it." I swiped at her tears with both thumbs before pulling her into me. "Talk to me."

"You don't have to be my husband." She sniffled. "My father and the board rescinded the contract."

It took a few seconds for the words to register and for my thoughts to connect. If she didn't have the contract, then she wouldn't have to get married. If she didn't have to get married, then we didn't have to be together.

"Why?" Was the only word I could manage because it felt like something had torn inside my chest.

"They didn't want to look bad in the media. Then you came aboard in another capacity to support the company. My father feels like you being there is a good thing."

Regina moved the heels of her palms up her face to combat the brigade of water flowing from her eyes.

"When did you find out?" I shouldn't have been concerned about the timing, when she knew or why they changed their minds, but the details mattered.

"Right before we went to London."

I took a moment to process that she had known that we didn't have to get married when I made all of those declarations in bed. She hadn't spoken a word about any contract changes, but her pattern of keeping information from me until the last minute was something that we could discuss later. My first priority was keeping her safe.

"I'm so sorry, Terrence. I didn't know how to tell you. I didn't know what to say. I didn't want it to end." Regina strung all of those thoughts into one breath and they roped around my heart pulling me closer to her and tying us together.

Leaning down to wrap her in a hug, I pressed my cheek against hers and whispered, "It doesn't matter."

Whatever the reason, however, the situation happened for us to come together, and who knew what, she was woven into my life now. We were together.

"What?" Her voice hitched and her eyes lifted to meet mine as she pulled back.

"I didn't have to wish for you, Regina," I admitted with confidence. "My heart knew the moment that you walked through Tyriq's front door that you would be mine. That hasn't changed."

The wheels of her mind had to be twirling if her gaped-mouth expression was any indication.

"I didn't trust that feeling at first." I continued. "I didn't believe that someone like you could walk straight into my life and love me too."

"And I do," she grabbed my hand before looking up into my eyes. "I love you. I want to be with you."

"I still want to marry you," I explained. "There's not a situation that I can fathom where you and I don't exist together. I still want us, do you?" I asked.

I assumed that the tears would have stopped, but my declaration only seemed to make the water stream faster.

"With everything in me, I want you, Trevion, and Amaya too. I want us." Regina wrapped her arms around me like I would disappear if she let go.

"We're here," I confirmed while sliding my hand up and down the length of her back for comfort. "I'll be here as long as you'll have me."

"But no street justice." She sniffled and took that moment to look up at me. "This is business; we can find a way to gut him financially or legally, but with everyone still alive and unharmed," Regina emphasized in the last part.

"You're the boss," I relented before kissing her cheek. "But I see either one of them, I'm fucking them up on sight."

Regina didn't argue, and for once kept quiet.

"I'm glad y'all worked your shit out and everything, but can I get some help getting Kinnesha on board with some black love?"

Regina shook her head and chuckled. "Those twins are another whole battle, that I don't know if anyone can win."

CHAPTER THIRTY-SIX

Regina

I didn't think twice about meeting my dad for dinner, but as time passed I grew more worried. In the past, I never had to consider if my father was capable of meeting me somewhere.

I checked my phone again and called his driver. I needed to know if something was wrong. The new medication he started had him present as the Reginald I knew, more often, but still, there was that small worry crouching in the corner of my mind.

Before his driver answered, my father walked in, his normal gait and confident expression in place.

"The driver took a wrong turn. He took me to the office for some odd reason." He kissed my cheek before sitting down.

He seemed the same, but I knew then that he was different. I was learning to accept the small and large changes in his character.

"Why did you want to meet tonight?" I asked.

"I'm proud of you Genie," he beamed. "You've been the best daughter that I could ever ask for."

"Thank you, daddy." It was weird how much hearing those words comforted me, how much hearing that I was enough, soothed some of the anxiety I felt since first being asked to get married.

"I know that you and Terrence have something brewing between you, but you don't have to rush it. You don't have to get married on my account."

"What about seeing me walk down the aisle? Your legacy? The Cricket Stadium?" I questioned because I wanted those things too. I wanted to have him there with me and be aware of those special moments.

"It was selfish of me to even ask you to do that." He reached an aging hand out to mine and held on. "I trust you, Regina. These last few months have taught me a lot. You are my legacy, the most important piece of me that I can leave behind."

"Thank you, daddy." I squeezed his hand and he squeezed back.

He summoned the waitress with a raise of his hand. "Will you bring a bottle of Champagne? We are celebrating tonight."

"Celebrating what?"

"I got unofficial word today that our company will be a part of bringing Cricket to the U.S."

"Really? I can't believe the positive media blitz worked." I grinned and moved around the table to hug him.

"You and Terrence did a hell of a job. " he acknowledged.

I took the same seat at the table but felt like a new, lighter person.

"Speaking of-" I nodded my head toward the door.

Terrence, Trevion, and Amaya walked toward the table. Amaya sat closest to me as the guys filled in around the table.

"Hey! The gang's all here." My father smiled and I could tell that he was genuinely happy to see everyone. "How are my favorite people under the drinking age?"

"I'm almost there," Trevion said. "Only a few years before you can show me your secret hangover recipe."

"His what?" I looked between the two.

Trevion's eyes fell on the menu in front of him.

"Don't worry about it." Daddy dismissed before changing the subject. "How's it going with the Y.A.M's?"

"Great, except everyone is jealous that I get to hang out with Mr. T all of the time."

"Trevion is on track to graduate and considering Rice for college." Terrence cut in.

"My man," Daddy reached out to slap Trevion's hand.

"Missy picked me up from school and all the girls thought she was pretty." Amaya piped in trying to grab some of the attention for herself.

"And who is Missy?" he asked.

"I'm little Missy and she's my Missy," Amaya explained as she looked up at me.

"When I went to pick Amaya up from school, one of the girls said, 'Your mommy is pretty,' and I was going to correct her, but-"

"I pinched her." Amaya smiled, a little too proud of that moment. "I never had a pretty mommy before and I wanted to pretend like she was mine for real."

"We talked about it in the car and we agreed on Missy since she already had a Mommy."

"She's my bonus mom, and I get to be her daughter because I'm pretty like her already," Amaya added,

"I love it!" My father clapped.

We ordered food, ate, and enjoyed each other's company. My mother showed up just in time for dessert and drinks. My little Missy finessed her way into a manicure and sleepover with Cherry. Trevion had barely finished his meal when he asked about going to see a movie. The guys texted during dinner and he actually wanted to go since Amaya had plans.

I was happy to see him being a teen and feeling comfortable enough to interact with people his age.

Terrence declined to go get cigars with my father since we hadn't had the house to ourselves in a while.

Outside, I watched my father slide into the backseat of the Towne Car, as we waited for the valet to bring Terrence's truck around. I had taken an Uber to the restaurant since we had ridden to work together that day.

"I can't believe that I get you to myself all night," Terrence whispered into my ear as he pulled me in closer to him.

"You get me for life," I added.

He smiled at that. "I am honored to love you."

I didn't get to enjoy those words for long.

It wasn't the loud bang that shook me. It was the violent jerking of his body against mine. It was the screech of tires tearing away. It was the thud of our bodies against the concrete. It was the blood trickling onto my skin.

CHAPTER THIRTY-SEVEN

Regina

I prayed like my mama's mother taught me. She was East Texas-born with copper skin, long jet-black hair, and red dirt in her soul. In the summer, we walked through pine trees, watched stars, and attended revivals. She taught me that when we, the little things, gave big praises, miracles happened. So, I listed each person, place, and thing that I was thankful for. Called out my blessings from the gut and let the tears fall where they may. I didn't care what I looked like. I didn't care who saw me rocking back and forth on my knees in the small chapel, Terrence was shot. One of my shoes was missing, but I kept my toes planted firmly. My elbows burned from the rough cotton upholstery of the bench. My knees ached from being pressed on the hard tile floor for so long, but I prayed. Before I could even ask, before I could gather the words to request that Terrence be spared, I knew that I was wrong. I had been given so much. I had been given him. He wanted to help people when everyone I knew wanted to take. He wanted to share. He wanted to give. He wanted to love. He wanted to love me, and I had been the one taking. I took his love, his time, and his knowledge, and when he finally asked me to give, I hesitated. I wanted another chance to give him and those children my all, and I planned to pray until my knees bled if it meant that he would be there to give me one.

"Regina," a familiar voice called out.

I stood and didn't try to fix my rumpled dress or smooth down my hair. If I was hurting, I knew that she was. I did try to mop up some of the tears from my face with my hand and swallow back the giant cactus that had formed in my throat. I hadn't seen anyone. Once the doctor said I was fine, I went to check on Terrence. A nurse informed me that they had taken him into surgery and I power-walked to the chapel.

"Are you alright honey?" Shirley asked.

I nodded because there was nothing else that I could do.

"I'm sorry." I barely eked out. "I knew I would mess him up somehow. I should have done something. I should have let Terrence take care of it. "

"Aww, baby." She was hugging me then, her round arms wrapped tight around my shoulders. "You didn't do this. You couldn't have predicted this. I know my son, and he wouldn't want anyone hurt. If he could take the pain for anyone, then I know he was glad to take it for you."

I shook my head against her shoulder. "You can't know that."

She patted my back, and I was thankful for her comfort. I should have been holding her. He was her son.

"The kids are here and looking for you," she said.

We went to the waiting room together, and I wasn't expecting my whole heart to press against my chest and open up. The second she found my eyes, Amaya's tiny feet pressed against the floor like they were starting blocks and she ran to me. She seemed so much smaller than she had that morning. When she ran to me, arms up and lip trembling low, she became mine. I hadn't carried her in my womb, but I vowed then to help carry her throughout life.

Tears pressed against her chunky cheeks when I pulled her from my waist.

"He's going to be ok," I crouched down to touch her face and pressed a thumb against her face to wipe away the water.

"I don't want to go," she whispered as she wrapped her tiny arms around my neck. I felt the words more than I heard them. Invisible cords tangled, reached between us and bonded us together. "Will you keep me?"

"Always, Amaya," I looked her in the eye and tried to push all of my love for her into my words. "I will always keep you. You're my little missy."

Amaya and I sat near the door of the waiting room. The Lewis family was there in full effect. The brothers, cousins, and parents.

Trevion looked worried. He worked through various combinations of sitting, pacing, and checking his phone. Then finally, he walked over to me.

"The guys from the shop want to know," he swallowed. "They want to know if it's ok to visit Mr. T."

He looked away from me and rubbed at his mouth.

"Not yet," I answered. "Terrence is still in surgery."

"I don't know why they asked me," Trevion added with a shrug. "It's not like he's my dad."

The tears started then, and I pulled him into a hug.

"I wished he was my dad," he blubbered on my shoulder. "I can't ever have nothing good. I want him to be ok. I don't want to do this by myself."

I held onto him because I knew that he was hurting. I knew that his world was crashing apart and burning to dust. That was not easy.

"We got this, Tre." I held him like the child that he was. I let him hurt out loud in my arms. I let him crumble because he had been so strong. "You, me, and Mr. T are a team. There's not anything in this world that would make me leave you. Terrence was given a chance to choose a son, and he chose you. I choose you."

"Don't forget about us," Tyriq added.

I wasn't sure how they did that- appeared together when needed, but Tyriq, Trystan, and Tyson surrounded us.

Trevion straightened to wipe his face like he was strapping on a manhood back-pack to look stoic in front of the guys.

"Things are going to work out, Tre," Tyson said placing a hand on his shoulder. "I see you at the shop, holding it together and staying consistent. Keep pressing."

"My mom is messed up, Mr. T is hurt, and it's just me and Amaya," Tre huffed.

"That's not true," Pops added.

"You're one of us, now. That part won't ever change." Tyriq explained. "We'll get through this together."

And then there were hugs for all of us, and I felt protected. I felt accepted. I felt that we would be alright, no matter what happened.

Mama Lewis, the name she asked me to call her, had gone to speak to the doctor at some point. When she returned, she asked me to come with her.

"You're the first person he asked for." She said.

"What?"

"He's awake. The surgery to repair his arm and leg went fine. He's going to be fine, and he's asking for you."

I walked with Mrs. Shirley out of respect. It would have been rude to take off in a sprint to his room ahead of her, so I wobbled alongside her with one shoe on gnawing at my bottom lip in anticipation.

She was right. He was conscious but bandaged and groggy-looking.

He looked too large for the bed, as if they had given him a medium instead of a large. His locks were loose and splayed out across the pillow and he was in hospital attire when I was used to seeing him in all black.

"Damn." He said in a low rumble. "You look like you got shot."

"That's not funny." I watched his eyes travel over me, and I wished that I had fixed myself up before I walked in there.

"What happened to your shoe?" He asked.

I hunched my shoulders. "I didn't take the time to look for it. When the ambulance came, I jumped in the back with you."

"I can't believe you left behind a shoe for me," he chuckled.

"You're a very important person Mr. Terrence Lewis."

His right arm and leg were bandaged, and there were a few scrapes on his face, but he looked like my Midnight. He looked like my Terrence, and I wanted to hold him. He must have read my mind because he patted the bed with his left arm, signaling me to sit.

"Don't be scared. They have stellar pain meds here."

I was supposed to be strong. He was the injured one. He was the one who was hurt, but the mix of sadness and relief that overwhelmed me was too much to keep in.

"I'm so sorry," I cried into his good shoulder as I fisted his shirt.

"Bloom, I will always protect you," he pulled me closer to him. "When I saw that car coming toward us and the window rolled down, everything went in slow motion. I was scared, Regina. I couldn't lose another love. The stadium, the company, all that other bullshit didn't matter. I love you, and no bullet was going to take that from me."

I could tell that he meant every word of it.

CHAPTER THIRTY-EIGHT

Regina

I don't like funerals. They were slow and sad, and I always wanted to spend more time living when I got news of someone passing. I wanted to dance, yell, drive, and maybe run somewhere. I wanted to use every ounce of my aliveness to do something besides sit and mourn. However, I was there. We were there together, as a unit. Terrence wore a boot over his leg cast that allowed him to walk for short distances without a crutch, and the wound in his upper arm was healing under his shirt. Trevion walked next to him for support, even though he didn't want it. Amaya held onto my hand as we walked along the fake green turf laid down over the real grass. A large blue tent had been set up to block the sun and cover the yellow casket in front of us.

Their mother didn't make it. Deep down, I think the kids knew that it was her time. I had taken them to see her at the nursing home a couple of times, but she didn't respond. She never woke up.

Between Sandy the social worker and Trystan working to make things right, Terrence was able to get indefinite full legal custody of the kids instead of just temporary. We were all together in the country house as a family, but not. The kids were connected to him. He loved me, but I was the odd man out. All of them felt like mine, but they weren't.

"The flowers are pretty," Amaya whispered.

"You did a good job picking them," I whispered back and she took my hand again. I could see the sadness flickering in her eyes, but she was very stoic about it. Stronger than I would have been in the same situation.

The service was short. It was only us, my friends, the Lewis family, and a couple of people who knew their mom from Grace Lake.

We made sure that all of the guests had transportation to and from our home where we had food and drinks in celebration of their mother's life. The caterer had a team to take care of the food. Terrence and I spoke, and we thanked everyone for their attendance. Amaya and Trevion had shaken hands and spoke to the guests until the only people left in the home were connected to the Lewis clan in some way.

"What's wrong?" Nailah asked after she walked through the sitting room to where I had landed in the corner on a small sofa.

"Nothing," I answered curtly.

"See," she said. "Something's wrong. One word?"

I sighed because she was right. The kids had just lost their mother and my little hurt feelings shouldn't mean anything at the moment, but I couldn't stop the rampant thoughts of being disconnected.

"I'm not anything to them," I said the words but I knew they weren't really correct. They were the closest thing to the feeling that I could find. "Terrence will be their adoptive father, Trevion and Mya are blood. I'm just Regina to them. I'm not even Terrence's wife."

"The man took a bullet for you, and you know that you'll be his wife eventually, right?" Nailah lifted an eyebrow.

I didn't get to answer because Jubilee piled in and sat between us.

"Bullets? I saw on the news that they caught the shooter." Jubilee stated.

"I'm so happy that part is over," I nodded. "They used the area cameras to get a license plate number and found the shooter at his aunt's home in Texarkana."

"Did they ever confirm that he was hired by Hendrix to complete the drive-by?" Jubilee asked.

"Yes. He took a plea deal and explained who hired him," I answered. "Basically, once I shut down my engagement Hendrix, the state shut down Grace Lake due to our reports, and he lost the stadium. Hendrix wanted me gone."

"That's heavy," Nailah added.

"I was hoping that once both the shooter and Hendrix were behind bars, Terrence would ask me to marry him. I thought maybe he would finally make it official since we really don't have to get married, but maybe he's not all in."

"Who's not all in?" Kinnesha asked, stepping into the conversation. She followed my eyes as I narrowed in on Terrence sitting in a chair and talking to Tyriq. "Oh. Give him some time. It's been like three weeks since he got out of the hospital."

"You're right."

"I know I am- oops." Kinnesha slid to the left and crouched down behind the sofa. "hide me."

"What are you doing?" I asked.

"I am hiding," Kinny whispered from her safe space.

"From who?" I asked.

"Tyson." She whispered. " He kind of asked me out, I agreed, and then I didn't go."

"Why would you do that?"

"It's complicated." She sighed before peeking her head around the arm of the couch. "I agreed to take on this extra job that is literally consuming me and I don't have the time."

"Tanisha isn't the reason for this crazy extra job is she?" I asked. Kinny was always doing something for her sister.

"Not really, this is a 'me' thing." She answered. " Just help me sneak out, please."

***

No one would guess that we had been to a funeral earlier that day from the sound of laughter in my new SUV (*because neither the Mercedes nor Maserati could fit the whole family*). I wanted to get everyone out of the house. I wanted to lift their spirits.

I drove since Terrence would have the cast and boot on for a few more weeks. If anyone had told me that a perfect night would include driving a man around in a cast and two kids who needed a home, I would have argued them down. But it happened.

I turned the car into my favorite twenty-four-hour donut shop.

"What are we doing here?" Amaya asked.

"I want to share something with you all." I took the time to look at the three people who had changed my world.

Making our way into the shop wasn't as smooth as I had pictured, but we got in there, found a table, and ordered donuts for the table. Terrence's choice was always the simple plain glazed; Trevion loved the maple glazed, and Amaya wanted anything with sprinkles.

I returned with a wrapped box for each of them. I ordered a dozen extra to graze on in the morning. I handed the boxes to them.

"This is where we found your dad that night," Terrence mentioned as he received his box with his left hand and placed it on the table.

"My dad brought me here anytime life didn't seem right when I felt like everything was going wrong. This is our special place."

"It's a good special place." Amaya smiled. "Can I open it now?"

"Yes, go ahead and open it, but let me show you how," I answered. "Every day is a gift, and you know that better than anyone. You have to take the time to untie the ribbons."

I modeled what my father showed me when I was a little girl for Amaya as she opened the box.

"You got me sprinkles." She clapped.

"Sometimes it takes time to get to the good stuff inside," I added. "There are great things ahead for us, and I want to share that joy with everyone at this table."

"Thank you." Amaya jumped up and hugged her small arms around my neck.

"Thank you," Trevion added. "You didn't have to do any of this. I don't know what we would have done without your kindness."

CHAPTER THIRTY-NINE

Terrence

Regina reworked her original wedding day to celebrate her role as head of her family company. I thought it was weird that she changed the venue to her grandmother's East Texas farm, but I went along with it. A huge white tent was set up, and at least 20 tables were decorated in the Rose Gold color she chose. It reminded me of all the work she put into the day. Getting married had started as her father's idea, but I knew that deep down, she still wanted to tie the knot. I wanted to give her that, but there wasn't enough time to pull everything together, not the way that she deserved.

"Take a walk with me." Tyson placed a hand on my shoulder. I needed a moment to gather my thoughts. I had to suck up my disappointment that I wasn't marrying Regina. *It was too soon. We had too many life changes at once. We should wait.*

The party barely started, but I watched our family and close friends dance to old-school jams.

Regina was near the DJ booth speaking to her dad, and I nodded in her direction.

She beamed a smile before she walked over to me. It took all of my restraint not to lift her into my arms and kiss her face. She was everything to me.

"Real quick," her hands fell into mine. "Do you want this?" She asked as she guided her fingers between our chests. "Do you want me forever?"

My eyebrows folded. *What kind of question was that?* "Completely. I love you. I wished that this was still our wedding day."

She shook her head, and I couldn't tell if it was regret or disbelief tugging at the lines of her mouth.

"Thank you for loving me." She gave my hand a quick squeeze and nodded toward Tyson.

"Don't ever forget that I do."

Regina blew me a kiss as she found Mali across the room. I was happy to see that they were friends again.

"Let's step into the house. We can talk there." Tyson nodded toward the door, and I followed him through it.

My walk was closer to normal now that the boot was off, and my arm wound had healed up nicely. I felt better than my old self. The Y.A.M's won their competition with Tyson's help, the empowerment center plans were coming along, and Regina had started scouting locations and partners for the Cricket stadium. Life was better than good.

I entered the room where my brothers and cousins, Chad and Cairo, had gathered. They were all dressed in tuxedos with rose gold accents and accessories.

"What the hell? Where did the tuxes come from? Y'all know this isn't a wedding, right?" I shot out all the questions at once.

"Do you want it to be? Do you want to marry her?" Tyson asked. "She sure wants to marry you."

"Regina got the tuxes done in a rush and the bridesmaid dresses too,,, if you want to do this."

Tyson lifted his phone, and I saw Regina's face on the call.

"Terrence Lewis, you saved my life in more ways than one," she said. Even through the phone, I could see the glassiness of water drawing at her eyelids. "You have been more than I ever could have expected. I want to commit my life to you today."

The delay didn't happen because I was unsure of my feelings for her. I loved Regina with everything in me. The delay came because Regina deserved everything she ever wanted in a wedding. She deserved an over-the-top lifestyle of the rich and famous Hollywood event with flashing lights and thousands of people.

"Like this?" the two words were slight. They must have hit her like a sonic wave because her face seemed to crack her face in a million pieces. "Regina, don't you want something fancy?"

"I want you," She sighed so earnestly that I felt terrible for even asking her. "Do you remember the first time that you held my hand?"

I smiled first, picturing her distress on the plane that day. "Yes, I remember."

"You asked me where I would want to get married, and what did I tell you?" She asked.

The laugh burst through me as the only way that I could express the joy that I felt.

I could see the expressions of confusion marring the faces of my family members.

"She told me that she wanted to get married where she felt most like herself, the place that shaped and molded her, where love began."

Tyson nodded. "It sounds like a pretty special place to me."

"Yes, it is." I turned my attention back to Regina on the phone. "Put on your dress. I'll be waiting for you."

Her glee radiated through the phone as Tyson ended the call.

I always thought dudes who cried during their wedding were feeling guilty, that all those tears were for the misdeeds and bull shit they put their women through. Standing next to my brothers, watching my daughter Amaya throw petals across the path, I pushed tears to the back of my eyes. It had nothing to do with guilt. From head to toe, I felt loved. I felt accepted. I knew that right or wrong, good or bad, I had found a partner. When my son walked out with rings, the first tear fell. I wiped it away with my thumb, but there was another to replace it.

When Regina entered on Reginald Strong's arm in a sweeping gown, I felt my knees weaken.

"Hold up, Big Bro. You gotta stay upright to marry her." Tyriq gave me a steady hand and lifted me, just like he had always done.

There was a light chuckle from the people in the front who had heard.

Tears were raining from my eyes when she made it to me.

Regina let go of her father's arm and wiped my cheeks.

"I'm here, Night. I'm not going anywhere." She said. "We got this."

She didn't understand. Cupping her chin, I brought our faces nearer to let her know.

"These are grateful tears. I have never been this full of love. I have never been this happy. I have never been so myself. Thank you. Thank you."

I pepper her face with kisses, trying to show her my gratitude.

The minister cleared his throat as he tapped my shoulder. "Uh, Terrence. We're not at that part yet."

Reluctantly, I released Regina, and the ceremony continued amid laughter.

After we were official, the party commenced, but I couldn't stop looking at her, at them, my family, and I couldn't stop smiling.

THE END

About the Author

SUBIRA MILES

Although life can bring hard times that require patience, there are also amazing opportunities that are worth the wait. Subira, which means patience rewarded, has experienced this often in her life. A recurring theme throughout her work, Subira is a living testimony that it gets better.

Subira writes the stories that she wants to read and then shares them with anyone willing to listen or read them. Her stories open the door to her mind for others to experience characters that they will root for and grow to love. Her goal is to share hope through stories that make people feel good.

Subira enjoys simplicity in her spare time: Read. Write. Vibe to music. Eat good food. Repeat.

Join her on this adventure, exploring the worlds she's created and finding a piece of your own story in the characters she developed through patience and love.

Instagram: SubiraMiles
Facebook: Subira Miles Books
TikTok: SiennaOchreBooks